D1048261

THE LAST HIGHLANDER

Claire Cross

JOVE BOOKS, NEW YORK

TIME PASSAGES is a registered trademark of
Berkley Publishing Corporation.

THE LAST HIGHLANDER

A Jove Book / published by arrangement with
the author

PRINTING HISTORY
Jove edition / August 1998

The Penguin Putnam Inc. World Wide Web site address is
http://www.penguinputnam.com

ISBN: 0-515-12337-4

A JOVE BOOK®
Jove Books are published by The Berkley Publishing Group, a member
of Penguin Putnam Inc.,
200 Madison Avenue, New York, New York 10016.
JOVE and the "J" design are trademarks belonging to
Jove Publications, Inc.

PRINTED IN THE UNITED STATES OF AMERICA

10 9 8 7 6 5 4 3 2 1

THE LAST
HIGHLANDER

$\mathcal{P}$rologue

EDINBURGH CASTLE, MARCH 1314

"HAVE ANOTHER SWALLOW of the old barley bree, laddie!"

"Aye, let us see what the lad is made of!"

Alasdair choked on the healthy measure of whisky being poured down his throat by his gleeful compatriots. 'Twas not the first he had sipped this night, and his difficulty in focusing on the faces of those about him showed the result. At one and thirty, he was no wee laddie, but he did not correct the old codgers.

After all, this was a moment to celebrate! This very night they had routed the English and claimed Edinburgh Castle for Robert the Bruce. Now, flushed with victory, they roamed in victorious exploration of their newly gained prize.

'Twas only a matter of time before Robert the Bruce took Stirling Castle as well. Then Scotland would be free, for once and for all, of England's heavy hand.

The men jostled each other good-naturedly, peered down darkened corridors, dashed up and down twisted stairs like children granted free rein. The goodly quantity of whisky they had imbibed did naught to aid their collective sense of direction.

Alasdair had just noticed that this corridor seemed particularly dark and rough-hewn when a voice rose from the shadows ahead.

"Halt, all ye trespassers!"

The men stumbled to a dumbfounded halt. Alasdair found himself unexpectedly at the front of the awkwardly silent pack. The two torches that the men held high illuminated the corridor with fitful orange light.

A pinched old harridan of a woman confronted them with a boldness that belied her humble garb. Her white hair hung tangled about her face, and her garments were tattered. Though she looked no better than a beggar, there was an authority about her that made a man shiver in dread.

But Alasdair folded his arms across his chest and braced his feet against the stone. He had faced foes much more deadly than this wraith of a woman.

"This castle is ours!" he declared. " 'Tis fairly won and we shall do what we will within it!"

The men muttered agreement, but the woman shook one finger in their direction. "Morgaine le Fee will not take kindly to your intrusion," she hissed.

The men took a collective step back, but Alasdair could not stop himself from snorting with scorn. "Morgaine le Fee?" he echoed. "You threaten us with a child's tale?"

The men gathered closer to Alasdair and murmured approvingly.

"Aye, a wee bairn's tale is Morgaine and Arthur's fable," said one with newfound bravado.

"A tale fit to frighten the wee ones, 'tis no more than that," muttered another.

At that moment, a roar rose from somewhere deep beneath their feet, and the stones trembled in a most unsettling way. Alasdair was not the only one to glance at his companions in uncertainty. When he looked back at the woman, he saw her eyes alight with a strange glow.

"Oho!" she cried and flung up her hands. "Morgaine's dragon awakens! Your bold words have disturbed its slumber and will tempt her wrath!"

"And who might you be?" Alasdair demanded. Even the

whisky was not enough to give him tolerance of this woman's nonsense.

His challenge seemed to reawaken a similar attitude in his companions.

"Aye, and how did you find your way here?"

"There was no woman in our ranks when we arrived, so you must be of the English!"

The woman's glance was chilling. "I have no name that you might care to say," she intoned ominously. "And to no country of men do I owe allegiance." She closed her eyes and swayed slightly on her feet. "To Morgaine alone do I pledge allegiance, and it is she alone who summons me."

Clearly the woman was mad.

All the same, she evidently knew another way into the fortress that they had yet to discover. It was Alasdair's duty to ensure that every passageway, however narrow, was secured against retaliation.

"Enough of your haivering about," he ordered when his companions fell silent. "Show us the way you entered this place."

The way the woman's gaze locked with Alasdair's sent a curious chill tripping down his spine. "So, you would meet my queen?"

"I demand only to know your means of gaining this keep."

The woman smiled, displaying crooked and yellowed teeth. "Then you must ask my lady Morgaine," she said simply and offered her hand to him in invitation.

Alasdair stared at the taut, pale flesh of the woman's hand, not the least bit certain that he wished to touch her, let alone follow her.

A great rosy orb of a nose appeared close by Alasdair's shoulder when he hesitated. Alasdair did not have to look to know that the nose belonged to Iain. All the same he did look and saw bushy silver brows working energetically up and down and eyes glittering.

The man fair lived to make trouble.

"Not afraid of witch's tales, are ye, laddie?" Iain demanded.

"I have naught to fear from a wee witch, if indeed she is

even one,'' Alasdair retorted. Though he led these men well, he knew Iain still liked to rile him because of his age.

"I, for one, would know if we sit atop a dragon or not," Iain declared. " 'Twas you who challenged her and you who should see the matter through." Before Alasdair could answer, Iain leaned closer to whisper. "Truly, if there be no Morgaine and no dragon, ye have naught to lose. And if there be, you might ask her the fate of our bonny land."

Alasdair cast a quelling glance at the other man. "Any fool knows that Scotland will soon be free again. Robert the Bruce will see it made so."

Iain smiled slyly. "Then naught have ye to risk by asking."

"Dare you, we do," asserted another.

Alasdair did not have time to consider the matter before Iain whispered a taunt. "Unless the lad is afraid?"

"Are you afeartie, laddie?"

That accusation and the men's chuckles hit a sore point. Alasdair had never shirked his duty or cowered before a challenge, however unpleasant either might be.

And he would not begin now.

"I am afraid of *naught* a woman might cast my way," Alasdair snapped, certain that this was all a bit of foolery that would cost him little. "I shall indeed meet this Morgaine!"

The men about him crowed with delight, and a flask of whisky was shoved into his hand. Alasdair threw back his head and took a long draught of the fiery liquid under the woman's steely regard.

He heard his blood pounding in his ears as he reached out and took her hand.

The witch's flesh was as cold as the grave.

Alasdair had noted no more than that before she began to run like a wild thing. Despite his greater height, he had difficulty in matching her pace. She led him down one convoluted path and another, and the sound of his pursuing companions fell away behind them.

Alasdair quickly lost his bearings and could only cling to the harridan and dog her steps. She flew down a shadowed corridor and darted up a course of unevenly cut stairs, but Alasdair galloped directly behind her.

And caught his breath at the cold when he gained the top.

Witch and warrior stopped as one, the puffs of their breath mingling in the chill of the air. Innumerable stars dotted the indigo sky, their twinkling light surely just beyond the reach of Alasdair's fingertips. The rise of Arthur's Seat was a still darker silhouette against the blackness of the night far to his left.

Evidently, it was to the top of some tower that they had climbed. Alasdair wondered at its age. The stone rim of the parapet was broken here, and he had a dizzying view of the drop, straight down the side of the mount to the market far below.

He swallowed and looked skyward. A lump rose in his throat as he recalled how brightly the stars had burned on his last night at home. His heart had been heavy then with the weight of what he had wrought and what he must do to make it come right.

Could he ever have imagined 'twould take so long?

Alasdair deliberately looked out toward the hills, fighting against the unruly tide of emotion that set his heart to pounding. He could not bear to think what had become of those he had left behind—he did not dare to consider it.

He had never imagined that the good fight would take so long to win. But soon Robert the Bruce would reign victorious and Alasdair's debt would be paid.

Soon he would be able to go home.

The stillness of the night was disturbed when the first man stumbled onto the small landing behind Alasdair. The remainder of his companions spilled out in quick succession, their breathing heavy after their race.

"A fair chill night it is, indeed," muttered one man.

"Aye, enough to steal the warmth of the drink away from a man's bones."

"Surely the witch's nonsense need not take all the blessed night."

Alasdair met the still gaze of the woman who yet held fast to his hand. A glimmer in her eye made Alasdair wonder whether she read his thoughts, his doubts, his fears.

"It is time," she said simply and released her grip. The

men fell silent as she dug into a concealed pocket in her dress. Alasdair frowned when she shoved something dry into his hand.

Heather.

"From the bonny hills around the Stone of Scone," whispered the woman. "Where all grows thicker, for the old forces are stronger there."

Alasdair looked at the plant again and noted that the flowers were white, not the usual plum shade. Uncommon luck, his gran had foretold, whenever anyone found the rare white heather.

Would he have uncommon fortune this night?

The old woman pushed something cold into his other hand. "And from the regalia itself is this," she confided as Alasdair touched the smooth edges of the gemstone.

"The regalia?" Alasdair's frown deepened, and he felt his own displeasure echoed in the mood of the men around him. "But what . . . ?"

"Morgaine said a tall man would come to this place—a man young yet bold, a man with hair of gold," the woman intoned hoarsely. " 'Twas he, she said, who should be the one to venture into the beyond. 'Twas he she would have for her very own." The woman leaned closer, and a shiver of trepidation rippled over Alasdair's skin.

"You are the one," she confided.

"Bollocks! I will be no witch's toy!" Alasdair squared his shoulders, well done with listening to this lot of haivers. "Summon your lady Morgaine for me. She and I have matters to discuss if she thinks to make a captive of *me*!"

The woman cackled. "Nay, laddie, you must go to her!"

"Where?"

"Ah, my lady lurks in the hidden corners of the beyond." Before Alasdair could ask for explanation, the woman pointed a bony finger at his feet. "Turn thrice in this place while I chant her spell."

Alasdair could not keep his brows from rising skeptically. "And then?" he prompted.

"And then we shall all have another sip of whisky!" concluded one of the men boisterously, an idea that was greeted with great approval.

"And *then* . . ." the woman said loudly enough for her voice to carry over the men's foolery. They fell silent and eyed her with wariness. "And then you will have the opportunity to ask of Morgaine your questions." She leaned closer and her voice dropped yet lower.

"If you dare."

There was such certainty in her voice that Alasdair suddenly feared there was more to this matter than he had suspected. A shiver danced down his spine as the cold wind ruffled his hair. He stared into the mad witch's eyes and for a fleeting moment doubted the wisdom of taking his men's dare.

"Are you man enough to confront a harridan?" teased one of the men.

Alasdair aimed an unappreciative glare over his shoulder. "Man enough?" he scoffed in turn. "Well it seems to me that I have fallen into a company of whispering old women. Turn thrice and see myths come to life that you might ask about the future! Dragons beneath the mount!" He spat with vigor. "Nonsense, all of it!"

Alasdair braced his feet against the parapet and nodded to the hag. "Chant your ditty, woman, and I will turn as you bid me, if only to prove this whimsy for what it truly is."

"Hold tight to the charms," the woman cautioned ominously. "They might well be your only route of return."

Return? Surely he was not going anywhere? Alasdair frowned, but the woman began to drone an old Gaelic verse that was vaguely familiar. At her imperious nod, he started to turn.

Once.

The spinning disoriented him, but he closed his eyes tightly.

Twice.

Alasdair's annoyance rose as the air seemed to swim about him. Curse the strength of that whisky!

Thrice.

"Wish!" the witch hissed.

Alasdair wished with all his heart and soul to see the future of his beloved Scotland, to see the freedom he fought to ensure his son would inherit.

He stumbled then, the woman's chanting faint in his ears. His heart stopped cold when his steadying foot encountered naught at all.

He had stepped off the staircase!

Alasdair swore vehemently as he fell, at once bouncing off the walls of the crooked staircase and roundly cursing his companions, who did naught to aid him all the way down. Blithering fools! His neck would be broken for their foolish dare!

Alasdair landed at the foot of the stairs with a thump so resounding that it stole the breath from his lungs. His hands flew open. The gem danced away and the heather crumbled to naught, though but a moment before it had been green and fresh.

Then his head cracked on the cold stone floor and Alasdair knew no more.

"Hoy!"

"Stop, lad!"

"Hold up!"

A dozen besotted men stumbled down the stairs in pursuit of their fallen companion. They rounded the last corner and burst as one into the hall below, half afraid of the bloodied sight each and every one of them anticipated.

Naught greeted their bewildered eyes but the dancing shadows cast by their blazing torch.

Alasdair was nowhere to be seen.

That was enough to sober the most drunken of them all.

"But where . . . ?" Iain whispered as the others carefully checked the corridor.

After a fluster of searching, the men faced each other once more, their eyes dark with suspicion.

"Perhaps he but plays a prank upon us," muttered Iain skeptically. "Alasdair is not above a trick." The others turned on him, unanimous in their conclusion that this was no jest.

"Then where has he gone?"

"There is no sign of the lad!"

"And where is the old crow?"

It was the first they had noted she was not among them.

One of the younger men ran to the parapet again, his foot-

steps slower as he descended to the expectant group. His eyes
were wide when he came into sight.

"Gone as if she had never been!" he whispered.

A chill fell over them, and they glanced at each other in
trepidation.

"They will think us mad."

"Or that we played foul with Alasdair."

"Robert the Bruce will be ill pleased. He favors the lad,
'tis well known."

That thought was not received well, and more than one
frown darkened a brow in the huddled group.

"He was a good man."

"A fine soldier."

"A man of determination and honor."

"And a man with nary a whisper of his past," Iain concluded. The men exchanged worried glances. "What did we
know of Alasdair MacAulay, in truth?"

"All the better reason to hold our tongues," advised an
older man.

The men nodded slowly, then their glances lifted to the
heavy stone walls around them. Suddenly the castle they had
considered no more than a strategic site seemed alive. Danger
lurked in every shadow, and the men instinctively drew closer
to each other.

For if the doughty Alasdair could be taken so readily, what
caprice of fate left them untouched?

A woman's laughter echoed suddenly, carrying from everywhere and nowhere all at once.

"Morgaine le Fee!" Iain muttered.

"She comes for *us*!"

It took no more than that to set the entire group running for
the gates.

Some time later, they halted, panting, in the same camp where
they had lain the night before. The spot seemed haunted by
Alasdair's measured tones, and more than one could fair see
him crouched in the midst of them as he described his plan of
attack.

''Look!'' Iain whispered and pointed to the high mount of
Edinburgh's keep.

Every heart sank like a stone as a line of ascending torch-
lights pronounced the English reclamation of Edinburgh's
prize.

They had failed.

And the English would not succumb to the same deception
again.

What would this turn in the tide mean for the course of
Robert the Bruce? For the freedom of all Scotland? Could the
witch have stolen more than Alasdair from them this night?

Chapter 1

EDINBURGH, SEPTEMBER 1998

By THEIR SIXTH day in Scotland, Morgan was beginning to suspect that this trip had not been one of her better ideas.

It had sounded so good—using a plump advance to research her book on site in Scotland. But instead of the relaxing meander that Morgan had envisioned, the trip had become a nightmare in military precision. Vacationing with Blake and Justine was proving to have a more demanding schedule than Morgan's working life.

As they trudged through Edinburgh Castle in the wake of a kilted guide, Morgan thought their relative positions said it all.

Her brother-in-law, Blake, was right behind the tour guide, his pencil and notebook at the ready, interpretive guidebook— heavily marked with fluorescent yellow Highlighter—tucked in his windbreaker, Day-Timer and map stashed in the opposite pocket. He pushed his wire-frame glasses up his nose and obediently looked, as bidden, his profile reminding Morgan of a hawk on the hunt.

Six feet two and so lean that his Adam's apple looked like a golf ball lodged in his throat, dark-haired Blake was a font of information on bonny Scotland, as he was on everything else.

Blake was certainly not Morgan's idea of a knight in shining armor, though she had learned the hard way that her romantic ideals were unrealistic, at best. Her brother-in-law was good-hearted, if overly driven, but she supposed a successful corporate player had little choice. And organization had proved to be an addiction for Blake.

Justine, poised, elegant, and groomed with a perfection that Morgan had long ago given up trying to emulate, strolled beside her spouse. Justine exuded tranquillity in the most harried circumstances, a trait that balanced surprisingly well with Blake's intense drive. Her serene smile and easy assurance had been known to calm the most stressed mother of the bride and had given her catering business a definite edge in the wedding market.

Justine carried the camera, changing lenses before her husband even asked, and she had the enviable ability to find their location the minute Blake cast the map over his shoulder in disgust.

But then, Justine had always been the Problem Solver.

In contrast to her composed sister, Morgan could get lost in an elevator. Her hair was unruly, her makeup and finesse non-existent, her culinary skills meager, and her inability to be punctual an old joke.

Morgan had the same coloring as her older sister and the same fine-boned build, but while Justine was tall and slender, Morgan was petite. Her hair, instead of being straight and thick, was a disorderly tangle of curls that fell to her waist. Like Justine, she had green eyes, though hers tipped up at the outer corners.

Justine often said that her sister looked like one of the little fairies from Morgan's own illustrations come to life. Certainly Morgan would rather have lived in one of the delicate paintings she created for children's books than in the modern world that she often found so challenging.

Morgan was the Artist. It was a role that fit her fairly easily, at least when she wasn't feeling inadequate in comparison to her sister.

And Morgan finally had a chance to build a fire under her artistic career. This book was a turning point for her—if it was on time and brilliant, she could be looking at years of good work. Morgan had bet the farm to gather the folk stories she needed right here in Scotland in order to give the book her best shot.

But her priorities hadn't quite made it onto Blake's agenda. Not out of malice or bad intentions—Blake just didn't understand anything that didn't come with a decimal place. It wasn't in his nature to sit still and listen to the voices in the wind.

Morgan's other objective—and her ulterior motive for inviting Justine and Blake along—had suffered pretty much the same fate. Morgan was running zero for two and wasn't happy about it.

Having a child was the one goal that so far had eluded Blake and Justine, and that was the one thing they both wanted most of all. Morgan was convinced that their hectic lifestyle lay at the root of their fertility troubles. And she hoped that a niece or nephew would fill a little of the void that love had left in her own life.

Now it seemed almost a joke to remember her conviction that a leisurely vacation would solve everything. She *had* talked Blake and Justine into taking a vacation that they would never have gotten around to booking themselves, but victory had ended early.

Morgan looked longingly toward the city below, wishing she could escape the Scottish Invasion, as she had come to call it, and wander through Edinburgh on her own.

As though he had heard her thoughts, Blake Macdonald made his way back to her, Justine trailing behind. He leaned toward the sisters and spoke in a low voice, tapping his perfectly sharp pencil on his Day-Timer as he checked his watch.

"It's eleven-oh-nine. This tour should be finished by half past the hour. We'll have an early lunch here in the castle so we don't have to pay admission again to hear the one o'clock gun."

Justine walked her fingertips up her husband's arm. "Then we could go back to the bed-and-breakfast for a couple of

hours to relax before dinner," she suggested with a provoca-
tive smile.

Finally! At last something was going according to plan!
And Morgan could have some time to herself. Three was definitely a crowd when conception was on the agenda.

"Great idea," Morgan concurred. The tour guide cleared
his throat and eyed them sternly.

Blake frowned. "Don't be ridiculous, Justine. There's not
enough daylight in this country to risk wasting any of it. Besides"—he consulted his notes while the women exchanged
glances of exasperation—"we can zip down High Street and
make the last tour of Holyrood Palace before teatime."

"Then, we'll go back to the room and put our feet up?"
Justine suggested more gently.

Blake shook his head. "We *have* to have high tea at this
hotel on Princes Street, Justine. All the books say so. Then,
we'll wander down to the Grassmarket . . ."

Trust an accountant to make every moment count, Morgan
thought mutinously. She had an idea that Blake's understanding of "wandering through the Grassmarket" would differ
enormously from her own.

"And now, ladies and gentlemen, take a look down the rock
wall of Edinburgh Castle," their kilted guide instructed in his
brisk brogue. The band of tourists looked, as bidden, and
Blake craned his neck to see.

Morgan, though, tipped her head back and watched the
Scottish flag—the white cross of Saint Andrew on a pale-blue
field—flutter overhead against the azure sky.

She closed her eyes, dismissed the real world, and thought
of medieval pennants and banners flying above fairy-tale turrets. In her mind's eye, Morgan saw knights in shining armor,
riding proud-stepping horses with ribbons braided in their
manes.

"It was here in March of 1314 that a small band scaled the
rock, then entered a hidden passageway," the guide declared.
"That night they easily routed the English and reclaimed the
keep in the name of Robert the Bruce."

The guide rolled the "*r*" of the Scottish hero's name with
gusto. "Not four months later, the English were soundly de-

feated at the Battle of Bannockburn. If you visit Stirling Castle, the battlefield and site of the reclamation of Scottish independence are not to be missed.''

The guide cleared his throat. ''As many of you may have heard, there was a referendum last year in Scotland. The Scottish people voted overwhelmingly in favor of reestablishing a Scottish National Assembly. This decision will effectively make Scotland an independent nation by the turn of the millennium, bringing the legacy of Robert the Bruce full circle yet again.''

Morgan did not have to look to know that Blake was scribbling a notation in his Day-Timer. No doubt they would soon be bundled into their teeny rental car and headed for Stirling.

Blake flipped to a map of Scotland, frowned, then whispered confidently to Justine. ''Up at six, out by seven, we could be in Stirling and tour the castle before lunch tomorrow. We *have* to go to Bannockburn!''

He tapped his pencil decisively. ''We'll do Bannockburn in the afternoon—it probably has an interpretative center—hmmm . . . we could still make Perth for dinner.''

''Blake!'' Justine murmured through her teeth with a pointed glance at her sister. She dropped her voice, but Morgan still heard her words. ''How will Morgan meet anyone if you keep rushing us on?''

Blake blinked owlishly at Morgan, clearly not having considered this side of things. Morgan shrugged, assuming her sister was talking about the research for her book.

It was to be a children's volume of Scottish fairy tales, one that Morgan would both compile and illustrate. The book was destined to be part of a new hardback series and, with luck, she would be entrusted with future volumes.

Morgan hoped to collect some unusual stories on site, but she didn't think Edinburgh was the place to do that. ''I don't need to meet anyone here,'' she said. ''In fact, the smaller towns will be better for finding folktales.''

Blake grinned once more. ''See? No problem. Stirling in the morning, then.'' He snapped his notebook closed and nodded with the conviction of a man who has just successfully settled a dispute.

Justine sighed in a way that told Morgan there *was* a problem and that Blake's thinking on the issue would shortly be straightened out.

The guide cleared his throat portentously. "Now, ladies and gentlemen, we shall return to the keep proper and descend into the vaults." The older man, in the full dress of the Sutherland Highlanders, turned a corner smartly and summoned his brood of sightseers with a flick of his wrist.

"These vaults date from the sixteenth century and are best remembered for their use to contain foreign prisoners of war in the late seventeenth century. If you look carefully, you will see initials carved by the prisoners, mostly Frenchmen, in the very walls during their incarceration . . ."

Blake clicked his teeth. "Nothing like a little gory detail," he whispered in his terrible imitation of a Scottish accent. He winked and trotted behind the group, alert and attentive. Justine raised a slender eyebrow and singled out a man from the group with a glance.

"*He* keeps looking at you," she whispered to Morgan. "He's alone and he's cute. Why don't you hang behind and see what happens?" Justine winked conspiratorially and sailed after Blake.

Morgan didn't even look at the man in question.

Nor did she follow the tour.

Now she understood who it was that Justine expected her to meet! But Justine *knew*! Morgan fumed silently, then pivoted and stalked to the outer wall of the keep. She wanted no part of anyone's matchmaking schemes and Justine, of all people, should know why!

Oh, *now* Morgan saw the signs she had ignored. How often had Justine "accidentally" invited one of Blake's coworkers—always a *male* coworker—over while Morgan was there? How often had the sisters "bumped into" an old friend while they shopped together? An old friend who just happened to be a single man.

Morgan gritted her teeth. Trust Justine to have a scheme of her own! Trust Justine to think she knew best!

There were moments when being the younger sister was a distinct disadvantage. Morgan glared out over the city, certain

she could happily live out her life without having her older
sister—or that woman's husband—trying to improve it.

Morgan was never going to be dumb enough to get involved
with a man again and that was that.

A crisp wind made her jacket snap and tousled her hair, as
she looked down on the city of Edinburgh arrayed in the dap-
pled sunlight. The sounds of the city that rose to her ears were
so muted that they might have been passing through a layer
of cotton batting.

She was alone, as she hadn't been since coming to Scotland,
and slowly her usual even temper returned. It was easy to
forget Justine's meddling and Blake's organizing with a view
like this. Morgan took a deep breath and studied the maze of
streets below as the tension eased from her shoulders.

This was the Scotland she had come to see.

Edinburgh was unspeakably old and deliciously romantic.
Mist still clung to the distant valleys, which Morgan could see
but not name. Below was a labyrinth of countless nooks and
alleys, little passageways that led to secret courtyards and hidden doorways. Wrought-iron signs creaked in the wind, and
lace curtains fluttered from open casement windows. Morgan
observed the way the fortress walls rose steeply from the rock
face and deliberately let her imagination take flight.

What secrets did these heavy old stone walls keep locked
within themselves? What great power plays had they witnessed? Had lovers once trysted in that twisted alley below?
There must be dozens of ghosts rattling through these old
stone corridors.

She stared down the rocky outcropping and remembered the
guide's words. What kind of men had scaled this rock face?
The artist within Morgan painted a starry night in her mind's
eye and a luminous moon riding high above the determined
silhouettes of the climbing men.

Rough men, and strong, in kilts that showed their legs to
advantage. Their faces would be somber with determination.
Maybe one would carry the blue-and-white flag they intended
to plant atop the high tower, another would glance down in
apprehension. Dangerously gleaming dirks would be clenched
in their teeth for the battle that awaited them at the summit.

Morgan shivered with delight. The past was always more romantic than the present. She tried to put her brother-in-law in the ranks of the rebels and laughed aloud. They might have had accountants in the fourteenth century, but Blake would have been lost without his Day-Timer.

Morgan strolled toward a small tower, letting her fingers skip across the old gray stone. A sunbeam danced amid the shadows inside the tower room, the narrow band of light creeping through an arrow slit.

The narrow vertical opening would frame a perfect picture of the city. Far, far below, thousands of daffodils were blooming in the park alongside Princes Street, the memorial to Sir Walter Scott rising in dark Gothic splendor from the midst of the flowers. On the far side of the street, bright awnings above the shop windows fluttered in the morning breeze.

Perfect. There were even red double-decker buses cruising along the street at intervals. If she timed it just right . . .

Morgan briefly studied the Polaroid camera that Blake had declared "idiot-proof"—a label Morgan had already challenged twice—making sure she wasn't going to waste another shot.

Just as she raised the viewfinder to her eye and a bus slid into the perfect spot, somebody moaned.

Morgan froze. Was her vivid imagination playing tricks on her?

The moan came again, echoing from below.

Ghosts?

Once more she heard it, this time a very human sound of pain. Her eyes grew used to the shadows and she saw the stairs within the slender tower.

"Hello?" Morgan peeked down the stairs but could not see their end.

"Oh, my bleeding head," a man muttered, as though he hadn't heard her.

Blood? He must have fallen and hurt himself!

Maybe she could help. The stairs were tightly curved and narrow—it was easy enough to see how someone could have lost his footing.

"Are you all right?" Morgan called out, starting down the stairs.

The only answer was another very miserable groan.

Morgan looked back over her shoulder, but there was no one in sight. She couldn't leave him if he was bleeding! Morgan gripped the rail and descended purposefully.

She found a man sprawled on the floor, cradling his head, but there was absolutely no sign of blood.

He looked as though he had stepped right out of her imagination. Morgan froze and gaped.

His hair was a dark gold, his hands were strong and deeply tanned. He was wearing a kilt, and Morgan understood for the first time how masculine a garment it was. His legs were superbly muscled, tanned and dusted with golden hair.

A second glance showed, however, that he was less fastidiously attired than most of the men in kilts Morgan had seen since her arrival. In fact, even calling his garment a kilt was a loose usage of the term. It was plaid, woven in earthy hues of green and deep red, shot with the occasional line of white, but it wasn't pleated with anything close to perfection.

It looked like he had just wound it around his waist and tossed the end over his shoulder. It was far from pressed and more than a bit dirty. His lace-up boots were encrusted with mud, and he had shoved his linen shirtsleeves up to the elbow, revealing tanned, muscular forearms.

All the same, he was the most assertively masculine man Morgan had seen in a long time. The little tingle within her that had been in exile came awake with a vengeance.

He looked up and impaled Morgan with a bright blue glance, a slow smile stealing over his firm lips.

The tingle became a roar.

"Well, well, well," he mused in a voice as languid as honey in the sun. "I have not seen you about before."

The intensity of that look stole any words Morgan might have said right from her mouth. He could not have been called a handsome man, but he had a rugged appeal, even with several days' growth of beard.

Perhaps because of it.

Certainly there was the air of the rogue about him. And

Morgan knew plenty about rogues. She took a cautious step back.

His jaw was solidly square, his nose had a kink in it that told her he had lost at least one fight in his life, and a long-healed scar graced his cheek. Morgan found herself wondering just what kind of troublemaker he was.

But his eyes blazed blue with breathtaking intensity. His slow smile made Morgan feel feminine and incredibly desirable.

Even Matt had never looked at her like this.

Morgan had an odd certainty that this man wouldn't do anything by half measures, and her skin tingled at the prospect. She realized with sudden clarity exactly how long it had been since a man had touched her.

To the minute.

His gaze danced openly over her dark green leggings and hiking boots, lingered with some puzzlement on her purple Polartec fleece pullover and a green Gore-Tex jacket, then lighted on her face with what could only have been astonishment.

Morgan bristled at the disapproval she sensed from him. She looked like a tourist and she knew it, but this sort of clothing was practical for traveling. And it wasn't as though she was the first American tourist he had ever laid eyes on!

"I asked whether you were all right," she repeated in her best facsimile of Justine's businesslike tone. "You said you were bleeding."

His eyes narrowed assessingly, though he did not answer her directly. "Well, I would well recall a lass as bonny as you, that much is for certain." His words rolled in a brogue that was delightfully Scottish and totally unaffected, and to her own dismay, Morgan couldn't think of a single thing to say.

He then winked with devilish charm. "Be a good wench and fetch me a wee dram of whisky."

Whisky! Now Morgan smelled the telltale whiff of the liquor and guessed how he had come to fall down the stairs.

Her tone turned harsh, but she didn't care. "You don't seem to have hurt yourself too badly for falling down drunk!"

His smile flashed unexpectedly, and he fingered his head.

"Ah, lassie, you are only thinking as much because you have not got the ache between your ears that I have."

Morgan bristled at further confirmation of his state. "You're lucky to have only a headache to show for your drinking," she charged, hearing the heat of an old wound in her words.

The man whistled under his breath, then winced. "Bold as brass. That will not be earning you much in your trade." He eyed her legs again with open appreciation, then shoved himself to his feet.

Morgan, dismayed to realize how much he towered over her, darted up another step so she could at least look him in the eye. When his fair brows drew together, she wasn't at all certain this was a good place for her to be.

Maybe trotting down these stairs had not been the best idea. She did have a tendency to act first and think later. She looked around and realized the only way out of the small chamber was back up the stairs.

"Do not be getting skittish on me now, lass." He pushed his hand through his hair, his blue gaze fixed determinedly upon her, and his voice rumbled in a most unsettlingly confidential way. "You have got to know that I was only thinking of your fortunes. Fetch me a wee dram and I will see that you have a roll unlike any other, and coin for your own as well."

His bold wink left no doubt as to what kind of roll he meant.

Of all the nerve!

It wasn't reassuring in the least that Morgan was still simmering from that first glance. She sputtered for a moment before she managed to take refuge in indignation. "How dare you talk to a perfect stranger like that!"

To Morgan's dismay, he laughed, the rich sound filling the tower room. "You must be the most cheeky whore I have yet to meet," he murmured, a grin still lingering on his lips.

"I am *not* a whore!" Morgan snapped.

He blinked, then his fair brows drew together. He shoved a hand through his hair, leaving it tousled in a boyish manner at odds with the severity of his expression. "Nay? What manner of spouse would let a woman run about dressed as you are?"

The idea of a husband telling Morgan what she could or

could not do struck a nerve, and she heard her own voice rise.
"If I had a husband, he wouldn't tell me what to wear!"

"Would he not, then?" The man's sapphire gaze was assessing, though he seemed to muse as much to himself as to
Morgan. "And why would he be listening? Why, a man could
just toss a wee lass like you over his shoulder . . ."

Morgan's mouth went dry as he stepped closer, a sensuous
gleam in his eye.

"Morgan!" Justine's call came at the perfect moment.

"Here!" she cried in response. With one last glance at the
man, Morgan scampered up the narrow steps.

But in her hurry to escape, she slipped.

She yelped, clenched her camera, and gritted her teeth. She
bounced off two stairs before landing with a *thumpity-thump*
all the way at the bottom again. The jolt of her landing made
her camera go off, since her finger was still on the shutter.

The flash was blinding.

"Ach! The light!" The man swore vehemently under his
breath, but Morgan had a few curses of her own.

Another shot wasted! Morgan shoved the camera back into
her bag in frustration, hating that she was so useless with me-
chanical things.

She didn't even have a chance to think about what Blake
would say before the kilted man squatted down beside her. He
braced his arm against the wall above her shoulder, effectively
trapping her in her ignoble sprawl. Morgan couldn't take a
breath, he was so close.

His blue, blue gaze was fixed upon her again, and Morgan's
mouth went dry. She was far too aware of the tanned strength
of those legs, let alone how close they were to her own. Beneath the tang of the whisky, Morgan could smell the musk
of the man's skin, and her traitorous toes curled inside her
boots.

She could really pick 'em.

"Are you all right, lass?" he asked with surprising gentleness.

"I have to go," Morgan said hastily, but he did not move.

Then the Polaroid clicked, and the sound of the emerging
picture echoed loudly in the tiny room.

Her companion glanced pointedly at her bag, his eyes bright
with curiosity. "What manner of sorcery made that light? You
had only a wee box in your hand." He cocked his head at the
sound of the whirring. "It hums like some fey insect in
there!" He reached out a hand. "Let me see, lass."

Morgan's fingers closed proprietarily over the straps of her
bag. Was he a thief? The last thing she was going to do was
display her recently acquired camera to this man! "No! It's
just a camera."

"Just a *what*?" He looked, remarkably, as though he did
not know the word, though his eyes shone with intelligence.

Where had this man been for the last century?

"A camera. You know."

His firm lips twisted. "Nay, lass, I know of naught that can
blaze that brightly with such speed. Let me have a look at it."
He leaned closer with obvious curiosity. Morgan inched backward, convinced that he was trying to trick her.

It was disconcerting how quickly she found the stairs at her
back.

Morgan swallowed and looked up at the determined man
leaning over her. "You can't see it," she insisted and hitched
the bag higher over her shoulder. "You have to let me up."

The way his gaze darted over her made Morgan's blood
heat in a most troubling way. He might have spoken, but Justine's voice again sounded from overhead.

"MORGAN!"

The man's head snapped up. "Morgaine!" he whispered.
His gaze blazed into hers. "She called you *Morgaine*!" His
voice was low, as though he barely dared to voice her name.
"Why?"

"Because it's my name. Morgan Lafayette."

Alarm flickered through those blue eyes. "You *are* Morgaine le Fee!" he hissed through his teeth.

Before Morgan could make sense of that, he jumped backward—as though he were suddenly leery of her—and seemed
surprised to find a solid wall behind himself.

Morgan took advantage of the opportunity to scramble to
her feet.

His gaze flicked between the wall and Morgan. Evidently

he was noting escape routes just as she had been doing a minute earlier. If she had been more composed, she might have found the change of roles funny.

"Sealed up the passage, have you?" he demanded suspiciously. Then his eyes narrowed to sapphire slits. "I suppose that is all the proof a thinking man needs of your powers."

Morgan had never met anyone whose eyes so clearly revealed their thoughts, even ones as inexplicable as his seemed to be.

"And I must pass you to escape," he mused. "Some sort of test, is it, then?"

A test? What on earth was he talking about?

Suddenly Morgan recalled his demand for whisky and understood. The man was drunk as a skunk! No wonder he made no sense!

Trust her to find the only drunk in this place and to find him attractive! Hadn't she learned her lesson?

Morgan reached for the railing, determined not to make the same slip twice—in more ways than one. "Well, at least you weren't hurt by your fall. Perhaps you'll think about this the next time you have a whisky." Morgan smiled brightly. "I'll just be going now."

And she fled up the stairs.

"Wait!" he cried, with such dismay that Morgan halted to look back at him and saw that he was about to follow after her. His eyes were bluer than blue, the appeal within them as clear as crystal, and he certainly didn't look drunk.

Something within Morgan melted with dangerous ease.

"What are you wanting from me, Morgaine?" he asked huskily. He put one foot on the bottom step, revealing those bronzed legs to singular advantage.

Morgan's mouth went dry. Her impish mind immediately recalled the offer he had already made, before she forced herself to remember where she was.

And what kind of man he was. A drinker, a troublemaker, possibly a thief, apparently a womanizer.

A man a whole lot like Matt.

His question alone should have been enough to remind her

of those last ugly months with Matt. How often had Matt asked her what she wanted of him?

And how seldom had he *listened* to her simple answer?

Hundreds of broken promises flooded through Morgan's mind, the memories alone enough to make her heart ache once more. She blinked her tears away, tears not for Matt but for her own stupid trust, and squarely met the stranger's gaze.

Been there, done that, Morgan reminded herself forcefully. And never again.

"Nothing," she said firmly, though she might have been answering Matt rather than the attractive stranger below. "I don't want *anything* from you." She waved a hand toward the top of the stairs, wanting to make sure he understood that she wasn't alone. "They're waiting for me."

Without waiting for a reply, Morgan turned and ran as though her life depended upon it.

Chapter 2

THE BUMP ON Alasdair's head throbbed as he watched the delicate marvel of Morgaine le Fee dance up the stairs. Aye, she was all he had heard of her and more, an enchantress of the highest order. What manner of woman would flaunt such shapely legs before the eye of a red-blooded man?

Incredible as it seemed, Alasdair had indeed been sent to confront a powerful sorceress within her own den. He thought furiously, but there was no other explanation. It did not help at all that the whisky, the fall, and Morgaine herself had left his thinking all tapsal-teerie.

His first idea, that she was a whore hired by the lads to muddle his wits in good fun, had been a reasonable one given her garb. But then the other details had not added up.

If the bite of her tongue—another attribute held to be Morgaine's, he reminded himself—had not made the truth clear, then that flashing box had made her identity obvious. That Morgaine had hidden it away after he caught a glimpse of it only hinted further at the power of its sorcery.

And every laddie knew that Faeries had eyes the shade of new grass.

Alasdair liked to think that there was a more sensible explanation for his plight, but he had a terrible feeling it was not to be.

For what mortal woman could have been so fetchingly beautiful as she? Just the sight of her made a heat unfurl in Alasdair's loins—the unnatural power of it should have told him sooner who stood before him. Like a blood-red rose Morgaine was, delicate and alluring, yet the barb of her viper's tongue was as brutal as the rose's hidden thorns.

Aye, he should have guessed the truth sooner.

'Twas fortunate for Alasdair that she'd had her dark tresses bound back. Had her hair been loose, who could have guessed what havoc she might have wreaked! He remembered well enough the tales of what could happen when a sorceress unbraided her hair.

Aye, Alasdair would do well to recall the manner of foe he had engaged. She was a wily one, one who caught men in the net of her allure and never set them free. Already she had sealed off the passageway that led to his compatriots, and so seamless was the barricade that Alasdair knew it must have sorcery at its root.

'Twas clear enough that he had already riled Morgaine with his accusation that she might be a whore. He was a fool and then some! He could think of a thousand options of how she might torment him, each lovingly detailed in his gran's tales, and he liked not a one of them.

He was in a mess of trouble, there was no mistake. He took a deep breath and raked a hand through his unruly hair, wincing as his fingers brushed the bump on his skull. The only way out was the same way the enchantress had gone.

But what cruel fate awaited him at the top of the stairs?

"Morgan! *There* you are!" A woman's voice rose above, drawing Alasdair's gaze reluctantly upward once more. "Are you ready for lunch?"

'Twas clear enough that the only way he would ever see the mortal world again would be to convince Morgaine to send him there. Perhaps he had only to ask her of Scotland's fate. He had no idea, but one thing was evident.

He could not afford to let Morgaine le Fee out of his sight.

Alasdair took a deep breath, swallowed his trepidation, then climbed the stairs two at a time. After the shadows below, the brightness of the sunlight made him blink.

How long had he slept?

A castle was spread before him, its towers and turrets of fantastical design. Alasdair immediately spied the sorceress, her shapely legs snaring his gaze with beguiling ease. He deliberately looked to those Morgaine met and found a pair of men attired in garb strange to him, yet similar to her own.

Well, he had never been one to avoid a deed, however unpleasant it might threaten to be. Alasdair stalked in pursuit, determined to see this matter settled as soon as possible.

He had obligations to fulfill, after all.

To Alasdair's surprise, the threesome were engaged in a dispute by the time he reached them.

To his further astonishment, one of the "men" proved on closer inspection to be a woman, flaunting the same shocking garb as the enchantress herself. She looked enough like Morgaine to have been her sister, but there was a polish about her that the enchantress did not share.

'Twas as though this pair copied the garb of their queen to win her favor. The man tapped a curiously slender quill on a pad of uncommonly fine vellum. A clerk, Alasdair concluded, though his implements could only have been wrought so fine by dark sorcery.

These must be Morgaine's advisors. All leaders gathered a cadre of like-minded men about them, in Alasdair's experience. Perhaps including the woman, whose function Alasdair could not discern, was a concession to Morgaine's own gender.

It seemed his eye was already bewitched by her, for his gaze kept dancing back to linger on those boldly displayed legs. Alasdair could not seem to stop it. She had fine legs, that was true enough, but still his attraction for her was unsettling.

Could Morgaine have already cast a spell over him?

"But I thought we were going to Stirling tomorrow," Morgaine was saying as Alasdair drew near. She looked confused, and he paused to eavesdrop on this unexpected development.

"Stirling?" The man frowned and shook his head with disdain. "There's no reason to go there, nothing to see at all."

That was true enough, to Alasdair's thinking—Stirling was

the last of the royal burghs still held by the English, after all. Why would a right-thinking man want to go there, unless it was to attack? Alasdair warmed to the lanky man, despite the unnatural contraption fixed over his eyes.

The device was wrought of two wire circles, hooked securely to the man's ears and linked over his nose. Some torture tool of Morgaine's devising, Alasdair concluded, feeling sympathy for the man when he pushed it further up his nose.

It must be fiercely uncomfortable.

"Nothing to see?" Morgaine echoed. "But you just said you wanted to visit Bannockburn!"

"Visit the site where Scottish independence was lost forever?" The man rolled his eyes. "Morgan, there's no way I would go there!"

Now, there was the sound thinking of a Scotsman! Alasdair himself could not have been persuaded to visit such a place, wherever it might be.

But Scottish independence was hardly lost forever. Alasdair conceded that 'twas not unreasonable that an advisor of Morgaine's—who clearly supported the English—should appear pessimistic about Scotland's success in the current bloody fight.

"Don't be ridiculous!" Morgaine argued. "Bannockburn was the site of a Scottish *victory*! The guide was just telling us so."

"Morgan!" The man looked down his nose at the enchantress. "What are you thinking? The guide just told us that the Scottish were soundly *defeated* at Bannockburn."

The advisor's manner was quite bold, to Alasdair's thinking.

The other woman shook her head. "Honestly, Morgan. Didn't you pay any attention?" she chided. "Remember—we're going to the Palace of Scone tomorrow."

"Where the kings of Scotland were once crowned," the male advisor added with gusto.

Aye, that was true enough. Robert the Bruce himself had been crowned there but a few years past.

Still, the manner of these advisors was inexplicably forthright. Alasdair could only conclude that this pair must be close to the enchantress to challenge her so openly, especially when she looked distressed. Were they not terrified of her reprisal?

"You've got this backward, Blake," Morgaine insisted. She fanned through a book with an ease that belied the volume's obvious value, then began to read aloud.

"After the effort to reclaim Edinburgh Castle from the English in 1314 failed . . ."

Morgaine's voice faded, and her dark brows pulled together in consternation. "But that's not what he just told us!" She looked to her companions. "And it's *not* what I read in this same book this morning!"

The woman rolled her eyes. "For the last time, Morgan, you've got to keep real life separate from your imagination."

"But it said . . ."

"Morgan, you have to pay attention," the woman interrupted crisply.

Morgaine closed her mouth firmly, but Alasdair knew she was not pleased.

The man pushed the device up his nose and glanced around himself, his face lighting up when he spotted Alasdair. "Ha! We'll ask a real Scotsman for Scottish history," he declared and beckoned to Alasdair. "Excuse me, sir, could you answer a question about your homeland for us?"

A real Scotsman. That was Alasdair. Alasdair stepped forward with pride at the advisor's astute appraisal.

Morgaine turned slightly, her vivid emerald gaze lighting on Alasdair. Her eyes widened slightly, as though she were alarmed to find him so close at hand, and Alasdair's gut clenched.

The force of his attraction to her was no less the second time—it could only be magically invoked. Alasdair was suddenly achingly aware of how delicately wrought the sorceress was.

Had she guessed his weakness for petite women and somehow taken this form to deliberately tempt him? Oh, he could toss her over his shoulder and find a quiet corner to show her a thing or two, that much he knew!

But he needed to court Morgaine's favor if he meant to escape her kingdom and 'twas clear that a liaison was not the way to do so.

Alasdair summoned his best memory of fine manners and bowed slightly to her. "My lady Morgaine," he murmured.

"Morgan!" the other woman whispered with undisguised delight. "Who is *this*?" She gave Alasdair a perusal that was openly assessing, and he felt awkward at her obvious approval.

Then she looked to Morgaine and arched a questioning brow. To Alasdair's amazement, the sorceress blushed like a young girl, and that heat returned to his loins right on cue.

There was nothing softer or sweeter, to Alasdair's mind, than a woman's unwitting blush. Had she guessed his vulnerabilities so completely as that?

"We, um, we just met, in the tower there," Morgaine said, with markedly less than her earlier assurance. Her cheeks turned steadily more crimson when she dropped her book, though the woman advisor seemed quite pleased by this news.

"Aye, that we did," Alasdair contributed, certain that his urge to help the faltering Morgaine was purely the result of his need to earn her goodwill. He scooped up the volume, presenting it to her with a slight bow.

Their fingertips brushed in the transaction, and an unholy tingle danced along Alasdair's flesh. He made the mistake of glancing into those beguiling green eyes and found himself marveling at the thickness of her dark lashes.

But wait! He could not be feeling gallant toward an enchantress who held his fate within her cruel grasp. He forced himself to tear his gaze away, though the deed was more difficult than he'd expected.

Morgaine fumbled with her book, and Alasdair knew that her discomfiture resulted from the failure of her attempt to charm him. Faith, but she had a rare power! He would have to doubly brace himself against her allure.

"You're a *real* Scotsman," the man commented.

"Aye, and proudly so," Alasdair confirmed and squared his shoulders with pride. It was a relief to turn his attention to the advisor, though the weight of Morgaine's gaze was heavy upon him. "I am Alasdair MacAulay, pledged to the chief of Siol Tormod and sworn to the hand of Robert the Bruce, King of Scots."

To his amazement, the advisors stared at him for an instant, then laughed aloud. Alasdair glanced at the sorceress and found even her lips twitching.

There was naught amusing about his name!

"Bravo!" The man clapped his hands. "I didn't know they hired actors to bring history alive here. What a wonderful idea!" He turned to the female advisor, who nodded agreement.

"Very convincing," she added with a gracious smile. "And your costume is so authentic!"

Alasdair frowned at Morgaine, uncertain what to make of this. The smile she was fighting to hide won the battle and curved her lips as she met his eyes. She touched the man on the sleeve, her gaze locked upon Alasdair.

"Go easy on him," Morgaine said quietly. "He fell down the stairs and hit his head."

Her soft tone undermined Alasdair's resistance to her charms. He forced himself to watch the advisors. What the enchantress said was true enough, but the pair made more of this revelation than Alasdair had expected. They nudged each other knowingly, exchanged a wink, then offered him bright smiles.

The man pushed the torture device up his nose once more. "But all the same, you must know your Scottish history. Can you settle this dispute for us, once and for all? What happened at Bannockburn?"

"Bannockburn?" Alasdair racked his brain but could not remember anything of a place with such a name. It did not help his memory to have the enchantress's emerald gaze locked upon him. With eerie certainty, he knew she watched him without even looking her way.

Yet, despite her obvious interest in his response, Alasdair could not lie. "I do not even know of such a place as Bannockburn," he admitted.

"Aha! You see—they don't even teach their children about such a humiliating loss!" the man crowed. He pulled a shiny and colorful volume out of his pocket, then handled what must be a very precious manuscript with abandon. Fanning the pages, he bent the book open and tapped the vellum with a knowing fingertip.

"Says all about it, right there."

Alasdair leaned forward, as he was evidently expected to do, but could make no sense of the myriad black lines.

He supposed this would not be an opportune moment to admit that he had never seen much point in learning to read. That was the business of monks and clerics, not men who had battles to fight and a living to wrest from hostile soil.

Or so he had long maintained.

'Twas Morgaine, to Alasdair's astonishment, who seemed to guess the truth.

She sidled up beside him, some enticingly feminine scent rising from her skin to tease Alasdair's nostrils. He thought immediately of a pallet piled high with coverlets and pulled close to a fire, the sorceress Morgaine securely in his lap.

Alasdair clenched his fists as a fantasy that could only be magically induced possessed his mind.

But he could not stop the image of himself peeling away those garments that revealed Morgaine's form so temptingly, kissing those luscious lips all the while. He guessed that she would have skin as creamy as fresh milk, softer than soft and smooth from her head to her toe. He saw his hand sliding over the curve of her shoulder, slipping downward to cup her breast . . .

"*After the failure to regain Edinburgh Castle,*" she read crisply, her finger tracing the path of the script, "*Robert the Bruce rapidly lost ground in his attempts to wrest control of Scotland from the English. In the wake of his failures, Bruce died forgotten . . .*"

The words slowly penetrated, and Alasdair straightened with a snap. This fiendish creature had laid claim to his very mind!

"That is a lie!" Alasdair interrupted, outraged that even Morgaine would insist on such a travesty. "That is a clarty lie! Robert the Bruce is a hero, yet full of vim and vigor! And Edinburgh Castle was taken from the English just this last night!"

The trio blinked, clearly unconvinced.

"Last night?" Morgaine breathed. She stood right beside

him, her breast nearly touching his arm, but Alasdair steeled himself against her charms.

"Aye, last night it was," he said firmly, his certainty in the timing faltering slightly before such skepticism. "Or perhaps the night before, I am not certain how long I slept."

The three were still openly dubious.

"I led the attack myself!" Alasdair insisted. He turned to Morgaine, certain that he could persuade her of the truth. "You have but to take me there! Take me to Edinburgh keep and I will *show* you the truth!"

Her eyes were filled with sympathy. "We are there," she said quietly and offered him an apologetic smile.

Nay! It could not be true! Alasdair looked about with alarm. "This is not the keep of Edinburgh! It cannot be!"

It certainly was not the Edinburgh that he had seen just the night before. The town spilling below the mount where the keep was built stretched in every direction, spreading from the foot of the mount and belching mire into the air. The keep itself was larger and more ornate, rife with towers and walls where none had been before.

This place was irreconcilable with Edinburgh!

But then Alasdair saw the similarities in the sweep of the land itself. The mound of Arthur's Seat rose behind the tower of the fortress before him, the smooth water of the Firth of Forth sparkled in the distance. He examined the hills and could not deny their similarity to those that he knew surrounded the city.

The hillock where they had camped still rose as a curve against the land, although now it was piled with buildings of some manner or another. Alasdair frowned. If he ignored the buildings, 'twas not *that* different from the land he had so recently looked upon.

This truly could be the site of Edinburgh, but with a dark and twisted town of Morgaine's imagination imposed upon the land he recognized. Too late, Alasdair recalled that in his gran's tales of the land of Faerie all was familiar but contorted from the world of mortals.

And the worlds overlaid each other, intersecting only at certain points, where the portals were guarded vigilantly. He spun, seeking the tower he had climbed, but he could not distinguish it from its companions.

Evidently that portal had already been veiled.

Any lingering doubt Alasdair might still have had, any conviction that good sense could explain away all he had seen this day, died a quick death.

He was truly trapped in the domain of Morgaine le Fee.

And he did not know quite how to proceed.

The male advisor, who Alasdair had already thought showed good sense, now exhibited a measure more. "You look like you could use a drink," he suggested with a friendly smile. "How about joining us for lunch?"

Morgaine inhaled sharply, but Alasdair had to risk her annoyance for the moment.

After all, if a man did not deserve a healthy measure of whisky when he has been whisked unexpectedly to the land of Faerie, then when could events merit a drink?

"Aye, a wee dram would be welcome just now!" he agreed with enthusiasm.

"It was your whisky that landed you square in the trouble you're in," Morgaine said disapprovingly.

She was right, of course, for if Alasdair had not been celebrating the night before, he would never have taken the lads' dare. All the same, he felt in need of something fortifying at this moment.

"Aye, that would be true enough, and I have the bump to show for it," he conceded, giving her a sample of his most winning smile. It had earned the favor of a reluctant lass on more than one occasion, and Alasdair reasoned that it could not hurt to try his charms on the enchantress too. "Just a wee sip to set matters straight, my lady Morgaine, then you can have your way with me."

Her eyes flashed dangerously, and Alasdair knew he had overstepped a mark. Before he could make matters right, she stepped away and tossed her hair like a flighty filly.

"Go on and have your whisky!" she snapped. "What does it matter to me if you waste your life?"

And with that the sorceress turned and stalked away.

Alasdair started in pursuit, but the woman advisor laid a

hand upon his arm. "It's all right," she purred with a reassuring smile. "Morgan is a bit sensitive about alcohol."

The man appeared on Alasdair's other side. "But that's no reason not to have a 'wee dram' ourselves, is it?" He smiled cheerfully, and Alasdair saw that he was being corralled by this pair. "Maybe a wee bit o' haggis to keep it company?"

The familiar words echoed strangely in the man's flat tones, as though they were not pronounced quite right. Alasdair had seen enough of battle to understand that these two were deliberately befriending him.

Though *why* he could not say.

"But you do not understand," Alasdair protested, flicking a worried glance toward the rapidly disappearing Morgaine. "I cannot let her out of my sight!"

The pair exchanged a quick look that Alasdair did not miss. Indeed, if he had not been between them, he knew the woman would have given the man a nudge with her elbow. That intent glance—and the elbow nudge—was a signal he had endured many a time from Fenella.

Particularly at family gatherings, where much was left unsaid. Were these two a pair, then?

"I'm Blake Macdonald," the man said cheerfully. A Macdonald of which persuasion? The clan had cleaved into those who avidly followed the Bruce and those who just as avidly did not.

This Blake had not been upset at the mention of Alasdair's name, so he must be with the Macdonalds who followed the Bruce. And 'twas clear that Blake did not realize what Alasdair had done to Fenella, a member, however distant, of his clan.

Alasdair shook Blake's hand and had a good look into the man's eyes. Reassured, he looked after Morgaine.

She had disappeared back through the doorway where they had met only moments past. Alasdair suddenly had a niggling feeling that there was something he should remember. His head throbbed vigorously at the effort, and that whisky—not to mention a bite to eat—sounded even better.

Aye, he had been fou as a puggie the night before, that

much was certain, and now he had the aching head to show for it.

"And this is my wife, Justine," Blake continued. "We're just here on vacation, from Chicago, you know, and we'd love to buy you lunch. We were going to eat in the restaurant here—do you know whether it's any good?"

Because they seemed to be waiting for an answer, Alasdair shook his head. Vacation? Chicago? Restaurant? How could he understand anything about their world when he had only just arrived?

"Well, we'll try it anyway. You know, there's nothing like hearing the perspective of someone right from a country . . ."

"But Morgaine!" Alasdair protested as they turned in the opposite direction.

"Will join us later, I'm sure," Justine interjected, then linked her arm with Alasdair's with a smooth grace.

She reminded him of Elizabeth de Burgh—Robert the Bruce's wife—always the perfect hostess and never at a loss for the right thing to say. Alasdair found such women slightly dumbfounding. They were so different from his gran, who was feisty and spoke plainly.

As Morgaine did.

Now there was an unsettling thought! Oh, he had need of a bite in his belly. Alasdair stifled a desperate urge to turn tail and run from all of this.

An eerie scream carried below the mount, something setting the very ground to rumbling. Too late, Alasdair recalled one detail of Morgaine's domain and jumped despite himself.

Aye, he was in a fine fankle, to be sure.

"Morgaine's dragon!" Alasdair muttered.

Blake shook his head, frowning at a band strapped to his wrist. "No, no. Eleven-thirty." He fanned through another book. "That would be the *Highland Chieftain* leaving Waverly Station for London. Right on time." He glanced up at Alasdair. "*Morgaine's Dragon* isn't on my train schedule. Are you sure it leaves from here?"

"Nay," Alasdair conceded, not having any clue what the advisor was talking about. Blake fumbled through his book, evidently looking for something, while Justine tapped her toe.

Perhaps it would be a wise course to curry the favor of these trusted advisors of Morgaine's. They might be able to help him escape the clutch of her spell.

Alasdair could not outrun the land of Faerie, that much at least he knew, as well as he knew his own name. 'Twas those who outsmarted the enchanted folk who returned to the world Alasdair knew to tell their tales.

"Look, Blake, just leave it for now," Justine said smoothly. "We've invited Alasdair to join us for lunch, after all." She smiled up at Alasdair. "So, you like Morgan. You know, I just have the strongest feeling about the two of you . . ."

"Oops, bad news," Blake interrupted, glancing up from his ledgers. "Says here that they only have tea and snacks at this restaurant." He frowned indecisively.

Alasdair did not know of this tea and snacks, but it sounded less than promising, given Blake's response. "A man has need of a proper drink when matters go awry," he said firmly.

Blake winked at Justine. "And we're *real* men, aren't we, Alasdair? No quiche and tea for us!" He fanned through his book before Alasdair could make sense of that, jabbing victoriously at the page. "Hey, here's a pub in the Grassmarket." He looked up brightly.

Alasdair had to ask. "A pub?"

"Public house. We can get our wee dram there, or a beer."

Ah, a tavern. Alasdair nodded understanding as Blake consulted his volume again. "It's called the Hangman's Drop. What do you think?"

Justine rolled her eyes, but Alasdair thought the name oddly appropriate. Those lost to the world of Faerie might as well be dead, after all.

"What about your one o'clock gun?" Justine asked enigmatically.

"Maybe tomorrow," Blake said with a dismissive wave. "Today, we'll just enjoy a bit of local color." He grinned. "Hey, Alasdair, stand with Justine, will you? I've *got* to take your picture!"

Alasdair watched as Blake held a small black box to his eye and made it click. They were a strange lot in the world of Morgaine le Fee, that much was for certain.

Alasdair could not be trapped here for all eternity. Nay, he had to escape.

And Morgaine le Fee herself held the sole key to his release.

Chapter 3

WHAT WAS IT with men and booze?

And why did Morgan invariably find men who couldn't stay away from the stuff so attractive? She should have learned her lesson by now! She stormed across the grassy bailey, as angry with herself as with the highlander, jumbled memories crowding into her mind.

Matt with his insincere promises.

Matt laughing at yet another party, the consummate charmer even when he drank far too much.

Matt snoring in the car as Morgan—stone-cold sober and deeply unhappy—drove home.

Again.

And again and again and again.

Then the final straw.

But Morgan would not think about it. The subject was closed. Old business. Nothing to do with her life anymore. That chapter was done and best forgotten.

What she should be thinking about was her new book.

Or more to the point, why she hadn't a clue how to start.

Well, she could hardly collect stories by racing through one town after another at breakneck speed. What she needed was a few hours alone with her sketchbook. Then everything would start to flow.

Morgan knew she had to stop fretting about Blake's sched-
ules and Justine's chances for conception and just treat herself
to a little time to think about the work.

And Morgan would start by following the first creative impulse she'd had all week. She would go back and take that
picture of Edinburgh through the arrow slit, the one she had
planned to take before finding Alasdair.

Morgan knew she *could* work the camera, and she would
prove it.

The shot looked as good in the viewfinder—in fact, the
angle of the sun was a little better than it had been before—
and Morgan carefully snapped the picture. The Polaroid
whirred as it spit out the print and she lingered in the tower
room while it processed.

No point in leaving until she knew for sure she had done it
right.

Morgan refused to admit that she might be deliberately
avoiding any chance of being swept along with her sister's
plans. Irritation surged through her at just the thought of Justine's unwelcome interference.

Honestly, fixing her up with an actor pretending to be a
historic figure in an old castle. Couldn't he find any better
roles to play?

Of course, the drinking could have ruined his chances of
serious acting. What would he do next? Detergent commer-
cials? Couldn't Justine see that Alasdair was trouble with a
capital *T*?

Although he did have awfully good legs.

And Morgan had a picture of him. Unable to deny her impulse, she rummaged in her bag for the Polaroid that she had
inadvertently snapped of Alasdair.

The picture, though, showed only the room below.

Morgan frowned at it in disbelief. The last step was there
and the wall opposite, where she was certain Alasdair had been
when the camera went off.

But he *wasn't* there. The photo showed only barren stone.

And Morgan's own toe. How could he have avoided being
in the picture? Was the room below bigger than she had
thought?

Intrigued, Morgan trotted down the stairs. She held up the picture and compared it to the small room, squinted between the two, but was unable to avoid the truth.

The room was so small that Alasdair couldn't have missed being in her shot somewhere. Even Morgan hadn't been able to stay completely out of it, as evidenced by the tip of her out-of-focus boot.

So, why wasn't he there?

Morgan felt goose bumps rise on her flesh, but she told herself it was just the damp chill of the air. There had to be a logical explanation for this. She studied the picture for a clue.

There was a funny glimmer on the floor in the shot. She checked the room again and saw something catch the light in the same place.

It was a stone.

Without a second thought, Morgan crossed the room and picked up the large quartz crystal, cradling its weight in her palm. She turned it over and over, fighting against a sense that she had seen it somewhere before.

But where? Morgan knew she hadn't noticed it here earlier. She'd been too busy noticing Alasdair's legs.

Morgan climbed back to the sunlight thoughtfully. She watched the light play within the stone, unable to shake the feeling that it was somehow familiar.

Where had she seen this stone?

The memory came in a sudden flash. The regalia! She had seen it this morning on the castle tour.

But how could she be holding part of the Scottish crown jewels in her hand? They were locked away in a display case in the castle.

Unless Alasdair had stolen the stone.

A sick feeling coiled in Morgan's stomach. It was a perfect plan—take a job working inside the castle, get to know the staff, be amiable enough to be trusted, and then steal a precious antiquity.

All the same, Morgan had a hard time believing that the man she had found could be a thief—at least on such a grand scale.

But he was an actor, wasn't he? And she *had* thought he intended to rip off her camera.

Well, there was only one way to find out the truth.

To Morgan's relief, the others had disappeared from view when she peeked out the tower door. She sprinted across the lawn to the entry of the special exhibit about the castle's history. She elbowed her way through the crowds, pushing to the front of the group gathered around the display case in the last room.

The Scottish regalia were the vestments of royal authority gathered over the nation's long history, now finally displayed for all to see. The crown of Scotland perched on a crimson pillow, the crown ringed with ermine and lavished with garnets and pearls. The massive sword lay the length of the display, its ornamented hilt and scabbard indeed fit for a king.

But Morgan stared at the scepter as the tourists flowed around her. A golden shaft spiraled with inscriptions and said to have been a gift from the pope in the Dark Ages, its gold had been reworked numerous times. Now it culminated in a trio of porpoises, nosing a golden setting skyward.

An *empty* golden setting.

Morgan swallowed nervously. The crystal in her pocket had been mounted in that gold filigree this morning when she first saw the regalia. She knew it. She fingered the stone guiltily, unsure what to do. She didn't know how Alasdair had done it, with so much security around, but the truth was right before her eyes.

Alasdair was a thief.

And she had the goods!

Not even Justine would believe her little sister could get into such trouble so effortlessly.

Morgan glanced over her shoulder, but the guards stood as implacably as they had when she had been here earlier. Wouldn't they have closed the hall if there had been a theft? Wouldn't the case be damaged? Or an alarm set off? This place looked to be Security Central.

Morgan recalled suddenly how everything about Bannockburn had turned around while she was in the tower. She dug in her bag for her guidebook.

"The Crown Jewels and Scottish Regalia are part of a special exhibit at Edinburgh Castle and the culmination of a tour re-creating the fortress's past. The regalia were given to Edward I of England in 1296 as a token of Scotland's subservience to England. They were taken to Westminster Abbey, then returned to Edinburgh Castle in 1996 to commemorate the seven hundredth anniversary of the joining of both nations' fates."

That didn't sound right to Morgan. She was sure there had been something this morning about Sir Walter Scott finding the regalia here in the castle. But Sir Walter Scott wasn't even in the index anymore.

That was too weird.

What had happened to her book? Morgan closed it with a snap and eyed the untrustworthy volume with new suspicion. It looked exactly the same as it had this morning, complete with turned-down pages at places she wanted to visit.

But the text was all different. Morgan turned her scrutiny on the display cabinet, which seemed oddly undisturbed. The goose bumps returned, even though it was comfortably warm in this room.

If Alasdair had stolen the crystal, then how had he managed to change the text in her guidebook? And in Blake's? And how had he gotten the stone out of the display case without anyone noticing?

None of this made any sense. She probably just didn't have a devious enough mind to see how the con job worked. She never could figure out magicians' tricks, that was for sure.

Okay, Morgan *knew* she had seen the stone firmly lodged in the regalia this very morning. But it wasn't there anymore—it was in her bag because she had found it on the floor in the tower room where Alasdair had been.

Obviously, he had dropped it.

Now, if Alasdair was a thief who had managed to conjure the stone out of the scepter, then maybe he had similarly substituted pages in Morgan's and Blake's guidebooks. That would be nothing compared to getting a gemstone out of a protected display.

But why? Morgan frowned.

Of course! Alasdair must be intending to use Blake, Justine, and herself to smuggle the stone out of here! Ha! He would follow them and steal the stone again, once they had done the dirty work for him.

Morgan hadn't been given a four-star imagination for nothing, and it was working overtime now. Clearly, they had just been in the wrong place at the wrong time, looking like hapless tourists.

And a hapless tourist was exactly what Alasdair must have needed. Morgan groaned inwardly that she had played along so well.

The whole scheme was far-fetched and weird, but she couldn't think of any other possible explanation. The way those blue eyes sparkled with intelligence told her that Alasdair had it in him to concoct a brilliant plan.

But what should she do with the stone? She glanced toward the guards, standing with their stoic passivity, and knew they would never believe her story if she handed the crystal back.

After all, it sounded nuts. Did *they* think the stone had been lost for seven hundred years? The guard standing to one side had been here this morning. She had answered a question for Blake and just might remember Morgan.

She certainly would remember whether the crystal had been in the scepter.

Morgan smiled as she walked toward the uniformed guard, her heart pounding, her fingers unable to stop toying with the quartz deep in her pocket. "Excuse me, I was here this morning, maybe you remember me?"

"Oh, yes, miss." The guard summoned a professional smile. "Are you having a pleasant visit?"

Morgan swallowed. "Yes, but I was wondering something. Wasn't there a crystal in the scepter this morning?"

The guard looked astonished. "Oh, no, miss, there's never been one as long as I've been here and it's nigh onto five years."

Her words were probably meant to be reassuring, but Morgan frowned. "I was sure I saw the stone this morning."

The guard shrugged and kept her tone light. "With all respect, you canna have done so, miss. It's been lost since the time of that scoundrel Robert the Bruce.''

Robert the Bruce a *scoundrel*?

Morgan blinked in surprise, but the guard leaned closer and dropped her voice. "There are those to say he stole it and sold it to pay for his petty uprising against the good British." She clicked her teeth in disapproval while Morgan gaped.

The *good* British?

The guard's words were so irreconcilable with everything Morgan had heard since her arrival in Scotland that she thought the woman might be joking.

But she was perfectly serious.

Was the guard in on Alasdair's scheme?

Morgan frowned and tried another tack. "Can you tell me anything about the actors in period costume within the castle? Where do you find them?"

The guard looked confused. "Actors, miss? We hire no actors here."

"But there was a man in a kilt . . ."

The guard drew herself up proudly. "If you are thinking of the Sutherland Guard who proudly conduct the tours of the castle, I must assure you, miss, that they are no actors, but loyal veterans of Her Majesty's Highland Military."

"No, no, not the tour guide." Morgan hastily tried to make amends. "It was another man, in a different kilt."

The guard's glance was cold. "I assure you, miss, that there are no other kilted men in the employ of the castle. Perhaps you have confused another guest with our staff." Her cool smile returned. "Perhaps you might be moving along now, miss, and make way for other visitors to see the regalia."

No actors in the fortress.

And no crystal in the regalia.

Morgan eyed the other security guard, who nodded crisply in her direction. He hadn't been here this morning, but surely not everyone could have been in on the scam, could they?

Morgan crossed the room, repeated her questions, and received exactly the same answers from this second guard. In fact, the man seemed bemused by her curiosity, and Morgan didn't miss the tolerant glance the guards exchanged. The male guard must have seen her note the look, for he smiled coolly.

"With all respect, miss, we often have American tourists with fanciful ideas about Scottish history. There has been no stone in the regalia for at least seven hundred years, you have my word. In fact, of late there has been some question as to whether the stone was really a quartz crystal." He rattled off a series of academic citations obviously intended to put an end to Morgan's questions.

It worked.

She stalked out of the gallery, knowing that she wasn't some fanciful American tourist. She had seen the stone this morning!

Somehow Alasdair had bamboozled the guards! Not only was the highlander a con man, he was a very, very good one.

But just because Morgan was the only one who had noticed his crime, that didn't mean he was going to get away with it. She wasn't going to return the stone herself—because that would be the quickest way to get herself in this up to the neck—so, she would make sure that Alasdair did.

Which meant that she had to find him, and the sooner the better.

Well, her sister had spirited him off for a "wee dram" and a confidential lunch. She knew that look in Justine's eye: Alasdair would at this very moment be embroiled in an interview for Eligible Bachelor of the Year.

Which couldn't be further from the truth.

If that trio was anywhere between here and Holyrood Palace, Morgan was going to find them. She wanted some answers from Alasdair MacAulay, answers that probably wouldn't show him in a very flattering light.

Morgan smiled despite herself and headed for the castle restaurant. She couldn't help looking forward to proving her always-knows-best older sister wrong.

Just once.

By the time Morgan headed back to the bed-and-breakfast, it was getting dark and her feet were aching. When Blake and Justine weren't to be found in the castle restaurant, she waited for the one o'clock gun, certain that they would return for that.

But they hadn't.

Even though it had been on Blake's itinerary.

Which just added to the oddities of the day. Thinking she had missed them somehow and they had gone on to Holyrood Palace, Morgan had walked the length of the Royal Mile and back. She hadn't caught so much as a glimpse of Justine and Blake, or even of the con man Alasdair.

After a while she became distracted from her mission by her surroundings. Morgan couldn't help but enjoy the opportunity to dart down one mysterious "close" after another. The crooked little streets leading to tiny squares were all named after trades—Advocate's Close, Fleshmarket Close—and Morgan loved their engraved mottoes, wrought-iron signs, and tiny windows.

She wandered as she searched and felt a guilty pleasure at finally having the time she'd wanted. This was the Edinburgh Morgan had hoped to see. She got lost at least half a dozen times, but without Justine to roll her eyes at the inconvenience, Morgan enjoyed her unscheduled detours.

She was incredibly proud of herself not only for finding the hotel on Princes Street where they had intended to go for tea but also for getting there before four-thirty.

Half an hour late was nothing for Morgan.

But Justine and Blake hadn't been there. Hungry and determined to celebrate her own success, Morgan had high tea anyway.

And it was wonderful. She convinced herself in the midst of her second scone with Devon cream that Blake and Justine had gone back to the bed-and-breakfast for a little afternoon interlude.

Following *her* itinerary for a change.

And Alasdair, having charmed Blake into buying him one drink, had flunked his interview for Hot Date of the Day. Justine was pretty perceptive, after all. The con man actor must have gone on his way, leaving Morgan with his prize.

She wouldn't think about what would happen when he realized his loss. With luck, they would be merrily on the road to wherever. For once, Morgan was grateful for Blake's killer schedule.

And then she could ship the stone back to the castle anonymously, and all would be put right in the end. It sounded so easy that she treated herself to another cup of very hot Earl Grey tea.

By the time she found the bed-and-breakfast—after only four wrong turns—Morgan was sure everything was back to normal.

But she couldn't have been more wrong.

Justine checked her watch for the fifth time, then demanded that Blake give her the time again. "Seven!" she repeated with rare irritation. "We're going to be late, and all because of Morgan! When will she ever start paying attention to the time?"

Justine could manage anyone else's stress with one hand tied behind her back, but when it came to her baby sister's prospects for male companionship, she was more jumpy than a cat on a hot tin roof.

She *had* introduced Morgan to that rat, Matt, after all.

And she really, really, *really* hated being wrong. Morgan might not have known that her accidental meeting with Matt had been carefully contrived by her sister, but the truth ate away at Justine.

And Auntie Gillian hadn't just guessed the truth—she had charged Justine with fixing her mistake. Her aunt needed only to give Justine a stern glance—the two women thought enough alike that Justine understood her mission.

She had to find Morgan a real man to take care of her.

Because Morgan was the kind of person who really needed a guardian angel, if not a whole team of them. Auntie Gillian was definitely pulling whatever strings she could from upstairs, but Justine was the on-the-ground correspondent.

And this time she wasn't going to screw it up. Justine was going to fix this if it was the last damn thing she did.

"You already bought her a watch," Blake commented with a shrug. "But it's not much good if she forgets to look at it."

Justine paced the tiny lobby of their bed-and-breakfast, her mind going a mile a minute. "But what if Alasdair gives up on us? You know he's just perfect for Morgan, don't you? And he *likes* her!''

Justine ground her teeth when Blake—cleverly—kept silent. ''And she—if she would just give him a chance—would like him, too. I just know it! There's something between them, I can feel it.''

''How can you be sure? He's not much of a talker,'' Blake dared to comment. ''I don't think he said two things today, just sipped his whisky, listened to *us*, and ate all the sausage rolls.''

''Don't you see?'' Justine demanded with exasperation. ''He's not the type to talk on about nothing!''

''Ah.'' Blake shoved his hands into his pockets. ''Why don't you just give it a rest? Morgan can find a guy on her own.''

''But, Blake, she won't! Not after Matt—and that was all my fault! Can't you see that I have to . . .'' Justine flung out her hands in frustration just as a jingling bell announced the opening of the front door.

In the blink of an eye, Justine summoned a warm, completely unfrazzled smile. Not for the first time, she acknowledged that catering weddings was great practice for real life.

''Morgan!'' she exclaimed with delight. ''We were wondering where you were.''

''You weren't in the restaurant,'' Morgan said without accusation. ''I looked. And I looked at Holyrood Palace and the hotel where you were going for high tea.''

Blake blinked. ''You found them all? By yourself?''

Morgan smiled sunnily. ''Yes, I did. And almost on time.''

''Phew!'' Blake wiped imaginary sweat from his brow. ''For a moment there, you had me worried!''

Morgan smiled at his teasing, but Justine ached to see how the amusement did not reach her sister's eyes.

How long had it been since she'd heard Morgan really laugh?

How long before Morgan forgot how? How long could a giving person go without having someone to give their affection to—at least without drying up inside? Justine didn't want to find out.

She knew her matchmaking instincts were right on the money with Alasdair. The guy looked like he had just walked off the cover of one of those historical romances Morgan loved to read. And he was so worried about keeping track of her!

Justine looped her arm through her sister's and guided her to the stairs. "We spent the afternoon with Alasdair," she said conversationally. "You know, he's very charming. But hurry up and change for dinner—we'll tell you all about it then."

"What's the rush?" Morgan asked with a trace of suspicion.

Justine silently cursed herself for revealing her hand. "We have reservations, remember?"

Morgan flicked a suspicious glance at her sister that Justine chose to ignore. "No, I don't, actually."

"Maybe I forgot to tell you. Remember that place Blake's boss recommended? Beside the Lyceum Theatre? Well, we booked it for dinner tonight. It's kind of fancy, so wear the dress you brought." Justine gave her sister an unceremonious shove toward the stairs. "And hurry! We don't want them to give away our table!"

"Yeah," Blake concurred. "Peter said it's the best place to eat in town—he's a real gourmand, after all. And I'm starving. Let's go!"

To Justine's relief, Morgan did as she was told. Justine pivoted, so her retreating little sister couldn't see her pleased expression, and winked boldly at Blake.

Damn, she loved it when he helped move things along! His boss wouldn't know a four-star dinner if it was labeled with flashing neon signs.

"Liar!" she mouthed silently, knowing her delight showed.

Blake smiled slowly, and the air in the foyer heated on cue. "Got a problem with that?" he murmured, his eyes darkening.

Justine strolled across the floor, knowing her husband was devouring every move. She leaned against him, making sure he could feel the curve of her breasts, and she stretched to roll her tongue in his ear.

Blake closed his eyes and shivered.

"With luck, we'll be back nice and early," Justine whispered, punctuating her words with a kiss. "Morgan will be in very capable hands."

Blake grinned wolfishly. "And so will you."

Justine could hardly wait.

All of Justine's assurances that she would bring Morgaine seemed worthless to Alasdair as he waited restlessly at their assigned meeting spot. He paced in front of the glittering building, well aware of the curious glances of all who passed.

They could not come quickly enough to suit him.

This place dazzled him with its myriad lights, never mind that those lights were without visible flames. The glass that composed its wall was large and smooth beyond any glass Alasdair had ever seen before—clearly a product of magic!—and he refused to look overlong upon it lest it bewitch him.

To be sure, he had enough troubles as it was.

A fierce tapping upon the magical glass brought Alasdair's head up with a snap. A woman with very pale skin smiled at him from the other side. Her eyelids were shaded purple, her lips were the color of wine, her black dress clung to her virtually nonexistent curves. She waved her fingertips playfully, but Alasdair recognized dangerous temptation when he saw it.

She could only be the succubus that the priest warned men to beware! Oho, Alasdair had heard tales aplenty of these wraiths who came to men in the night, enslaving their desire and drawing them forever into the depths of Faerie.

Nay! She would not make his entrapment worse! Alasdair jumped back.

And, unbeknownst to the highlander, it was the change in the angle of the light that transformed the curtain of glass into a massive mirror.

Alasdair saw only more magic at work.

He could scarcely marvel at this wizardry before his own reflection dismissed all such thought from his mind. That it was the clearest rendering of his own image he had ever seen was little consolation, for his curiosity was dismissed by dismay.

Alasdair was filthy. There were no two ways about it.

To be sure, the fount he knew at Mercat Cross was replaced

here with a clogged replica that was a sorry excuse for a source of water. None of the strangely attired inhabitants of Morgaine's world would point him to an alternative washing place.

And he dared not wander farther astray, lest he not be able to find this place again. This place was fair confusing. To be sure, it mattered little how Alasdair looked if he lost track of the only means of his return to the world he knew.

He could not lose Morgaine, at any cost.

All the same, the truth was worse than he had feared. Alasdair fingered four days' growth of beard on his chin and eyed the mark of another man's blood on his chemise. His golden hair was wild, his kilt was askew, his boots were muddy. A long scratch on his leg, earned during their scaling of the mount, had closed but still sported a dried dribble of his own blood.

He had no doubt there was whisky lingering on his breath. Aye, the bits of meat that Justine had declared constituted "lunch" had scarce been enough to sustain a man. His belly complained mightily of its emptiness at that very moment.

Nay, Alasdair was in no shape to court a woman's favor, particularly one who kept a fierce dragon as a pet.

But what was he to do? He must remain here and wait! Alasdair muttered a colorful curse and glowered at his reflection before turning to pace anew.

How the lads would laugh if they saw him, long reputed to be one who had a way with the ladies, turned tapsal-teerie by a wee scrap of a woman!

Never mind that Morgaine was the most bonny lass he'd ever seen.

And still she did not come. A thousand worries crossed Alasdair's mind, a thousand possibilities of his own dire misfortune. How could he return home if he had no chance to appeal to the queen of this domain herself?

How could Justine have lied to him, when so much was at stake? Could he have made some slip of the tongue this day that offended Morgaine's advisors? He had been careful to hold his tongue, understanding so little of their chatter as he did.

But 'twould have been fair easy to err and never guess the

truth. That did little to reassure the pacing highlander.

Alasdair growled in dissatisfaction, pivoted to pace the length of the theater entry again, and froze in his tracks. Justine and Blake were stepping out of one of the black horseless chariots that he had been seeing all day.

And Morgaine, radiant in a fitted and flared kirtle, dismounted behind them.

Alasdair's heart thumped. She had come, garbed fetchingly in Faerie green.

Now all Alasdair had to do was figure out how to earn her favor. A hard lump rose in his throat. Any vestige of charm he possessed disappeared like a morning mist burned away by the sun.

"Alasdair!" Justine exclaimed, as though surprised to see him here. "What a delight to see you again."

"You remember Morgan?" Blake gestured to the tiny, perfect queen and winked slyly at Alasdair.

They had warned him that this meeting would have to look uncontrived. Endeavoring to look pleased with a chance encounter, Alasdair summoned his best smile and turned to the lady in question.

Only to catch a flash of fear in her eyes.

This was not good. All of Alasdair's comments in their first encounter tumbled into his mind, and he feared that he had given grave offense in assuming the lady to be a whore.

Oh, he was the most simple daftie ever to draw a breath!

"My lady Morgaine," Alasdair said as smoothly as he could.

The lady took a step back.

Suddenly Alasdair recalled how the lairds greeted Robert the Bruce's wife. The way to a woman's approval, as any man knew, lay in sweet words.

Though any compliments he granted this sorceress would be far from insincere. Alasdair captured her hand with a quick gesture, then bent low and kissed its back. The scent of roses that emanated from her fed his highly inappropriate desire. "Might I say you look lovely on this evening."

Justine sighed and Alasdair dared to be encouraged.

But Morgaine snatched her hand away. "Why, you . . ." she began.

Before the enchantress could finish whatever she had intended to say, Justine intervened quickly. "How wonderful to cross paths again! What a small world. Alasdair, you'll just have to join us for dinner."

"Why, look, we're almost late for our reservation," Blake declared with a glance at the black band on his wrist.

Justine laughed lightly. "Maybe they can find us a table for four. We'd better hurry inside." She flashed a meaningful look at Blake, who began herding them all toward the restaurant like a brood of wayward chicks.

The entire transaction occurred so quickly that Alasdair's head fairly spun. They were accomplished at seeing their objectives met, these two, and Alasdair felt a grudging respect for the manner in which Justine kept her pledge.

Morgaine was clever to have such advisors close to her.

"Justine!" Morgaine sputtered. "What are you doing?"

The advisor, to Alasdair's surprise, slanted a coy look at her monarch. "Just being friendly," she responded enigmatically.

Morgaine flushed scarlet, and Alasdair's heart melted at the sight. Had he ever had the good fortune to meet a more entrancing woman? That her charms were wrought by magical means did not seem to be pertinent—at least, not to one part of his anatomy.

Blake ushered them into the restaurant, where they lingered in the doorway, obviously awaiting some attendant. By accident or by design, Morgaine was directly beside Alasdair. He could smell that bewitching blend of roses rising from her very flesh.

This was his moment.

Alasdair gritted his teeth and cleared his throat. "My lady Morgaine," he murmured with a slight bow of his head. "I must say what a great pleasure it is to enjoy your company again."

The lady fired a hostile glance in his direction. "Don't even pretend this is an accidental meeting. I know Justine too well for that."

Alasdair felt the back of his neck grow hot, a sign of guilt if ever there was one.

But no one was going to aid him here.

Justine deliberately ignored her monarch's comment. Alasdair wondered how anyone could be so cavalier with their own hide.

A man garbed in black, with a length of linen inexplicably over his arm, chatted with Justine, nodded, then led the way across the glittering hall.

Justine sailed across the floor, Blake right behind her, and Alasdair seized the opportunity to speak to the queen without her advisors listening.

He looked into Morgaine's green eyes and felt the pull of her enchantment. "I must admit," he said quietly, "that I greatly desired to see you once more."

The lady's lips thinned. "Look, I know what you've done. And contrary to some people's expectations, I'm not *that* desperate for a man!"

Alasdair was quite certain that she had enough immortals at her beck and call to satisfy whatever desires she had. "My lady, I must apologize for my earlier assumptions. As you might understand, I was confused by what had occurred and fear I did not present myself well. On this night, I wished only to speak to you that I might present my plea . . ."

Morgaine's eyes flashed, and she waved a finger indignantly under his nose. Alasdair fought the instinct to retreat. "I don't need to hear any pleas from you! Whatever you might have told Justine, I know all I need to know about the kind of man you are! I'm not interested in anything you have to say."

Alasdair caught his breath, then anger surged through him. How dare she judge him without a hearing? "You know naught of the manner of man I am!" he retorted.

"Is that right?" The enchantress dug in her small black satchel and hauled out a faceted crystal that was breathtakingly familiar.

Alasdair gasped.

The crowning stone from the regalia! 'Twas the stone the witch had bade him hold when she sent him to Morgaine's kingdom.

'Twas the stone he would need to return home.

Without a second thought, Alasdair snatched at the gem, but Morgaine danced out of his range. Understanding burned bright in her green eyes, and she shook her head in displeasure.

"What kind of a man would stoop to stealing from the regalia?" she hissed—and Alasdair's hand fell limply to his side.

He could well understand her revulsion. Indeed, Alasdair would have shared a low opinion of anyone who resorted to thievery of Scotland's crown jewels.

But the witch had *given* the token to him.

"I can explain," he protested, but the sorceress shook her head.

"Save your lies," she said coldly. "You may have fooled everyone else, but I know what you've done and I'm going to make sure it gets fixed."

With that, she swept away in Justine's wake.

But her words made no sense. Alasdair could not quite understand how Morgaine, who stole men away to her world without remorse, could judge him harshly for stealing from the regalia.

A crime of which he was not even guilty.

Did she nurse a secret affection for the Scottish dream of independence—despite the fact that she flew the English standard above her abode?

Was that why it required the regalia stone to come to her domain?

Alasdair did not know. Annoying the powerful enchantress had certainly not been on his agenda for this night. How should he proceed?

Justine solved the issue.

"Alasdair!" she summoned him with a smile, indicating a vacant seat beside Morgaine. "Come along, we're waiting."

Alasdair gazed across the glittering restaurant and felt as kenspeckle as a fart at a funeral. But there was naught for it. Somehow he had to win the Lady Morgaine's favor. And this might be his only chance.

Surely, even given his current run of luck, he could not manage to make matters worse.

Chapter 4

SOME ACTOR! ALASDAIR certainly hadn't been able to hide the fact that he recognized the crystal Morgan had found.

Well, she was on to him now, and even Justine would see that she had been wrong about this man.

Morgan marched to the table the maître d' indicated and sat down without looking back at the highlander. She cringed when her sister called out to Alasdair, but bent her attention on the menu.

The menu, however, was not sufficiently fascinating to keep Morgan from noting a very muscular leg sliding under the table beside her. The dusting of golden hair on Alasdair's leg caught the light, and Morgan had an impulsive urge to test whether his muscles were really as firm as they looked.

She gripped the menu harder instead.

Moules marinara, avec une baguette de l'ail.

Morgan swallowed when Alasdair's knee bumped against her own and she felt her cheeks blaze with self-consciousness. She ignored her sister's not-quite-concealed nudge of Blake. Those two huddled behind their menus, smugly satisfied co-conspirators.

Strong fingers landed on the table within Morgan's peripheral vision. She hated how she noted their lean strength and

deep tan. Morgan imagined those fingers sliding up her flesh
and swallowed awkwardly.

"My lady Morgaine?" Even his voice was low and husky,
a perfect pitch for intimacy. If she drew him, Morgan would
put Alasdair against a fiercely blue sky, his hair blowing in
the wind.

Wait a minute! She wasn't going to *draw* some con man!

"My lady?" Alasdair murmured again, and Morgan didn't
have it in her heart to ignore him.

Auntie Gillian had always said there was no excuse for
rudeness. Morgan composed her features in an unencouraging
expression. She glanced up and nearly drowned in fathomless
blue eyes. Her heart stopped, then lurched forward again.

Why, oh, why, did this scoundrel have to be so attractive?

Alasdair cleared his throat, obviously uncomfortable with
what he had to say, and glanced at the menu. His ears red-
dened, and Morgan remembered that he hadn't been able to
read the guidebook in the castle.

A tiny, traitorous part of her heart melted in sympathy when
he leaned closer. Alasdair's voice dropped to a husky burr that
eroded Morgan's resistance even further. "My lady, I fear that
I do not know how to proceed in such circumstance . . ."

Surely it couldn't hurt to help the man order a meal?

"It's in French," she explained before she could question
her compassionate impulse. "They have a lot of steak and
seafood, it seems."

He looked blank.

"Beef and fish."

"Fish?" Alasdair grimaced comically. "Who would have
fish when they could have good beef?" He gave her a suspicious look. "Unless the beef here is tainted?"

Morgan decided not to get into the whole "mad cow" business, especially since she didn't understand the specifics very
well.

Instead, she stuck to the tried and true. "Studies show that
it's not healthy to eat red meat every day," she informed him.

Alasdair scoffed openly. " 'Tis a far sight healthier red than
any other shade."

Morgan knew that this time *she* looked blank.

But Alasdair's firm lips twisted and his fair brows drew together in a frown. "Aye, there's many as think they can fool a man with stewing and spices, but when meat is gone, 'tis *gone,* and no kitchen wizardry will disguise the truth from a man's belly."

He seemed to be speaking from experience. Morgan supposed that if she had ever been served bad meat, she would be similarly opinionated.

She deliberately did not think of her own culinary efforts, many of which had not been fit for a dog.

Alasdair shook his head, then turned those beguiling blues upon her. Morgan, astonished to find a twinkle glimmering in their depths, could not look away. "When the pigs will not consume it," he confided in a low rumble, "any cook must be compelled to face the truth."

His words were such a close echo of her own thoughts that Morgan felt as though he had seen right into her mind. She felt herself blush furiously.

Alasdair's gaze danced over her face, and the resolute line of his lips softened. If Morgan thought his tone had been low and confidential before, the way it rumbled now proved this man had considerable charm still to spare. "My lady Morgaine, would you do me the courtesy of choosing some viand to fill my belly?"

Morgan tried to act unaffected by his appeal but was pretty certain she failed. Fumbling with the menu and dropping it on the floor was a big clue.

Alasdair gallantly dove to retrieve it at the same moment as she did, and they bumped heads en route. She sat up hastily when she saw his strong fingers close over the laminated sheet.

By the time she was sitting straight again with the menu securely in her grip, Morgan's face was so hot that she was sure it was as red as a beet.

One glance at Justine's smug smile was enough to revive her. This guy was a crook! And she was going to prove her sister wrong on this matchmaking venture!

Morgan took refuge in the details of the menu. "How hungry are you?" she asked, proud of her businesslike tone.

"Very."

Morgan refused to let Alasdair's low chuckle affect her attitude.

A waiter carried a tray of hors d'oeuvres, including escargots, past their table. Alasdair sniffed appreciatively at the waft of garlic butter, then looked alarmed as the food was deposited on the next table. He was obviously shocked when the diners tucked into their appetizers.

"They eat *snails*? Like some vermin in the fields?" he inquired in an incredulous whisper. The woman in question apparently heard his comment, because she shot a hostile glance toward their table.

Morgan swallowed her smile. "It's an acquired taste."

"Indeed, I would expect so!" Alasdair inhaled sharply and looked toward the other diners with unconcealed horror. "I beg of you, my lady, find me some decent fare."

Decent would be big, red, and dead, in the vocabulary of a man like Alasdair, Morgan was sure. She scanned the menu. "There's a Delmonico steak in a pepper sauce."

A glint of interest in Alasdair's eye told her she had made a good choice. "Aye? 'Tis good fresh meat?"

"Oh, I'd think so. They serve steak tartare, after all."

He frowned. "What is this Tartar's steak?"

"It's raw, with onions and an egg and some spices," Morgan explained. "But the meat has to be very, very fresh."

Alasdair nodded firmly. "I will try this."

"But it's just an appetizer . . ."

"And the other?"

How could he even wonder about a Delmonico steak? The only time Morgan had ordered one—the "house special"—she'd taken two thirds home and had pieces of it for dinner for the next three nights. "That would be a main course."

Alasdair nodded approval, his glance straying to Morgan's black clutch. He leaned toward her, capturing one of her hands in his great warm one. His voice was low with intent, and Morgan felt that tingle awaken in the depths of her belly. "My lady Morgaine, you must understand that I *need* that stone . . ."

That's what she got for trying to help!

"I'm sure you do," Morgan snapped and easily pulled her

hand out of his gentle grip. She snatched up her purse and slapped it definitively on the table at the furthest point from Alasdair. Just for good measure, she shifted her chair a good foot closer to Blake.

Alasdair stiffened. "What do you think I mean to do?" he demanded, as though insulted. "*Steal* the token from you?"

Morgan arched a brow eloquently. "It would hardly be news, would it?"

Alasdair snorted and Morgan took refuge in her menu, pretending she hadn't already decided to order the filet mignon.

"Morgan!" Justine chided. "Don't you think you're being a little harsh? Alasdair is our guest tonight, after all."

"Yeah." Blake smiled at Morgan and Alasdair in turn. "We really enjoyed his company this afternoon. I'm sure you would, too, if you just gave him a chance."

Morgan deliberately set her menu aside. "That's only because you don't know that he's a thief."

Justine and Blake gaped at Morgan most satisfactorily.

"My lady, I told you that I could explain . . ." Alasdair murmured, but Morgan wasn't going to listen to anything a con man had to say for himself.

"A thief?" Blake echoed, adjusting his glasses with a frown. "Why on earth would you say that?"

Morgan snatched up her purse and rummaged in it, dropping the crystal from the regalia onto the white linen tablecloth with a victorious flourish. "Because he stole *this* from the regalia!"

The response was less than she might have hoped for.

Justine and Blake stared at the stone as though they didn't know what it was. Alasdair's hand landed on the table, but Morgan stilled any acquisitive move he might have contemplated with one cold look.

"From *where*?" Blake asked.

"*What* is it?" Justine asked simultaneously.

"It's the crowning stone from the Scottish regalia," Morgan explained impatiently. "Don't you remember that it was mounted on the top of the scepter in the display this morning?"

Blake rolled his eyes. "Morgan, you really have to start listening! What's the point of taking these tours if you don't pay attention? The guide specifically said that the stone had been missing for seven centuries or something." With a dismissive wave, he picked up his menu again. "That Robert the Bruce dirtball is supposed to have sold it."

Alasdair inhaled sharply, and Morgan glanced up to find his eyes blazing. "Robert the Bruce would never have committed such a foul deed!"

Blake shrugged. "Whatever. It's not like it matters now. The guy was a loser, no matter how you slice it." He ran a finger down the array of offerings and wrinkled his nose. "Do you think the lobster would be good?"

Justine clicked her tongue and winked at Alasdair. Morgan was irritated to hear her sister's soothing hostess-with-the-mostest tone. "Alasdair, I sincerely hope that you're not insulted. Morgan has the most active imagination."

"I'm not making this up!"

Justine laughed lightly. "Oh, Morgan. You always said that when we were kids too! Honestly, monkeys outside the window and pet dragons in the closet." Her lips twisted as though she couldn't help laughing, then she plucked the stone from the table.

The tension emanating from Alasdair was tangible. Morgan noted that his fists were clenched on either side of his chair.

If he grabbed for that stone, she wasn't going to let him get away with it!

"Don't you see?" Morgan said urgently. "He used us to get the stone out of the castle and now he's going to steal it back." She looked scathingly at Alasdair. "Probably sell it for a fortune."

"That?" Blake's glance was skeptical. "Might get five bucks for it—on a good day."

"It's kind of pretty." Justine turned it to catch the light, then tossed it to Morgan as though it were no more than a bauble. Morgan fumbled but managed to hold on to it. "Did you find it in one of those New Age shops? They're just nuts for crystals, aren't they?"

Morgan felt herself tremble as her fingers closed over the stone. "This isn't a joke," she insisted.

"Then why doesn't either of us remember the stone being

in the scepter?'' Blake asked mildly. "Face it, Morgan. Your imagination has gotten away with you again.''

Obviously they didn't believe her. Morgan didn't know how Alasdair had managed to fool everyone, but she was somehow going to prove that she was right. She shoved the stone back into her evening purse, glancing up when she felt the weight of someone's gaze upon her.

And one look into those blue, blue eyes told Morgan that there was one person who already knew that she was right.

The steak of Tartars was good fare, but hardly ample enough to satisfy. Alasdair was greatly relieved when the servant slid a great wallop of beef beneath his nose. The smell alone made his innards growl in anticipation.

Anxious not to give offense in this strange court, he had already noted and adapted to the use of the small, tined spear that had been awaiting him at the table. He surreptitiously watched the lady Morgaine herself as she carved a piece of her own much more meager serving of meat, then mimicked her actions.

And closed his eyes when the succulent flavor flooded his mouth. He was too hungered to care whether 'twas bewitched. The red wine was finer than any he had ever known, wine being a rarity in his life and one oft so musty by the time it ventured this far north that Alasdair preferred his ale.

All in all, he could not object to the quantity or the quality of the food in Morgaine's domain.

As long as one avoided the snails.

"I must thank you, my lady,'' he murmured. "For the fare is most fine.''

Morgaine looked unimpressed by his gratitude, although she nodded curtly. Conversation flared briefly as each commended the meal to the attentive servant, then silence reigned again. Alasdair took another morsel of meat and tried to think of a way he could win the crystal from Morgaine's clutches.

Let alone curry the queen's favor.

"You know, Alasdair, you just might be able to help us,'' Justine commented brightly.

"Indeed?''

"Yes." The advisor smiled. "You know, Morgan has a fascination with folktales and old stories. I was wondering if you might know some, you know, stories you heard as a child, that you could share with us."

Alasdair glanced sidelong at his adversary, only to find her expression murderous. Evidently she did not like this advisor sharing tales of her tastes. Why would she be interested in the tales of mortals, except to turn them to her own dark gain?

But all the same, this might work to his advantage. Alasdair summoned a winning smile. "Aye, that I do. My gran is a great teller of tales, and I have heard the lot of them from the cradle."

"Really?" Justine was obviously impressed by this news. "You see, Morgan, I just knew Alasdair would be able to help!"

Before Morgaine could comment upon this, a servant hovered at the periphery of the table and coughed discreetly. Blake looked up and beckoned to him.

"Excuse me, sir." The servant's manner was as deferential as though he addressed Morgaine herself. Alasdair wondered whether the common folk here were not permitted to speak to the great lady without intercession. "We did manage to obtain tickets for this evening's performance for you"—Justine cooed in delight—"although there is a small problem."

"Really?" Blake fastidiously wiped his mouth and laid his fine napkin aside. "And what's that?" He did not look surprised by this morsel of news, nor did he so much as glance at the sorceress Morgaine. Alasdair could not help but wonder whether these two had launched yet another scheme on his behalf.

He would not consider what he might owe them for their intervention.

The man cleared his throat. "Sadly, there are only two tickets available . . ."

"Ah!" Blake's face wore an expression of exaggerated dismay.

Justine pouted in a manner that Alasdair would have thought most uncharacteristic. "But I *really* wanted to see this play. It's our only night in Edinburgh."

The pair of advisors turned winning smiles on their patroness.

"Well, then, you should go," Morgaine said flatly and stabbed at her meat. "Don't worry about me."

"Oh, we couldn't," Justine protested, her bright glance dancing toward Alasdair so pointedly that he realized his role in all of this.

As did the tiny queen, evidently. Morgaine muttered an expletive beneath her breath that Alasdair was astonished she knew.

And then he was so sorely insulted that she found his companionship offensive that he could not summon a word in his own defense.

"Well, that's settled, then." Blake pushed himself to his feet and looked at the dark band on his wrist. "Almost curtain time." He presented a gold square to the man, who bowed and scurried away, then smiled at Morgan. "I'm glad this worked out so well. You and Alasdair just take your time here, everything's taken care of."

"Have dessert and coffee," Justine added as she got to her feet.

"And Alasdair, surely you wouldn't mind seeing Morgan back to the bed-and-breakfast?" Blake asked amiably. "Any city at night is no place for a woman alone."

Alasdair got to his feet politely and inclined his head. "I should be most honored to accompany the lady Morgaine wherever she so desires . . ."

"You can't do this to me, you know," Morgaine said tightly, sparing a glare for Justine that did not bode well for that woman's future. "I'll just go back to the hotel myself. This isn't going to work."

"Oh, don't be silly!" Justine protested. "Sit and enjoy yourself. Talk. Relax for once, Morgan." She slid her arm through Blake's and smiled for him alone. "I'm sure we'll all have a wonderful time this evening."

The pair exchanged a hot look that left no doubt in Alasdair's mind as to the status of their relations. Blake retrieved his gold square and they swept away, leaving Alasdair with the lady Morgaine.

Who was evidently not very happy with the situation.

No sooner had they left than Morgaine jabbed a finger to-ward Alasdair, giving him no chance to try another measure of his charm. "You may have fooled them, and you may have fooled the guards, but I know what you did and I'm not going to forget it."

"But I can explain . . ."

"I'm sure you have some story," she sniffed with disdain. She pushed her plate away, obviously preparing to leave.

"But my lady, I truly must speak to you . . ."

"I'm not interested in anything you have to say," Morgaine said crisply. She stood up and gathered her small satchel, the crystal making a little bulge in its softness. She met Alasdair's gaze coolly. "And you don't have to see me back to the hotel, regardless of what Blake and Justine have said."

And with that, she swept out of the restaurant.

Alasdair watched her go, grudgingly admiring the way she held her head high. She was a feisty bit of woman, that much was for certain.

And Alasdair was not going to let her out of his sight, re-gardless of what she had to say about the matter. His gran had always said the MacAulays were too cursed stubborn for their own good, and for once Alasdair was content to prove her right.

There was too much at stake to do otherwise.

It was probably the best exit Morgan had ever made in her life.

She hadn't tripped over a single thing, or tried to leave through the ladies' room, or had her words come out in the wrong order. She hadn't even inadvertently dragged the linen napkin away from the table. And she hadn't been to the ladies' room, so her skirt couldn't be tucked into her pantyhose.

But it was just her luck that there wasn't a single taxi in front of the Lyceum Theatre.

Something had to go wrong. It always did.

When a great blond man slipped out of the restaurant while she lingered indecisively at the curb, Morgan knew her luck had run out. She wouldn't be able to manage hanging around without talking to Alasdair again.

And Morgan didn't trust herself to say no to him again so quickly. She jumped off the curb to hail a cab flying past, but the taxi kept going. In its wake the street was dark and empty in both directions.

Well. If her options were talking to Alasdair or walking back by herself, there was no choice.

She would walk.

It was a nice evening, after all, Morgan told herself, and the exercise would do her good after that meal. And she could work off some of her irritation with Justine's meddling.

She hastily picked the road she thought led to the bed-and-breakfast, without looking back to see whether Alasdair was behind her. She headed off at a quick pace, despite her little black heels, and was momentarily alarmed by how quickly she became the only one walking in the street.

Morgan nervously glanced back at the brightly lit theater behind her. Her heart skipped a beat when she thought she saw a figure step quickly into the shadows.

No. She was imagining things. Again. Edinburgh was a safe city, probably a lot safer than Chicago, where she regularly walked by herself.

At least, she walked streets she knew were safe.

And in daylight.

Morgan scanned the front of the theater, but Alasdair was gone. She refused to feel disappointed that he had finally taken no for an answer.

After all, she didn't need an escort. She was sure it wasn't far to the bed-and-breakfast. And it was only eight-thirty—it just got dark early here.

There was no problem.

Morgan clutched her purse, her instincts screaming to the contrary, and trotted in what she was absolutely positive was the right direction.

Directionally impaired Morgan was, of course, completely wrong.

But by the time she realized her mistake, there wasn't much

she could do about it but keep walking. Periodically, she
thought she heard a stealthy tread on the pavement behind her,
but whenever she looked back, the street was vacant.

She wasn't sure whether to be relieved or frightened. Her
heart had no such indecision—it was pounding in her ears like
the sound track of a rock video.

But Morgan kept walking.

And cursing her own ability to get herself in a pickle.

The neighborhood she found herself in must have been part
of the university. It was completely, eerily deserted, the windows of the lecture halls dark and vacant. Her heels clicked
loudly on the pavement, and a candy wrapper rattled as it
tumbled across the road.

There wasn't a vehicle in sight, and the only light came
from the streetlights. Keep moving, she told herself firmly.

Morgan studied a building opposite, certain she had seen it
sometime during the day but unable to place it. Had she been
going to the castle? To the palace? For tea? Back to the bed-
and-breakfast? All the streets were twisted around each other,
their names made no orderly sense, and it was so very confusing.

She could have headed back to the theater, if she could have
managed to guess which way she had come. Morgan rounded
a corner and the dark silhouette of a park loomed three blocks
ahead.

She hesitated for a moment. Crossing that expanse alone
wouldn't be a clever move.

Morgan considered narrow streets to the left and the right
but didn't like the look of any of them. The street behind her
was filled with ominous shadows. Left without many choices,
she marched onward, ignoring the lump in her throat.

A cat yowled suddenly and Morgan jumped. She lost her
balance on the unfamiliar heels, tripped over the curb, and
took one step down into the gutter.

And broke the heel of her shoe in a sewer grate.

The heel disappeared through the metal grate and she heard
it splash into something unmentionable far, far below.

Morgan was almost ready to cry. She loved these shoes!
And she would never be able to get another heel to match.
She turned to head back to the theater, one way or the other,

then realized she had bigger problems than matching a heel.

Morgan wasn't alone anymore. She looked up into the cold
eyes of a truly Dickensian ruffian, standing on the curb right
beside her.

Complete with a very nasty little knife.

Morgan swallowed carefully. She hadn't even heard him
coming.

"C'mon, darling, give me all your lovely money." The
knife flashed as he waved it impatiently at her. "C'mon,
c'mon, hand over the wee purse. I've not got all night for
this."

Another shadow separated itself from an alleyway and ad-
vanced, this young man a close copy of the first. "Hey, she's
a cute wee bird." He chuckled darkly. "We could have us
some fun, we could."

Morgan's blood ran cold. Justine had been right.

Again.

But it was a little bit late for second thoughts.

"C'mon! C'mon!"

Morgan eyed the pair of thieves and realized she'd be lucky
to get out of this with just the loss of her purse.

Suddenly a bellow echoed through the empty street. It
sounded like a boar had gotten loose and wasn't too pleased
about its situation.

Morgan saw no more than a tawny blur before the glint of
the knife disappeared. She backed away from the scuffle, uncertain whether the new arrival had come to her rescue or
simply wanted the spoils for himself.

The first attacker went down with a yelp and his head hit
the pavement with a sick thud. Blood trickled across the side-
walk. A great shadowed figure pivoted and dove after the second attacker, who made the mistake of trying to flee.

He managed to take four steps before he was snatched up
from behind.

The boy gave a good fight and cursed eloquently. Morgan
caught a glimpse of dirty plaid and the brassy glint of her
defender's hair, and her heart began to pound. Although she
knew she should run, Morgan couldn't help but watch.

No more than a moment later, Alasdair kicked the limp

body of the second thief aside. He spat on the pavement between the two, who looked a lot younger than they had just
moments before, then his simmering blue gaze locked on Morgan.

She took a cautious step backward, her heart racing like a
freight train.

"What in the holy name of God do you think you are doing?" he roared, then came after her.

Now Morgan ran.

Actually, she hobbled, one heel up and one heel down. But
even as she ran, Morgan couldn't help but wonder what Alasdair intended to do to her. Hadn't he said he'd toss her over
his shoulder and have his way with her?

As much as she hated to admit it, a part of her really liked
that idea. She was running as much from that realization as
from the highlander.

But she didn't get far before Alasdair scooped her off her
feet and tossed her over his shoulder in one bold move, mut-
tering all the while. Morgan struggled, but his one hand was
clamped so firmly over her knees that she wasn't going anywhere Alasdair didn't want her to go.

Her mouth went dry.

"Of all the fool things to be doing, I never would have
imagined the likes of you to have so little sense as this!" he
raged. "And what manner of a foul kingdom is it you have
that the common folk show no respect for a queen within their
own filthy ranks?"

Alasdair stalked down a shadowed street, and Morgan was
surprised to note that it didn't look so bad on closer inspection.
Within moments, they emerged onto a brightly lit and very
busy thoroughfare.

"Never have I seen the like of it, though the fault is as
much yours as theirs. Did Justine not warn you to not walk
alone on these streets? What manner of queen employs advisors, then ignores their counsel?"

Morgan was embarrassed and annoyed to realize how close
she had been to comparative safety. Alasdair rounded the corner and strode into a throng of people who eyed them with
curiosity.

She wriggled, to no discernible effect. "Um, you can put me down now."

But Alasdair showed no signs of setting Morgan on her feet. She wasn't even sure he'd heard her.

"Mere lads they were! Not more than thirteen summers!" His disgust was evident. "What manner of town is it that a boy can find himself such trouble? Where are their sires and mothers? Have they not decent work to pursue, rather than thieving from women?"

Morgan struggled, not liking the way her skin heated everywhere she touched Alasdair. The strength of his hand locked around her knees sent unwelcome shivers all through her.

But he was evidently not interested in any thoughts Morgan had on the matter.

He ranted, waving his free hand as he stomped down the street. "And what manner of advisors have you by your side that they would be so quick to leave you unattended when such danger lurks at every turn?"

"They're not my advisors! Now, put me down."

Alasdair growled on as though Morgan hadn't said anything at all. "You may be assured, my lady, that they were not the first to have interest in your bonny curves. Had I not been busy with the last, these would never have gotten so close."

He muttered an expletive that made even more people turn to look, and his voice dropped to a growl. "Aye, were you a woman of mine, I would be having fine words for your lack of interest in your own safe keeping . . ."

"But I'm not a woman of yours," Morgan retorted. "So please put me down."

Alasdair stopped suddenly, and Morgan braced herself for trouble. She couldn't help but wonder why he had heard that one comment.

"Aye," he acknowledged in a dangerously low tone, "that you are not."

His hands suddenly were on her hips, moving with the sure touch of a caress. The heat of his palms launched a tingle over her flesh that she would have preferred to be without.

Then those hands lifted her high. Morgan's mouth went dry as Alasdair let her slide slowly down the length of him until they stood toe to toe. His hands rested proprietarily on her waist, his eyes blazed into hers. She barely dared to breathe as she stared up at her self-appointed protector and felt his thumbs tracing little circles against her back.

Morgan was fully aware of the erection she had slipped past. It throbbed against her stomach now as though there wasn't all this clothing between them.

And the glint in Alasdair's eyes was unabashedly sensual.

Nothing else could have fired her blood like the evidence of Alasdair's arousal. Matt's continued pursuit of other women—and his avoidance of intimacy with his wife—had left a deep scar in Morgan's belief in her own attractiveness.

To have this aggressively masculine man desire her was a siren's call Morgan couldn't refuse.

But Alasdair was waiting. And when Morgan looked deeply into his eyes, she understood why.

He was waiting for her to decide how to proceed. Morgan knew not only that Alasdair wanted her but that she could push him away with one fingertip.

And if she did, he would go.

Just having the choice made Morgan not want to make it. It had to be the glass of wine she'd had with dinner, she concluded wildly.

Or maybe it was the adrenaline rush of barely escaping a mugging.

But the truth was that Morgan didn't care. She wanted to kiss Alasdair, just once, just a little kiss, just because she had the choice.

And right here, right now, she had the perfect excuse.

Alasdair's grip tightened ever so slightly on Morgan's waist. "You are not going to be so foolish as to run off again, are you?" he demanded, his fair brows bristling. "You may be sure that I shall see you safely to your abode."

Morgan could smell Alasdair's scent, and her toes curled inside her mutilated shoes.

"No." Her voice was no more than a whisper. She was vaguely aware of catcalls and whistles around them, but couldn't have cared less about anything beyond this man.

Alasdair arched a brow. "Promise?"

The "*r*" rumbled in his chest, the vibration startling against Morgan's breasts. She felt her nipples tighten as her imagination concocted what she could have expected if she had been Alasdair's woman.

How would he kiss?

"Promise," she agreed breathlessly.

Alasdair smiled then and lifted one hand to gently touch her cheek. "Are you unharmed by those ruffians, then, my lady? Hale and hearty?"

His protective concern was the icing on the cake. No one other than Justine and Auntie Gillian had ever been so concerned for Morgan's welfare. Certainly, no one had ever saved her from thugs.

"Yes." Her voice was breathy, like some silver screen movie star. "I'm just fine."

"Good." Alasdair nodded emphatically and started to step away.

It was Morgan's last chance.

Before she could lose her nerve, she stretched to her toes. Alasdair froze, obviously uncertain of what she meant to do. Morgan paused, a finger's breadth from his firm lips and looked into those blue, blue eyes.

"Thank you," she whispered, then kissed him.

Morgan had been thinking of just brushing her lips across his, sort of a sisterly buss of appreciation, but Alasdair evidently had different ideas. He stiffened for just a moment, as though surprised, then made a quick recovery. He angled his mouth across Morgan's and lifted her against him.

But some of that tentativeness lingered in his touch, reassuring Morgan that she could rebuff him—if she wanted to. She melted at that certainty and wound her arms around his neck.

Morgan's imagination hadn't begun to do his kiss justice.

Her eyes closed in pleasure as Alasdair's one hand cupped her buttock and the other cradled her shoulder. Her lips parted of their own accord, and the sleek heat of Alasdair's tongue slid between her teeth.

The whistles Morgan had heard earlier were nothing compared to the ones echoing around them now.

But Alasdair tasted so good that she didn't care. Her arms twined around his sturdy neck, her fingers taking note of the muscled strength of his shoulders before tangling in the thick hair at his nape. Morgan could feel the thunder of his heart against her own as his kiss became more demanding.

Alasdair wanted her. *Her*. Morgan's skin heated, and the tingle of desire in her belly grew to a roar. She wanted to twine her legs around Alasdair and drag him back to her lair.

And ravish him all night long. Alasdair had unlocked a barricaded door, setting ten years of pent-up desire free.

Morgan didn't want to cage it again.

Alasdair must have been thinking along the same lines. He lifted his lips from hers, and his sapphire gaze locked with hers for an electric moment.

Then he swung her up into his arms and began to stride through the crowd.

And Morgan had a moment to think.

What on earth was she doing?

How could she have forgotten what Alasdair had done?

Chapter 5

THE SORCERESS CHANGED moods faster than an autumn sky. No sooner had Alasdair acknowledged the not unpleasant feeling of having her nestled in his arms than she twisted and fought his grip like a wild thing.

"Put me down!" she demanded.

Only then did Alasdair realize his own foolhardiness. He had lost himself in Morgaine le Fee's kiss! He was seven kinds of fool to be so careless with his own fate.

The enchantress did not need to repeat her request. Alasdair dumped her on her feet without ceremony and backed away. He wiped the taste of her kiss from his burning lips with the back of his hand and surveyed her warily.

What witchery had she cast over him?

Morgaine looked as distressed as Alasdair felt. Her cheeks were flushed in a most attractive way, her eyes were flashing, her hair was tangled.

And her lips were temptingly swollen. Anger rose hot within Alasdair that he had been so readily tricked.

"How dare you touch me?"

"I touch *you*?" Alasdair retorted. "You were the one as pressed yourself upon me!"

"You were the one who took more than was offered!" the

lady answered back, shaking an indignant finger. "I was only going to give you a peck of appreciation . . ."

Alasdair folded his arms across his chest and glowered at her. He refused to think about the fire this one would start when she *meant* to kiss a man soundly. "That was no peck, my lady."

"It certainly wasn't!" She glared back at him, so full of vigor that Alasdair was tempted to repeat the exchange.

Even if his better judgment demanded that he keep her at arm's length. Alasdair fought against his desire and slowly got his pulse under control.

His gallant words were forced through gritted teeth. "Clearly, 'twas no more at work than the fright we both have had."

Morgaine looked as though she would argue that point, then she nodded vehemently.

Alasdair wondered only for a moment whether she had deliberately been testing her allure. Then he shook such whimsy from his mind and offered Morgaine his arm, his manner as coolly impersonal as he could make it. "My lady? I would accompany you to your abode."

"You will not!" she snapped and danced backward. She tossed her hair like a flighty filly. "I can find my way there alone, thank you."

Did the woman have so short a memory as that? Alasdair folded his arms across his chest, knowing his skepticism showed. "Aye, you were doing a fine job of it when last I came along."

The lady flushed crimson and Alasdair's anger melted to naught.

"I gave my word to Blake," he added gently when she seemed at a loss for words. "And I would see it kept."

Morgaine stared at him for a long moment. "How do I know you don't want to hurt me? You said you want the stone—you might mug me and leave me in a gutter somewhere."

Alasdair snorted and looked pointedly around. "I should think that even in this place, on such a busy avenue, someone might notice a foul deed and intervene on your behalf." When she looked unconvinced, Alasdair felt himself scowl with impatience. "Why would I come to your aid just to attack you myself?"

Morgaine exhaled slowly, her bright gaze fixed upon him. "You might want me to trust you," she mused.

Alasdair studied her, liking the light of intelligence in her witchy eyes. She was a clever one—he had not even thought of such a ploy.

"My lady," he said in a tone that brooked no argument, "I grant you my word that I mean you no harm."

She lifted her chin proudly. "Then what do you want from me?"

Here was his chance. Alasdair sobered as he dared give voice to his only hope. "I only want to go home, my lady."

Morgaine stared at him, as though confused by his simple request, then bit the lip he had so recently tasted. Alasdair's desire roared to life.

"So do I," she admitted, a most fetching and shy smile curving her lips. "Except I don't know where it is."

A lie, clearly, for no queen could forget the site of her own lair. Yet Alasdair guessed this was a test of his ingenuity. Were his gran's tales not filled with Faeries requiring mortals to prove themselves worthy of any otherworldly gifts?

And to be released from the domain of Morgaine le Fee could only be considered a great gift. Alasdair had but to think of his son to have his determination renewed.

He gripped Morgaine's elbow and marched her into a brightly lit establishment, where the portly patron glanced up from his ledger. "I have need of direction to the lady Morgaine's abode," Alasdair said firmly.

The man blinked as though he had not the wit to understand, and looked to Morgaine.

"The Thistle Bed-and-Breakfast," she supplied, and understanding dawned on the man's heavy features.

How could he not know the home of his queen? thought Alasdair.

The man led them back to the door and pointed in the direction they had been headed. "Down thisaway a good six eight blocks to Leeds Avenue, then right for a few blocks, then left on Thistle Down, then it should be along on your right beside the off-license."

That might as well have been in Latin, for Alasdair understood little of it. The off-license? And Leeds was far to the south, in the Britons' country.

"Thank you," Morgaine said with a charming smile.

Alasdair squinted down the road. Right, left, right. He could remember that.

"Right, then," the man said with a nod and ducked back to his books.

Morgaine and Alasdair exchanged a glance, and he was reassured to see that she evidently understood no more than he did.

"We had best make a start of it," he said crisply. "My lady, you had best look for this Avenue of Leeds. I shall count these six eight blocks." He cleared his throat as they stepped onto the pavement. "What, my lady, would be a 'block'?"

Morgaine seemed to fight the urge to smile. "The distance between two cross streets." She pointed back at the last intersection, then to the next with a quick explanation, and Alasdair understood.

It was no small advantage that each intersection was marked with curious illumination that changed from green to amber to red. Indeed, a man could scarcely miss such a signpost.

Alasdair began to stride down the walkway with Morgaine's elbow firmly within his grasp, but the lady wriggled free and danced ahead of him.

"You can see me back to the bed-and-breakfast if you like"—she cast the words over her shoulder without looking back, but Alasdair heard in them that she was not as indifferent to his decision as she might have liked him to believe—"but don't even think about touching me again."

Oh, Alasdair *would* think about it, that much was for certain, especially with those hips twitching right afore his eyes. A man did not readily forget a kiss that left him simmering clear down to his toes.

The enchantress limped along as he watched, then stumbled over the shoe that yet sported a stilt. In a quick gesture, she ripped off the shoes, looked them over, then cast them aside, marching on without them. One pale toe peeked through her dark stockings and Alasdair feared for those tiny feet amidst the muck of the street.

He scooped up the shoes as he trailed behind her and easily broke the stilt off the other one. A perfect pair they were now.

If only she would accept them from him. Alasdair could not help but wonder whether the sorceress would grant him another token of her esteem when he showed concern for her tender toes. The very idea did hot and thick things to him that could only betray his desire to return home.

Aye, he was a fool and then some to lust after a Faerie queen.

Morgan stifled a howl of pain when she stubbed her toe hard on the pavement. She bit her lip, hoping Alasdair hadn't noticed her clumsy move, and fought back her tears as she tried to continue on her way as though nothing had happened.

He was beside her in a moment, his lips tight with impatience. "Have you no care for your own welfare?" he demanded, then bent and lifted her injured foot in his great gentle paw. He ran a fingertip over the bruise, his touch making Morgan shiver, then slipped her own discarded shoe onto her foot.

In the blink of an eye, Morgan had matching shoes on her feet. They felt strange without the heels, the toes curling up like Aladdin's slippers, but they were a lot more comfortable than the pavement.

Why hadn't she thought of that?

"Now, then," he said briskly, eyeing the street before them. "We seek six eight blocks. I count this crossroads ahead as one." He gripped her elbow and set off at a purposeful pace.

He probably couldn't wait to be rid of her, Morgan concluded.

The idea bothered her so much—and made so little sense—that she didn't have it in her to make conversation. With a heavy heart, she clumped along beside him, enjoying the way he cupped her elbow in his warm palm even though she knew she shouldn't.

And then Alasdair began to hum.

The tune was infectious, and Morgan found herself matching her steps to it without intending to do so.

Alasdair must have noticed, because he cast an amused expression in her direction. "Lifts your spirits, does it not?" he murmured, and Morgan couldn't help but smile.

"What is it?"

"Ah, an old ditty of my gran's. 'Tis a tune to walk upon."

"Are there words?"

"Aye, 'tis the song of True Thomas. Surely you know it?"

"No." Morgan was fascinated. When Alasdair hesitated, she took his arm and gave him a little shake. "Tell me."

Alasdair's eyes narrowed. "It would please you?"

"Oh, yes! Like Justine said, I'm here to find folktales from the countryside."

"Well!" Alasdair straightened. "This is no fey tale, for True Thomas was a man in fact . . ."

"Will you sing it?"

He assessed her with a glance filtered through his fair lashes, his gaze intensely blue. That look alone was enough to set Morgan's blood to simmering. "If it would please you." His voice was so low that Morgan had a hard time fighting her urge to kiss him again.

"It would," she managed to say.

Alasdair straightened his shoulders and hummed the ditty once more. Then he began to sing.

> True Thomas lay o'er yon grassy bank,
> And he beheld a lady gay.
> A lady she was brisk and bold,
> Come riding o'er the fernie brae.
>
> Her skirt was of the grass-green silk,
> Her mantle of the velvet fine.
> And woven into her horse's mane
> Hung fifty silver bells and nine.
>
> True Thomas he took off his hat
> And bowed him low down till his knee.
> "All hail, thou mighty Queen of Heaven!
> For your peer on earth I ne'er did see!"

People turned in the street to smile and nod in time to the tune. Alasdair's voice was magnificent, melodic and deep, and Morgan was fascinated.

Then she laughed as Alasdair changed the pitch to a falsetto to indicate the voice of the fairy queen. He winked at her in a roguish way and her heart skipped a beat.

>*"Oh, no, oh, no, True Thomas," she says.*
>*"That name does not belong to me.*
>*I am but the Queen of fair Elfland,*
>*And I'm come here for to visit thee.*
>
>*"But you must go with me now, Thomas.*
>*True Thomas, you must come with me.*
>*For you must serve me seven years,*
>*Through well or woe as may chance to be."*
>
>*She turned about her milk-white steed,*
>*And took True Thomas up behind.*
>*And aye, whene'er her bridle rang,*
>*The steed flew swifter in the wind.*
>
>*For forty days and forty nights,*
>*He wade through red blood to the knee,*
>*And he saw neither sun nor moon*
>*But heard the roaring of the sea.*
>
>*Oh, they rode on, and further on,*
>*'Til came they to a garden green.*
>*"Light down, light down, my lady free.*
>*Some of that fruit let me pull to thee."*
>
>*"Oh, no, oh, no, True Thomas," she says.*
>*"That fruit must not be touched by thee!*
>*For all the plagues that are in hell*
>*Light on the fruit of this country.*
>
>*But I have a loaf here in my lap,*
>*Likewise a bottle of claret wine.*
>*And now ere we go farther on,*
>*We'll rest a while and you may dine."*

When Thomas had eaten and drunk his fill,
"Lay down your head upon my knee."
The lady said, " 'Ere we climb yon hill
And I will show you pathways three."

They came to the intersection of Leeds Avenue, and Morgan
indicated that they should turn to the right. Alasdair paused,
pointing to the left with a smile.

"Oh, do you see yon narrow road,
So thick beset with thorns and briars?
That is the path of righteousness,
Though after it but few enquies."

Morgan grinned at his game, and Alasdair gestured to the
road ahead.

"And do you see that broad broad road,
That lies across yon lillie leven?
That is the path of wickedness,
Though some call it the road to heaven."

Alasdair pointed to the right and turned their steps in that
direction.

"And do you see that bonny road,
Which winds about the ferny slope?
This is the road to fair Elfland,
Where you and I this night must go."

His voice dropped low as they started down Leeds Avenue.

"But Thomas, you must hold your tongue,
Whatever you may hear or see.
For if a word you should chance to speak,
You will never return to your own country."

Thomas has gotten a coat of the even cloth,
And a pair of shoes of velvet green,

And 'til seven years were past and gone,
True Thomas on earth was never seen.

The shadows of the entwined branches over Leeds Avenue made Morgan feel as though they were following that road to Elfland. Even the streetlights seemed to dance, as the light was filtered through the rustling leaves. It was quieter here, an elegant neighborhood where a few townhouse dwellers wandered with their dogs.

"Isn't there any more?" Morgan asked when Alasdair didn't continue.

He shook his head. "Nay, that is the end of the rhyme."

"But what happened to him?"

"True Thomas? Ah, my gran says he spent his seven years in Faerie, though indeed it seemed to him to be no more than seven days and nights. When he returned to Erceldoune, the queen of Elfland granted him an apple that gave him the gift of prophecy and a tongue that could not lie. 'Twas then she explained why he was to be named True Thomas, though he was known by mortals as Thomas Rhymer. He made his way as a poet whose verses came to pass with uncanny ease."

Morgan's imagination was captured by the spell of Alasdair's song, a thousand images gathering in her mind, restless to be set on paper. She could easily visualize Thomas being surprised by the Queen of Elfland while he lay on a hill and the way his eyes would go round when she showed him the marvels of her world.

"Well, why did the Queen of Elfland pick him?"

"Ah!" Alasdair nodded sagely. " 'Twas said he had seen her once and lost his heart to her beauty. With her otherworldly arts, she heard his heart's song and came to him, binding him to her side with a single kiss."

"Oh, that's lovely!" Morgan sighed with romantic delight, her image of Thomas becoming stronger with every detail Alasdair added. "She must have loved him, too, to have given him such a gift."

"Aye." They navigated the next curve, this street busier but with fewer trees. " 'Twas said that even the barrier betwixt

the worlds could not keep them apart,'' Alasdair mused. ''She
sent for him years later, as my gran tells it, and Thomas passed
happily to the land of Faerie, never to be seen again.''

Morgan saw the liquor store that the locals called an ''off-
license.'' The bed-and-breakfast was right beside it, and the
blue Nissan Micra rental car was parked out front.

''There it is,'' she pointed. Evidently Alasdair had noted
the thistle on the sign, because he headed straight for it.

They paused as one at the base of the steps, Morgan toying
with her key. She hadn't dated in so long that she'd forgotten
how awkward this moment could be!

But then, this wasn't a date.

Morgan tipped her head back to find Alasdair's expression
unreadable. ''Thank you for walking me home,'' she said quietly, then smiled. ''And thank you for keeping those kids from
taking my purse. I really appreciate it.'' She cleared her throat,
unable to look away from Alasdair's steady gaze.

It didn't help that he didn't say anything.

''And thank you for singing,'' Morgan said finally. ''I liked
the story very much.''

Alasdair smiled suddenly, the sight stealing Morgan's
breath away. ''Anything to please you, my lady,'' he murmured, then bent low over her hand.

Morgan's skin tingled where his lips brushed across it. The
memory of their kiss unfurled in her mind, and she didn't trust
herself not to repeat her mistake.

Morgan turned and quickly trotted up the stairs, hating how
breathless her voice sounded. ''Well, good-bye. I hope you do
find your way home.''

Alasdair frowned at that, a sadness claiming his eyes that
tore at Morgan's heart.

But before she could say anything that she would probably
regret, he turned back to the street. ''Sleep well, my lady,''
he said gruffly and walked away.

Morgan hesitated for a moment, fingering her key. If Edinburgh wasn't Alasdair's home, then where would he sleep?
Did he even have any money? Her characteristic sympathy
rolled to the fore, and she almost called after him before she
caught herself.

He was trying to manipulate her! Obviously, he wanted the crystal back. Morgan had to remember that Alasdair was an accomplished con artist—and the consummate actor.

But all the same, his song had filled her mind with wonderful images. She let herself into the silent B&B and climbed the three flights of stairs to her room, thinking busily all the while.

Instead of going to bed, Morgan turned on the light over the desk and pulled out her sketchbook. She stared at the blank space for just a moment before she began to fill the page with drawings for the tale of Thomas Rhymer.

The work came with an ease that Morgan had almost forgotten. A border of curling ivy concealed half a dozen pointed and curious faces. Then, Thomas's grassy bank of Erceldoune grew across the page, filled with wildflowers and tiny hands and faces.

Morgan's pencil seemed to have a mind of its own. It felt as though she were simply setting the little sketched elves and fairies free of their pencil prison.

She smiled and bent over the work, thinking about Alasdair's wonderfully deep and expressive voice. There was something magical in the way he had made each character come to life. The old folk verses painted such vivid pictures in her mind that she could swear she had been to Elfland with Thomas Rhymer.

But then, a lot of actors could sing. And she had always had a weakness for a good baritone.

All the same, Morgan couldn't completely free herself of the spell of his voice. She stopped trying and let the illustration flow under its own momentum. Alasdair's song echoed in Morgan's ears as the Queen of Elfland's radiant outspread wings came to shimmering life on the page.

This was exactly what she had needed to begin on her book. Morgan refused to think about the man responsible for her inspiration—let alone whether it was more than his song that inspired her.

Little did Morgan know that in the tiny park opposite the bed-and-breakfast, a disreputable-looking highlander folded himself up on a public bench, his gaze fixed on the golden light spilling from her window, and settled in for the night.

Justine knocked on Morgan's door and then, when there was no response, knocked even harder. Honestly, it was eight o'clock! Blake was itching to get on the road again and head off to Scone Palace in Perth. And Morgan was late.

Again.

Justine was going to have to get her sister a watch with alarm bells or something. But then, Morgan would probably find a way to ignore that too.

Justine knocked again. Blake left their room across the hall, pushed up his glasses, and gave Justine an exaggerated wink. She smiled despite herself, knowing what had put the twinkle in her husband's eye.

She had no doubt there was an answering sparkle in her own.

"We could just go back to bed," he murmured. He strolled across the foyer and planted a kiss on the nape of Justine's neck that made her shiver. "Check out late. What do you think?"

"You'd never do it." Justine turned to Morgan's door. "Do you think anything's wrong?"

Blake grinned. "Maybe something's very right."

"What do you mean?"

"You didn't look out the window this morning, did you?"

Justine shook her head, mystified, and Blake pushed the door to their room open with a fingertip. "Go look," he invited.

"You're going to ambush me and we'll never get out of here," she accused, unable to keep herself from smiling at the thought.

"Scout's honor." Blake crossed his heart solemnly.

"Rats," Justine teased, then went to look.

Alasdair was sitting on a park bench, his long legs stretched out in front of him, his ankles crossed. His arms were folded across his chest and his expression was grim.

He was staring at a point that would exactly correspond to Morgan's window.

"Oh!" Justine spun around to face Blake with delight. "What do you think happened?"

He shrugged, unable to hide his smile completely. "It's not like Morgan to sleep once the sun is up."

"You're right! She's always been a morning person." Justine fought to keep her hopes from rising too high. She darted back out into the hall and rapped impatiently on Morgan's door.

"Morgan?" Justine leaned close and called quietly against the door. "Breakfast is on. Are you coming?"

She thought she heard sounds of life from within the room, so she knocked again. Louder.

Morgan opened the door a crack, her hair spilling around her face in a disorganized tangle. She was still wearing her dress from the night before, but it was wrinkled almost beyond recognition.

Something—or *someone*!—had kept Morgan up all night.

Justine dared to hope.

Then she saw the pencil smudges on her sister's fingers, and her heart sank. Alasdair might be smitten, but Morgan had just been working.

Drat.

"Good morning." Justine forced a bright tone. "Sleep well?"

Morgan ran a hand over her brow, then frowned toward the little desk in one corner. "It wasn't long enough to tell. What time is it?"

"Eight."

"And I was supposed to meet you at seven-thirty." Morgan groaned. "I'm sorry." She wandered away from the door and surveyed the room as though unfamiliar with its contents. "Do I have time for a shower?"

Justine, unashamed of her curiosity, followed and closed the door behind them. She immediately noticed the open sketchbook on the desk but tried to look as though she hadn't.

"Sure. If you pick what you're wearing, I'll pack the rest of your stuff. Then we can have breakfast together." Justine gave her sister a pointed glance. "This *is* a vacation, after all."

"Right. How could I forget?" Before Justine could interpret

that, Morgan yawned luxuriously. "I guess I can nap in the car." She peeled off her dress, plucked leggings and a sweater from her bag, then padded into the en suite bathroom.

Justine felt a teensy-weensy twinge of guilt as she unfolded her sister's suitcase on the bed. Were they running at too quick a pace for Morgan?

But then, if she had her way, Morgan would never get very far at all! Justine frowned at the jumbled contents of the bag and set to work reorganizing everything. "When did you go to sleep?" she called out.

"I don't know. I remember seeing the sun come up."

An all-nighter. Justine was itching to see the product of her sister's work, but she knew Morgan didn't like people looking at sketches before they were done. And she couldn't tell by Morgan's manner whether she was pleased with the work or not. The shower began to run as Justine folded and packed with surgical precision.

Only when her sister had disappeared into the shower stall did Justine dare to step over to the desk. Three pages were scattered there, each one covered with Morgan's trademark whimsical drawings.

Justine glanced guiltily toward the bathroom. She could hear Morgan humming something in the shower.

So she bent closer to look.

And caught her breath at the myriad little fairy faces peeking out mischievously from behind leaves and nodding flowers. The first page was titled "Thomas Rhymer"—this lanky man who had a passing resemblance to Blake must be Thomas himself. In one corner was a woman of such ethereal beauty that she could only be a fairy queen. Her horse was dressed with ribbons and pacing impatiently, her own wings as gossamer fine and iridescent as those of a dragonfly.

Justine was so engrossed that she didn't hear the shower stop.

"Oh! You found them."

Justine pivoted in alarm, one of Morgan's clean T-shirts clutched against her chest. "Morgan, they're gorgeous!" she declared before her sister could say anything. "These are more beautiful than any of your work I've seen before!"

Morgan glanced down, typically modest of her abilities, then smiled. "They are, aren't they?"

"They're absolutely wonderful! So, who's this Thomas Rhymer?"

Her sister, characteristically, flushed, and even the way she fussed with pulling on her sweater couldn't hide it. "He was a poet who said he had been captured by the Queen of Elfland. He kissed her and was imprisoned by her for seven years in her kingdom."

"Wow." Justine turned back to the magical drawings with fascination. The longer she looked, the more details she seemed to find. "Just the kind of story you wanted to find."

Morgan's flush deepened as she crossed the room. "Yes," she admitted, then hastily gathered the drawings together. "Look, these aren't done . . ."

"I know, I know, you'd prefer not to have me ogling them." Justine stepped out of the way, watching her sister carefully slide the drawings into a portfolio. Morgan's high color and the silence that descended told Justine there was something important she had missed.

And she immediately guessed what that was.

Justine leaned a hip against the desk with apparent idleness and fixed Morgan with a look designed to worm confessions out of war criminals. "So, who told you about Thomas Rhymer?"

Morgan turned crimson.

Ha! Blake had been right!

Morgan's attempt to shrug off the questions didn't fool Justine. "Alasdair told me."

"Really?" Justine forced her tone to remain calm even though she was gleeful inside. "So you *did* stay at the restaurant, after all." She ran a finger down the desk. "Did you have a nice dessert?"

"No, well, no, we didn't actually stay." Morgan shuffled her feet, the very image of a child caught with her hand in the cookie jar.

Even better—they had adjourned to more romantic surroundings.

"Alasdair took you somewhere else?" Justine asked.

"Where did you go? Some nice little coffee bar?"

"Well, um, no."

Justine had a sudden feeling that things hadn't gone perfectly according to plan. She impaled her sister with a look
that commanded a full accounting.

Morgan, tellingly, examined her toes. "Actually, we argued
and I, uh, left the restaurant alone."

Alone?

"You took a cab?" Justine knew her tone was icy.

"No, I couldn't get one."

"Morgan, tell me that you didn't walk *alone*!" Justine flung
out her hands and stalked across the room, hating that Morgan
could make her so very angry.

And that only when her baby sister showed no care for her
own safety. Honestly, sometimes she felt as though Morgan
needed a full-time keeper!

"How many times have I told you that you just can't count
on the world being a safe place? We're not living in Disney-
land, you know! Even though Scotland has Old World charm
by the ton, this *isn't* the old world anymore . . ."

"Justine, it was fine."

Justine felt her eyes narrow with suspicion as she turned to
Morgan again. There was more to this story than she was
hearing, that was for sure. "*Nothing* happened?"

Morgan shuffled her feet. "Well, it might have if Alasdair
hadn't followed me . . ."

Anger coursed through Justine, relief quick on its heels. To
hide her response, she turned to finish the packing, her gestures quick and efficient.

Had Alasdair appointed himself Morgan's keeper?

The thought appealed to Justine. "I like him better and better all the time," she restrained herself to saying.

That seemed to snap Morgan to attention.

"Justine! He stole the crystal from the regalia, and I have
it! He wants it back. Obviously he wants me to trust him and
will do anything to make me let down my guard."

Morgan flung out her hands in exasperation, but it was hard
for Justine to take her seriously when she was in no more than
Calvin Klein briefs and a sweater. "Don't you get it? He's a

con man! He probably set the whole thing up so he could pretend to rescue me.''

Justine treated her sister to her most skeptical glance. "And this con job—that would be the one to get back a crystal that only you remember seeing anywhere other than in your purse—would it also explain why he's waiting for you?''

"What?" Morgan's eyes rounded in alarm. "He's waiting for me? Where?''

Justine nodded toward the window and Morgan peeked out through the curtains. She jumped back as though the sight burned her. "He's out there!''

"Of course he's out there." Justine was calm again. "He *likes* you—despite the way you treat him.''

"Justine! What am I going to do?" Morgan paced wildly, more nervous than Justine had seen her in quite a while.

Which could only be a good sign. Justine folded with authority, her composure regained, and made short work of the rest of the packing.

"You're going to go down there and invite him in for breakfast," she said firmly.

Morgan paled. "I am not!''

"You are so." Justine spun to confront her sister and let her voice drop threateningly. "Because if you don't, I will.''

"You can't! Don't you get it? He's a con artist!''

Justine rolled her eyes. "Oh, Morgan, stop it. Not every guy on the face of the earth is like Matt." She shook her head, closed the suitcase with a decisive snap, and swung it off the bed. "Thank God for small mercies.''

Morgan got her Stubborn Look, but Justine would not be swayed.

She propped her hands on her hips. "Morgan, let's look at the facts. Your suspicions to the contrary, Alasdair has been nothing but a perfect gentleman. He even made sure you got back here all right. Now, go on down there and invite him in—it can't hurt to find out what he wants.''

Morgan sighed and frowned as she shoved one hand through the thickness of her hair. "He said he just wants to go home.''

Justine heard the wistfulness in her sister's tone and knew

that Morgan wasn't as immune to the highlander's charm as she'd like everyone to believe.

Which was the most promising sign of healing that Justine had seen in years. She liked that Alasdair was protective of her baby sister and also that he wasn't afraid to wear his own heart on his sleeve.

The man definitely had promise.

"Well, maybe we'll just have to take him there," Justine declared in her most authoritative tone. "It doesn't look like he has a lot of cash on his hands. Ask him for breakfast and we'll find out where his home is."

"But Blake has an itinerary . . ."

"Blake will get over it. It's about time his planning had a rest."

"But Justine . . ."

"But *nothing*." Justine let herself smile as she tried another tack. "You know, if we got off Blake's itinerary, we just might end up in some wonderfully romantic little hamlet, maybe in a castle turned into a hotel. Wouldn't it be lovely?"

Justine waited a heartbeat, then sighed with mock disappointment. "No, you're right, of course. We should follow Blake's plans. After all, he might get all amorous if we ended up in a place like that, and you'd be left to fend for yourself. That would be a horrible shame, especially since we're all on vacation together."

She shrugged, commandeered the suitcase, and headed for the door. "Forget I said anything. Let's have breakfast. Where did Blake say we were going today? Scone Palace, I think."

Morgan muttered something unrepeatable under her breath. "All right! All right! I'll ask him!" she declared with obvious irritation. "But don't blame me if you're wrong!"

But Justine was never wrong. Well, other than that one time.

She grinned as Morgan slammed the door of the room behind her. She liked seeing her sister this bothered about including the highlander in their plans.

It could only bode well for Justine's scheme.

Blake, just now lugging their own bag out of their room, arched a brow and glanced between spouse and door. "Problem?"

Justine's smile widened. "Not at all. Everything is going to be just fine."

Blake grinned. "Always is when you're in charge."

And he was right. Justine had, after all, made a science of knowing best.

Chapter 6

ALASDAIR SPENT A night tormented by the similarities between his own troubles and those of Thomas Rhymer. To be certain, it could be no coincidence that that particular tale of his gran's—out of ranks of thousands—came to his lips last eve.

Had he condemned himself to seven years' imprisonment in the land of Faerie with a single kiss? That it had been an embrace of rare power was beyond doubt, for the heat of Morgaine's salute had fairly melted his bones.

And True Thomas, 'twas said, had believed himself gone only seven nights upon his return to Erceldoune, though truly seven years had passed. It had been but one day since Alasdair found himself in this fey world—at least to his mind.

Could an entire year have already passed in the land of mortals? Alasdair's heart twisted that his gran should believe him dead.

Or worse, that he had abandoned his only son.

Alasdair sighed and glared at the sorceress' window, hating how a moment of whimsy had so meddled with his life. There were those, he well knew, who did not win a respite even after seven years but were trapped in Faerie for all eternity.

Surely this could not be his fate?

The enchantress emerged from her abode just when Alasdair

was convinced matters could get no worse. Her sour expression bode naught good, to Alasdair's mind. Garbed in green and gold she was this morning, as fresh as a new blade of grass, her hair bouncing in a dark cloud behind her.

Yet for all her poor temper, the woman was sufficiently beguiling to elicit a response from Alasdair's treacherous flesh. Everything tightened within him as she cut a path directly toward him, and he could think only of her lusty kiss.

He knew 'twas no more than a deception, for his gran's tales were filled with the marvels of Faerie folk making their own shapes. 'Twas a dark magic Morgaine summoned to delve into Alasdair's mind that she might design herself to fascinate him.

He felt no more clever than a fly, stumbling into an artfully baited web while the crafty spider lingered in the shadows, awaiting her prey.

But such whimsy would win him naught! Alasdair pushed himself to his feet and shoved one hand through his hair, determined to face this conflict squarely.

"Justine insists that I invite you for breakfast," Morgaine declared without sparing him a greeting. Her green eyes were shadowed with displeasure and her lips drawn to a tight line that belied their usual ripe fullness. "And so I am."

Alasdair was so surprised that she granted the advisor's counsel such weight—never mind that the advisor evidently still supported his own cause—that he held his tongue.

She grimaced. "Because if I don't, she'll do it anyway. That's how Justine is."

Alasdair absorbed this amazing piece of information. What would any ruler have to say of an advisor who did whatsoever he or she desired? 'Twas unthinkable!

Yet even more pressing, to Alasdair's mind, was the fact that Morgaine's opinion of him did not seem to have improved over the night. Had he won no esteem for recounting a tale that evidently intrigued her?

Morgaine wagged a warning finger at Alasdair, dashing any hope he might have had. "But don't get any ideas that I like you or anything. And don't think for a minute that I've for-

gotten the kind of man you are. You certainly aren't going to
get that crystal from me, so don't even try.''

'Twas more than clear that Alasdair's charm had won him
naught in Morgaine's eyes.

He cleared his throat and tried to show himself as respectful
of her powers. ''I mean no offense, my lady.''

Morgaine folded her arms across her chest, pushing the
curves of her breasts to surprising prominence beneath her
loose garb, and Alasdair's slumbering desire roared to life.

Ye gods, but she made his blood boil!

The sorceress, though, wore a skeptical expression. ''Justine
thinks we should take you home after breakfast,'' she said, an
assessing glint in her eye. ''If that's what you want.''

Alasdair gasped to have release so freely offered, especially
after her earlier words.

There must be a trick.

All the same, he would not show ingratitude. He bowed
deeply and tried to think of flowery words to impress her.
''Aye, aye, I should dearly love to return home. My lady, you
grant a great favor to me in this matter, and do not imagine
that I do not appreciate . . .''

''It's not my idea,'' the sorceress interjected flatly. ''In fact,
I'd rather not do this at all, but—'' she hesitated for a moment,
then waved her hand dismissively. ''Well, never mind. It's
complicated. Where do you live, anyway?''

Alasdair fought not to scoff at the question and to keep his
humble tone. Clearly, she mocked him, for a Faerie queen
would know all! ''Callanish, on the isle of Lewis, my lady.''

''Oh!'' Morgaine's eyes opened wide and her hostility
melted away. ''Where the standing stones are?''

And the sight of her softness nearly undid what remained
of Alasdair's resolve. He supposed he should not have been
surprised that Morgaine would be intrigued by a circle of
stones reputed to be magical beyond all. Had his gran not
declared Callanish to be the meeting place of the local Faerie
folk?

''Have you been to see them?'' Morgaine demanded with
a curiosity she could not disguise.

Was this another opportunity to win her favor? Alasdair had

never felt so buffeted by conflicting emotions. He seriously
longed for the previous simplicity of his life.

For the first time in years, his crofter's cottage held allure.
Aye, 'twould be good to be home again, with naught on his
mind but keeping the sheep from the garden and bouncing his
son on his knee.

"Aye, I know them well," he admitted carefully. "They
are said to be most powerful and are close to my own abode."

"Oh." Morgaine's lips twisted. "I bet they're wonderful."
She sighed and glanced over her shoulder at the portal of her
abode, before summoning a thin smile for Alasdair. Only now
he noted her exhaustion, where previously he had thought her
merely annoyed with him.

Her candle had burned all through the night. Was it possible
that she had been as sleepless as he?

For the same reason? Alasdair's heart skipped an unruly
beat.

"You know, I really wanted to go to Callanish on this trip,"
she confided, "but Blake thought it was too far."

Too far? She manipulated him again!

Alasdair's anger stirred that she would already change her
mind about her offer. And what was distance to a Faerie queen
who could be anywhere she desired with a snap of her fingers?

His manners had been impeccable, yet still she toyed with
him! Alasdair's tolerance of these Faerie games was wearing
dangerously thin.

"So you would stir a man's hopes, then snatch them
away?" he demanded impatiently. "I should have expected
no less! Do you mean to destroy my will that you might bend
me to your own ends?"

"That's not fair!" the tiny sorceress declared. "You're the
one with something to gain, not me! You only want the crystal
back!"

Alasdair took a fortifying breath, knowing a test when he
saw one. He had to remain calm. And charming.

Even if his frustration was rapidly coming to a boil.

Evidently Morgaine spoke of the magical stone.

Alasdair mustered his most sincere glance, and his voice

fell low. "If I grant you my pledge to not try to retrieve the stone, will you see me home?"

The words seemed to surprise Morgaine. She stared into his eyes for a long moment. "You'd promise me that?"

"Aye." Alasdair's tone was unequivocal.

After all, how could he guess whether or not he could make the witch's charm work in reverse, even if he did retrieve the stone? And he had little to gain from a mere crystal, if Morgaine herself would simply send him home in exchange for a vow.

Morgaine stared at him, her lips parting ever so slightly. Alasdair's gut tightened, and he knew he looked into the bewitching green of her eyes overlong. Once again he could think of naught but kissing her until she moaned against his lips.

'Twas too readily she had granted his request, he feared suddenly. Clearly there was another test Alasdair had to pass in order to win his way home.

Ye gods, was there no end to this nonsense?

Morgaine drew herself up taller so suddenly that Alasdair feared she had read his thoughts. 'Twas almost a joke to see her assume a haughty manner, for she had to be one of the softest-looking women Alasdair had ever met.

But who knew what darkness lurked in the shadows of her heart?

"All right. But don't be getting any ideas about me changing my mind about you," she said frostily. She pointed a finger at him. "You keep your distance."

Then she spun around and stalked back to her abode, the proud tilt of her chin so intriguing that Alasdair almost forgot that he was lost in the grip of a powerful sorceress.

Morgaine spun and wagged a finger at him. "And remember, I'm not talking to you."

When she continued to walk away, her hips twitched with such feminine allure that Alasdair's distrust melted like butter in the sun. Aye, had she been a mere lass, he would have followed her to the ends of the earth.

But Morgaine was no lass and Alasdair was already beyond the ends of the earth.

He gritted his teeth and crossed the park in the enchantress's wake. No doubt a meal would restore his even temper, though he had best ensure that his manners were impeccable. Everything he desired was so close, nearly within his grip. Alasdair did not dare risk erring now.

Morgan didn't miss her sister's quickly smothered smile as she entered the little room of their bed-and-breakfast that was designated for the morning meal.

Tables no bigger than card tables were packed into what had evidently been a parlor in the converted Victorian townhome. There was barely enough space to sit at each place, let alone to pull out a chair or cross the room. Plastic tablecloths punched in imitation of cutwork linen hung perfectly square on each tiny table, a printed place mat marked each place.

The room was packed with tourists, obviously in a hurry to get to the business of sight-seeing on a day that promised sunshine. Morgan noted, to her dismay, that Blake and Justine had claimed a corner table that would require considerable navigation to reach.

Blake had packed his long legs into the back place and was wedged against two walls. It didn't look as though he could manage to break free anytime soon. Justine perched beside him with the same grace she would have exhibited if breakfasting at Buckingham Palace, although her elbows were tight against her sides as she poured her coffee.

Their hostess, Maggie, was depositing racks of toast, cups and saucers, and individual pots of both coffee and cream amid the clutter of the condiments permanently set on the table. The plump matron expertly fitted everything around the pair's half-emptied cereal bowls and juice glasses.

As Morgan watched, Blake, trying to find a way to reach his knife without starting an avalanche, moved his pot of coffee to the other side of the table to make space.

Maggie swooped down on the offending pot, plucked it up, and moved it back into Blake's quadrant. "*Mr.* Macdonald! Must I remind you that that place is intended for another guest?"

"I'm sorry, I just needed a little space here . . ."

"Mr. Macdonald," Maggie sighed deeply in disapproval, "I can only ask you to be courteous and keep your breakfast to yourself."

Suitably chastened, Blake tried to edge his knife free without either hitting one elbow on the wall or jabbing the other into Justine's ribs. Morgan felt a momentary twinge of envy when he succeeded.

She would have sent the entire table tumbling to the floor. As it was, she still had to wind her way around four tables to reach the place opposite Blake. When she got there, Morgan resolved, she would certainly let Blake put his pot of coffee on her side of the imaginary line dividing the table into quarters.

Maggie came to a full stop on her bustle back to the kitchen and pointedly eyed Morgan, who still lingered on the threshold. The hostess then looked up at the prominently displayed wall clock and back to her guest, her brow furrowing.

"Breakfast is at eight-fifteen," Maggie admonished in her rollicking brogue. Her lips were so tight that Morgan wondered how the words broke free. "Not eight o'clock and not eight-thirty, Miss Lafayette, but eight-*fifteen*."

Every eye turned to see who had broken the cardinal rule, and Morgan felt her color rise.

This was a vacation?

But there was obviously only one thing to say.

"I'm sorry."

"Well! We are having our share of troubles from our American *friends* this morning!" Maggie sniffed at this inadequate apology and undoubtedly would have said more, but her eyes fixed on a space behind and slightly above Morgan.

The matron's entire face brightened.

Morgan didn't have to turn to know who had just arrived. She groaned inwardly as everyone in the room stopped talking and stared. Morgan was sure she heard a knife clatter on a plate.

Justine, of course, simply stirred her coffee, looking like the cat who swallowed the canary.

"My most sincere apologies, my goodwoman," Alasdair

said in his charming rumble. "My dalliance has delayed the lady in coming to the board."

"Oh!" Maggie's features melted into a smile that was obviously an unfamiliar expression. "Well, for such a braw man, I canna blame her for dawdling." Then she winked at Morgan and made for the kitchen with a definite swing to her hips.

Someone chuckled, and Morgan didn't need her imagination to know what they were all thinking. Her face went hot right on cue, and the whispering began.

When Alasdair's hand landed on the back of her waist, her heart skipped a beat, and Morgan knew she had to move. Now. She darted forward, thinking of nothing but reaching the relative safety of her seat.

Of course she snagged her toe on the corner of a table en route.

And everything went from bad to worse in a hurry.

The table jumped six inches, the blond woman there squealed as her tea spilled into the saucer. Her portly husband muttered in noisy disapproval, the china clattered, the vase holding one fake carnation wobbled.

They simultaneously erupted into a scold of German.

"I'm sorry! I'm so sorry!" Morgan danced away and backed into another table. The salt and pepper shakers from that one tumbled to the floor and rolled underfoot. The woman seated there said something uncomplimentary, just as the vase on the German tourists' table decided to fall after all.

It landed right in the blond woman's sunny-side-up eggs, sending a little splash of bright yellow yolk across the place mat.

Exclamations in several languages burst from all sides. The woman with the silk carnation in her eggs expressed her feelings about the matter in rapid-fire German.

Morgan didn't need a translator.

She stepped forward to help clean up, but the German woman took one look and cried out, "*Nein!* Not the little one again!"

As she protested, she spilled her tea, sending a dark flood across the plastic tablecloth. Her husband's mouth rounded in a little O, and he jumped to his feet, a dark, steaming stain on his trousers revealing just what the problem was.

He wasn't a small man and his quick move made his chair bump against Justine's table, immediately behind. Blake swore, china clattered, people stood up to get a better view, and Morgan felt Alasdair right behind her.

Just when it seemed things could get no worse, Maggie appeared in the doorway, clucking like a disapproving hen. "Miss Lafayette! What are you about? What have you *done*?''

Morgan looked back too quickly to explain and might have lost her balance if Alasdair hadn't snatched her elbows and lifted her clean out of harm's way.

"That would be enough of that," he said, his tone so dangerously low that Morgan froze.

The entire room breathed a collective sigh of relief.

Morgan could feel the solid thud of Alasdair's heart against her back, and the heat of his skin pressed against her own was enough to make her blush again. Her toes were dangling several disconcerting inches above the ground.

Morgan saw the sly smiles slide around the room and didn't know whether she was grateful for the highlander's intervention or not.

She wished the floor would yawn open and swallow her whole.

"Do not even move, my lady," Alasdair growled.

Morgan was smart enough to take his advice. She nodded and he set her back on her feet. One strong hand remained on the back of her waist, as though Alasdair didn't trust her to do as she was told.

"There's no harm done there," he told the one woman, as he gallantly retrieved her salt and pepper shakers. " 'Tis powerful good fortune to spill a wee bit for the pixies. Toss a pinch over your shoulder for good measure." He winked and the woman sat back with a smile.

"The left one," called someone, the room settling with a chuckle as she did exactly that.

Alasdair plucked the vase out of the German woman's eggs and treated her to a killing smile. " 'Tis no harm to an egg

already broken," he assured her. "Nary a bit of water in the
vase to spoil the meal."

He turned back to the matron, and Morgan seethed at the
way Maggie relaxed before his easy wink. "Maggie, lass,
would it be too much trouble for you to bring another pot of
brew? And a wee cloth to repair any damage done?"

Maggie, far from a lass, giggled—much to Morgan's astonishment—and darted away to do Alasdair's bidding. Everyone
returned contentedly to the meal, and the low hum of conversation filled the room again.

"Now, step there and there," Alasdair murmured, the flurry
of his breath on her ear making Morgan shiver. She did as she
was told and slid gratefully into her seat, knowing her cheeks
were hot.

Alasdair took his seat with unexpected grace for one so out
of scale with his surroundings. Morgan immediately realized
there was absolutely no way to avoid having his arm brush
against hers. His leg was planted firmly alongside her own,
and she swore she could feel the tickle of his hair through her
leggings.

"Well, good morning!" Justine said smoothly, as though
nothing had transpired. Morgan studied the bad drawings of
the local attractions printed on her place mat, as though they
were fascinating, and pretended not to notice the warm scent
of the man almost pressing her against the wall.

That damn tingle was humming warmly in her belly again—
and it had a companion tingle quite a bit lower. Morgan tried
to ignore them both and failed.

Alasdair took a deep breath, and to Morgan's surprise, when
he spoke, his tone was hearty and cheerful. "And a fine morning 'tis indeed," he agreed.

He glanced to the bowls of cold cereal before Justine and
Blake, and Morgan caught a glimpse of his dismay. Morgan
smothered a smile and eyed the drawings once more.

"Is the fare good in this hall?" he asked, his voice sounding
strained.

"Well, you can't eat eggs and sausages every morning,"
Justine declared.

"You cannot?"

Blake grimaced and indicated his wife. "I could if she let me." He winked at Alasdair. "A *man* needs a hot breakfast, right?"

"It's not good for you to eat so much saturated fat," Justine stated with her usual assurance about matters of nutrition.

Blake leaned forward with gleaming eyes. "What about kippers, Alasdair?" He pushed up his glasses. "Don't real Scotsmen eat kippers?"

"Aye, that they do! A plate of kippers with eggs and sausages, bread and ale would be most welcome indeed."

Morgan peeked through her lashes to find Alasdair looking much more enthusiastic. Maggie was hailed and was easily persuaded to provide two kipper breakfasts for the men, but she wouldn't go for the ale. Morgan supposed she shouldn't have been surprised that Alasdair got what he wanted.

Morgan had bran flakes.

At least, she tried to have bran flakes. The little boxes of cereal that Maggie provided were sealed far better than Morgan remembered. She cut along the perforated lines indicated but couldn't get the box all the way open. Oblivious to the fact that her three companions were watching her warily, Morgan put aside her knife and wrestled with the little box.

Now she remembered why she had hated camp.

Morgan gave the cardboard a determined tug and it tore unexpectedly. She saw that the wax paper lining was ripped just as bran flakes flew all over the table. They cascaded everywhere, oblivious of coffee, cream or anything else.

Fortunately, her family was used to this kind of thing. And the last container with which Morgan had lost a battle had been an econo-size jar of mustard.

Now, that had been a real mess.

Blake philosophically picked a few bran flakes out of his coffee, and Justine swept up little piles on the tablecloth. Morgan tried to get some of the cereal actually into her bowl before Maggie could chide her. Even retrieving the bran flakes from every relatively clean surface left Morgan with only half a bowlful.

She would have to open another. Morgan gritted her teeth

and reached for another box. She caught Alasdair's eye in time
to see his dumbfounded expression.

"You would go to such trouble for wood shavings?" he
demanded.

"It's cereal!" Morgan retorted. She waved the box at him.
"And besides, I'm not talking to you."

"Aye?" Alasdair picked up a flake from his table quadrant,
put it in his mouth and chewed for only a moment before he
made a face. " 'Tis wood shavings and naught else!" He took
the wet flake out of his mouth and fastidiously set it on the
side of a saucer.

Morgan ran her finger under the type and read aloud: "Bran
flakes. Eight essential vitamins. Part of a balanced breakfast."

Alasdair looked unimpressed.

Determined to do a better job of opening this one, Morgan
turned her knife on the box. But before she could really do
any damage, Alasdair scooped package and knife out of her
grasp with a low sound of exasperation.

"I can do it!" Morgan protested.

He flicked a wry glance her way. "Aye, I have seen how
well you do." Morgan flushed as he made short work of the
box, his gestures economical and easy.

He added the cereal to the remnants of the previous box in
Morgan's bowl, then looked her square in the eye. "If indeed
you must insist upon eating wood shavings, at least do not
compel the rest of us to wear them."

There was nothing Morgan could say to that. She tried to
look indifferent to him as she poured milk on her cereal, but
Justine's smug smile told her she hadn't succeeded.

But she knew one thing that would wipe the smile off her
sister's face.

"I told Alasdair we'd take him home," she informed them
brightly. Justine and Blake looked delighted, but before they
could say anything, Morgan continued, "He lives on Lewis in
the Hebrides. Near Callanish."

Both faces fell with comic speed.

"But that's all the way across the country!" Blake protested.

Justine dug her elbow hard into her spouse's ribs. "Well,

we'll be delighted to have such a tour, won't we, *dear*?''

Blake blinked, looked from one sister to the other, then shook his head. ''All right. All right. We'll take Alasdair home to Lewis.'' He dove for his guidebook. ''Lewis!'' he muttered to himself and started to scan his maps.

It served them right, Morgan concluded. If they didn't know by now that Alasdair was Mr. Wrong, they would by the time they reached his home.

''We can still go to Scone,'' Justine said, her tone conciliatory.

Blake didn't even look up.

''Where Robert the Bruce was crowned King of Scots,'' Alasdair interjected.

Blake looked up at that. ''As though that matters. Crowning that troublemaker would have tainted the place forever if the English hadn't already taken away the Stone of Scone.''

Morgan put down her spoon. Why didn't anyone remember that Robert the Bruce was a hero?

Alasdair's hands landed heavily on the table, and his voice was low with outrage. ''Robert the Bruce is no trouble-maker!''

Blake set down his map. ''Look, my own forebear Angus Og was fooled by him, so I can't blame you for thinking this Robert the Bruce guy was all right. But he caused a lot of trouble and cost my family a lot of land, so I'd rather we just didn't talk about him anymore.''

Alasdair sat back with a dissatisfied thump. Morgan saw that his hands had tightened into fists in his lap.

And why not? He was right!

Always ready to leap in and set a wrong to rights, Morgan tapped the edge of her bowl with her spoon. ''But you said on the way here that Angus Og *won* a lot of land for supporting Bruce. When Bruce was victorious at Bannockburn . . .''

''Morgan!'' Justine interjected. ''The Scots *lost* at Bannockburn!''

But they didn't and Morgan knew it.

Maggie brought breakfast at that point, laying it before the men with a proud flourish. Alasdair recovered himself enough to thank her politely for the meal, but Morgan heard his growled words as he tucked in.

"Robert the Bruce is a hero and the King of Scots. Naught that anyone tells me will persuade me to forget the truth."

Why was it that only Alasdair remembered the same details about Scottish history as Morgan did?

And how could Alasdair have changed Blake and Justine's *memories*?

Morgan thought about the Polaroid of Alasdair with no one in it.

And the guard who swore she'd never seen the crystal before. A little shiver danced down Morgan's spine that had nothing to do with the temperature in the room.

Morgan suddenly wondered whether this really was a con job—because it would have to be an awfully good one—or there was something Truly Weird going on.

Either way, the only one who knew the answer to that was Alasdair. Who was he? Where had he come from? And what was he up to? Morgan watched him out of the corner of her eye and wondered how she could find out the truth.

"I am begging your pardon for zis interruption of your meal." The German man at the next table leaned toward them with a broad smile. He turned his attention to Alasdair and fingered a fancy camera, his *r*'s rolled almost as much as Alasdair's. "But would you be minding if I take your picture? My vife, she zinks you are a *real* highlander."

Having conquered not only the unfamiliarity of driving on the left side of the road and shifting gears with the left hand, a North American tourist might consider himself an accomplished UK driver.

At least until he encountered the humbling experience of the roundabout.

Supposedly, this alternative to traffic lights is intended to make driving from point A to point B less of an ordeal—but the reality is a nail-biting contradiction.

The roundabout—as might be expected from its name—is a circular intersection, the converging roads radiating like spokes of a wheel. A given car enters at one spoke, merges

with the traffic on the roundabout, travels clockwise around
the circle, then exits at the desired spoke to continue on its
way.

The equation is complicated by the structure of the roundabout itself. There are usually at least two lanes: the outer one
for traffic exiting at the next outgoing road, the inner one for
vehicles continuing further around. Incoming cars must take
advantage of any break in the traffic and lunge into the appropriate lane.

Just to add to the sport of it all, the round format reduces
visibility to virtually nil, as do the frequently adverse climatic
conditions. Add to the mix the fact that drivers familiar with
the intersection tend to travel through the roundabout at breakneck speed, and you have one intimidating obstacle to driving.

With far too many opportunities for practice, to many tourists' minds. There are those who believe that some drivers
have been circling the same busy roundabout for years, desperately trying to escape at their desired exit.

Blake was determined to conquer not only the basics of
negotiating the roundabout itself but also the fine points of
merging and signaling protocol. A perfectionist in every phase
of his life, he could be no less behind the wheel of a Nissan
Micra with right-hand drive.

Sadly, Blake was not as familiar with a manual transmission
as might have simplified matters. After all, he had graduated
from his Honda Civic to a sleek silver Mercedes—with an
automatic transmission—a long, long time ago.

And shifting with his left hand was a new art.

Alasdair, however, understood little of these modern tech-
nicalities. He knew only that they were going to Scone, where
Robert the Bruce had been crowned King of Scots and from
whence the British had stolen the Stone of Scone. It was a
course that suited him well, as Alasdair knew that in the mortal
world Scone was on the way from Edinburgh to Callanish.

It seemed that Morgaine intended to keep her word. The
only question was when they would pass through the veil between the worlds.

Such lofty expectations were tempered when it became clear
that they were to ride within a strange blue chariot. Alasdair

was astonished by the vivid blue of what they called the Micra.

And he was even further amazed by the advisors' expectation that he clamber into the tiny rear seat.

Beside Morgaine.

But Alasdair could not risk their irritation now. He managed to pack himself into the small space, though he was far from comfortable.

Clearly the Micra was yet another implement of torment designed by the malicious Morgaine. That she endured its cramped conditions herself, apparently willingly, was a puzzle Alasdair could not resolve.

The threesome shielded their eyes with obsidian that shone in the sunlight, leaving Alasdair wondering what damage this chariot would do to his own eyes, for he had no such armor.

'Twas all so very strange.

Once they were all inside the chariot, Blake made a mysterious gesture. He muttered an incantation under his breath, repeated the gesture, and the Micra began a disconcerting humming. Alasdair surreptitiously looked for the flock of angry bees, but to no avail.

When the Micra slid away from the walk and moved along the road with no sign of a horse, Alasdair inhaled so sharply that his nostrils pinched shut.

Any discomfort was forgotten with his mistrust of this conveyance. The Micra vibrated like a country cart but moved markedly faster.

What powerful sorcery Morgaine granted to her minions!

The Micra darted down the curved streets with disconcerting speed, and Alasdair wondered fleetingly whether Morgaine intended to return him home in a shroud.

He glanced at his companions and was startled to find that they all clearly took its wizardry in stride. Alasdair strove to appear similarly nonchalant but was certain that he failed. He stared out the window and watched the streets hasten past.

No doubt this was some part of the magic necessary to move between Morgaine's domain and the mortal world. He gathered that they intended to be in Scone before midday. Indeed, he might be home sooner than he thought.

In one way or another.

Chapter 7

By THE TIME the humming Micra met its first major roundabout, Alasdair had only just managed to find a way to sit without doing any of his vulnerable parts serious injury.

"Shit!" Blake declared from the front seat. "This one has *eight* roads going into it!"

Alasdair peered through the space between the front seats and had to close his eyes at the dizzying rate their little chariot chewed up the road.

This was definitely not in the world of mortals—though he would endure even this wild ride to see his home island again. Alasdair was beginning to have very affectionate feelings for his humble cottage.

He was even thinking fondly of his sharp-tongued gran.

Justine touched Blake's arm, her voice low and soothing. "Don't worry, you can do it. We'll help. Right, Morgan?"

The sorceress fairly bounced on her seat, and her eyes sparkled with some challenge that Alasdair could hardly begin to guess. "You bet. Which one do we need?"

Justine consulted an intricately drawn manuscript, then squinted at the road ahead. "The fourth one."

"Got it," Morgaine said.

"Jesus Christ, here we go," Blake muttered. "Second gear."

"Right-turn signal," Justine murmured. She leaned forward in her seat, pulling off her dark eyeshields as she did so.

An astonishing stream of similar chariots sped across their path at breakneck speed. They looked like so many beetles, and when Alasdair looked carefully, he could see people trapped within each one. They had the same dark shields over their eyes as his companions did, making it look as though the insects had yet more insects in their bellies.

He thought of his gran's tales of Faeries riding the backs of moths and beetles.

Blake inched their chariot forward, watching the stream avidly. Evidently they were going to join this rush of shiny beetles.

Alasdair was not certain he wanted to watch.

"First gear," Blake gritted out.

"After the red one," Morgaine declared, her nose fairly pressed against the curved window.

Blake leaned forward, his knuckles white on the stick between himself and Justine. A red chariot not unlike their own flashed by.

"GO!" the women roared simultaneously.

The Micra squealed in protest, and Blake urged it forward. Alasdair's eyes widened at the proximity of an extremely large vehicle that was closing in behind them at great speed, and he nearly squealed in sympathy.

Instead he crossed himself. It seemed rather a timely moment to rediscover his long-misplaced religious beliefs.

"Three goddamn lanes!" Blake swore under his breath.

"Into the middle one," Justine directed.

"Second gear," Blake said to himself. "Turn signal."

"One!" bellowed the sorceress, as an alley flashed past on their left.

The huge chariot wheezed behind them, the entire back view of the Micra filled with the great one's massive silver teeth. Alasdair strove to keep his composure and simultaneously recall his rosary.

"Two!" cried the sorceress.

"Third gear, no signal."

"Left lane, left lane," Justine said.

"I can't because of that truck!"

"Three!" crowed the sorceress.

"You have to," Justine insisted calmly. "We can't go around and around all day like we did in Jedburgh."

"All right, all right. Left-turn signal," Blake concurred and checked over his shoulder. "Am I clear?"

As far as Alasdair could discern, there was naught to see but the complaining chariot behind.

It looked large enough to consume them whole.

"Go, go now," Justine urged.

"Four!" Morgaine interjected. She leaned between the seats and pointed at a road ahead on the left. "That's it, that's the one!"

Alasdair eyed the road she indicated and could not discern how they would get from here to there without being mangled by other chariots in the process.

Despite his religious skepticism, Alasdair saw no harm in a few Ave Marias under such circumstance. He muttered them under his breath and tried to hide his fear from the sorceress.

'Twas no small thing to know oneself immortal at such a moment; that was the only thing that could explain her sparkling eyes.

"Second gear," Blake declared, but this time when he moved the stick, the chariot made a high-pitched whine.

"If you can't find 'em, grind 'em," Morgaine whispered and giggled.

Blake glared over his shoulder. "I'd like to see you do this." He looked back to the road and cranked the wheel hard. The chariot obediently lunged into the outside lane.

A heartbeat later—if indeed Alasdair's heart had been beating—the little chariot darted along an open stretch of roadway.

"We did it!" Morgaine cried triumphantly, and Alasdair breathed a sigh of relief.

The humming Micra was filled with gleeful cheers, and Blake earned not only a pat on the shoulder but a sound kiss from Justine.

The car swerved dangerously close to the ditch during this exchange of esteem. Morgaine cried out, Justine gasped, and two pairs of hands steadied their path.

Alasdair felt a cold trickle of sweat run down his back. The comparative solitude of his cottage was sounding better and better all the time.

"Christ save me," he muttered gruffly. "You are all mad."

The enchantress took one look at him and laughed so hard it seemed she could not stop.

"You should see your face!" she managed to gasp before convulsing in yet more gales of laughter. Her merriment made her look so young and fetching that Alasdair nearly forgot the extent of her foul powers.

All the same, he could not look away.

He was so lost in her eyes that he missed the coy glance that Justine and Blake exchanged before they turned their broad grins to the road once more.

On the northern outskirts of Perth, Blake pulled the Micra into the generous parking lot of Scone Palace. Morgan thought the palace looked disappointingly modern for a site of such historical significance.

"Well, here we are!" Blake declared. "Scone Palace, Moot Hill, and all that jazz." He set the emergency brake, killed the ignition, and accepted his highlighted travel guide from Justine. "Let's make sure we know what we're looking at here."

Morgan noted from the corner of her eye that Alasdair seemed similarly unimpressed. In fact, his expression had turned quite grim. He slanted a very blue gaze in her direction and folded his arms across his chest.

The move made his shoulders nearly fill the entire backseat of the car.

"This is not Scone," he said with surgical precision.

"Of course it is." Justine folded her map and tucked it into the glove box.

Morgan was not nearly as unconcerned as her sister. Alasdair looked fit to kill, and she had an inkling that he could break the neck of any of them with his bare hands.

All that advice about not picking up hitchhikers came to mind a bit late for comfort.

"You have lied to me." Alasdair declared through clenched teeth. He was positively seething.

"Get serious. This is Scone," Blake countered dismissively. "Listen." He leafed through the pages and lifted one finger in his best imitation of a professor about to lecture learnedly.

"Scone Palace took its current form in the sixteenth century, although it contains fragments of earlier construction. It is located near Moot Hill, where the Stone of Scone, or Stone of Destiny, was the traditional crowning site of the Scottish kings."

"Until the English stole the stone away," Alasdair muttered. He looked so lethal that Morgan tried to edge away from him.

The Micra offered little chance of that.

Blake glanced over his shoulder, his finger running down the page. "No, it says here that the Scottish *gave* the stone of destiny to the British as a token of esteem when they welcomed foreign rule."

Alasdair's snort made his opinion of that clear.

The really scary thing was that Morgan agreed with him— and not with Blake's tour book.

Blake read on, oblivious to raised hackles in the backseat. *"Originally, the kings of Dalriada—an ancient name for Scotland—were crowned at Dunadd, a hillside fort in Argyll. But in the ninth century, the Stone of Scone was purportedly carried to Scotland from the high seat of Tara in Ireland and installed on Moot Hill."*

"That at least is not a lie," Alasdair acknowledged tightly.

Blake fired a glance between the seats. "They brought it *here*. This is Scone."

"That it is not."

The two men locked gazes in some silent challenge of testosterone, and Morgan knew she wasn't the only one holding her breath.

Blake was the first to look away. He abruptly cleared his throat and continued. *"Eventually, the seat of royal power moved southwards, first to Dunfermline Abbey, then to Edinburgh. Holyrood Palace in Edinburgh remains the official residence of the monarch in Scotland."*

"And which monarch would that be?" Alasdair demanded coldly. "Some poppet from south of the wall, that much is certain, and 'tis just as certain that no rightful monarch could come from such ranks.''

Blake twisted in his seat to face the highlander. "Look, I don't know where you learned your history, but you've got it wrong. The Scottish *welcomed* British rule.''

"A filthy lie!'' Alasdair retorted hotly. "The Scots would NEVER welcome British rule!''

"Look.'' Blake took off his glasses and jabbed them through the air toward Alasdair. "All this kilt business is very showy, but I really would have expected a true Scotsman to know his history . . .''

"I AM A TRUER SCOTSMAN THAN YOU WILL EVER SEE!'' Alasdair bellowed, the volume of his voice enough to rock the Micra. He looked like a cornered bear and his eyes flashed lightning. " 'Tis clear enough which camp of Macdonalds you call your own, for there is naught but lies falling from your lips!''

"Lies?'' Blake inhaled sharply and color rose on his neck. "I haven't told any lies!''

"It is one lie after another as I hear it,'' Alasdair shot back. "With nary but a broken promise betwixt and between! THIS IS NOT SCONE!''

Justine laid a restraining hand on Blake's arm and used the same tone that had successfully talked down countless hysterical brides. "Maybe it's just changed. When were you last here, Alasdair? Have they added some new signs or something?''

The tone—which should have been patented for its unfailing success—had no effect on the highlander.

"Nay!'' Alasdair looked fit to explode. "There is not a bit of it that resembles the Scone I know!'' He gestured angrily. "That very building was not here, nor this foul expanse of blackness spread upon the ground! The land was not cluttered with your fearsome chariots, nor crowded with folk in such odd garb.''

Alasdair flung out a hand. "And I know *naught* of this sixteenth century you tout. Sixteenth century since *what*? Always have I known right-thinking men to count their years from the birth of Christ!''

Morgan blinked, for the reference *was* to the sixteenth century since Christ.

Blake frowned, and picked his issue. "Well, it *is* Scone. No doubt about it."

"I have my doubts, 'tis clear enough." Alasdair leaned between the seats and Morgan watched Blake draw back ever so slightly. The highlander's voice deepened with a threat so tangible that Morgan shivered.

"You have *lied* to me, Blake Advisor. You do not take me to Scone this day, nor do you ever intend to take me home. Be man enough to confess the truth."

"Of course we'll take you home," Justine assured him. "This is just on the way."

"Another lie in the company of many!" Alasdair roared. He pushed at the confining wall of the little car and growled when nothing moved. Morgan was torn between a desire to put as much space between him and herself as possible and an unexpected urge to reassure him.

Alasdair tipped back his head and shouted, "For the love of God, let me out of this foul prison!"

Before Morgan could sort out her feelings—or Alasdair could explode—Justine opened her door and leapt out onto the pavement. Alasdair pushed the front seat forward with enviable grace and couldn't seem to get out of the car fast enough.

He shook back his hair when he was on his feet and glared down at them with his hands on his hips. Morgan couldn't help but stare. Alasdair was magnificent in his anger, larger than life, snapping with vitality.

He belonged outside, in the wind and the sun, and before she could stop herself, Morgan had updated her mental image of how she would paint him.

"Make no mistake, this is not Scone." Alasdair savagely bit out the words. "Second, the Stone of Scone was stolen! And third, Robert the Bruce is no treacherous dog, but a hero through and through! And *that*, Blake Advisor, is the ungarnished truth."

And with that, he pivoted and strode away.

Morgan could almost feel the aching of his heart. It was

disconcerting to find her own memories perfectly reconciled with his view of history.

The only question was *why*.

"Alasdair, come back!" Justine cried, but Alasdair didn't even look back. His long strides took him across the parking lot in record time. Instead of going to the palace, he stalked right into the woods, his tartan quickly disappearing into the shadows.

Justine turned back to Blake, and Morgan almost laughed at her sister's dismay. "Blake, stop him!"

Blake took his time putting his glasses back on. He leafed through his tour book. "Let him go," he said grumpily. "If he won't even pick up a book and read the truth, there's not much I can do about it."

"He *can't* read!" Morgan retorted, surprised to find herself defending Alasdair. She climbed out of the car impatiently. "And until yesterday, *you* were the one going on and on about Robert the Bruce."

Justine and Blake both looked blank.

That was enough. Some of Alasdair's impatience must have transferred to Morgan, because she was suddenly fed up with all of Alasdair's mysteries. She was going to find out the truth and she was going to find out now.

Justine caught her breath. "Are you going after him?"

"You promised him a ride home," Morgan reminded her sister firmly. "I guess I'll have to make sure you keep your promise."

At least that was the excuse she would use. She turned to follow Alasdair, deliberately ignoring her sister's quick smile of satisfaction. While she walked, she took the crystal out of her purse and buried it carefully in the back of her money belt, then retucked T-shirt and sweater to hide the money belt's bulge.

The stone dug into her ribs, but Morgan ignored it.

It was time to get to the bottom of things. Alasdair MacAulay was going to have to be straight with her about who he was and what he was up to if he really wanted that ride back to faraway Callanish.

And if he was as broke as Justine thought, Morgan was sure she'd get the answers she wanted, but quick.

Alasdair glared at the chapel perched on Moot Hill as the anger drained out of him.

And left him feeling like seven kinds of fool.

Of all the glaikit things he could have done! 'Twas no consolation to find his gran right about his temper at this particular point.

Alasdair kicked at a clump of heather and berated himself silently but thoroughly. Would he ever get home now? Or had he trapped himself in Morgaine's world for all eternity?

He deserved no less for being such a fool.

Yet he was still seething. How dare the advisors promise to win Morgaine's favor, pledge that they would see him home, then break their word? Was a vow worth naught in this twisted world? Such faithlessness nearly made him growl aloud.

A man's honor was the only thing of value he could call his own. But calling Blake Advisor the liar he evidently was had undoubtedly not made Alasdair any friends. What an addlepated fool he was to have thought he could not make matters worse!

What would he not give to be home this very moment? There was a certain irony in wanting no less than to be back in the cottage that had not been able to hold him seven years past, but Alasdair was not particularly appreciative of that.

He chose to forget that he had not been able to shake the dust of Lewis off his boots—nor sweep the guilt from his mind—fast enough in those days.

Alasdair was dirty. He was tired. He was befuddled and frustrated beyond all by Faerie games. And he had an erection that simply would not say die.

Curse Morgaine le Fee!

Alasdair pivoted at the sound of a light step, only to find the sorceress herself closing the distance between them. A man with naught to lose—and one with a temper still simmering—Alasdair spoke his mind before he could stop himself.

"Come to smite me, have you?" he demanded boldly.

Morgaine's chin snapped up and her green gaze fixed upon

him. Her footsteps faltered a dozen steps away, but Alasdair was interested in little she might have to say.

"Smite me, then, and be done with it!" he cried and flung out his hands. "Surely there could be naught worse than this? Filthy and tired I am, surrounded by your adder-tongued advisors whose words cannot be trusted even while they are uttered."

"Blake means no harm."

Alasdair spat on the ground. "He can mean no other when he breaks his word as readily as he makes it!"

The enchantress visibly bristled. "He didn't break his word. This is Scone, and it's on the way to Lewis."

A bald-faced lie!

Had Blake acted under her dictate?

Ha! Alasdair should have expected no less!

Alasdair shoved a hand through his hair and glared at Morgaine. " 'Tis naught but lies from start to finish. Why tell me this is Scone, when any thinking man can see 'tis not? Why call that keep of yours Edinburgh, with its clarty English flag waving above it? Why insist he would see me home, when 'tis clear he intends no such thing?"

Alasdair swore in exasperation and paced the width of the hill with rapid steps. "And *why* does Blake Advisor wear that torture device over his eyes if he has the power within him to remove it?"

Morgaine made a choking sound at that, though when Alasdair turned to look, she tried to hide her laughter from him with her hand. Something within him softened at the sight.

Another part of him did precisely the opposite.

'Twas an unwelcome reminder of his predicament.

"Do not push me, my lady fair," Alasdair growled, shaking a warning finger in her direction. "If you mean to twitch your buttocks and tempt me with maidenly flushes, you had best keep your distance."

Morgaine pinkened, which only made matters worse, from Alasdair's perspective. "I have never twitched my buttocks . . ."

"Oh, I would insist the contrary!"

She gasped and stared at him, as though uncertain what to

say. 'Twas all a game to her, no doubt, a game she played
most artfully. And how could she not, privy as she was to
Alasdair's hidden desires? 'Twas no small advantage she had
in reading his very thoughts.

Aye, but Alasdair could make her moan aloud, he could,
and in this moment, the prospect was promising indeed. On
all sides, the heather grew knee-high and waved in the sunlight, fairly inviting man and lass to make use of its soft con-
cealment.

"Be warned, mistress Morgaine," Alasdair growled, though
a different heat had laid claim to his tone. "Venture too close
and I'll be buried to the hilt afore you can gasp a breath."

Morgaine took a cautious step back, as though she should
be afraid of him. "You wouldn't!"

"I would, with nary a regret," Alasdair asserted and knew
the truth when he heard it. "A man can only be tempted so
long, my lady, and make no mistake my threshold is near."

Morgaine looked so alarmed by this earthy reality that Alasdair turned his back on her. And what was she expecting of
him? He raked a hand through his hair again and paced across
the mound Blake so fecklessly called Moot Hill.

From first glance, she had set a fire within him, and that
blaze showed no signs of dying down to embers soon. Alasdair
took a deep breath and struggled to curb his raging desire.

He deliberately recalled the last time he had stood on the
true Moot Hill. It had been a gloriously clear day, one not
unlike this one, with a crisp wind on his face and a blue sky
arched overhead. And Robert the Bruce himself had lounged
amidst them all, smiling in reminiscence as his squire shared
the tale of his crowning on that very spot.

Well aware of the sorceress's bright gaze resting on him,
Alasdair turned. She had not moved, the dark tendrils of her
hair lifting in the wind, her eyes wide, her manner uncertain.

"What is it you want with me?" he asked, a new gentleness
in his words. She seemed to be encouraged by his question,
for she drew nearer as he watched. "I thought you were not
speaking with me."

"I'm not," she asserted, then evidently realized the whimsy
of her claim.

And she smiled tentatively. The winsome sight sent the frustration easing out of Alasdair as surely as if it had never been. The sunlight stretched golden between them, and Alasdair forgot everything his wary mind was telling him about this woman's danger to his very hide.

Indeed, he felt an answering smile tug on his own lips. "Aye, I can tell."

The lady laughed, an enchanting sound if ever there was one.

Alasdair's heart took a dizzying leap, and he suddenly felt the cur for railing at her so severely. "I would apologize, my lady. 'Tis true I have a fair temper when riled, but 'tis all bluster, as my gran is wont to say."

Morgaine's eyes danced. "I think I might like your gran. Wasn't that one of her stories last night?"

"Aye, that 'twas."

Morgaine took a tentative step closer. "I meant to thank you again for sharing it with me."

Alasdair felt his brow arch in skepticism. "Even though you are not speaking with me?"

She chuckled again and shook a finger at him. "Don't let this go to your head."

They stared at each other for a long, very warm moment, Alasdair recalling all too well how she had thanked him once before. When her lips quirked so playfully, 'twas hard to believe that this fragile creature held Alasdair's fate in her tiny hands.

She tilted her head. "Why don't you think this is Scone?"

"Because it cannot be." Alasdair frowned at the palace, regal enough but unfamiliar, the strange chapel, the clusters of people garbed as oddly as she.

"Why not?" the enchantress whispered, and Alasdair was surprised to find her by his side. He looked into the splendor of her eyes and saw the myriad shades of the sea reflected there. A part of him acknowledged the danger of staring too long, but Alasdair did not even want to look away.

He was beguiled by the Queen of Faerie, and in this moment he did not care.

Indeed, he wanted no more than to win her favor. Alasdair

recalled suddenly her fascination with the tales of mortals.

"I shall tell you of the Scone I know and what befell there," he vowed softly. "Though this is a tale of truth, not some fable told to keep bairns tight in their beds."

Morgaine's eyes glowed. "Tell me."

Alasdair took her small hand in his own and led her to the far side of the hill, where the view was of woods and fields. Here the sound of the crowds and chariots was less and the heather waved freely in the breeze. He sat down, then tugged the length of plaid off his shoulder and gallantly spread it across the greenery, his back to the palace.

Morgaine seated herself regally beside him, her bright eyes fixed upon him. Seated on the end of his tartan, she was dangerously close, and every fiber of Alasdair's being was aware of her soft warmth. He could smell the sweetness of her skin, and a part of him insisted there were better things to be done here than share tales.

But Alasdair stared determinedly into the trees as he braced his elbows on his knees. A promise made was a promise kept.

"Long ago, a part of Scotland was known as the kingdom of Dalriada, established by men who sailed bravely from Ireland to settle a new land. Those men claimed Kintyre and called the ancient hill of Dunadd the crowning place of their kings. 'Twas there on the rocks that each king pledged to his people and had a circlet of gold set upon his brow.

"There came a day when Saint Columba's own kinsman was to take the kingship and Columba came himself to seat the crown upon that man Aidan's brow. 'Twas said that then the Stone of Scone made its first appearance, and there are rumors that Columba himself brought it out of the mists of Ireland. 'Twas said to have been a gift from the High King of Tara to his distant kinsmen in Kintyre.

"From thence, the stone became known as the Stone of Destiny, for the future of his countrymen was secure in the hands of any king crowned upon it.

" 'Twas not long after that the first Norsemen came to make war, to claim slaves, capture bonny lasses as their women, steal plate and jewels. In time, they saw the beauty of Scotland and came to stay, invading islands and planting their seeds and seed. The land was hotly contested in those times, for there was precious little of it fertile, and the men of Dalriada lost more than their share of battles.

"For fear of capture, the Stone of Destiny was moved northward, along with the king, to Dunstaffnage. A tale there is that the stone itself was mortared into the wall of the fort to ensure that none might steal it away.

" 'Twas there that Kenneth the Hardy, son of Alpin, became the first King of Alba. A fair king he was and one with a dream for Scotland unified. Crowned upon it, he later moved the Stone of Destiny to Moot Hill, where it would be safe from the raiding Norsemen. Even in those ancient days, Moot Hill was a council place of great authority, and the king wisely blended old and new beneath his hand. Kenneth made Moot Hill the site of his court and so it was for many a year."

Alasdair laced his hands together, and stared into the trees. He was well aware that the sorceress attended his every word.

"The years rolled by, the kings birthed and died, feasted and killed, yet despite their battles, Scotland endured. The Norsemen settled on the islands, the Norman knights were granted lands, and all grew to prosperity. Alexander III was the last of the great kings, a man who witnessed the death of his kin, of his wife and three babes, yet was known to be religious, holy, wise, and kind.

"Aye, those were fine days for Scotland, days of prosperity and peace beneath a just king's hand."

Alasdair paused, and the sorceress leaned closer. "What happened to him?"

"Late in his days, he took a wee wife to his side, a French lass name of Yolande de Dreux, and 'twas his love for her that drove all sense from his mind." Alasdair shook his head. "But I stray from the tale in telling of this too soon."

He frowned at the woods. "There were portents of doom in the last year of Alexander's kingship, for foul weather welcomed the new year. 'Twas on the lips of many that the Day of Judgment was at hand, though the king believed naught of it. 'Twas the eighteenth day of March, the date foretold by many to be that Judgment Day, when Alexander—perhaps in defiance of popular belief—called his council to Edinburgh.

"They conferred long hours, then the good king entertained his favored ones with a fine meal that stretched long into the night. A storm began to rage as they dined, making more than one man shiver in dread. The king laughed, though, and lifted his chalice high, urging all to fill their bellies.

"Perhaps 'twas the influence of good Gascony wine, but when all made to retire, Alexander wanted only to be with his beloved new bride. Yolande slumbered at his abode of Kinghorn, not too far distant but across the Firth itself.

"He called for his ostler and he called for the ferryman, and he rode to the port, though the storm was ripping through the trees. All begged that he wait for the dawn, but Alexander would not be swayed.

" 'Twas the blackest hour of the night that they sailed across the Firth, fighting the waves all the way to Inverkeithing. The innkeeper there again begged the king to tarry, but he would have none of it. Naught would suffice for him that night but his sweet bride's own bed, and he began the long ride along the coast to Kinghorn. The heat of his desire sent Alexander ahead of his party and the wind stole away their warning cries."

Alasdair looked to his boots. "They found him in the morn, a victim of his own recklessness," he said quietly. "In his haste, he had ridden carelessly. His steed had fallen from the road, the necks of both broken on the rocks below. And so it was that Scotland had no king."

"Didn't he have an heir?"

Alasdair shrugged. "A wee lass, who died shortly thereafter." His frown deepened. "And Edward of England saw his long-sought chance to make Scotland his own."

He plucked a stem of heather and twirled it in his fingers, remembering all too well the tumult of those times. And later, the distant uproar in Alasdair's homeland had been echoed before his own hearth.

For a Fenella displeased was a Fenella impossible. And there had been much in the early days of their match—indeed, throughout the match—that Fenella found displeasing.

Alasdair shifted awkwardly at the unwelcome recollection.

Morgaine waited silently, and he suddenly realized that the heather he held was white of bloom.

Alasdair granted it to Morgaine with a wry smile. " 'Tis said to be uncommon fortune," he said before realizing that an enchantress had no need of such tokens.

But she accepted it all the same, giving him a smile that twisted his heart. "By your gran?"

"Aye."

"It sounds as though she has a lot of folk wisdom to share."

Alasdair grimaced. "Aye, oft too much." He smiled ruefully. "Would that I had listened." Then the smile vanished, the visage of Fenella invading his thoughts for the first time in years.

And the ardor that raged in his loins in Morgaine's presence felt the equivalent of a winter's daunting chill.

Morgaine leaned against him, the press of her breast against his arm banishing the unwelcome Fenella from Alasdair's mind. And beneath his kilt, there was a definite promise of summer's heat. "Was there a war?"

Alasdair nodded and fought against his earthy urges. "Aye, there was, and nasty 'twas indeed. Edward had women and children put to death for no reason at all, he razed entire towns and terrified the people. He taxed and murdered and slaughtered until all bent to kiss his hand. He would have all grovel before him, whatever the cost."

Alasdair fixed the sorceress with a stern look. "If any had a doubt about the English and their intent for Scotland, years of bloody savagery put it to rest. It might have been a short war indeed, for so many bellies had gone soft in those good years, were it not for one William Wallace of Elderslie."

"Oh, I know all about Wallace," Morgaine declared. "I saw *Braveheart*, you know."

Alasdair could make no sense of that comment, but he continued nonetheless. "Aye. Well, Edward captured Wallace after years of war and years of hunting. He put the valiant man to a gruesome public death."

Morgaine grimaced. "I know. I couldn't watch the end."

Alasdair frowned at this easy reference to her powers. "But though Wallace died cruelly, he did not die for naught. Edward

showed the truth of his cruelty in his pursuit of Wallace. He
stole away both the ancient regalia and the Stone of Scone
when he considered himself victorious, showing one and all
that he did not intend Scotland to have another king of her
own. A broken promise it was, for he had promised Scotland's
crown to one loyal to his side, name of Robert the Bruce.''

"But I thought Robert the Bruce was a rebel?''

"Aye, in the end he was, though there was a time when he
too bent his knee to England. Such is the burden of those who
hold property and must think of their responsibilities as well
as their own hearts' demand.

"There was more than one Robert the Bruce, for the first
son of each generation of Bruces had the name of Robert. The
one I follow is the grandson of the one to whom Edward broke
his word. One of two powerful families in Scotland, the Bruce
clan knew 'twould be they or the Comyns who retrieved the
Scottish crown, if any had the valor to do the deed. 'Tis said
the Comyns did not want the crown but agreed to aid the
Bruces in exchange for land and wealth.

"At any rate, 'twas no coincidence that Robert the Bruce
took council with John Comyn the Red in Dumfries, nor that
a church was chosen for their parlay. Many's the account of
what happened that day, for they two were fiercely competitive
and ambitious both, and neither afraid to use his blade. In the
end, there is but one fact clear—they argued and John Comyn
left the chapel in a shroud alone, while Robert the Bruce rode
away.''

Chapter 8

Morgaine's eyes were round. "He killed him?"

"Aye, or at the least his man finished the deed once 'twas begun. To have done so in the holy sanctuary of a church was no small sin, and I can only believe that the Robert the Bruce I know and serve would have had just cause. I heard tell that John had betrayed Robert's plans to the English and done so far too soon for comfort, but 'tis not a topic upon which Robert the Bruce will tolerate discussion."

Morgaine frowned at that and might have protested, but Alasdair continued determinedly with his tale. " 'Twas certain the English would hunt any man who killed one of their own—let alone one conspiring to make himself king—and war was in the wind once more. Robert the Bruce hied himself to Scone, his supporters in his wake."

Alasdair smiled, recalling that sunny summer's day they had lolled on Moot Hill and heard the tale recounted. "Imagine the sight, if you dare. A fine spring day, a heather-clad hill and pennants snapping in the breeze, great stallions of war stamping on the perimeter.

" 'Twas the twenty-fifth of March, some twenty years after the death of Alexander III, that Robert the Bruce was crowned King of Scots in the Abbey of Scone. He was attended by three bishops and four earls, together the eight most powerful men in this bonny land.''

Alasdair leaned toward the sorceress and lowered his voice. '' 'Tis said the MacDuff clan have the ancient right to set the crown upon the brow of the Kings of Alba—this blood courses through the veins of the Earl of Fife. That man was imprisoned in England, but his sister, Isobel of Buchan, defied her husband's allegiance to both Edward of England and John Comyn. She rode in haste and at considerable risk to herself to fulfill her family duty.''

''How exciting!'' Morgaine's eyes sparkled.

''Aye, there were those who said Isobel loved the Bruce more than her own spouse and 'twas that alone that set her course.'' He shrugged. ''Whatever the truth, the lass was two days late for the coronation, by all accounts. All the same, Robert the Bruce had her place the golden circlet upon his brow once again. 'Twas Palm Sunday and Scotland again had her rightful king.''

The enchantress frowned. ''But you said that Edward took the Stone of Destiny away.''

''Aye.'' Alasdair smiled at the intent sorceress, pleased that she listened well. He dropped his voice to a conspiratorial whisper. ''There are those who say he stole a fraud and that the true stone was hidden away. Those who knew the truth unveiled the real stone for the crowning of the Bruce.''

Morgaine sighed. ''That's so romantic.''

Alasdair nodded grimly, not able to pinpoint precisely why it troubled him so to find the sorceress prey to the Bruce's legendary allure. ''Aye, Robert has always been one to turn a lassie's eye, that much is for certain.''

''But wasn't Edward still ready to make war?''

''Aye, that he did. You may well believe that once he heard the tale of the coronation, he bayed for blood. Robert the Bruce managed to flee and came himself to my island, seeking recruits to his cause.''

Alasdair cleared his throat as he pushed recollections out of his mind. ''At the time, it suited me well to join his ranks.''

''But . . .'' Morgaine looked perplexed.

''But *what*?'' Alasdair echoed irritably. There had been protests aplenty when he joined the Bruce, but Alasdair had no interest in hearing them again now. "Do you think it so unnatural for a man to wish to see his homeland freed of the iron fist of the English?"

Morgaine looked dumbfounded.

In truth, for a sorceress of rare power, she was markedly easy to surprise.

"But the war is over . . ."

"*Over?*" To think that she would tell him another falsehood after he had shared this noble tale! " 'Tis far from over and you know that truth as well as I!"

Alasdair bounded to his feet in outrage, tugging his tartan from beneath her with such force that she nearly rolled away. "I know well enough that you support their cause, but listen to me well, my lady. There can be no excuse for the rape and slaughter Edward and his kin have made of this fair land."

Morgaine looked exasperated. "But they're all dead!"

Alasdair straightened and impaled her with a stare. "Who would be dead, by your account?" he asked coldly.

"Robert the Bruce, for one." She ran a hand over her brow. "I mean you talk as though you know him, but . . ."

"*I do know Robert the Bruce!*" Alasdair set his hands on his hips. "I have served beneath his hand for seven years and have yet to regret one single day of that service."

"But . . ."

"Morgan! There you are!" Justine crowed.

The sorceress looked as dismayed as Alasdair felt at the interruption of her advisors. Justine and Blake descended on them, their wide smiles remarkably at odds with Alasdair's jaggly mood.

"Should we head out? Blake's found the most wonderful little place where we can stay tonight."

The pair acted as though there was naught amiss.

"Is it to Lewis you would take me?" Alasdair asked suspiciously.

Blake pushed the device up his nose. "Look, I'm sorry we misunderstood each other before. It's going to take a couple of days to get there, you know, it's pretty far."

Alasdair knew well enough that the road was long from

Faerie to the mortal world. But how much earthly time passed
with each moment here?

Blake smiled. "Trust me, that's where we're going."

Trust him.

Alasdair hated that he had little option other than to do
exactly that if he meant to see his home again. Morgaine
frowned now, as deep in thought as Alasdair had ever seen
and clearly not following the conversation around her. The
sorceress looked as though she intended to be of little use to
him in this, although she could addle his wits in splendid fashion.

Was his fate no more than a game to her?

Alasdair wondered at his own sense that Justine fairly held
her breath, awaiting his approval. "Please, Alasdair," she cajoled, with a smile that appeared genuine. "We're on the way
now, anyway."

Alasdair had never been fond of moments when he had few
options. He thought of his wedding day and his mood wors-
ened considerably.

He sighed, then nodded grimly. "I will continue to journey
with you." When Blake and Justine smiled happily, Alasdair
turned to Morgaine.

One last matter was there to resolve.

The advisors trotted back toward the Micra, evidently busily
planning some scheme or other, and he waited until they were
out of earshot.

Then, Alasdair bent low to growl to Morgaine alone. "Understand that I travel with you because I have no other choice.
But make no mistake, my lady, I will not readily countenance
your lies about the man of honor I follow."

"But . . ."

"But naught!" Alasdair interrupted her savagely before she
could concoct some tale to beguile him. He glowered at her
sternly. "So long as you insist the English have vanquished
the Scots and that Robert the Bruce is dead, 'twill be *I* who
is not speaking with *you.*"

With that, Alasdair followed Blake and Justine, leaving
Morgaine to trail in his wake.

                    *   *   *

Alasdair said he knew Robert the Bruce.

Personally.

Was he nuts?

Or was he telling the truth? From their first meeting, Morgan had thought those blue eyes revealed his thoughts with unreal clarity. He believed without a shadow of a doubt everything he had just told her.

Morgan could see it in his eyes.

But did that mean she should believe it too? Because if Alasdair was telling the truth and he wasn't nuts, then he had to have come from the past.

Morgan watched him stride away and wondered.

What if he *were* lost from another time? His attitude about nearly everything could be explained if he had just arrived from the fourteenth century, but even Morgan's imagination had a hard time accepting that.

Maybe he was an actor who really got into his roles. That was easier to accept, but it left three really big loose ends dangling.

How could Alasdair have changed their guidebooks?

And, even tougher, how could he have changed Blake's and Justine's memories of Scottish history?

And why didn't he show up in her photograph? Morgan chewed her lip and trailed behind the trio.

Unless Alasdair's coming forward in time had *changed* history.

It couldn't be true. There had to be a logical explanation, but logic had never been Morgan's strong suit. She was intuitive, and her intuition was screaming *Yes!* at the very idea of Alasdair traveling through time.

Morgan rubbed her temple as the trio marched away and tried not to flash back to math class and the torture of geometric proofs. Not having had enough sleep didn't make thinking this through any easier.

She meekly piled into the Micra, vaguely aware of Justine describing some romantic hotel that a nice woman from Cincinnati had told them about.

Morgan twiddled the heather, liking that Alasdair had given it to her and not liking that she liked that.

But if Alasdair was a fourteenth-century highlander, then he wasn't a con man. In fact, if he had had the crystal from the regalia in his possession before he traveled through time, that could explain why it was missing and no one remembered it ever being there. Alasdair could have changed history.

Morgan really didn't like how reassuring she found the logic of that. No one could zip across six or seven centuries.

Could they?

And if they did, would it turn Robert the Bruce from hero to scoundrel?

It was all just too confusing. Morgan leaned back in her corner of the backseat and pretended to doze, all the while watching Alasdair through her lashes.

Okay, first the con man scenario. For a smooth talker, Alasdair hadn't seemed to be particularly goal-oriented or even very smooth. He had promised *not* to try and get the crystal from her, which was supposedly the only thing he wanted.

And he had saved her from those thugs.

And if Alasdair was after bigger spoils than the crown jewel of Scotland, well, wouldn't he at least have asked what kind of asset base the three of them had?

Nope, the con man scenario had some definite weaknesses.

Blake pulled out onto the highway, and silence descended in the car. The humming of the Micra was quite soothing, as were Justine's murmured directions. Alasdair seemed slowly to relax beside Morgan, and Morgan herself realized just how tired she really was.

Now, if Alasdair was an actor, she reasoned, staring out the window, he might just be really getting into playing his role. But the castle guides said they didn't hire actors, and he never missed a beat in not understanding modern stuff.

In fact, Alasdair seemed to find the contemporary world awfully confusing. She would expect a medieval guy to be just about as frustrated as Alasdair obviously was.

Morgan suddenly remembered how the highlander's manner had changed in the tower when he heard her name. What had he called her?

Morgaine le Fee. And he still insisted on calling her Morgaine. Well, Morgan had read enough fairy tales to catch that reference.

Morgaine le Fee, the sister of King Arthur who went over to the Dark Side. Morgan chewed her lip. Was that who he thought she was? He did talk a lot about her kingdom and this foul world.

Did he think he was trapped in some domain of sorcery?

Morgan's lips twitched unwillingly. She didn't want to laugh at him, but it was funny to think of herself as the powerful Evil Queen of all she surveyed.

"Luke," a tiny voice in her mind breathed raspily, *"come over to the Dark Side."*

It would be funnier if it didn't make so much sense.

And it would make even *more* sense to a fourteenth-century man. How else could he explain the modern world? It was obviously a magical illusion that couldn't be trusted.

The capricious realm of Faerie.

Morgan's mind ran in circles, trying unsuccessfully to find another explanation. The only option that accommodated everything that had happened was that Alasdair really had come from the past.

After all, he thought Blake's glasses were a torture device.

Morgan fidgeted but couldn't get comfortable against the hard, vibrating wall of the car. She eyed Alasdair and noticed that his head had dipped forward.

Her heart contracted in sympathy. If she was right—and Morgan's gut told her she was—he was probably one confused highlander. And he probably hadn't slept too well on that park bench, either.

She couldn't blame him for getting a bit testy about the whole thing. Of course he didn't think that was Scone—it would have changed an awful lot in almost seven hundred years. Why, Blake had said the palace dated from the sixteenth century.

Morgan's natural compassion came to the fore. Somehow she had to help Alasdair—the only question was how.

And that was a biggie. Morgan watched Alasdair doze and felt her own energy run low. All this thinking was making it easy to remember that she hadn't slept much the night before either.

And Alasdair's shoulder looked like a much better place to lean her head than the side wall of the car, especially since she now knew that he wasn't some dastardly criminal.

His gran was right, she thought with a little smile. Alasdair was all bark and no bite. He made a lot of noise, but right now he looked as easygoing as a big, warm pussycat. She couldn't imagine a safer place to curl up and sleep than right beside him.

Of course, Alasdair might have other ideas.

Morgan straightened cautiously, but the highlander didn't stir. Justine and Blake seemed oblivious to anything going on in the backseat.

Morgan sidled closer and leaned her arm tentatively against Alasdair's muscled strength.

He didn't even move.

In fact, he seemed to breathe more deeply.

Morgan took that as encouragement and carefully leaned her head against his shoulder. She closed her eyes, letting herself luxuriate in the masculine heat of his skin.

It had been so very long.

She stared at his hand through her lashes, liking how his strong fingers splayed across his knee. Morgan gave herself permission to imagine just a little bit.

What if she had been born in the fourteenth century? What if she, like Isobel of Buchan, had been a woman smitten with a brave and bold man? She let her mind wander as she drifted closer to sleep. In her mind's eye, the pennants snapped and the horses stomped around that heather-clad hill.

Fierce isosceles triangles bristled around the perimeter, threatening the idyllic setting with protractors and sharp compasses, each demanding that two of their angles be proved equal without delay. They came closer, their points menacing, and Morgan forgot everything she had ever pretended to know about mathematical proofs.

She was at their mercy!

A single lusty roar sent the triangles suddenly scattering to the four winds. Angels sang, Morgan heaved a sigh of relief, and the world was safe from geometry again.

The hero responsible, garbed in disreputable-looking plaid, stormed through the proud steeds. He dispatched a few errant slide rules with a sweep of his broadsword, then headed directly for Morgan with purpose in his step.

And when Morgan lifted the golden circlet of Scotland's crown in her hands, it was Alasdair who dropped to one knee before her, flashing those magnificent legs as he did.

Then he tipped back his head and met Morgan's gaze. She stared into the fathomless blue of his eyes and smiled ever so slowly.

And Alasdair smiled back, the twinkle in his eye sending a flush of anticipation dancing over her skin. Morgan felt herself bend toward him, cup his face in her hands, and lower her lips to his.

It was a good thing for Morgan's resistance that she was too tired to tingle from head to toe. She managed to savor the dream moment for about that long, then her eyes drifted completely closed.

Alasdair was having a wonderful dream. 'Twas such a rare marvel that he had no desire to awaken.

Because indeed there could be naught finer than having a compliant Morgaine le Fee nestled in his arms.

His memory supplied the sweet, rosy scent of her, his hands recalled the softness of her fair skin as well as if they yet held her close. Alasdair could even feel the tangle of her dark hair winding around his fingers.

And in his dream, her allure held no hidden serpent's bite.

Through the filter of his lashes, Alasdair could see Morgaine lying within his embrace, her own eyes closed, her ebony lashes stark against her skin, her ruby lips parted in soft invitation. She was nearly in his lap, the sweet weight of her curves pressed so wondrously against him.

And Alasdair wanted her. The urge that had tormented him since first he spied the sorceress seemed to have trebled in his sleep. And while he dreamt, he was safe to indulge his desire.

Unable to deny temptation, Alasdair leaned over the lady.

She stirred and her witchy green eyes opened lazily.

The welcoming smile that curved her lips was lethal to any uncertainty lingering within Alasdair. Before he risked awakening, he bent and captured her lips with his.

To his astonished delight, the sorceress rose to meet his embrace. Her hands slipped around his neck and she pulled him closer, as though she hungered for his touch as desperately as he desired hers.

Morgaine was sweeter than the first spring honey and made him more dizzy than the strongest mead. Alasdair gathered her close and slanted his lips possessively across hers, swallowing her low moan of delight. His hand slid over her delicacy and cupped her breast of its own accord.

When his thumb found her turgid nipple—a sure sign of her arousal—it near undid him. Alasdair caressed the taut bead, sliding his fingers over her, rolling the nipple betwixt thumb and finger.

Morgaine gasped and arched against his hand, her tongue tangling provocatively with his own. Her kiss turned demanding, as though she would devour him whole, and Alasdair was more than willing to return her ardor.

He feasted upon her, sampling her sweetness deeply, inflamed by the way she clutched his hair in her tiny hands. He gathered her up and her breasts pressed against his chest, the tautness of her nipples making his heart thunder in his ears. His exploring fingers found the ripe curve of her buttocks just as she moaned and rolled her tongue within his ear. The heat raged over his flesh, and Alasdair made to roll her beneath him.

Only to bump shoulder, knee, and head against some confines that seemed vaguely familiar.

Alasdair's eyes flew open, and his heart sank when he found himself battling the enclosure of the blue Micra.

Blake and Justine were gone, the tops of the doors somehow open to the crisp bite of the wind. The chariot sat on a point of land, a mirror of shimmering water stretched before them.

Yet on the far shore stood a stone keep, its walls crumbling but obviously of Alasdair's own world. He could smell the faint tinge of salt in the wind and knew the sea could not be far away.

He truly was home in the land of mortals!

But there was one particular immortal yet sprawled in his lap.

A hard lump rose in Alasdair's throat as he realized he had indeed kissed the sorceress with rare abandon. His dream had held some vestige of reality, indeed, but the lady's pleasure could not be the truth of it. Alasdair barely dared to look down and see Morgaine's wrath.

But look he did. And the flushed Morgaine he found looking shyly up at him did not look wrathful at all.

In fact, the delicate blush gracing her cheeks and the mischievous glint in her eyes moved the hard lump somewhat lower than his throat.

"Wow," she breathed, then smiled enchantingly. "What a way to wake up."

And awakened Alasdair undoubtedly was. He was home! Or close enough that he could return to Lewis alone. These hills could be nowhere other than his own beloved Scotland, and he knew he could find someone to direct him on his way.

He had returned from the land of Faerie.

And the Lady Morgaine had made it so.

Alasdair's delight was such that he wanted to sing aloud, bellow some long and boisterous tune that would set every toe to tapping.

But then he thought of a much better way to celebrate. Alasdair bent and kissed the sorceress again with the thoroughness the situation deserved.

Morgan was drowning in sensation.

And the last thing she wanted was to be saved. Alasdair's kiss was the best thing she had tasted in a long, long time. His strong hands moved over her in an endless caress, the gentle sweep of his touch almost reverential.

Morgan had never felt so treasured. And yet, the heat of his erection pressed against her hip, the size of it leaving no doubt of his desire.

He wanted her. Morgan could barely wrap her mind around the incredible concept, but she didn't care.

She just didn't want this moment to end.

And she didn't want Alasdair to change his mind. A decade of denied desire came to her rescue, and Morgan kissed him as though she would never have another chance to kiss a man.

Because she might not.

The reassurance of her expertise thrust against her hip. Alasdair groaned and gathered her closer, and Morgan rubbed her breasts against the broad strength of his chest. One hand cupped her nape, the other slipped beneath her sweater.

Morgan caught her breath when his hand closed with gentle possessiveness over her breast. The heat of his palm was bare against her skin and Morgan praised the day she had abandoned brassieres. She opened her eyes and stared into the endless blue of Alasdair's gaze, their noses almost touching.

He slid his hand across her tight nipple and Morgan moaned softly. It was more than a little reassuring to hear him catch his breath as well.

"What would you have of me?" he whispered huskily, and Morgan knew they both knew the answer to that.

Before she could question her impulse, she moved to straddle him. He gasped when she sat down and wriggled herself against his hardness. Her leggings and his kilt seemed to be no barrier at all, and Morgan rocked before she could stop herself.

"Morgaine!" Alasdair leaned forward, captured her lips with his and simultaneously drove himself against her in one lightning-quick move.

Morgan barely realized that she was pinned against the back of Justine's seat before the seat unexpectedly flopped toward the dashboard. It wasn't a very timely reminder of how the front seats tipped to allow access to the back.

Morgan squeaked at the sudden release of the catch, Alasdair growled, then he was sprawled clumsily on top of her. They came to an inelegant halt when the seatback was almost completely horizontal.

It wasn't exactly a picture-perfect love scene. Alasdair looked so astonished that Morgan almost laughed out loud.

She caught a glimpse of one very tight and muscular buttock beyond a sea of plaid.

Then she did laugh.

Alasdair looked at her as though she were crazy, his astonishment changing slowly to outrage when Morgan couldn't stop laughing.

"I see naught amusing about our embrace," he began to huff, but Morgan pointed to his bare butt.

"It's true!" she managed to choke out. "It's really true."

"You find my buttocks a source of amusement?" Alasdair demanded.

"Not at all," Morgan retorted. "They're magnificent."

Alasdair inhaled sharply. "Then, you mock my embrace!" He shoved open the car door, no doubt intending to sweep regally out of the Micra.

Instead, opening the door proved that they had been braced against it. They tumbled together to the asphalt outside and landed with an ungracious thump.

Morgan was delighted to note that, even though he was miffed, Alasdair ensured that he took the brunt of the blow. She heard a click as her favorite hair clip took a hit and a clattering as more than one piece of it fell to the ground.

It had only been a matter of time before she broke it. Morgan confronted the sad truth that she was such a klutz she couldn't even make out in a car with the most handsome hunk she'd ever met.

Before she could think too much about that, Alasdair bounded to his feet. He snapped his kilt back into place with a self-righteous flick of his wrist and glared at her.

From her vantage point, sprawled on the parking lot, Morgan could see straight up those legs with their dusting of golden hair. She squinted, caught a glimpse of something swinging free, and giggled again.

It *was* true!

Alasdair harumphed, but Morgan held up one hand. She wiped away her tears while he glowered at her, clearly not inclined to share the joke.

"Scotsmen really don't wear anything under their kilts, then," she said when she caught her breath.

Alasdair raised a fair brow and crossed his arms over his chest, looking only a little less insulted. "And what would my lady suggest a man wear beneath his kilt?" he demanded coldly.

Morgan propped herself up on her elbows, her grin still tugging at the corner of her mouth. "Ever heard of Calvin Kleins? Harvey Woods? Maybe something nice from Mr. Brief?"

If Morgan thought Alasdair had taken umbrage before, that was nothing compared to his outrage now.

"I would suffer no man mucking about beneath my tartan, of that you can be certain!" he roared. "No matter in what esteem you might hold this Calvin and Harvey, neither is welcome beneath my plaid!"

He thought she thought he was gay?

Alasdair stormed a few paces away and pivoted to jab a finger through the air at Morgan. "Of all the lies that have been told about me, my lady, that is far and away the most loathsome!"

Despite herself, Morgan started to chuckle again. She had never before been so absolutely positive that a man was straight. As the laughter spilled from her lips, Alasdair's ears turned bright red.

Then he stalked farther away.

And this time he didn't look inclined to stop.

That stopped Morgan's laughter cold.

"No, wait, that's not what I meant. I wasn't laughing at you." Morgan stumbled to her feet. "Alasdair, don't be angry. I can explain . . ."

Suddenly Alasdair seemed to notice his surroundings for the first time. He halted and looked about himself with such dismay that Morgan took a look too.

The Micra was parked on a point facing a romantic little lake complete with a photogenic ruined castle. Behind the car sprawled a perfectly pedestrian asphalt parking lot, a little inn on the far side with cars clustered near it. Apparently the inn had a pub, because a neon Guinness sign shone red in the window.

Morgan almost died when she saw the big tour bus parked

less than twenty feet away from the car. Dozens of Japanese tourists studiously pretended not to have noticed her and Alasdair, snapping pictures in every other direction. Morgan looked back at the car and saw that the front and rear windows were fogged.

She couldn't help but blush.

Alasdair spun abruptly to confront her, looking as though he found their surroundings morally offensive. "This is not my home!" he roared, and everything feminine within Morgan delighted in his masculine indignation.

Whether Alasdair was a time traveler or a nutcase, at this moment Morgan didn't care. She wanted to grab him by the hair and pounce on him until he begged for mercy.

And maybe even a little longer than that. Alasdair's kiss had more than demonstrated how thorough he would be about any amorous adventure, and part of Morgan regretted that she had declined his invitation that very first day.

It really might have been a roll like none other.

And she was sure he could teach her a few things she didn't know about lovemaking. Her experience was pretty limited, after all. Morgan had already picked up some kissing pointers from this highlander.

Alasdair clenched his fists when she didn't respond. Morgan heard a murmur from the Japanese tourists, then the clicking of cameras turned on her and Alasdair.

Which reminded her that Alasdair didn't photograph well.

He *had* to be from the past.

And she had to help him.

"Unleash me from your spell, Morgaine le Fee," Alasdair demanded with obvious impatience. "Release me and send me home to my son!"

His son?

Morgan blinked, but he glared at her. Had she heard right? "You have a son?"

Alasdair's expression turned ominous. "Already I have told you that there's naught amiss beneath my plaid." He shook a finger at her. "But do not be thinking that I will stand by and let you seize him for your own. I will fight you for my son with every last fiber of my being, make no mistake about that.''

His fierce protectiveness of his child warmed Morgan to her toes. But all the same, this shouting had to stop. She held up her hands in a peaceful gesture and slowly walked toward him, trying to remember every hostage movie she'd ever seen.

''I don't want your son,'' she said in a low, even voice, making sure she maintained eye contact with Alasdair. ''And I really do want to help you get home.''

Some of the skepticism eased out of his shoulders. His eyes narrowed slightly with suspicion. ''Aye?''

''Aye,'' Morgan agreed and smiled. She stopped before him and tilted her head up to hold his gaze. ''I promise you that.''

Alasdair sniffed. ''Is your word worth as little as your advisor's pledge?''

''No. I keep my word.''

His lips thinned as though he believed her but wished he didn't. Alasdair folded his arms across his chest and his expression turned stubborn. ''Swear it to me, then.''

''I swear to you, Alasdair MacAulay, that I will do everything I can to send you home,'' Morgan vowed softly. ''Wherever—and whenever—that is.''

Alasdair eyed her carefully and Morgan felt some of his resistance dissolve. Then he arched a fair brow. ''Whenever?''

Morgan frowned as she tried to think of how to begin, then she looped her arm through his. ''It's kind of a long story,'' she confessed, urging him to walk toward the inn.

To Morgan's relief, Alasdair easily fell into step beside her.

''And I have an idea that you might want one of those wee drams to make it all go down a little easier.''

Despite everything Morgan had against alcohol, this was one time when she couldn't have blamed anyone for having a drink to dull the shock.

In fact, if she was right and Alasdair had skipped through the better part of seven centuries in the blink of an eye—never mind leaving a child far behind—she wouldn't blame him for getting stinking drunk.

Morgan's heart contracted with a compassion of frightening intensity.

Surely she was only worried about a little boy, left alone?

Surely. There couldn't be any other reason. Morgan knew that she didn't need—or want—any man in her life, especially one who was more lost than she had ever managed to be.

Obviously, she just felt sorry for Alasdair's son.

It couldn't be anything more than that.

Alasdair fingered the dram of whisky that had been placed before him and studied the sorceress. 'Twas unsettling how somber she had become. What was amiss?

He did not drink the spirits, fairly certain that if matters were as dire as her expression suggested, he might need it more once she had had her say.

Was she going to tell him that he could never go home? Alasdair's gut went cold at the very thought. Was it because of some deficiency in her power? Or the terms of the witch's spell that had sent him here? Had he failed a test?

Or was she simply unwilling to release him?

Morgaine pushed her glass of water across the table, making circles with the wet mark it left on the wood. Playing she was, as though she knew not where to begin.

And it was making him mad.

Alasdair captured her glass with one resolute gesture. When his fingers closed over hers, Morgaine met his gaze with obvious reluctance.

"Tell me," he urged in a low voice. "Tell me the worst of it."

The lady licked her lips and looked from one side to the other before she began. "It's not good," she admitted, such a vision of maidenly softness that Alasdair actually longed to reassure her.

Her fingers trembled slightly beneath his grip, and Alasdair gave them a reassuring squeeze before he could stop himself. " 'Tis true that tidings are always worse before the telling. Giving voice to the worst lessens its bite."

"You're probably right. And there's no point beating around the bush." She smiled sadly, then squared her shoulders. "Alasdair, where do you think you are?"

Alasdair sensed a trick, but her expression was guileless. "In your domain."

"Which is where?"

Would he earn some loathsome fate by giving voice to such names? Alasdair's mouth went dry, but he forced out the words.

He would balk before naught. "In the land of Faerie."

"And that would make me who?"

"The sorceress Morgaine le Fee."

She shook her head slowly, and Alasdair feared he had erred in naming her occupation so boldly.

But before he could apologize, Morgaine took his hand in the two of hers and looked deeply into his eyes. Alasdair knew 'twould be fair dreadful whatever she meant to say. He braced himself against the worst calamity.

But he could never have prepared himself for what she did say.

"Alasdair, you're wrong. I'm not Morgaine le Fee and this isn't the land of Faerie."

She was deadly serious, her gaze devoid of guile. A cold tremor of fear rolled over Alasdair's flesh.

What was this?

"You've traveled almost seven hundred years into the future, I don't know how." The sorceress gave his fingers a squeeze, her expression now turning apologetic. For a fleeting instant Alasdair was almost fooled by the sincerity in her steady green eyes.

If he was not in Faerie, then where could he be?

"I can't explain it, Alasdair, but the year is 1998, and I'm guessing that you think it's a good bit earlier than that." She stared deeply into his eyes as he slowly absorbed what she had said.

1998?

But that could not be! The sorceress held his gaze, as though she would will him to believe her.

'Twas impossible! Alasdair blinked. Indeed, 'twas such a daft load of bunk that his lips twitched. 'Twas a jest, no more than that. Or a test of his gullibility.

And one he had nearly failed.

Nearly fooled him, Morgaine had. Traveling through time—stuff and nonsense! 'Twas beyond belief! As though the world could have turned to such a hellhole, even in seven hundred years.

Alasdair grinned.

Morgaine did not smile. Instead her expression grew concerned. "You have to believe me," she insisted, her gaze intent. Aye, she was a clever one, to stick so firmly to her lie!

But the way he had fallen prey to her allusions of doom was so perfect that Alasdair chuckled. What a daftie he was!

Aye, he had fallen like a witless rock for her jest! He, Alasdair MacAulay, who was broadly considered to be a man of good sense, had nearly swallowed Morgaine's feckless tale whole! How the lads would mock him for this!

Beneath the sorceress's astonished gaze, Alasdair began to laugh and could not stop.

Chapter 9

OH, SHE HAD led him on beautifully, teasing him with portents of doom, when she meant to make a joke! The more Alasdair thought about it, the harder he laughed.

And 'twas so good to feel laughter rippling through him again that he did not want to stop. An errant tear trickled from the corner of his eye.

But the sorceress stared at him. "Alasdair, you don't understand." Her words were emphatic. "My name is Morgan Lafayette. I'm a book illustrator. I'm not a dark queen, or even an enchantress."

The intensity of her manner captured Alasdair's attention more securely than anything else could have done. His eyes narrowed in consideration, and his laughter came to an abrupt halt.

Why did she deny her own identity?

Why would a sorceress want him to believe she was not her own powerful self? There could be no import of good in this.

Had Morgaine decided not to aid him in returning home? A cold weight settled in Alasdair's belly. Had her advisors decided his cause was not worth the trouble?

Morgaine shook her head, her green eyes filled with concern. "And that's not the worst of it, Alasdair. Your coming forward in time has somehow changed the past." She toyed

with the glass again, and his gut clenched at the sight of her
distress, despite his certainty that she toyed with him.

She grimaced. "And I don't know how to fix it."

Those words recalled him to the truth.

'Twas a lie! Morgaine le Fee could repair any matter, that
much Alasdair knew without doubt. Her dark powers were
boundless and far-reaching, as any laddie learned at his gran's
knee.

Morgaine could only have chosen not to aid him and yet
had not the audacity to tell him flatly as much. Alasdair could
not guess what he had done to earn her disfavor.

Indeed, he had made efforts to accommodate himself to the
vagaries of her world! And he had been gracious beyond all!
Alasdair's annoyance rose a notch—not unlike many another
mortal who strayed into the world of the unseen, his cause
had been poorly served. Certainly, he had not had any fair
hearing in Morgaine's court!

But his anger would serve him poorly in this matter. Alasdair fought to control his response, very aware of the sorceress's gaze locked upon him. Could she read his rebellious
thoughts? Were those thoughts what had wrought his doom?

He did not know.

And worse, he did not know what to say.

Alasdair clutched the wee pewter cup of whisky, feeling in
dire need of its consolation. Suddenly he wondered whether
there was significance in Morgaine's choice of water.

Was this another game?

Was there aught awry with the whisky?

Alasdair cleared his throat, as he considered flinging the
dram against the wall. Would it leave a trail of flames there?

But when he spoke, his words were icily polite. "You do
not join me?"

"I don't drink," Morgaine declared with a toss of her hair.

It was loose since their adventure in the car, a great tangle
of ebony witchery behind her shoulders, and Alasdair suddenly feared what she might do to him. There was no telling
what a wee witch with her locks trailing loose might conjure,
and Morgaine had powers far beyond such mortals who commanded only a fraction of her abilities.

Alasdair recalled well enough Morgaine's displeasure when he had been drinking before. He had the eerie sense there was something of import here that he was missing.

Alasdair arched a brow and watched Morgaine's response carefully. "It sounds a matter of principle with you."

Her lips tightened and she took a quick breath. "It is," she said fiercely.

"Why?"

Morgaine was clearly discomfited by his soft question. Her full lips tightened and she looked away. "I don't want to talk about it."

But Alasdair knew that he was close to learning something that could lead to his salvation. 'Twould be good indeed to have some understanding of the enchantress's thinking.

"But I do, my lady," Alasdair insisted quietly. He leaned forward, trying to compel her to meet his gaze. "I would know what troubles you and why."

Twin spots of color burned brightly in her cheeks. Morgaine looked from one side to the other, then finally locked her gaze with his. She took a quick breath and fairly bit out the words, apparently responding against her will.

"Because it changes people," she said heatedly. "Drinking makes them act differently and do things they would never do otherwise. It makes them break promises and hurt people close to them."

Morgaine choked on her next words, then shook her head, and the shimmer of tears in her magnificent eyes was unmistakable. "It ruins everything. *Everything.*"

She snatched up her glass and gulped the water, but Alasdair was not fooled. He had seen these changes of which she spoke. In most folk, the whisky brought a lightheartedness, but there were those who turned dark when whisky was in their belly.

'Twas clear enough the lady had experienced this.

"Aye," he agreed carefully. "I have seen it make a docile man turn bloodthirsty."

She pressed her lips tightly together and nodded.

"And I have seen that man hit his woman for no reason at all."

Morgaine looked away.

And there was the meat of the matter, unless Alasdair missed his guess.

Well, he was not such a fool to alienate his Faerie hostess, particularly when she was already ill-disposed to aiding him. And if the prospect of a man with whisky in his belly unsettled Morgaine, there was but one thing to be done.

Alasdair deliberately lifted the wee cup and set it on the edge of the table. Morgaine's gaze brightened with interest, though she only flicked a glance at him.

The servant appeared in a flash. "Something wrong with the whisky, sir?"

Alasdair shook his head, his gaze fixed determinedly on the sorceress. "Nay, there is naught amiss. My taste has but changed. Would you be so kind as to bring me a vessel of water, as that of the lady?"

The servant sniffed and swept up the pewter cup, striding across the tavern in poor temper. No doubt he disapproved of the waste—though Alasdair was certain the whisky would not be cast on the ground.

And he only had eyes for Morgaine's tentative smile. "You don't have to do that," she murmured, though there was a thread of delight in her tone that he had.

The sight of Morgaine's pleasure with his choice emboldened Alasdair as naught else could have done. He could win her favor yet!

He *would* win her favor yet.

Aye, he had never been one to back down from a challenge—and Morgaine's endorsement could be the greatest challenge that ever he faced.

But the prize was well worth the winning.

Suddenly Alasdair recalled his gran's certainty that Morgaine le Fee was one to grant favors to those mortals who shared her bed.

And Alasdair knew exactly where he was going to be, as soon as it could be managed. The very idea made his heart pound, though he was certain 'twas only because his goal was in sight.

It seemed his first instinct had not been far wrong, after all.

"Aye, I do." Alasdair leaned forward and captured Morgaine's tiny hand within his own. Her fingers quivered ever

so slightly, this minute sign of her awareness of him embold-
ening Alasdair as naught else could have done.

Was it possible that he, a mere mortal, already held some
sway over the tiny sorceress?

Alasdair stroked the back of her hand with his thumb and
dared to stare directly into her eyes. "For I pledge to you this
moment, my lady—as you have sworn to take me home—that
I shall let no whisky touch my lips while yet I am in your
domain."

"It's not my domain!" Morgaine protested, but 'twas clear
she was pleased. There was no doubt of that, though she
seemed embarrassed by his intensity as well. "Why would you
do that?"

"Because you wish it to be so."

"I never said that!"

Alasdair smiled slowly, noting how the defiance in her hand
melted away. He dropped his voice to a seductive rumble.
"Your eyes, my lady, did all the telling."

And it was true. Even now, a heat lit their emerald depths,
and Alasdair knew he had embarked well upon his new quest.
His lips reminded him of the sweet heat of her kiss and his
loins tightened with enthusiasm.

Suddenly Alasdair wondered why he had been so intent
upon winning the goodwill of her advisors and not that of the
lady herself. As he stared into Morgaine's eyes, he could not
for the life of him think of a single reason.

Wanting naught other than to see her smile fully again, he
squeezed her hands and winked at her, then sat back to drink
heartily of his water. 'Twas not half bad when 'twas cold like
a mountain stream.

She liked tales. And Alasdair had a thousand of them.
Should he need to sing them all to win his way between her
thighs, 'twould not be too high a price to pay.

And if a day in this enchanted land made a year in the world
of mortals, Alasdair had best begin his conquest now.

"I have a tale for you, my lady," he said quietly and knew
that only one would do. " 'Tis a tale of the knight Tam Lin,
a knight stolen away by the Faerie Queen but won back by
his mortal love."

"But we have to talk. You really need to believe me about this time thing . . ."

"There will be time enough for talking, but this be the time to see a fair lassie smile." Before she could argue any more, Alasdair tapped his toe and began to sing.

> Janet has kilted her green kirtle,
> A little above her knee,
> And she has snooded her yellow hair,
> A little above her bree,
> And she is to her father's hall,
> As fast as she can be.
>
> Four and twenty ladies fair
> Were playing at the ball,
> And out then came the fair Janet,
> Once flower among them all.
>
> Four and twenty ladies fair
> Were playing at the chess,
> And out then came the fair Janet,
> As green as any glass.

The few other patrons of the tavern turned and lifted their glasses in silent toast to Alasdair's tune. He nodded his acknowledgment and continued on, delighted to see a sparkle of interest in the lady's eye.

> Out then spake her father dear,
> And he spake meek and mild.
> "And ever alas, sweet Janet," he says,
> "I think thou is with child."
>
> "If that I am with child, Father,
> I must myself bear the blame.
> There's never a laird about your hand
> Shall get the babe's name.
>
> If my love were an earthly knight,
> As he's an elfin gray,

I would not give my own true love
For any lord that you claim.

The steed that my true love rides
Is lighter than the wind;
With silver is he shod before,
With burning gold behind.''

Blake and Justine came into the tavern then, their faces lighting up when they spied Alasdair and Morgaine. They made their way across the room and sat beside them, and soon Blake's fingers were tapping lightly on the rim of the table.

Meanwhile, Alasdair sang about Janet seeking out her beloved Tam Lin to tell him of the babe she carried. Tam Lin, it turned out, was not of the Faerie, but a mortal captured by them. Janet demanded the tale and the knight Tam Lin complied.

''And once it fell upon a day,
A day most cold and foul,
When we were from the hunting come,
That from my horse I fell.
The Queen of Faeries she caught me
And took me to her domain to dwell.

And pleasant is the Faerie land,
But, an eerie tale to tell,
Aye, at the end of seven years,
We pay a tithe to Hell.
I am so fair and full of flesh,
I fear it be myself.

But the night is Halloween, lady,
The morn is Hallowday.
Then win me, win me, as you will,
For well I want you to.

Just at the murk and midnight hour,
The Faerie folk will ride.
And they would their true love win,
At Miles Cross they must bide.''

Alasdair changed the pitch of his voice to sing Janet's part.

> *"But how shall I know thee, Tam Lin,*
> *Or how my true love know,*
> *Among so many uncouth knights,*
> *The like I never saw?"*

Alasdair leaned closer to Morgaine, lowering his voice to confide Tam Lin's wisdom.

> *"O first let pass the black, lady,*
> *And then let pass the brown.*
> *But quickly run to the milk-white steed,*
> *And pull his rider down.*
>
> *For I'll ride on the milk-white steed,*
> *And always nearest the town.*
> *Because I was an earthly knight,*
> *They give me this renown.*
>
> *My right hand will be gloved, my lady,*
> *My left hand will be bare.*
> *Cocked up shall my bonnet be,*
> *And combed down shall be my hair.*
> *And there be the clues I give thee,*
> *No doubt I will be there.*
>
> *They'll turn me in your arms, my lady,*
> *Into an asp and adder.*
> *But hold me fast and fear me not,*
> *I am your babe's father.*
>
> *They'll turn me to a bear so grim,*
> *And then a lion bold.*
> *But hold me fast, and fear me not,*
> *As you shall love your child.*
>
> *Again they'll turn me in your arms,*
> *To a red-hot rod of iron.*

But hold me fast, and fear me not,
I'll do to you no harm.

And last they'll turn me in your arms,
Into the burning gleed.
Then throw me into well water,
Oh, throw me in with speed!

And then I'll be your own true love,
I'll turn a naked knight.
Then cover me with your green mantle,
And cover me out of sight.''

The server brought two tall tankards of ale for Justine and Blake and another glass of water for Alasdair. He looked pleased at the song, for a few more patrons had slipped through the doors to listen.

But Alasdair had eyes only for his lady's dawning smile. His voice dropped low to tell of that All Hallows' Night.

Gloomy, gloomy was the night,
And eerie was the way,
As fair Janet in her green mantle,
To Miles Cross did she go.

About the middle of the night,
She heard the bridles ring.
This lady was as glad at that
As any earthly thing.

First she let the black pass by,
And then she let the brown.
But quickly she ran to the milk-white steed,
And pulled the rider down.

So well Janet minded what he said,
That young Tam Lin did win.
She covered him with her green mantle,
As blythe's a bird in spring.

Out then spake the Queen of Faeries,
Out of a bush of broom.
"Them has gotten young Tam Lin,
Has stolen a stately groom."

Out then spake the Queen of Faeries,
And an angry woman was she.
"Shame betide her ill far'd face,
And an ill death may she die,
For she's taken away the bonniest knight
In all my company."

"But had I known, Tam Lin," she says,
"What now this night I see,
I would have taken out thy two gray eyes,
And put in two eyes of tree."

Applause broke out around the tavern, and Alasdair was heartened by the shining of Morgaine's eyes. "That's wonderful," she breathed. "Another from your gran?"

"Aye! She has a thousand of them, but Tam Lin is a favorite."

"I want to hear them all," Morgaine said firmly.

Well, if that was the price of freedom, 'twas one Alasdair could easily pay.

What a wonderful story!

Morgan's mind filled with flowing images of the Faerie host riding at a moonlit midnight, their queen at their head and mortal Tam Lin in their ranks. She envisioned his mortal love, round with child, waiting and waiting, her features drawn with anxiety.

The planning of the page layout came in a flash, and Morgan knew she'd show the reunited lovers embracing at the lower right corner, a symbol of love conquering all. She sighed with satisfaction, her fingers itching to get to work, and felt Alasdair's gaze heavy upon her.

He had a true gift for making a story come alive.

Alasdair smiled, as though he had guessed the praise she hadn't even uttered. Morgan smiled back at him, welcoming the warmth that spread from her own heart. Alasdair really was the kind of man she had always wanted to meet.

Protective, strong, gentle, and tough by turn. A man of honor who valiantly defended those around him. A warrior who sang folktales without embarrassment. A man unashamed to show his concern for his son.

But men didn't get sons all by themselves. Alasdair must have a wife in the fourteenth century, too.

The unexpected thought blindsided Morgan—as did the intensity with which she disliked it. She fought against a completely unreasonable jealousy, but still couldn't dismiss her feelings.

Trust her to be attracted to a man who had been married for more than seven hundred years!

"Well, we have the most exciting news!" Justine declared.

Morgan, having learned to be wary of Justine when she looked so delighted with herself, didn't encourage her sister. She could feel Alasdair watching her, and she knew that that sexy smile still toyed with his firm lips.

And she remembered all too easily just how good those lips felt on her own. Morgan fidgeted in her chair, wanting something she didn't dare to name.

And hating Alasdair's eagerness to go home to be with his wife.

Irritation coursed through Morgan. It wasn't her fault that she was thinking of the highlander in a sexy way.

After all, *he* had kissed *her*.

And what kind of man did that make him? How dare Alasdair kiss her the way he did and smile at her the way he did when he had a wife?

Maybe he wasn't that different from Matt, after all! Anger pulled Morgan's lips into a thin line, and she sat stiffly as she simmered.

Men. They *were* all the same. Take away the great legs and the charming accent and the timely promises that they never meant to keep and they were all the same. Every man was only interested in sex.

She should have known better by now.

"Yes, we certainly do," Blake agreed.

When no one asked for details, Justine still provided them.

"We're going to stay at that marvelous old inn! It has the most wonderful view of the lake and the hills and the castle . . .''

"And the rooms are reasonable enough," Blake interjected.

"And they serve a wonderful breakfast. The hostess is so nice, she even showed us the rooms, and they're divine.'' Justine sat back with resolve. "We've booked two nights.''

Two nights stuck here. And all Morgan wanted was to toss Alasdair back at his wife ASAP.

"But I thought we were going straight to Lewis," she protested.

Justine's gaze bored into Morgan's, and she pronounced each word with precision. "But it's so *romantic* here. How could we resist?''

Indecision warred within Morgan. Justine had finally caught on to the Baby-Making Plan! At least that was going right.

But the price was a bit higher than Morgan had anticipated. She glanced sidelong at Alasdair and found him looking a bit confused.

"You granted me your word that we went directly to Lewis," he said in a low voice.

But Blake obviously didn't hear the danger lurking in the other man's tone. "Well, what's another day? We have to stay somewhere tonight anyhow," he maintained, ever the heart and soul of practicality. "It's too late to drive further, and I'd kind of appreciate a day of not driving.''

Morgan blinked. A day of not driving? Someone had stolen away her brother-in-law and replaced him with a living, breathing replica.

Then Blake gave Justine one of those sizzling smiles that they shared all too seldom, to Morgan's way of thinking, and she knew she just couldn't disagree.

By the looks of it, this would be her only chance to hold a bouncing baby on her knee.

Somehow she'd have to survive.

Alasdair leaned forward to protest, but Morgan sent a lethal glance across the table. It not only silenced him but seemed to stun him.

"I think it's a great idea," she said firmly, before Alasdair could voice his opinion. "I can hardly wait.''

Alasdair sat back, his expression wary.

At least he hadn't argued with her. All the same, Morgan was a bit surprised that this change of plans hadn't brought on another volcanic eruption, as it had the last time.

He hadn't even called Blake a liar, which was most unlike Alasdair. Morgan sneaked a peek through her lashes and found the highlander looking thoughtful. What was he up to now?

Nothing good, that was for sure. Morgan had an uneasy sense that things were going to go from bad to worse.

Shields up, phasers on stun.

But the anticipated shot came from friendly territory.

"Great!" Blake dropped a key on the table. It had a plastic tag labeled "Room 7." "Well, if you don't mind, we'd kind of like to spend the evening on our own. There's a little restaurant on the other side of the hall, if you tell them you want dinner."

One key?

Morgan waited, but no other key joined it on the table.

In fact, Blake and Justine got to their feet, linked arms, and smiled, looking like a united—and hurried—front. "Have a good one, then!"

"But where's the other key?" Morgan asked. She snatched up the key and waved it at the departing pair as though they had missed this critical detail.

Justine wouldn't have.

Justine *couldn't* have!

But when that Mona Lisa smile slid across Justine's lips, Morgan knew she'd been had.

She wouldn't share a room with Alasdair! She just wouldn't.

"Oh, they only had two rooms left. One for us and one for you. Didn't I mention it?" Justine waved off Morgan's sputtering and practically hauled Blake toward the door. "Oh, well, I knew you wouldn't mind." She stretched and pressed a kiss to Blake's cheek, whispering something in his ear that made him inhale sharply.

"We've got to go! We've *really* got to go." Blake almost tripped over his words in his haste to make tracks. "Hey, Morgan, I'll take your bag up to the hotel when I get ours."

"You can't do this!" Morgan cried and bounced to her feet. "I won't let you get away with this!"

But they were gone.

And most of the other patrons in the bar were getting a really good look at Morgan shaking that key.

She spun around, sat down on the edge of her chair, and fixed Alasdair with a stern eye. "We have to go and sort this out," she said in a low, firm tone. "There *has* to be another room. After all, we can't share a room."

To Morgan's dismay, a seductive smile slid over Alasdair's lips. "Can we not, my lady?" he purred.

An almost forgotten heat spread languorously over Morgan's flesh, leaving her tingling and weak-kneed in its wake. Damn him! How could she be so susceptible to his charm?

He was *married*!

Of course, that hadn't stopped Matt.

How could Alasdair imagine that Morgan would willingly be little Miss Here-and-Now, knowing full well that he had a family waiting for him in the past? It was disgusting!

Morgan could just about spit.

Justine was going to regret this one, that much was for sure.

"No, we cannot share a room," she insisted hotly. "And we aren't going to." With that, Morgan sailed out of the room, determined to set matters to rights, one way or the other.

'Twas not very flattering, the way Morgaine responded to what Alasdair saw as an admirable opportunity. Mercifully, she had absolutely no luck in weaseling another key out of the proprietors.

Alasdair wondered whether there truly were no other accommodations available or the advisors had bribed the staff overly well.

Either way, he had nary a complaint. Someone looked fondly upon him and his quest, 'twas clear, for he could not have arranged matters more to his satisfaction.

Perhaps he should indulge in prayer more frequently than was his wont. Those few Ave Marias in the Micra seemed to have had marked results.

At any rate, Alasdair had two entire nights to seduce Morgaine. And he knew the merit of his amorous talents well enough to smell success in the wind.

Her hand had trembled within his, after all.

'Twould be a slow and thorough loving. The very prospect heated his blood to a boil. He would taste every morsel of her delectable flesh, nuzzle and caress her, memorize every mole and freckle that graced her skin. Alasdair would make Morgaine moan aloud, make her cry out in her release, grant her untold praise for the delicious form she had taken. He would pleasure her as never she had been pleasured before.

And Alasdair would do it again and again, until they both were languid and exhausted.

Then they would do it again.

His pulse began to resonate in his ears, his palms were damp, and 'twas not because the stairs were overly steep. Morgaine's hips rocked beguilingly right before his very eyes, and he decided he would remove the tights that hid naught of her charms with his teeth.

Slowly.

Aye, they would have to be dragged from Room 7 two days hence.

But the sorceress, clearly unaware of the delights in store for her, looked fit to spit sparks as she marched up the stairs to the second floor.

Alasdair, in contrast, found himself whistling in anticipation.

Morgaine whirled on the landing and glared at him. "Would you stop that? You really haven't been a lot of help here. You could have insisted they find another room."

"And what need have I of another room," Alasdair murmured, letting his amorous intent shine in his eyes, "when 'tis Room 7 where you will be?"

Morgaine wagged a stern finger at him, obviously taking advantage of being able to look him in the eye, since he was still three stairs below her. "Don't even go there, mister. Save your bedroom eyes and romantic talk for someone more likely to fall for it."

Before Alasdair could answer that, she stormed down the narrow hall, peering at one door after another in the dim light. To regain some control over his raging desire, Alasdair glanced around the corridor and was not particularly taken with the dozens of flowers painted on the walls.

A fearsome amount of work 'twould be—and for what?

Without a good torch in the sconce—merely some flickering
wee glow—a man could barely see them anyway.

Feminine frippery—it could be naught else.

Finally, Morgaine fitted her key into the last door on the
right and shoved the door open with one toe. She marched
over the threshold and gasped.

Alasdair knew the moment of the hunt was upon him. He
lunged after the sorceress, only to catch the closing door with
his nose.

"No! You can't come in!" Morgaine desperately tried to
push the door closed, a hopeless task against a man so much
stronger than she.

Had he not known better, Alasdair might have thought her
afeartie.

But of what?

Surely not of him?

That thought was far from reassuring.

Had she merely guessed his plan and wanted to halt his
conquest? Alasdair could not be certain—but he had no interest in leaving a woman afraid of him. Alasdair wedged his
boot into the opening and let her valiantly struggle to close
the door.

He folded his arms across his chest and waited with consummate patience for her to realize the futility of this battle.

'Twas not long before the lady saw his toe. She muttered
an eloquent curse and glared at him through the narrow opening. That flicker of trepidation danced in the depths of her
eyes. "You can't come in. I won't let you."

"Aye?" Alasdair kept his tone amiable. "Then where am
I to sleep this night?"

The sorceress looked dismayed—a good sign, to Alasdair's
mind. She was concerned about his welfare, which could only
mean that she was not immune to his charms. "Um, you'll
have to sleep in the Micra."

Alasdair snorted his opinion of that. "There is not room for
a dog to sleep in that chariot."

Morgaine glanced wildly over her shoulder. "In the pub,
then. Can't you sleep in the tavern?"

If he had not realized it was so critical to share her bed,
Alasdair might have been tempted to agree, if only to ease the

concern in her wide-eyed gaze. She had an unholy allure herself, that much was certain.

Alasdair gave her a doubly stern glance. "Those feckless
days of my youth are long past, my lady."

"Well, you can't sleep here!" Her voice rose again, and
Alasdair knew he had to reassure the lady somehow.

"It does not look such a foul establishment." Alasdair tried
to peek around the door without success, then let his voice
drop to a confidential rumble. "You cannot have found lice
so quick as that, my lady. Or is it a mouse that has sent the
wind up you?"

"There is no mouse! And no lice—at least I don't think
so."

"Then what has made you so fey?" Alasdair leaned against
the door frame and lowered his voice to a whisper. "What is
it I could do to set matters to rights?"

"Nothing! I don't want anything from you!" Her words
were breathless now, her eyes so wide and dark that they
seemed to be bottomless pools. "Just go away!"

She stared at him, and Alasdair could see the flutter of her
pulse beneath the fine skin of her throat. She was so delicately
wrought, both fragile and resilient. 'Twas no lie that he had
never met the like of her.

And never would he again.

Before he could stop himself, Alasdair slipped one hand
through the opening and gently touched that dancing pulse. It
fluttered beneath his hand like a butterfly.

Had ever he felt anything so soft? His own hand looked
heavy and rough against the smooth silk of her skin. The
lady's eyes widened, but she did not move away, merely stared
up at him through the crack.

Alasdair wanted her as never he had wanted a woman before, yet the sight of her trepidation stopped him cold.

"Do you truly want me gone, my lady?" he whispered.

She closed her eyes, as though she hated the truth, and
shook her head ever so minutely. A single tear stole from
beneath the dark abundance of her lashes and made its way
down her cheek.

Alasdair was humbled by the sight.

"Surely you cannot be afraid of me?" He heard his own voice catch.

Morgaine swallowed with an effort, and her throat moved beneath his gentle touch. "No, not of you exactly," she whispered unevenly. A relief stunning in its power coursed through Alasdair.

"Then what troubles you?"

She stepped away from his touch, letting the door open with a defeated sigh. Morgaine indicated the bed with one sweep of her hand, as though she did not trust herself to speak.

The bed looked fine enough to Alasdair, wide enough for coupling and long enough for sleeping and plump with coverlets. 'Twas framed by a pair of fine windows that he guessed would let the morning sun fall upon the mattress.

Indeed, he could scarcely have hoped for better.

But clearly the lady found the bed fearsome.

Could it be that there was more to her tale of disliking drink than she had told him?

"I would never hurt you, my lady," Alasdair asserted, his words ringing with conviction though they were no louder than a whisper.

Her lips twisted, but her skepticism did not reach her eyes. There lurked the hopes and dreams of a lassie who had been sadly disappointed by what she had been granted.

Had some lover left her wounded? Alasdair determined then and there that he would do whatever was necessary to see at least one of this lady's hopes fulfilled.

"You do not wish to share the bed." 'Twas more a statement than a question.

Morgaine shook her head.

Alasdair smiled crookedly and leaned back against the door frame, leaving the distance between them that she had made. To his relief, some of the tension seemed to ease from the sorceress.

"But why not the room, my lady?"

She arched a dark brow. "It's the same thing."

Alasdair had to convince her to let him stay. If he were locked out of her presence for two days and nights, who knew what decision she could make about his fate?

But Morgaine had to make the choice. 'Twas a critical step in earning her trust. Never had Alasdair forced a woman to his way of thinking, and he would not begin now.

"I say it is not." Alasdair smiled ruefully, hoping to appeal to her compassion. "Would you not show mercy to an old warrior and let me sleep on the floor?"

She blinked. "You'd do that?"

"By your leave. 'Tis a far sight cleaner than a tavern bench."

Morgaine shook her head. "You'll just pounce on me when I'm asleep."

"Nay!" The accusation straightened Alasdair's pose. "I would never force myself upon a woman!" She still looked unconvinced, and Alasdair determinedly ignored her low opinion of his character. "I would give you my word," he insisted, then held his breath.

The sorceress chewed her lip as she eyed the room, evidently weighing his proposition.

Then Morgaine shook her head. "No. You can't stay here. I'm sorry, but it just won't work."

Outrage rippled through Alasdair, and now he stood ramrod-straight. "You would doubt my pledge?"

Morgaine looked uncomfortable, and his irritation died a quick death. "Well, no, not exactly." She frowned. "Look, I just don't know you that well," she admitted, her wondrous eyes filled with an appeal for understanding.

Aye, some foul mutt of a man had served her poorly, that much was for certain! Alasdair's fists clenched by his side as he imagined the reward he could grant such a scoundrel. No man of merit left such shadows in a woman's eyes, be she sorceress or nay!

But the problem remained: How could he convince the enchantress to let him stay? If his pledge meant naught, what else could he offer her? Somehow he had to win her invitation, then her trust, then make his way to her bed. Indeed, it seemed a test he was doomed to fail.

For the love of God, what had Alasdair done to deserve such a fate?

Chapter 10

THUNDER RUMBLED SUDDENLY in the distance, and Morgaine paused to listen. Her gaze flicked to the window, back to Alasdair, then away.

"It's going to rain," she observed, and there was a seed of doubt in her tone. When she chewed her lip, Alasdair understood the direction of her thoughts.

Ha! She dreaded casting him out in foul weather! Alasdair had only to feel the tide turn in his direction to seize the opportunity.

Already he had seen that she could have a soft heart and now he hoped he could win her sympathy.

"Aye, the Micra will be cold and damp, no doubt." He shrugged, feigning indifference. "But if you cannot bring yourself to trust a man who would grant you his word, then what else am I to do?"

Her eyes flashed, and Alasdair pretended a disappointment he was far from feeling.

"Nay, the Micra 'tis, though do not be surprised, my lady, if you barely recognize my twisted body in the morn. With a damp night like this, 'twould be a fortunate man indeed who could unfold himself from that vehicle."

He let his shoulders roll in dejection and turned in the doorway. The thunder rumbled, louder and much closer, at the perfect moment.

Indeed, it seemed there was something to these matters of faith. Alasdair resolved then and there to be more studious about his prayers.

"Wait!"

Alasdair did not permit himself to smile, though his heart began to skip victoriously. He deliberately schooled his expression before looking back at the sorceress. "Why postpone the worst? I had best be on my way, my lady." He bowed low. "Sleep well in your fine bed."

Morgaine frowned. "No, wait. Are you serious about giving me your word?"

Alasdair slanted a glance toward her. "I have no qualms about pledging my honor."

Morgaine folded her arms across her chest. Alasdair forced himself to look away from her tempting curves, though his body still responded to the fleeting glimpse. 'Twas some spell she had cast over him, to be certain, but any sign of arousal could have the sorceress doubting his honor again.

Alasdair forced himself to think of his wrinkled old gran washing her tired breasts in the morning when she thought he was asleep.

The image had immediate results on the suspicious rise under his kilt. Just for good measure, he recalled exactly how chilling the winter wind could be when it whipped beneath the plaid on those frosty January morns that he fetched firewood.

"All right," Morgaine conceded, though her expression remained wary. "Will you promise not to get into the bed during the night? No funny stuff—you sleep on the floor and I sleep in the bed."

Alasdair leaned against the door frame, perfectly capable of imagining many other places to couple with the sorceress. 'Twas only a man without resource who limited himself to a mattress, to Alasdair's mind.

And he truly had no intention of pouncing on the lady unaware. Nay, Morgaine would invite him between her thighs before this was done.

The first rain splattered against the windows. 'Twas a chilling sound, and Morgaine could not keep worry from sliding over her visage.

She was concerned for his welfare! The battle was half won. Alasdair vowed to recite his entire rosary this very night.

He folded his arms across his own chest in turn, and his voice resonated in the small chamber. "I pledge upon the blood of my forebears not to invite myself into your bed, my lady Morgaine, on this night or any other."

The enchantress shifted her weight from one foot to the other as the rain gained intensity and splattered more loudly. Alasdair held his breath again, fearing she would change her mind in the last moment.

"All right, then," she said finally. "You can stay. But any garbage and you're out of here. I don't care what the weather's like or what time it is. All right?"

At his nod, she spun on her heel, but Alasdair was not quite as convinced that the conversation was over. The road might be taken, but Alasdair would press on to attack the gates while the wind favored his cause.

"One moment, my lady."

Morgaine looked over her shoulder.

Alasdair dredged up every increment of charm at his disposal and poured it into his smile. "Should we not seal our bargain?"

She turned and stuck out her hand, but that was not the manner of sealing that Alasdair had in mind. 'Twas clear enough that she had other tokens of esteem in mind, as well, for that fluttering pulse appeared at her throat once more.

And Alasdair needed no further encouragement than that minute sign that their thoughts were as one.

The worst thing wasn't that Alasdair's blue, blue eyes showed his intent to kiss her.

The worst thing was that Morgan couldn't wait. The simple truth was that she wasn't afraid of Alasdair, or even of the bed. She was afraid that the power of her own attraction would make her act like a fool.

Like right now. Even knowing he was going to kiss her,

that she shouldn't let him, that she *couldn't* let him, Morgan just stood there, like a lovesick idiot. She stood and *yearned* as she watched him step closer. She didn't move when he lifted his hand toward her.

Morgan even shivered a little when Alasdair's strong fingers curved possessively around her jaw.

And when his thumb, with the rough callus on one side, slid languidly across her lips, Morgan thought she would melt like a stick of butter left out of the fridge in a Chicago July.

She actually leaned closer to him. Alasdair's other hand slid up her back to her nape, his fingers working their way through the thick mass of her hair. He pulled her gently against his chest and Morgan went willingly, drawn by the magnetic blue of his eyes and the sensuous smile that curved his lips.

It was his tenderness that undid her. If he had tried to force her, Morgan would have fought him tooth and nail, but this gentle assault was irresistible.

She promised herself to pull away after just one second more.

But how could she resist him? Alasdair had given her his vow that he wouldn't press his attentions on her. He had pledged not to drink anymore. Morgan was half certain that he was lying to her, but right now she wanted to believe.

Even if it was just for a single, tantalizing second more.

Alasdair's hand slid along her jaw as though he were marveling at the touch of her, that thumb crested the curve of her cheek and made her shiver.

Morgan was sure one more second wouldn't hurt anything.

He bent and brushed his lips across her brow, the heat of his breath on her skin making her tremble. Her eyes drifted closed as his warmth surrounded her and Alasdair's lips brushed across one eyelid, then the other.

Just a little bit longer.

Alasdair kissed the tip of her nose, his strong fingers spearing into her hair. He paused and Morgan knew what he was going to kiss next. That would definitely take a lot longer than another second.

But she couldn't pull away. Fortunately, she didn't have to wait long to have those firm lips claim her own.

And Alasdair's gentle, languid kiss was more than worth the wait. His lips slid across hers once with aching deliberation, then returned like a butterfly landing on a tempting flower. The heat of his mouth imprinted on hers ever so slightly, as though he asked her permission to continue.

He *asked*, instead of simply taking what he thought his due.

And given that, there was only one possible answer. Morgan's hands slid around Alasdair's neck without a second's hesitation. She arched against him, she swore she heard his heart thump at her small surrender, then his cajoling lips captured hers.

It was a kiss designed to melt her defenses. If Morgan hadn't been so lost in sensation, she might have been dismayed at how readily those defenses fell. There was a surety in Alasdair's embrace that coupled with his gentleness to make Morgan completely forget about anything other than his kiss.

His hands dropped to her waist, and he gathered her protectively into his arms. It was pure heaven and Morgan gave herself up to bliss.

Until one strong arm slid over her shoulder and a very pungent waft of masculinity recalled Morgan to her senses.

What was she doing?

Alasdair was trying to take advantage of her—and she was letting him! Somehow, he had figured out exactly how to get to her—and she wasn't stopping him!

Had she lost her mind?

But the languid heat of Alasdair's kiss wouldn't be that easily dismissed from her lips, especially since he chose that very moment to slip his tongue between her teeth. Morgan just couldn't think straight with everything in her body wanting more from Alasdair's beguiling touch.

The resonance of his pledge echoed stubbornly in her ears. He hadn't pressed his attentions upon her, so she couldn't say he had lied. But she wasn't exactly holding fast to her own ideas here.

What Morgan needed was a little time to think.

By herself.

Which meant Alasdair needed to be kept busy. Morgan

pulled away, hating how her heart lurched when his lips broke free from hers.

And she hated even more that the drowsy indigo of his gaze made that same heart take off at a gallop. She noticed the key in the bathroom door and knew exactly how she was going to get out of this muddle.

All by herself.

"You need a bath!" Morgan declared breathlessly.

The highlander grimaced ruefully and gave his shirt a theatrical whiff. "Aye, I have not had a clean shirt for at least . . ."

"I really don't need to know details," Morgan interjected. "First things first. You need to get clean, but quick."

His lips quirked, his gaze was warm. "Do I, then?" he rumbled, obviously mistaking her meaning.

Well, she wasn't going to look a gift horse in the mouth. She pulled Alasdair into the charmingly Victorian bathroom and deliberately ignored the way he looked around. It was a feminine bower in the worst way, a totally romantic room with ruffles and bows and a claw-footed tub big enough for two.

Morgan refused to think about any of that. Summoning her most businesslike manner, she turned on the taps in the tub. The water was steaming hot. "Look, they have one of those clothesline things, so you can wash out your shirt and leave it overnight to dry."

She rummaged through a basket of toiletries and laid them out in hasty succession, refusing to look back at the man who lurked right behind her shoulder and practically oozed sensual allure. Morgan heard a rustle of cloth and saw his shirt fall to the floor out of the corner of her eye.

Dear God, he was getting naked! She had to get out of here while she still could.

"And look!" Morgan was chattering, but she couldn't stop. "Soap and shampoo. Even toothpaste and a brush! Why, you'll be clean in no time at all. There's even detergent, for when you wash out your shirt . . ."

Alasdair's hands landed on Morgan's shoulders, and his breath feathered across her nape. All Morgan could think of was that bronzed chest almost against her own back.

She glanced up at the mirror and her heart stopped at the sight of him looming behind her, his strong hands closed possessively around her.

"Aye, my lady, I will not keep you waiting long at all," he murmured. A smile quirked those lips, then Alasdair bent to nuzzle her ear and sent an army of shivers down Morgan's spine.

Yikes! Morgan jumped and spun more quickly than she should have. She caught the edge of the basket with one flailing hand and sent all the toiletries scattering.

Alasdair bent gallantly to retrieve them and Morgan saw her chance. She ran for the door but couldn't help pausing for one little second.

She had a look. A really good look, because Alasdair without his shirt was worth it. His back was superbly muscled and tanned to golden perfection. He looked up, his hair tousled, those eyes flashing vivid blue as he evidently guessed her intention.

He lunged for the doorway.

Morgan slammed it shut behind her in the nick of time and turned the little key in the lock. She backed away, the key safe in her grip, as Alasdair wrestled with the knob.

The lock held. It was one of those really old-fashioned locks, with a key that worked from either side.

Morgan hoped desperately that there was only one key.

"My lady?" he called finally, his voice low and heavily disciplined. "What is this you do?"

"I think you need time to cool off," Morgan said brightly. "I'll go see about some dinner."

Alasdair muttered his dissatisfaction and rattled the door knob again, but Morgan beat a hasty retreat. It was only when she was safe in the corridor, well out of the range of Alasdair's dangerous charm, that she let herself recall her fleeting glimpse of his powerfully muscled chest.

Oh, she would definitely have to keep her distance. She knew that with her body defected to Alasdair's side, she couldn't trust herself to be alone with him.

But she couldn't put the kibosh on Justine and Blake's conception plans, either. Nope—somehow Morgan would have to make it through one night with Alasdair in her room. That seemed a fair compromise to her. In the morning she'd lay down the law.

Justine was going to owe her baby sister a big one for this. At that thought, Morgan knew exactly how she was going to solve this dilemma. Justine had long ago unwittingly given Morgan the solution she needed tonight.

Sleeping pills that Morgan carried around but had never taken.

Perfect.

Alasdair was not amused.

The wily sorceress had tricked him again. The prison she had chosen was an artful one, for there was but a single tiny window—and this secured so firmly that Alasdair could not even open it enough for a proper view of the world outside. The rain beat against it now with cold intensity.

And a lot of good that rain had done him in the end. 'Twas true enough that there was more room here than in the Micra, but Morgaine's bed was just as inaccessible to him.

In foul temper, Alasdair surveyed his prison, intrigued despite himself by the water steaming into the tub. He toyed with it a bit, then resolved he might as well see himself clean.

That such a deed would please the sorceress was more than clear. Alasdair set his lips grimly and set to work, wondering how much else he would do to win Morgaine's approval before this battle was won.

Things were not looking encouraging, that much was clear.

Perhaps 'twas time again to indulge in a few appeals to the laird above. The idea was not all bad, and Alasdair raised his voice to sing a hymn that was his gran's favorite.

Alasdair had long been clean, the room had fallen into shadows, and the metal on the wall had been radiating heat for a goodly while when he heard the room door open. He was on his feet in a moment, determined to take advantage of any opportunity Morgaine saw fit to grant him.

But the bathroom door remained locked.

"My lady?"

"Hi!" Morgaine called cheerfully. "How's your bath?"

"Quite finished." Alasdair couldn't keep his tone from being wry.

Morgaine laughed, which could only be a good sign. "Sorry to be so long," she called again, much too loudly, to Alasdair's thinking.

A murmur of voices made him snap to attention. A male voice 'twas! Had she brought some minion to deal with him?

Or would she taunt him with the sounds of her lovemaking with another? Alasdair fairly growled at the prospect, though he told himself 'twas only her own spell that fed his protectiveness of the tiny, perfect sorceress.

But a moment later there was a rattle of crockery and a most intriguing smell wafted beneath the bathroom door. Alasdair's stomach growled mightily at the prospect of a meal.

Or was this yet another kind of torture?

"Thanks very much," he heard Morgaine say. That man murmured in response as the door to the corridor closed once more.

Alasdair listened closely and heard only one pair of footsteps treading across the floor.

She was alone once more. Relief coursed through him and he dared to hope that all turned to his favor again.

He steeled himself to leap upon the door when first it opened. A thousand appeals for her indulgence had been composed and discarded while he waited, and now he knew only two things.

He had to remain in the lady's presence.

He had to persuade her to trust him, despite whatever had befallen her before. To that end, he snatched up a towel and wound it 'round his waist that she would not be immediately confronted with the evidence of her effect upon him.

There was a great deal of banging and rustling on the other side of the door, and Alasdair pressed his ear against it to listen. He still could make little sense of what he heard, but 'twas clear that Morgaine did not immediately come to his aid.

Surely she did not mean to leave him trapped in here?

"My lady?" Alasdair asked, forcing his words to be polite. "Will you not release me?"

"In just a moment," she called. Then, to his relief, he heard her steps grow louder.

He checked one last time in the mirror, reassuring himself that he was cleaner than he had been in many a day, then summoned his best smile.

"They only had bangers and mash—it looks like sausages and mashed potatoes—and beer," Morgaine confided cheerfully, her voice very close to the door. "But you have to take what you can get in these places, I guess."

Her tone was so friendly that Alasdair marveled at it. Had he misread her earlier disapproval of him? Indeed, she sounded almost willing to continue as they had ended.

Had she only wanted him clean before they proceeded?

Had she only feared he might not await her return? Ha! Alasdair would set her straight on that poor thinking!

"Hungry?" she asked pertly, her voice close.

Immensely relieved that his fears of failure were not about to be realized, Alasdair nodded, even though the sorceress could not see the gesture. "Aye, that I am."

And hungered he was for more than his dinner.

The key turned in the lock and Alasdair's heart began to pound.

Then the door swung open—to reveal an empty room.

Alasdair stared. A wee table was set before one window, a goodly quantity of food steaming upon it. A large bag stood beside the bed, an array of feminine frippery cast across its width. The rain pattered on the windows and a low light illuminated the room. There was a cot set on the far side of the room, turned down with fresh linens.

But there was absolutely no sign of the sorceress.

Fearing a trick, Alasdair took a cautious trio of steps into the room, only to straighten in shock when something—or someone—darted past him.

He pivoted just in time to see the door slam and hear the key grind in the lock again.

Alasdair swore. He darted back and jiggled the knob, knowing even before he did that 'twas futile. Finally, he strode across the room, folded his arms over his chest, and glared at the door.

"You might as well eat," Morgaine declared. "I'm not coming out anytime soon."

"But you must eat as well! Will you not join me at the board?"

"I already ate. Enjoy."

And any further protest Alasdair might have made was drowned out by the rushing of water into the tub.

Outsmarted again! Alasdair's pride rankled that he had been so readily fooled. Curse her!

Did she bathe as well? The prospect conjured a tempting image, and one that Alasdair would see in truth.

Unable to stop himself, he crossed the room on silent feet, crouched down, and peered through the tiny keyhole.

"Ha!" Morgaine cried from the other side. "I see what you're doing!"

Alasdair blinked and sat back with a start as she jammed something white into the tiny opening. "Do you come to the board after you bathe?" he dared to ask.

"I'm not coming out at all," she retorted. "You might as well eat and make use of that bed."

She had beaten him on every front. Alasdair hung his head and examined his toes with disinterest. When he heard Morgaine's clothing hit the bathroom floor, his mood grew even more foul.

All women were filled with trickery, be they mortal or immortal! But Morgaine's trick would not work thrice, Alasdair resolved as he stomped across the room and sat down before his meal. He took a long draught of ale, ignoring its peculiar bitterness, and frowned toward the bathing chamber in thought.

Aye, 'twas the key that gave her such power over him.

And 'twas the key that Alasdair would be rid of, at first opportunity.

Somehow Morgan's bath wasn't quite as relaxing as she thought it should have been. It should have been a perfect moment, with the rain beating down and the heat pumping out of the radiator. The bathroom itself was a delight, the bath oil smelled wonderful.

But the lingering scent of a man was more than unsettling. Morgan had a hard time keeping herself from looking through the keyhole.

Especially when things got very quiet very fast.

She couldn't have put too many sleeping pills in the beer, could she? But Morgan hadn't had that many in the first place, since Justine wouldn't trust her sister with anything near a lethal dosage.

What if Morgan hadn't put *enough* sleeping pills in the beer? He was a lot bigger than she was, after all, and would need more of the sedative to fall asleep. What if Alasdair never went to sleep? She'd be trapped in here all night!

Morgan didn't even want to think about what Alasdair would do to get even with her for tricking him. He'd think she didn't trust him—when really, she just didn't trust herself.

But confessing that would effectively give him a green light for seduction.

On the other hand, he would wake up eventually. And he wasn't going to be very happy about all of this. Morgan splashed the bathwater in poor temper.

In retrospect, her whole plan didn't seem to have been a very good one—at some point in time, she'd have to face Alasdair.

Or worse, share the backseat of the Micra with him.

And men, in Morgan's experience, didn't take well to being made to look like fools.

It shouldn't have come as a surprise that she had stepped right square into something one more time. Morgan bobbed in the water and worried about the silence emanating from the bedroom.

Was Alasdair all right?

Finally, she couldn't stand it any longer. Night was pressing against the little window, the chill of the highlands penetrating the cozy little room. It seemed a long time since she'd had a good sleep, that little nap in the Micra notwithstanding.

Morgan just wanted to snuggle in her bed.

She got out of the tub, tried to take her time pampering and moisturizing, but ended up spilling a great gob of cream on the tile floor. The rose-scented talcum powder billowed in clouds fit to choke a horse and Morgan started to cough. She flung on her nightgown and carefully turned the key in the lock.

There wasn't a sound from the other side.

Morgan inched the door open.

No one jumped on her.

She opened the door all the way and looked out. On the far side of the room were the remnants of Alasdair's dinner. There wasn't very much left—it looked as though he had licked the plates clean—but Morgan wasn't interested in the meal.

It was the highlander collapsed on the cot that caught her eye.

Alasdair's eyes were closed, and his chest rose and fell with the easy rhythm of sleep. He sprawled across the little cot, almost overwhelming it with his size and looking as though he had practically fallen there. The towel that had been knotted around his waist had slipped free, revealing an intriguing stretch of hip. The glass of beer, now empty, dangled from his limp fingertips.

But was he *really* asleep?

Morgan took a deep breath and stepped out of the safety of the bathroom.

Alasdair didn't move.

She took a couple of steps, then hesitated. Reassured that he was asleep—or was still pretending to be—she continued in that halting fashion. She felt like a mouse on midnight prowl circumventing a large, dangerous cat.

When she reached Alasdair's side, Morgan was sure he would leap up and snatch at her. She braced herself to flee as she took that last step.

But Alasdair slumbered on.

She bent ever so slowly and lifted the glass from his hand. Alasdair's hand slid away from it as though he had no bones at all. She froze when he frowned slightly and murmured something in his sleep.

But then Alasdair rolled over to face the wall and started to snore.

Morgan refused to take the chance to have a good look at his tight butt. She had done it! She had actually managed to pull off a scheme!

Now, she just had to check how soundly he was sleeping.

Morgan put the glass on the table with a victorious thump, but he didn't move. She then gathered the dirty dishes onto a tray, taking no pains to be quiet.

The sound didn't elicit any response.

Morgan carted the tray to the door, making no end of noise setting it down, opening the door, and dropping it in the corridor with a clattering *thunk*.

Alasdair snored away, lost in the land of sleeping pills.

And Morgan, well satisfied with herself, turned out the lights and went to bed. The trick would never work again, but she didn't need it to. First thing in the morning, Morgan would trot down to Room 11 and convince Justine that they had to continue *immediately* to Lewis.

Do not pass Go. Do not collect $200. They had to get out of here.

The sun eased golden through the window when Alasdair awakened and looked around the room for the rat that had evidently slept in his mouth.

But he was in the sorceress's chambers—and the sorceress slumbered peacefully not half a dozen steps away. His first impulse was to slide into her bed beside her, but he forced himself to think matters through.

His tongue was thick and furry, the lingering taste most foul, and his thinking as foggy as the valley on a November morning. A dull thud pounded behind his eyes, but he had no recollection of an evening merry enough to have won such a state of affairs. Alasdair had fallen asleep after his meal, 'twas clear, and the lady had neither joined him nor invited him to her bed.

Perhaps Alasdair was not as close to victory as he had believed.

Too late he recalled the sharp tang of the ale she had brought him, and then he understood. 'Twas clear enough—

the lady Morgaine had concealed a noxious potion in the guise
of good ale. She had tricked him again!

And he had been fool enough to drink of it—even knowing
what he did of her feelings toward drink!

Alasdair nearly slapped his pounding forehead in disgust.
How could he have been so slow-witted? So angry had he
been by her trickery that he had fallen for another prank.

Well, 'twould not happen again! 'Twas clear enough she
only slept because she believed him safely enthralled, so Alasdair resumed his slumbering pose.

And he waited, watching her through his lashes.

'Twas not long before the sorceress stirred. To Alasdair's
mingled delight and dismay, she turned immediately to him,
her brow drawn in a worried frown.

Her chemise gaped at the bodice, revealing the creamy perfection of her breasts. But naught would reveal his wakeful-
ness more clearly than a rise in the linens. Alasdair gritted his
teeth and thought of his gran's morning libations again.

And of cold, cold winter winds.

Morgaine rolled gracefully out of bed, raking one hand
through the darkness of her curls. She came to his side, and
Alasdair closed his eyes, feigning sleep as well as he was able,
inundated as he was by her perfume of roses.

Did he breathe too fast? Too slow? Did his eyelids flicker
as she watched? How could he truly expect to fool a powerful
sorceress, especially one who could read his very thoughts?

An eternity later, Morgaine straightened and yawned. Alasdair treated himself to a glimpse through his lashes of her
stretch and it nearly undid his carefully composed state.

But mercifully, she turned away in that moment. She hauled
her gown over her head, the perfection of her buttocks making
his mouth go dry. Indeed, he forgot to pretend anything and
'twas his own good fortune that Morgaine clearly had other
matters on her mind.

For within the blink of an eye, she had dressed and was
opening the door to the corridor. With a single backward
glance—one that Alasdair fortunately had anticipated—she
slipped out into the silent establishment.

Alasdair waited only to hear her footsteps fade before he

rolled out of bed. He captured the bathroom key in one smooth move, padded across the room, and flung it out the window. It flashed in the pale-gray morning light, then disappeared, never to be seen again.

Well satisfied with what he had wrought, Alasdair resumed his sleeping pose and waited to see what the sorceress would do next.

He did not have long to wait.

Room 11 was not particularly different from any of the other rooms in the hotel. Morgan refused to think about how early it was when she came to a stop outside the door.

Surely Justine wouldn't mind? This was important, after all!

But Morgan had a funny feeling her sister wouldn't see matters that way. The DO NOT DISTURB sign hanging jauntily from the doorknob made her hesitate.

Still, her point of view counted. This was Morgan's vacation too! Despite Justine's obvious matchmaking, Morgan didn't want to spend her holiday locked into a romantic bed-and-breakfast in the highlands of Scotland with a wildly attractive man bent on seducing her.

That didn't sound quite right, but Morgan knew it was true anyhow. She raised one hand to knock on the door.

And froze as the squeak of a mattress carried clearly right through the door.

It squeaked again.

And again.

The rocking rhythm was pretty unmistakable.

Morgan chewed her lip, her fist an inch away from the door. Did she want to get out of here badly enough to interrupt a Moment of Potential Procreation?

She grimaced and backed against the far wall, thinking furiously. What was the rush? After all, Alasdair was still out cold.

And Blake and Justine couldn't "do it" forever. Morgan was sure Blake had other items on his agenda today.

Maybe this would be a good chance to zip back to the room and have a long, relaxing shower.

Morgan hadn't washed her hair the night before and it

needed it. And on a sunny morning like this, being without her blow dryer wasn't necessarily a precursor to pneumonia.

The bucking tempo of the mattress squeaks increased and a slight moan escaped under the door. Morgan had the sudden, quite definite sense that this was not exactly where she wanted to be.

A shower. Alasdair would sleep right through it and she'd be back here in half an hour. At least Morgan knew that Blake and Justine were already awake.

There was nothing to worry about, she told herself as she trotted purposefully to her room. The closer she got to Room 7, the faster her own pulse pounded. But her sleeping potion had worked on Alasdair, Morgan knew it.

And besides, she could lock the bathroom door.

At least, she could have locked the door if the key had been anywhere in sight.

But it wasn't.

She looked high and low, careful not to make any noise that might disturb her sleeping companion, but to no avail.

What had she done with it? Morgan propped her hands on her hips and glared around the room, willing the errant key to appear.

But the fact was, she just couldn't remember where she had put it. She had been so intent on checking on Alasdair and making sure she hadn't killed him. The rhythmic sound of his deep breathing distracted her even now. Morgan stared at Alasdair and tapped her toe, halfway feeling that this was *his* fault.

With increasing irritation, Morgan checked the desk, the end table, even the closet. She had a rummage through the dirty dishes still waiting outside the door, but no luck.

The key was gone.

It was old news that she would lose her head if it wasn't screwed on. Frustration rolled through Morgan but there was nothing she could do about it.

The damn key was probably somewhere "safe." Morgan gritted her teeth. She'd find it in her luggage the next time she planned a trip, or something equally stupid. It happened to Morgan all the time.

But what about her shower?

Morgan eyed Alasdair dubiously, feeling as though her scalp was itching with the need to wash her hair. Did she dare take a chance?

As though he had heard her very thoughts, Alasdair nuzzled his pillow, then rolled to face the wall and started to snore softly.

Well, that decided that. Morgan smiled. Alasdair wasn't going to wake up anytime soon, that was for sure! She had really knocked him out cold. With luck, he might even sleep most of the day, and she could work, too.

Maybe this hotel hadn't been such a bad idea, after all. Morgan picked up her toiletry bag and bustled purposefully toward the shower, merrily thinking up baby names to suggest to Justine.

It was, at best, a poorly calculated risk.

Chapter 11

ALASDAIR ROLLED OVER in time to see the sorceress stroll into the bathing chamber. She pushed the door closed with one toe, and when he heard her clothing hit the floor, he smiled to himself.

As soon as the water began to run, he was on his feet.

Alasdair cast aside his towel and stealthily made his way across the room, eyeing the half-closed door all the way. He flattened himself against the adjacent wall and edged toward the narrow opening.

What would Morgaine le Fee do to a man who surprised her in her bath?

Alasdair refused to think about it. He had to win her approval, he had to gain her affections, and some hard thinking had given him an idea of precisely how to manage the deed. The lady was wary of men, that much was certain, and 'twas clear she had been poorly used in the past.

But Alasdair had a plan. He took a deep breath, tried to slow the pounding of his heart, then peeked around the corner.

A creamy buttock flashed as the sorceress stepped into her bath. That cascade of dark hair bounced behind her, and Alasdair caught a glimpse of her face.

Had she seen him?

Alasdair snapped back against the wall and held his breath.

His heart thundered with the certainty that he had been discovered. He half expected Morgaine to explode out of the
chamber to smite him.

But instead she began to sing quietly.

'Twas clear she had little confidence in her voice, for she
sang softly, but Alasdair strained his ears and was delighted
to recognize the tune he had sung just the night before.

He needed no more incentive to round the corner on silent
feet.

A curtain was drawn round the tub, the water was running
merrily, and steam rose toward the ceiling. Alasdair could
faintly discern the enchantress's silhouette behind the curtain
and his mouth went dry. He would have but one chance.

He had best put his all into this.

To say Morgan was shocked when someone eased the shower
curtain open would be the understatement of the century.

The curtain moved, Morgan squealed, she dropped the soap
at the sudden draft of cooler air. Her mouth fell open when
she found a naked Alasdair watching her with steely determination.

What was he doing awake?

Had he guessed what she had done? Morgan took a wary
step backward, her foot landed squarely on the soap, and she
yelped as her feet flew out from underneath her.

Alasdair swore expressively and before Morgan could
panic, she had been snatched up and trapped against a very
firm, very masculine chest. Her hands landed on his shoulders,
because there was really nowhere else for them to go.

And a powerful arm locked around her waist.

Morgan refused to think about anything she could feel below that, but her nipples tightened instantly, nestled as they
were in the thick, tawny hair on Alasdair's chest. Her heart
pounded so erratically that she was sure he would feel it.
Warm water rained down upon their entwined limbs and trickled between them.

Now what was she going to do? Morgan wriggled, but Alasdair's grip only tightened, his broad hands spanning her back.
He turned and decisively closed the shower curtain behind

himself, and Morgan had to face the fact that a very naked highlander was in her shower to stay.

For better or for worse. She felt herself blush in consternation.

But Morgan just couldn't look up and meet those blue eyes. If she did, she'd be lost. If she did, she'd want Alasdair to stay, and that could only lead to Big Trouble.

Somehow she had to get rid of him.

"Well, good morning! Um, did you sleep well?" Morgan tried to sound as though there was really nothing unusual about having a large, sexy man join her in the shower. The water beaded on Alasdair's muscled shoulders in a most intriguing way and slid through the hair on his chest like a caress.

Morgan told herself that she was only having a good look for research. Who knew when she'd have to paint a man in the rain?

Alasdair snorted, and Morgan's cheeks burned hotter with the certainty that he had guessed what she was thinking. He braced his feet against the porcelain tub and drew Morgan up to her toes. The heat of his skin pressed against her and awakened that damn tingle in her belly.

Was he going to kiss her?

Morgan kept talking in hopes of avoiding that eventuality. "Yes, well, it was too bad you fell asleep last night, but I'm sure you're well rested now . . ."

Evidence of Alasdair's well-rested state pressed against her thighs, and she had a very good idea of what compensation he considered to be due.

Clearly, men joined women in the shower for only one reason—and it wasn't to ask when breakfast would be ready. What wasn't clear was why Morgan was having a hard time finding the idea offensive.

"Aye, I slept well enough." The highlander's voice was low, a thread of humor lurking in his tone. Morgan glanced up at that and was snared by the intense blue of his eyes.

"Though you had naught to do with that, hmmm?" Alasdair arched a fair brow, and his lips twisted in a smile so intimate that it nearly stopped Morgan's heart.

In fact, the whole world stopped right then and there. Morgan stared, her mouth went dry, her heart started to hammer. She felt that languorous heat slide through her that she was quickly coming to associate with Alasdair, and she couldn't have summoned a single word to save her life.

Her toe slid experimentally over his foot, then continued up the muscled length of his calf, as though it had a mind of its own and liked what it found. Morgan had the sudden sense that she had no chance in this battle—after all, her body was already on Alasdair's side.

He looked away then, examining the shower head, then smiled down at her once more, his eyes nearly indigo with intent. " 'Tis a fine circumstance for what I have in mind," he rumbled.

And Morgan had a very good idea what that was.

Before she could convince herself that she should bolt, Alasdair bent and kissed her ear in a most distracting fashion. What little was left of her resistance eroded dangerously.

She had to keep him talking, at least until she could collect her thoughts! "Um, well, you know, I won't be long, and then you can have the shower all to yourself . . ."

"I wish only to be where you are, my lady," Alasdair breathed into her ear.

Morgan hated that she shivered at the sensation, then she caught her breath as he nibbled on her earlobe. His hands fanned across her lower back, the way his fingers spanned her waist, making her feel infinitely small and delicate.

He cradled her in his arms and ran a line of kisses along her jawline. One more time, Morgan had the intoxicating sense that she was treasured and she couldn't turn away. Such tenderness was irresistible—as was the certainty that one word of protest from her would stop the whole interlude cold.

But Morgan was honest enough to admit that she didn't really want him to stop. When Alasdair's mouth locked over her own in gentle demand, she actually heard herself sigh with satisfaction.

And every single argument she had went AWOL. Alasdair's hand closed possessively over her breast, his thumb sliding across her taut nipple until Morgan arched against him. His hand eased lower, the other one cupping her buttock, then he ducked to flick his tongue across her nipple. Morgan gasped and clenched fistfuls of his hair as Alasdair suckled.

Morgan thought she would explode. A throbbing took up the beat between her thighs, and her wandering toes slid over his knee.

Alasdair groaned and lifted her, holding her against the tiles so that her feet dangled freely. He lifted her errant foot, caressing her instep before placing that foot on his thigh. His kisses distracted and disoriented Morgan, and she could do no more than hold on to his broad shoulders and enjoy.

Which wasn't so bad. Morgan writhed when Alasdair's strong fingers slid over her thigh, across her hip, then through her pubic hair, but he was undeterred. His fingertip landed with gentle assurance on her throbbing clitoris and moved with a surety that stole her breath away.

And Morgan couldn't find it anywhere within herself to fight this amorous assault. She had never had anyone touch her with such tender persistence, had never had any man awaken such longing inside her. Alasdair's thumb locked onto the nub of her desire and caressed it with slow persuasiveness.

Morgan kissed Alasdair with newfound abandon as her hands slid over his strength. To her amazement, he moaned into her kiss. When Morgan felt the heat of his erection bump against her, her hips began to buck in intuitive demand.

His finger slipped inside her and Morgan caught her breath. Their gazes locked and Alasdair smiled slowly as he moved his thumb once more. Morgan's heart thundered, the heat rose beneath her skin, and she couldn't look away from the hypnotic sapphire of his gaze. They rocked together in instinctive rhythm, the water bore down on them, and Morgan felt the crest of a wave rising deep within her.

She must have given some small sign, because Alasdair captured her lips with his in that very moment. He trapped her between the wall and his chest, his scent filling her lungs, his tongue in her mouth, his fingers inside her. Morgan writhed demandingly, pulling him closer, wanting more, wanting all he could give her.

Alasdair slanted his mouth over hers, his fingers danced

with persistence. Morgan cried out as her orgasm exploded through every pore in glorious unison.

And she sagged against Alasdair, trembling, in the wake of the torrent he had summoned.

It took several moments for Morgan to realize that things were not proceeding exactly as she had expected. Gradually, the numbness retreated from her mind, and she noticed that the amorous intent had left the highlander's touch.

When her pulse slowed, Morgan found herself standing on her own two feet with Alasdair busily soaping her down. Her breasts were all lathered up, as were her arms and belly. But it was obvious from the deft purpose in Alasdair's touch that this wasn't some game—he was simply washing her.

That wasn't what she had expected next in the script. Morgan frowned and looked, but his erection was as ferocious as ever. Before she could ask what was going on, Alasdair pivoted her purposefully beneath the cascading water, and she sputtered for a moment beneath its torrent.

"Rinse," he commanded. "Then bend over that I might scrub your back."

Morgan did as she was told, still trying to make sense of what was happening. His fingers were turning the tense muscles of her back to putty, but she knew she didn't imagine that the mood had changed. Morgan sighed as Alasdair found the souvenir kink that a day of sleeping in the Micra had left in her shoulder, but she forced herself to ask.

"What are you doing?"

"Bathing you, my lady." Alasdair's low voice was amiable. "Is that not why you came to this chamber?"

Morgan couldn't really argue with that. "Well, yes." His thumbs moved rhythmically against the knot, and Morgan closed her eyes with pleasure. She let herself enjoy his ministrations and savored the luxurious feeling of being pampered.

By a rough warrior. Morgan smiled at the contrast, then gasped in delight when Alasdair scratched her shoulders. She stretched like a cat, directed him left, right, and down, and knew she had never felt so good.

"Rinse," he commanded again and Morgan straightened as

bidden. When the highlander squatted down in front of her and started to lather up her legs, Morgan eyed him assessingly.

What was going on?

"Did I do something wrong?" she asked tentatively.

Alasdair's grin was fleeting. "That would be my question," he joked, then flicked a glance at her so intent that she caught her breath. "Were you well pleased?"

Morgan flushed scarlet. "Well, yes."

"Good." Alasdair nodded and frowned slightly as he focused on the task at hand. He worked the soap between each toe, then rinsed her foot before placing it back on the porcelain. Then he lifted her other foot.

"Um, what about you?"

One fair brow arched. "I can wait well enough," Alasdair murmured, and Morgan couldn't help but wonder how long he intended to wait.

Was he just softening her up for a big sensual attack? Morgan wondered whether she was the only one feeling awkward—Alasdair certainly didn't seem to have any doubts about how things should proceed.

His erection seemed to be mocking her, dancing between his thighs as he moved as though daring her to ask about it being so obviously left out of the loop.

Then Alasdair pushed her under the shower's assault and Morgan closed her eyes. She felt the weight of the water in her hair, then Alasdair's strong fingers began to massage her scalp.

She was being spoiled, and Morgan decided right then and there not to worry about what was to come, but just to enjoy. The hum between her thighs was already starting again as Alasdair's hands worked through her hair.

"Um, there's shampoo in that little bottle," she directed with one finger, taking the excuse of not wanting to open her eyes under the shower of water.

"Shampoo?"

"To wash my hair."

"Ah!"

Then Morgan was folded against his chest, her lungs filled with the scent of him, his hands working a lather in her hair like an expert. Her breasts were slightly crushed against his chest, the languor of her orgasm still throbbed through her veins. His erection bumped against her belly, and Morgan melted beneath those hands.

She felt as divinely pampered as a prize Persian. If heaven was anything short of this moment, Morgan didn't want to go.

All too soon, Alasdair gripped her shoulders and backed her into the shower stream once more. "Rinse," he dictated and when Morgan lifted her hands to ease the shampoo out of her hair, Alasdair's hands cupped her breasts.

Morgan's heart jumped but she didn't step away. Alasdair teased her nipples in a most distracting way, and she admitted she was prolonging the moment as much as possible.

Because Morgan knew that this was It. She braced herself for him to make a move on her and opened her eyes, but Alasdair had stepped out of the shower.

Leaving Morgan alone.

She peeked out through the curtain and watched him dry himself off, then cleared her throat. "Um. What about you?"

"I believe I am clean, as well."

"No, I mean about, well, about *that*." Morgan's face burned as she indicated Alasdair's erection.

He grinned, then shrugged. " 'Tis a state I grow used to in your presence, my lady."

Then he wrapped the towel around his waist and left.

LEFT?!

"Wait a minute!" Morgan stumbled out of the shower, nearly slipping on the slick tub as she turned off the water. She darted out of the bathroom, leaving a trail of wet footprints.

Alasdair stood at one window, watching her, arms folded across his chest. Morgan pointed back to the bathroom with rising frustration, hating how one good look at him awakened all those impulses that were safer locked away.

Morgan felt ruffled and disoriented, and didn't like it. Did Alasdair find her unattractive after all? Was he just teasing her? But then, shouldn't she be *glad* they hadn't done anything? She tried to blame her feminine pride for the confusing jumble of relief and disappointment.

"I thought you wanted me!" Morgan blurted out, hating the tinge of hurt revealed in her words.

Alasdair's slow smile heated her blood with dangerous ease. "Make no mistake, my lady, I do."

"Then, what . . ."

"Morgaine." The single low word silenced Morgan's outburst, that blue, blue gaze made her words stick in her throat.

His voice was low with intent. "Believe me, my lady, I desire you as never I have desired a mortal woman before. But know this. I see that men have played poorly with your charms, and I would have you trust me, for naught good happens between the linens before trust is forged."

Alasdair crossed the room with quick steps, capturing her chin in one broad palm. Morgan was stunned at the sincerity gleaming in his eyes.

"Believe this, Morgaine," he insisted with an intensity that melted Morgan's bones. "You have but to invite me to your bed, and I will spend my every breath in bringing pleasure to us both."

Morgan blinked, but he was perfectly serious. And she did believe him.

Part of her wanted to issue that invitation right now.

The other part, though, managed to speak up. After all, Alasdair had a *wife*.

Didn't he?

"What about your wife?" Morgan croaked.

Alasdair grimaced. "Ah, the beautiful Fenella." His expression turned grim. "What would you know of her?"

The confirmation that this wife existed, the admission of her name and her beauty combined to make Morgan's heart clench. And that packed a more powerful punch than Morgan had suspected. Before, she had only feared that Fenella existed—knowing the truth changed everything.

Especially Morgan's assessment of Alasdair's character. Men *were* all the same. Disappointment choked Morgan, and her words were hoarse. She felt sick with what she had nearly done.

She had very nearly replayed a familiar scene, and she didn't like the role she found herself acting.

Revulsion made her tone harsh. "How dare you touch me like that?" Morgan flung out her hands in frustration. "How can you practically dare me to invite you to bed, then calmly ask what I want to know about your wife? Don't your marriage vows mean anything to you?"

Alasdair frowned, then shook his head, his gaze locking with hers once more. " 'Tis a long tale."

Morgan knew her skepticism showed. Matt would have said pretty much the same thing. There was always an excuse.

"I'll bet." Morgan heard the bitterness in her tone. She stalked back into the bathroom and began to towel herself off roughly.

It made absolutely no sense that she was fighting against tears. How could she have misjudged Alasdair so completely? He wasn't at all the man she thought he was, let alone as compassionate and wonderful as she had believed.

How could she have been so stupid?

Morgan completely ignored the large shadow that loomed in the bathroom doorway just a moment later.

"I shall make you a bargain, my lady," Alasdair finally said softly. "I will tell you of my wife, if you share with me the tale of your hatred of whisky. 'Twas a man at root, unless I miss my guess, and I would know the manner of cur who has scarred you so deeply."

Morgan's head snapped up and she stared at Alasdair. He looked so sincere that she was tempted once more to trust him. And that made her doubt her conclusions.

Was she judging him too harshly? What if he really did have a good reason?

Didn't she at least owe him a chance to explain?

Alasdair *had* promised not to try and get the crystal from her and he hadn't. He had saved her from being mugged, he had sworn off whisky apparently just to please her. He let her know he was attracted to her, but what happened was always up to Morgan.

She fingered the towel and considered the facts. Alasdair did rant and rave a bit, but flinging words was not the same as flinging fists. She had to concede that his situation couldn't be easy. He made a great fuss over keeping his word, a trait that Morgan found quite admirable. And Alasdair apologized.

Matt had never done any of those things.

Morgan peeked through her lashes at the highlander. The simple fact was that Alasdair *hadn't* broken his marriage vows. He had pleasured her and stepped away.

And Morgan wanted to know the whole story. She dared to hope that all men weren't like Matt.

No, she dared to hope that this man wasn't like Matt.

Not only that, but Morgan found it oddly appealing to be offered the chance to talk about Matt. No one knew what he had done, not even Justine, and Morgan had the sense that it was time to let the pain of the past go.

And the best way to do that was to share the story.

Morgan had an instinctive sense that Alasdair would not judge her because of what had happened. It was time to tell someone, and Morgan wanted to tell *him*. Hadn't he been the one who insisted that the telling took the sting out of bad news?

"All right." Morgan nodded agreement. "But maybe we should get some breakfast first."

Alasdair grinned. "Aye, I knew from first glance that you were a woman of good sense."

The sorceress fiddled with the last of her toast as though she knew she could delay no longer. She had donned another pair of those tights that tormented Alasdair, tossing a vivid blue and green sweater over her shoulders. Her yet damp hair had been bound back in some semblance of order. The sunlight streaming through the window above the table painted blue lights in its drying curls.

But 'twas the vulnerability in her emerald eyes that tore at his heart this morning. Alasdair waited patiently, sipping at the vile brew she called tea. 'Twas clear enough that this tale would not be easy in the telling for her, and he was humbled that she had accepted his invitation to recount it.

Morgan flicked him a very green glance, and Alasdair knew 'twas time.

"I was married before," she confessed tightly. This was part of her history that Alasdair did not recall from his gran's tales, though he supposed he should not have been surprised. Within the eternity of an immortal's life, surely there would be moments of love?

Morgaine sighed. "I'm not really sure *why*, although at the time, it seemed to be the thing to do. We met at art school, you know, and he always knew what to do when I didn't." She shrugged. "I guess I admired him. He had so much self-assurance."

"Had he a name?"

She smiled quickly then, though the curve vanished as soon as it came. "Matt. Matthew James Reilly. He graduated and got a good job in an advertising agency, then he thought it was time to get married, so we did."

Her school of arts was obviously where the great sorcerers went to hone their skills, though Alasdair had no understanding of an advertising agency. It seemed to have little import, other than motivating this Matt to propose marriage, so he did not interrupt her tale. No doubt 'twas only a sign that Matt had proved himself.

Morgaine frowned into her cup. "For a while everything was wonderful. We found a good apartment overlooking the lake and I kept on with my classes. He came home from work and we cooked together, that kind of thing." Her lips twisted. "Maybe because it once was good, when it got bad, things seemed even worse."

Alasdair felt a pang of jealousy. There had never been a single day without strife in his marriage. That it had always been strife created by the willful Fenella purely for her own amusement made the truth no easier to bear.

Morgaine leaned forward. "You see, I thought it would be nice to start a family. I really *like* kids." Alasdair's heart clenched at the sparkle that just the thought brought to her eyes.

He had to look away when the spark was quenched. "But Matt didn't want any ties. At all. We started to fight, about every stupid little thing. He started to not come home, I started to wonder whether those ties he didn't want included me."

The shadow that fell over her delicate features showed the pain that even the memories caused. Her next words were husky. "We even stopped making love. It was awful. He didn't touch me at all—he went out of his way to avoid touching me."

This, then, was why she had such doubts of her allure. Alasdair realized why she had been so upset when he stepped away from her in the shower and wished he had known this tale sooner.

"There is naught amiss with your charms, my lady," he assured her heatedly, and that wan smile flashed briefly again.

"Well. Maybe." She shrugged. "Anyway, when I finally worked up the nerve to ask what was wrong, things got ugly fast. Matt accused me of wanting to trick him into creating a child, but I would *never* have done that." She looked sadly at him. "How could I have brought a child into a marriage where it wasn't wanted? How could I have done that to a little baby?"

Alasdair shook his head firmly, hating that he had not been as farsighted as the sorceress before him. "You could not."

She shook her head adamantly. "I couldn't have done it." She heaved a tremulous sigh and tears shone in her eyes. "But he didn't believe me. It was terrible, being married to someone who thinks the worst of you."

" 'Twas no more than a reflection of his own heart," Alasdair declared. The sorceress looked up, a question lurking in those wondrous eyes. "Those with dark hearts accuse all those around them of planning foul crimes. I have seen this often."

"Maybe." Morgaine played with her cup, and Alasdair knew there was yet more. He leaned forward and captured her nervous fingers, alarmed to feel them tremble within his grip.

The sorceress heaved an uneven sigh but did not look at Alasdair. "He, um, he started to drink. I mean, he always drank, but he started to drink a lot."

This then was the source of her concerns about whisky. Alasdair closed his fingers firmly over hers and held on.

"And he changed so much when he was drunk. He was awful, shouting accusations and throwing things, storming out and not coming home all night. It was horrible." Morgaine grimaced as Alasdair watched. "But it was worse when he wanted to have sex."

"When he was fou as a puggie?"

Morgan frowned, clearly not understanding.

"When he was drunken," Alasdair clarified.

Morgan smiled slightly, though the merriment did not reach her eyes. "Well, it didn't work most of the time. You know how it is. And he blamed me for that, calling me all sorts of names." Her voice caught. "Then I found out that he was sleeping with other women. We had a huge fight. I refused to let him into our bed." Her expression turned rueful at the recollection.

Morgaine fidgeted, but Alasdair did not release his grip on her fingers. She unwillingly lifted her gaze to his, and he saw the truth he would have her utter.

"Did ever he strike you?"

A tear shimmered in her luminous eyes. "Just once."

Anger erupted within Alasdair. She was so finely wrought, so tiny and perfect, even the fingers trapped within his own were delicate beyond all. How could any man lift a hand against her? What manner of boor would see the need to strike such a creature?

"Once is once too often, to a decent man's way of thinking!" Alasdair angrily leapt to his feet. "Tell me where I should find this Matthew James Reilly that he might be taught what is right and proper!"

He glared down at the sorceress in outrage, his hands on his hips. She looked up at him and slowly smiled, as though she barely dared to believe his anger on her behalf.

"You really would, wouldn't you?" she asked softly.

Alasdair's heart twisted that she had been so poorly used. "Aye! Do you doubt my pledge?"

Morgaine looked at him for a long moment but did not answer his question. "Sit down," she urged, "and I'll tell you what happened."

Alasdair did as he was bidden, but his indignation was not so readily dismissed. He wanted dearly to break the nose, if not more, of this Matthew, but he fiddled roughly with the cutlery instead. 'Twas not within him to sit still while his anger boiled, but he forced himself to do the lady's bidding.

Morgaine folded herself up on her seat, and her gaze slipped off to the distance. "Things had been really bad, but then suddenly they started to get better. He made all sorts of promises, and although I know now what they were worth, at the time I really wanted to believe him. I really wanted my marriage to work, maybe just on principle.

"I thought that we had reached the bottom and all those promises, well, they had me believing everything could be fixed. Where there's a will, there's a way and all that." She swallowed. "So, I trusted him."

"And he lied to you," Alasdair interjected savagely.

Morgaine's face was full of disillusionment. "Yes. It seems so obvious now. He kept doing what he was doing, but he didn't rage at home anymore. He still 'worked late' and everything, though. I guess I was too stupid to see the signs."

" 'Tis not stupidity to trust someone held within one's heart."

Morgaine's gaze locked with his own, and Alasdair feared she saw more deeply into his heart than he might have liked. Her lips parted, as though she would say something, then she shook her head and concentrated on her interlocked hands.

"It was our anniversary. Two whole years together. And I thought we had weathered the storm, that things were getting better and that we had a rosy future to celebrate. I was finishing my degree that year and had an offer for a full-time job. Everything looked great."

"But 'twas not."

"No." Morgaine swallowed. "I came home early from class, planning to make a great dinner as a surprise. I had bought a bottle of sparkling non-alcoholic wine and some flowers." Her eyes misted with unshed tears. "I think I might have been singing, probably quite badly."

Her lips thinned and her voice turned hard. "I walked in on him humping some woman in our own bed."

Morgaine plunged on with the telling before Alasdair could even blink.

"Well, all hell broke loose. I dropped the wine, so there was no mystery that I was there, and it splashed all over the place. The woman ran out half-naked, Matt started to yell at me for interrupting him, if you can believe it. And I finally snapped.''

The sorceress flung out her hands. ''I couldn't believe that he had lied to me like that, I couldn't believe that everything I had hoped for wasn't going to happen. But I *had* to believe it. It was literally laid out right in front of me.''

Morgaine drew herself up taller. ''And so, for the first time, I told Matt exactly what I thought of him and what he was doing. He yelled and''—she flushed—''I yelled back.''

Her gaze flicked to Alasdair. ''That was when he hit me. He punched me in the eye.'' She swallowed and frowned. ''It was like time stopped. We stared at each other, both of us stunned at what he had done. I don't know how I did it, but I just turned and walked right out of there. I went straight to a hotel, hired a lawyer, and never set foot in that place again.''

''He must have tried to speak to you.''

Morgaine's lips set stubbornly. ''After what he had done, there was *nothing* to say.''

''Aye,'' Alasdair acknowledged and leaned forward to reassure her. He touched her shoulder, alarmed to find her trembling. ''There is no excuse for striking a woman, whatever tale such a man might concoct. You are well rid of him and his kind.''

Morgaine's full lips twisted with the bitterness of what she had borne. She looked up at him, doubtless showing more vulnerability than she might have liked. Alasdair's heart twisted.

''Aren't all men of his kind?'' The words were uttered softly, as though her scar demanded she ask the question, but her eyes were filled with the hope that Alasdair would prove her wrong.

He captured both her hands in his own. ''Never would I strike a woman or break a pledge!''

''But you might twist out of it on a technicality.'' Her expression was sad, and Alasdair suddenly understood the full weight of the damage this Matthew had wrought. Here was the measure he had to prove himself beyond.

She propped her chin in her hands, the very image of disappointment. Alasdair could well sympathize with the shattering of her dreams, for marriage had fallen far short of his own expectations too.

He felt a curious bond with the sorceress.

"You leave the inviting to bed up to me, so that you won't be the one to actively break your wedding vows," she observed quietly. "In the end, it's all the same, isn't it?"

"Nay, 'tis not at all the same," Alasdair declared with resolve.

"Why not?"

"Because Fenella is dead."

Morgaine blinked.

But Alasdair had no time for her surprise. He ran a hand through his hair as the guilt flooded through him anew. He had to tell her how it had been.

"Yet you must understand, my lady, Fenella's death eats at my very soul. Though never I struck her, her blood stains my hands all the same." He pivoted to face the astonished enchantress.

" 'Twas I who killed my wife as surely as if I had fitted my hands about her neck."

Chapter 12

ALASDAIR HAD KILLED Fenella?

Surely Morgan had misunderstood!

But the highlander was staring at the floor, his expression pained. He heaved a sigh and paced the width of the room and back, as restless as a caged tiger.

It couldn't be true. Morgan just knew it. "What happened?"

"I wanted a child, much as you did," Alasdair confessed hoarsely. "But, my lady, I fear I did not show your foresight in thinking of that child's future."

He shook his head suddenly, frowning down at his feet. "But let me begin with the first of the tale. I met Fenella Macdonald first on the day of our nuptials, but I had long heard repute of her wondrous beauty."

Alasdair scowled in recollection and Morgan's blood ran cold. "Never will I forget the sight of her when she swept from her sire's ship. She was blonder than blond, as fair as the new snow, with lips as red as blood. Fenella was tall and straight, slender and supple as a willow. She moved with the grace of a queen and smiled at all who turned their faces upon her."

He swallowed visibly. "She was more beauteous than any might have warned me. I was stunned that she would be my bride."

Morgan fought against an irrational wave of jealousy. Fenella was dead, she reminded herself fiercely, but she couldn't help thinking that Alasdair's heart was buried with her.

It shouldn't have bothered Morgan, she knew.

But it did.

She fought to sound disinterested. "Why was she?"

Alasdair shot a bright glance Morgan's way. "Fenella's sire ran a fearsome risk in taking the side of Robert the Bruce in those days. The MacAulay legacy is a powerful one, and the wily old man saw advantage in having yet more warriors to his banner. 'Twas the blood of Olaf the Black her sire wanted in the veins of Fenella's sons and 'tis that very blood that courses through mine. My chieftain declared the match fine, and my fate was made."

Alasdair had kept the word of his chieftain and put his own plans aside, whatever they might have been. Despite herself, Morgan felt her sense that he was a man of honor grow.

Alasdair passed a hand over his brow. "Perhaps all might have been different if the expectations of the Macdonald had not weighed heavily upon my heart. Nay, that is not honest enough—'twas my own hope for children alone that drove my insistence."

"And Fenella did not want children?"

Alasdair's features darkened and he turned away. His single word was hoarsely uttered. "Nay."

Morgan watched his hands clench behind his back, working and gripping each other as though he would fight the demons that haunted him with his fists. She waited, and finally he tipped his head back to stare at the ceiling.

"I insisted," he confessed in a low voice, "no doubt more than I should have. And Fenella conceived. My gran saw bad portent in the scattering of blood from the sow we slaughtered that fall, but I was jubilant. A child! I was to be a father!"

He pivoted then, and Morgan glimpsed the flash of pain in his eyes. "But at what price?" he asked, so low that he might have been asking himself.

"What happened? I thought you had a son?"

"Aye, a bonny boy, healthy from the first. He gave such a

bellow when first he drew breath that the dead stirred in the cemetery three miles distant.''

A proud smile came to Alasdair's firm lips as he recalled that day. Morgan's breath caught as she imagined this man and the father he would be.

Alasdair suddenly sobered and stared down at his feet for a long moment. When he spoke, his voice caught. ''But Fenella died in the delivering of him.''

That was why he held himself responsible? Because he had wanted a child? Morgan was on her feet in an instant, compassion making her rush to reassure him. ''But you can't blame yourself! You couldn't have known!''

Alasdair's glare was fierce. ''I *should* have known!''

''How could you have known? Was she a delicate woman?''

Alasdair glared at Morgan. ''As hale as a horse was Fenella, nigh as tall as me and strong beyond all. But 'tis no small risk a woman takes in bearing a child. I *knew* this but could not look beyond my own hopes!''

Before Morgan could argue, Alasdair cast his hands skyward and stalked across the room. ''Fenella is *gone* because of my selfish desire, and I, I have only my guilt to warm me at night.'' He caught his breath, and Morgan's heart ached in sympathy.

He still loved his wife, with the same passion he had loved her then. And Alasdair would spend the rest of his life blaming himself for what he had done.

What would Morgan give to have a man love her the way Alasdair loved Fenella?

''What about your son?'' she managed to ask.

Alasdair exhaled raggedly. ''I have not seen him these seven years.''

''What?''

''He was but a babe when I left, a babe with his mother's eyes.''

A reminder of his lost beloved that would torment Alasdair every time he looked at the boy. Morgan's heart twisted. No wonder he had left the island—he hadn't been able to bear looking at his child.

"Is that why you left Lewis?" she asked softly.

Alasdair glanced over his shoulder. "I left Lewis to prove I am the man I know myself to be."

Morgan frowned. "I don't understand."

"There are those, my lady, who share your low esteem of men in general, or of me in particular. After Fenella's death, many cruel words were aired regarding the fate she had met in the embrace of the MacAulay clan. There were tales that I had treated her as this Matthew treated you. There was talk that I had failed to fulfill my clan's obligation to the mighty Macdonalds, and they are quick to take offense."

His eyes narrowed dangerously. "But I am not this manner of man, though indeed I erred in pressing her to bear a child. The burden of that I will bear for all my days."

He stared fiercely at Morgan. "Never would I raise a hand toward a woman. And never would I break a vow granted to another. I followed Robert the Bruce, a man of valor, to prove that I am of his ilk. I took the cause of Fenella's sire to prove to him that I am the man he believed me once to be. I risked my hide, I left my son, I abandoned my home to prove my clan's loyalty to the Macdonald allegiance."

His determination was a tangible force in the room. Morgan felt ashamed that she had ever doubted him.

"A man's word is his bond, my lady. Already you have witnessed my resolve in this—I repeat my pledge to not drink whisky in your domain. Your protest against the spirit is one all too common, and I respect your will in this."

Morgan tried to be nonchalant. "It's not that easy, you know. You could be setting yourself up here. I mean, if you drink a lot, you can't just stop like that."

"Is this the excuse your Matthew granted you?" Alasdair's lip curled, and he dropped into the opposite chair once more. "Know this, my lady, I have granted my word and will keep it, regardless of the cost. Robert the Bruce has shown that a man has only to believe in a thing to make it so. Do you know the tale of the spider?"

Morgan shook her head, intrigued.

Alasdair sighed and tapped his finger on the table. "I have told you well enough of his vision for Scotland and his meeting with John Comyn. After that day, all looked dark for Robert the Bruce. His allies had turned against him, he had been driven from his own lands, the king put a high price upon his very head, the taint of sin clung to his hide. He took exile in the islands not far from my home and made an abode of a cave beside the ocean, convinced he was naught but a failure.

"And while he sat there, lost in his own despair, he noted a spider spinning a web. The spider meant to attach its web to a point on the wall far out of range, but it swung valiantly toward its goal. Once it swung and missed. Again, it mustered resource, swung, and missed. Undeterred, the tiny creature attempted a third time, and failed.

"As Robert the Bruce watched, the spider attempted thrice more, failing each time but still going back to the battle, despite its inadequacies.

"And on the seventh attempt, the spider was victorious. It had only to believe it could be done to make it so, and thus it did. And Robert the Bruce took this lesson to his very heart. He left the cave of his exile, he summoned what men he could, he came to Lewis, told this tale, and I joined his ranks. And since that day, he has pressed on toward victory. Naught can stand long in his path.

"A man has but to believe a thing to do it," Alasdair repeated heavily. "And I believe in what I pledge to you, my lady. You fear all men are like this cur who treated you poorly—I say nay. Further I say, I shall prove it to you. I am a man of honor and a man of my word and before we part ways, you too shall know the truth of it."

He stared into Morgan's eyes for a long moment and she couldn't look away.

Because she believed him.

Then Alasdair's lips twisted in frustration. "Robert the Bruce trusted me with his troops, men who now are without my leadership. 'Twas at his dictate that I led the attack on Edinburgh keep."

He braced his hands on the small table and leaned toward Morgan, his gaze so intense that she couldn't look away. "My lady, you have snatched me away from the very moment of victory. The only thing I ask of you, in exchange for my keeping my pledge to you, is that you return me to my own domain that my son can carry his head high.''

And that was the crux of it. Morgan suddenly remembered the one pesky detail about Alasdair that she didn't know how to fix. She leaned forward and took his hand in hers, looking into his eyes in an echo of his sincere pose.

''But, Alasdair, I told you already. You've traveled through time. I don't know how to send you back! I don't know how you got here, even, and I'm really not Morgaine le Fee . . .''

''LIES!'' Alasdair roared as he flung off her grip and sprang to his feet. ''I grant you a tale from my heart and you have naught for me but lies! Why? *Why* do you deny who you are? What would you have me do to win your will in this?''

His blue eyes blazed into Morgan's. ''If you will not do this for me, why will you not aid my son?'' Anguish was etched on his features. ''My gran is elderly, she will pass, and he will be left alone. How can you compel me to abandon my son?''

Morgan felt more helpless than she ever had in her life. ''Alasdair, I can't fix this . . .''

''I care naught for your lies!'' he roared, then charged out of the room.

''Don't go! Come back!'' Morgan ran to the door.

Sharing the tale of Fenella had obviously opened old wounds, but she couldn't let him just go! They had to figure out how to send him back to the past—and only he knew how he had gotten here in the first place.

Alasdair hesitated at the top of the stairs and looked back at Morgan with frustration. Slowly, the anger filtered out of his eyes and his voice lowered. ''You know well enough that I cannot risk straying far from your side,'' he confessed heavily. ''I will be back, my lady Morgaine.''

And Morgan knew it would be so.

''I will keep my pledge to you, I will yet try to win your favor.'' Alasdair ran one hand through his hair and sighed. ''Indeed, I can do naught else.''

And before Morgan could respond, he was gone.

Morgan was very tempted to run after Alasdair, but she hesitated as his footsteps sounded heavily on the stairs.

She had to respect his desire to be alone. She could understand the need, even if the room seemed a lot emptier without him there. Morgan closed the door and leaned against it, thinking about everything he had told her.

Clearly, Alasdair loved Fenella to distraction. And he was fiercely determined to do what was right for his son. Morgan could only admire the kind of man she was beginning to see Alasdair to be.

He was as different from Matt as oil was from water.

Morgan had been wrong.

She wandered back across the room, absently picking up the breakfast dishes. Alasdair would be back, once his temper cooled, Morgan knew it. His word was his bond.

She kind of liked that—but Morgan refused to think any longer along those lines. She couldn't figure out how to send him back in time without knowing how he got here in the first place, which meant she'd just have to wait for him to return.

Morgan opened her sketchbook on the cleared table and studied the drawings she had made. The sunlight flickered across the top page, making Thomas Rhymer seem to come to life. She remembered the tale of Tam Lin and her smile turned bittersweet.

It was awful, really. Alasdair thought he was trapped like Tam Lin in the land of Faerie, except Alasdair's one true love couldn't help him return home. Morgan sharpened a pencil, turned to a fresh page, and began to draw the anguish of the lovers' separation that she had glimpsed in the highlander's eyes.

As much as Blake didn't want to leave the cozy haven of Room 11, his stomach was starting to argue the point. He didn't even know what time it was, but the sunlight had come and gone, and the room was getting darker. Justine poked him with one toe after their umpteenth round, just as Blake was thinking that his blood sugar must be nonexistent.

"I want french fries," she said, her tone making it all too clear who was going to bring them to the room.

"What do you take me for?" Blake retorted in mock indignation. "Some kind of lackey?"

Justine grinned. "A boy toy." She looked him over, the way a starving dog eyes a bone, then slowly licked her lips.

"Too much saturated fat," Blake managed to say, mostly because he didn't want to leave just as things were getting interesting.

Again.

Justine's lips quirked. "What can I say? You've stripped away every last one of my inhibitions."

Blake frowned, pretending to be stern. "But they're really fattening." He patted his belly. "I have to keep lean and mean."

Justine smiled the slow, sensuous smile that drove him crazy. She dropped her voice to a purr and walked her fingers up his chest. "Then we'll just have to think of a way to burn off all those extra calories."

Blake was suddenly quite sure he could go one more round before they ate. Justine must have read his mind, because she laughed, then dove beneath the covers.

She tickled his ribs, experience guiding her to the most sensitive spot. Blake hooted, he squirmed, then he threw off his glasses and resorted to finding his wife by touch.

A good fifteen minutes later, they ended up in a tangle of sheets on the floor, breathless with laughter. Justine plopped Blake's glasses back on his nose and he grinned at how uncharacteristically disheveled she looked.

"I'm starving," she complained, a twinkle dancing in her eye.

"Sheesh! Women and their one-track minds."

Justine laughed. "Oh, yeah, you've been a real mine of options this afternoon."

"I thought I'd done quite well."

Their gazes locked and held, the temperature in the room nudging up a few degrees. Justine crawled toward Blake on all fours, a knowing smile curving her lips.

"You do know that this kind of service will have to be considered in your tip," she murmured provocatively.

They looked at Blake's lap simultaneously. "Not on your

life!'' He cupped his hands protectively over himself and they both burst into laughter.

''That's not what I meant!'' Justine protested, but Blake made a show of jumping to his feet and covering himself from prying eyes. He finished dressing while his wife lounged on the floor, then bent to kiss her nose.

''Try to get out of bed for dinner,'' he coaxed.

She feigned a pout. ''I'll have to if you won't get back in.''

Blake grimaced theatrically. ''You'll get salt on the sheets.''

''You said you'd never throw me out of bed for eating crackers.''

''But you want french fries. Changes everything.'' Blake winked, then headed for the door.

''Don't forget that brown vinegar!''

''You're kidding? That malt stuff?''

''I'm starting to like it,'' she insisted, then raised a brow playfully and did a very bad Mae West imitation. ''Don't you want to please me, honey?''

Blake rolled his eyes. ''You do need food. I'll be back in a jiff.'' And he bounded out the door, the quintessential man on a mission.

And in a hurry to fulfill it.

Unfortunately, the cook in the restaurant wasn't so easy to convince. He wore a white T-shirt and sported a day's growth of dark beard. The way the cigarette dangled jauntily from the corner of his lip made him look as though he belonged in the galley of an oil tanker instead of a quaint inn in the Scottish highlands.

Maybe he didn't have quite the same motivation as Blake did.

''Now, you see, I don't heat the fryer up for a good hour. Makes no sense to waste the power before there's lots of orders coming in.''

''But my wife wants french fries!''

The burly cook rolled his eyes. ''American, are you?'' he asked, the words more a statement than a question. He rolled his eyes again and strolled away, as though that explained everything.

Blake appealed to the matronly waitress with the unlikely bright orange hair. "Don't Scotsmen get hungry in the late afternoon?"

"Of course they do, love, but it's *teatime*. What you're wanting is tea and scones, a wee meat patty, maybe a sausage roll. That will set you straight until dinner."

"But she wants french fries!"

The waitress looked sympathetic, but a stern glance from the cook had her shaking her head. "This isn't no McDonald's, you know," he said testily and slammed the oven door behind a tray of meat pies.

The waitress clucked her tongue. "There's no reasoning with him when he's in a mood, don't you know," she counseled in a low voice. "Highland temper, where would we be without it?"

"I heard that, Gladys!" the cook bellowed.

Blake leaned on the counter and tried for his persuasive best. He wasn't going back upstairs without Justine's fries. "Look, my wife *really* wants french fries. I'll give you twenty pounds to heat the fryer up early."

The pair exchanged a look. "American, all right," the cook declared sagely, then turned away.

The waitress patted Blake's arm. "Look, love, he's gone and dug in his heels. Why don't I make your wife a nice cup of tea . . ."

But Blake wasn't interested in tea because Justine wasn't interested in tea. He flung out his hands and said the first thing that came to mind.

"But she's *pregnant*! And there's no reasoning with her. She wants something and I'm supposed to just get it! Pickles in the middle of the night, french fries in the afternoon. It's making me nuts, but she has to eat *something* for the baby, and what am I going to do when all she wants is french fries?"

"Pregnant?" echoed the waitress.

"Pregnant?" The cook pivoted to face Blake with surprising grace, his cigarette dangling at an angle that was far from jaunty. "Why didn't you just say so, man? There's no reasoning with a woman during her time!"

And he flicked the red switch on the deep fryer to On.

"He's seven bairns of his own," the waitress confided in an undertone as the cook set to slicing potatoes. "And not a one of them over ten years old. This be a man who knows pregnant women."

Blake didn't ask how many women had contributed to that impressive pool of children. He shoved his hands in his pockets, feeling like an idiot for telling such a lie, yet perversely proud of himself for coming up with something that worked.

"It'll be a while, love. Why don't you sit and have a pint?"

Blake turned back to the nearly vacant restaurant that doubled as a pub—or vice versa—and for the first time noticed Alasdair. The highlander was sitting alone in the far corner, pushing a glass of water across a tabletop.

"Hey, Alasdair!" Blake waved as he crossed the room, not waiting for an invitation before he pulled out a chair. "How's it going?" He noticed belatedly that the other man looked morose. "What's the matter? Morgan kick you out?"

Alasdair glared lethally across the table. "What do you know of this Matthew James Reilly?" he demanded grimly.

Blake barely kept his mouth from falling open. "She *told* you about him?" Alasdair nodded and Blake whistled between his teeth. "Wow! She never talks about him at all. Hey, you want a 'wee dram'? Just us guys?"

Alasdair shook his head slowly, the move making him look like a stubborn lion. "I drink whisky no longer. I have pledged this to Morgaine."

Blake sat back and considered his companion. Justine would be pleased that things were getting so serious so fast.

But Alasdair sure didn't look like a happy camper. He leaned forward now and tapped his finger slowly on the table. "What do you know of this so-called man?"

Blake frowned in recollection. "Well, it's been ten years now. Um, he and Morgan were already together when I came on the scene. Married and everything." He rolled his eyes. "Though no one was very pleased about that."

"No one?"

"Well, Justine, but especially Auntie Gillian. Wow! Now there was one opinionated old babe. She was something else."

"I know naught of any Auntie Gillian."

"You're not alone there." Blake grimaced. "No one knows much about her, and those who do aren't telling. They never talk about her, but she was the one who raised them."

"I do not understand."

"Justine and Morgan are sisters. Sorry, I thought you could see the resemblance. Most people do. At any rate, when they were little squirts, their parents went away, maybe to a wedding, I forget, but they left the girls with Auntie Gillian."

Blake flagged down the waitress and ordered a pint. Alasdair declined with a shake of his head. Once she was gone, Blake resumed. "Well, there was a car accident—really horrible—and the girls were orphaned. They must have been four and two at the time, and real handfuls, as kids that age usually are. Busy, not bad. And if Auntie Gillian wasn't their closest relative, she was certainly the one most determined to give them a home."

Blake waved gratitude as his beer came, and after a long draught, he warmed to his story. Alasdair was listening intently.

"You see, she wasn't really their aunt—something like the aunt of a cousin of their mother or something. Some distant relative, at any rate. And possession is nine-tenths of the law, right? She had the girls and she kept them, the rest of the family be damned." Blake snorted. "I sure wouldn't have gone head-to-head with Auntie Gillian over anything."

A faint smile curved Alasdair's lips. "She was a woman of determination?"

Blake laughed. "More like one with an iron will. She was incredible—but she put everything into raising those two. *Everything*. They went to dance lessons and piano lessons and to the best schools. For an older person, Auntie Gillian kept up one helluva pace. She was bound and determined that they were going to have the *best*. Yet at the same time, neither of them got away with anything."

"She sounds most fierce."

"Yeah." Blake grinned in recollection. "I've gotta tell you, I was pretty worried when it was time to meet her. I mean, I knew that if Auntie Gillian put the kibosh on me seeing Jus-

tine, that would be the end of it. And I *really* didn't want that
to happen.''

''But you met with approval?''

Blake still felt surprised by his certainty of that. ''Yeah! I
remember that day like nothing else. We drove out to this little
town in Michigan—we were living in Chicago even then. It
was just as cute and apple pie as you can imagine. One of
those places where the feed store is the biggest building in
town and all the houses are these old wooden jobs from the
turn of the century. Big porches, people sitting out watching
what everyone else is doing. Norman Rockwell stuff.

''Well, Auntie Gillian's place wasn't one of the big showy
ones, just a cozy little place complete with white picket fence.
Of course, I was shaking in my boots, I was so worried that
this woman would hate me on sight.''

Blake took a sip of beer. ''I can still see her standing on
the walkway, waiting for us to get out of the car. Mauve pol-
yester pantsuit, blue hair all tucked up, and eyes that just
snapped. You could swear that she never missed a thing. She
stood staring at me, and I felt like she knew everything about
me before we were even introduced. I was surprised when we
got up to her that she was only as tall as Justine's shoulder—
about the same height as Morgan—because her presence was
so . . . formidable.''

Blake turned his glass in the wet circle it had made on the
table. ''We went into her living room, it was all this curvy
old furniture with red upholstery and horsehair stuffing that
itched your legs. We had tea in these little bone china cups,
and she ranted about Matt.''

Blake laughed. ''It was so anticlimactic. I was ready to be
interrogated to the nth degree, but she didn't ask me *anything*.
Once she got done with her list of Matt's crimes, we actually
had a very pleasant dinner.''

Alasdair's smile widened. ''She must have approved of
you.''

''Yeah, well, Justine gave me a big kiss in the car and told
me that I'd seriously won the compare-and-contrast game.''
When Alasdair looked blank, Blake continued, ''I don't know
that I would have done so well in Auntie Gillian's estimation

if Matt hadn't jumped in first and showed her how bad things could be.''

"What manner of man was he?''

Blake frowned. "You know, it wasn't anything you could put your finger on. He was a good-looking guy, a smooth talker. He worked out and played sports and stuff. Seemed like an okay guy, actually. At the beginning, I thought Auntie Gillian was just being overprotective of Morgan and Justine was chiming in. You know, 'There's nobody good enough for our girl' kind of thing.''

"But later?''

"Well, gradually I started to see it. You know, Morgan was completely head over heels. She thought the sun rose and set in this jerk, and she would have done anything for him. And over time, I started to get the feeling that it wasn't all mutual. Just a comment here or there, nothing you could really pinpoint, but the impressions added up.''

"He did not love her.''

Blake shook his head. "I don't think Matt loved anyone besides himself.'' He drank heavily of his beer, remembering a hundred little things.

"Yet he married Morgaine.''

"Yeah. I think he liked that she was in love with him. Kind of his own little fan club.'' Blake grimaced. "She was young, she had been really sheltered from his kind. He was flashy. Lots of women go for that—at least until they know better.''

Alasdair's disapproval of that was clear. "And what happened to this Auntie Gillian?''

"Well. Justine and I got married about six months after the Interview That Could Have Ended It All. A couple of months after that, we got a call from the hospital in the town nearest Auntie Gillian's.'' Blake swallowed. "She'd had a stroke and was barely hanging on. Morgan turned up begging a ride, and the three of us drove down together within half an hour of getting the call.''

"And this Matthew?'' Alasdair's voice was thick with disapproval.

Blake shrugged. "There was some excuse, I don't remember what it was, just that I knew it was a lie. Morgan looked like she'd been crying, Justine gave me one of Those Looks, and I just shut up and drove. You know how it is."

Alasdair nodded grimly. "Aye, that I do."

"So, we got there, it was too late to visit, but Auntie Gillian told the nurse in the ICU that she was holding on for her girls and they had damn well better let them in because she couldn't make it to morning. And they did. Like I said, you didn't mess with her. I guess she was in pretty rough shape because they seemed pretty surprised that she had hung on. Every blue hair still in place, though—that was Auntie Gillian."

Blake shook his head in admiration. "You know, it looked as though she was in charge of the place, not dying there. Justine and Morgan sat one on each side and took her hands. I kind of lingered in the background, you know, watching that little red light on the heart monitor go *beep-beep-beep*.

"She told them that now that her chicks were married, for better or for worse—Morgan got a Look for that one—it was time for her to go. She said good-bye to them both, reminded them to mind their manners, then gave them each a kiss. Then she laid back, closed her eyes, and the little red light didn't beep anymore."

Blake could see the sparse hospital room in his mind's eye and felt again the sudden absence of Auntie Gillian's commanding presence. The room had suddenly seemed emptier and colder, and he had known her formidable spirit had slipped out of her body before he even looked at the monitor.

"It was like a movie," he confessed quietly, still awed by the memory. "Perfectly planned, brilliantly executed. She even died on her own terms. Amazing woman. It turned out that she was a good fifteen years older than any of us had imagined."

"She sounds a woman of rare good sense," Alasdair said gruffly.

Blake frowned as he recalled where he had been going with this story, and his voice turned grim. "Yeah. And Auntie Gillian was right about Matt, that's for sure. Now, I don't know exactly what happened and I know better than to ask"—Blake punctuated this with a significant glance at his companion—

"but I know what I saw and I bet that's not what Morgan told you."

Alasdair leaned closer, his eyes gleaming. "Tell me."

If this guy wasn't nuts about Morgan, Blake would eat his Day-Timer.

And given that, Alasdair deserved to know everything Blake knew. Justine would think otherwise, but she wasn't here to know about it. Blake looked from side to side, then leaned across the table himself, dropping his voice even though he knew neither sister could hear him.

"About a year after that, Justine couldn't get ahold of Morgan and she was starting to worry. She was always edgy about Matt, said he was too smooth. So we went over there and knocked forever before Matt opened the door. He was half-stinko, but that wasn't much of a surprise. He gave us some cock-and-bull story about Morgan having a big assignment due for school, but I could tell he was surprised she hadn't called Justine, either."

Blake sighed. "All the way home Justine was talking about calling the cops. She was sure the bastard had hurt her baby sister. She said she had a bad feeling and was really wound up about his drinking. I think she thought she should be doubly protective of Morgan because Auntie Gillian was gone."

" 'Tis not an ignoble impulse."

"No." Blake smiled wryly. "But when we got home, the phone was ringing and it was Morgan. She was at a hotel, said she'd been there a week and a half, that she'd left Matt and wasn't going back. Well, Justine flat out said she couldn't stay at the hotel, that she had to come and live with us. Morgan argued, but we all knew she'd lose that one.

"So, we went and picked her up, and man, she was upset. She was pale and had lost some weight, one sad little lady. Never said anything more about the whole thing, though. I know Justine asked, but for the first time ever, Morgan completely stonewalled her. Justine couldn't figure out why she'd waited so long to call, but Morgan wasn't talking."

"You have an idea."

"Yeah, I sure do." Blake gritted his teeth and looked Alasdair in the eye. "I think Morgan was waiting for a bruise to fade."

What Blake saw simmering in the other man's eyes confirmed every suspicion about Matt's behavior that he had ever had. He had been right! And that made Blake feel damn good about what he had done for Morgan.

"Finally, she said she wanted a divorce. Justine didn't even have a chance to give me That Look—I wanted to make sure that everything went Morgan's way. So I called this buddy of mine from college—who just happens to be the meanest goddamn divorce lawyer you've ever seen." Blake straightened and mimicked his friend's formal manner. "Peter Ellis Thompson III."

Blake rolled his glass between his hands and let himself smile slowly in recollection. He'd been right there on Pete's shoulder throughout the whole thing, prodding him to go for blood. "You know, money may just be a way of keeping score, but it's a damned good one. Pete carved that boy a new asshole so big you could drive a Mack truck through it."

Alasdair looked slightly alarmed by this revelation, but Blake wasn't ashamed of the toll that he'd ensured would be extracted from the other man's hide. He pointed a finger at his companion.

"The important thing was that Morgan had herself a nice little nest egg, which was well worth Pete's bill. She never knew how much that was, because I paid Pete before he could even think about sending the bill to her.

"So, Morgan got herself a cute little studio loft not far from our place and started over again. She and Justine had a little nesting frenzy decorating that place. And when Morgan wanted to start her own business, she had the money to fall back on while she built up her contacts. She's done really well for herself."

Alasdair cleared his throat. "And once this Matthew was buggered and penniless, what became of him?"

Blake knew he didn't imagine the undercurrent of anger in the other man's tone. Alasdair was protective of Morgan, and Blake silently conceded that this was the man for his sister-in-law.

Justine had been right.

As usual.

He shrugged now and leaned back in his chair. "Well, it's funny, but things didn't go so well at his agency after that. He and Morgan moved in the same circles, you know, and people *like* Morgan. There was a well-deserved feeling that he hadn't treated her right, and when he lost a lot of business, they turfed him out. Eventually, he moved out west to start over again. We've never heard anything more."

Alasdair nodded approval, his expression fierce. "An outlander. 'Tis a finer fate than such a man deserves."

"That's for sure."

"French fries!" cried the waitress, and Blake quickly drained his beer.

"Oops, gotta go." He got to his feet, then cocked a finger at Alasdair, his tone only half joking. "Hey, don't make me send Pete after you."

Alasdair smiled. "There is little fear of that. Morgaine believes I am cut of the same cloth as this foul man and fears to trust me."

Blake leaned on the table. "You can't really blame her for being cautious, can you? And you're not like him, anyone can see that. It's only a matter of time before Morgan sees it, too."

Alasdair glanced up, a heat burning in his eyes. "Aye, you speak aright, Blake Advisor. Your counsel is good."

He got to his feet and finished his water with one swallow, setting the glass back on the table with a thump of resolve. "I shall prove to Morgaine that I am different. I shall prove to her that I can be trusted. I shall prove to her that I am worthy of sliding between her thighs!"

Blake blinked at the bluntness of that statement, but Alasdair had turned away. He strode to the door, the very image of masculine confidence, and Blake couldn't think of a thing to say that wouldn't sound silly after such a pronouncement.

So, he went to get Justine's french fries instead.

And wondered if that would prove him worthy of sliding between *her* thighs.

Chapter 13

ROOM 7 WAS ominously quiet, but the door was unlocked. Alasdair nudged it open with his toe, wincing when the hinges creaked slightly.

But the sorceress slumbering on the bed did not stir.

Alasdair crept into her lair on silent feet, closing the door securely behind himself. The room was filled with the soft rhythm of her breathing. The last rays of sunlight slanted orange through the windows and gilded the edges of the papers spread on the table.

Curious, Alasdair went to look, then gaped in amazement.

Pages of intricate, fanciful drawings spilled across the surface. Script rolled between the images, evidently some verse written in an elegant hand.

'Twas like the great illuminated Bible that the monks consulted and had shown Alasdair once when he was but a boy. He reached out as though he would touch the script, but fearful of smudging it, ran his hand a finger's breadth above the page.

And let himself feel the fullness of his old longing to read.

Alasdair swallowed and bent closer, examining the elfin faces peering from behind leaf and blossom. His heart leapt in recognition of a woman who could only be the lovely Jenny, her hair flowing long, her hand cupping the fullness of her womb as she waited at a crossroads beneath a starry sky.

And here! Here was Tam Lin himself, his bonnet cocked, his white steed prancing beneath him as he rode among the Faerie host, his gaze straining ahead as he sought some glimpse of his beloved Jenny. Alasdair sat down and bent over the page, smiling as he identified countless details of the tale he had told Morgaine.

'Twas clear the words were those he had sung to her. And on the right were the embracing lovers, Tam Lin brilliantly shown in contortions of change, Jenny stoically holding him fast, the Faerie Queen's lovely face twisted with malice.

And there they rode together, the moon hanging low over the victorious lovers, their limbs entwined, their faces shining with happiness.

Alasdair stared long at the marvel of this work, then carefully laid it aside. Beneath were several pages recounting the tale of Thomas Rhymer, he recognized it immediately. And half completed to one side was a sketch that could only be the tale of Robert the Bruce, contemplating the spider, then kneeling before a radiant Isobel of Buchan as she set the crown upon his brow.

But Alasdair's fingers continually strayed to the words he could not read. His gran's voice echoed in his ears, admonishing him to recall his station, but not even the knowledge that his place was to sow and to fight could dispel Alasdair's desire. The monks had seen the urge in him, he realized now, which was why they had been so welcoming to him.

His gran had undoubtedly feared her wee lamb would go to the church, leaving her to fend for herself.

Alasdair's lips twisted. Indeed, he had gone much farther, leaving his gran no less alone in his quest to aid Robert the Bruce. And with a squawling babe, as well.

Alasdair glanced guiltily at the sorceress, recalling well how her eyes had burned with her own desire for a child. She had wanted the child for its own sake—yet put her own wishes aside when she feared her home would not be adequate for that child's happiness.

Alasdair was ashamed to realize that his own motivation had been markedly less noble. He had desired an heir, a child to carry his name, a son who would grow to become a warrior straight and true.

He had never considered whether Angus would be happy or not. The boy was his son, his responsibility, and the honor of Alasdair's name—or the lack thereof—a weight upon Angus's shoulders. Alasdair wanted to ensure that his son could walk tall, but in his zeal to correct an error he saw that he had lost the child.

If indeed Alasdair made his way home successfully, Angus would not know him. Nor would he know Angus, unless the child strongly resembled Fenella or himself, though that would at best be a guess.

For the first time, he questioned the wisdom of the choice he had made seven years past. Indeed, Alasdair had never expected the conquest to take so long. And at the time, with rumors of his dishonor ringing in his ears, it seemed he had no choice.

But now he wondered. He had missed seven years of his son's life. Morgaine's fervor made him see the gold that had slipped through his fingers.

But what manner of sorceress yearned so for a child? Could Morgaine not have simply summoned one from her cauldron?

Alasdair stood back with a frown and looked from drawings to sorceress and back. Morgaine, he well recalled, denied that she was an enchantress, and beneath the current assault of doubts, Alasdair dared to give credence to her words while she slept.

Her right hand lay unfurled before her on the bed and he took due note of the smudges upon her fingers and the heel of her hand. They were of the same gray as the drawings themselves. And she slept like one exhausted by her efforts.

Alasdair frowned. A powerful enchantress like Morgaine le Fee need do no such labor to summon such images.

And he wondered whether Morgaine had told him the truth. She had said she was an artist, that she illustrated books, that she was not the Queen of Faerie.

Alasdair rubbed his chin. A sorceress had no need to labor with her own hands. A sorceress had no need of a protective Auntie Gillian—nor even of a sister or brother-in-law. A sorceress had no need of a spouse—especially one like this Matthew James Reilly. A sorceress need not long for anything, for all was within her power.

And a sorceress would not need an advocate to exact the pound of flesh due for indignities suffered by her. Indeed, could any man smite a sorceress and live to tell the tale, even as an outlander?

Nay, Morgaine's tale sounded all too mortal for her to be a great sorceress. Her impulses were all too human—her sympathy for the plight of others, her compassion, her concern. The vulnerability that oft shone in her eyes belied Alasdair's conclusion.

Though indeed, were she a mortal woman, Morgaine was a woman beyond compare.

Alasdair frowned. What if she *had* told him the truth? He paced the room silently, glaring out the window at intervals while he puzzled the matter through. Could the witch in Edinburgh have sent him forward in time, as Morgaine suggested?

'Twas a numbing proposition, but Alasdair could find naught to refute it, beyond the basic lunacy of the idea. The world certainly could have changed markedly in seven hundred years, perhaps even as markedly as this. His heart clenched as he recalled one assertion Morgaine had made.

Alasdair's traveling in time had vastly changed the course for Robert the Bruce. 'Twas true enough that Blake certainly had no esteem for the man Alasdair knew to be a hero.

But what could have happened? Alasdair fought to recall every detail of that night in Edinburgh. He must have disappeared when he fell down the stairs. And what then?

Could it be that the men had not held the keep without his leadership? Alasdair suddenly felt cold, and he paced with renewed vigor. His only dream had been to see Angus grow to manhood with a name he was proud to call his own, in a Scotland free from England's heavy yoke.

Had Alasdair unwittingly jeopardized that dream by taking a wee witch's dare?

'Twas madness! 'Twas impossible for a man to travel across seven centuries in the blink of an eye!

But Alasdair had a strange conviction dawning within his heart that that was precisely what had happened.

Though 'twas not a conclusion he could accept readily. His gran's tales of the Faerie realm echoed within his mind, and though Alasdair had never been a fanciful man, they made more sense to him than did this wild tale of Morgaine's.

Alasdair grimaced, wondering whether he simply took refuge in the familiar. How would he ever know the truth for certain?

Then the certainty dawned in his heart. Blake and Justine had pledged to take him home, back to Callanish. And in Callanish, Alasdair would know the truth.

Naught could lie to him there. In Callanish, he would know. His gran would be there, his son, his home, his livestock.

Or they would not.

Alasdair swallowed with difficulty at the possibility.

What if he could not return home? What if he had sacrificed not only seven years with Angus but all eternity? Too late, he saw the value of what he had left behind, and he desperately wanted to set matters aright.

If only he could have the chance.

Morgaine stirred, and Alasdair spun to face the bed. His heart softened as he watched her sleep, for if she spoke aright, she was no Faerie Queen. Alasdair frowned as he considered his behavior of the past day, and now he could not blame Morgaine for defending herself against his amorous plans.

But 'twas a different matter, to seduce a woman of good heart and abandon her, than to win the way to a sorceress's bed and earn her indulgence. The chance that Morgaine spoke truth demanded that Alasdair abandon his plan to seduce her, though, indeed, he had no alternate plan.

At least not until he saw the isle of Lewis with his own eyes.

Alasdair rubbed his brow in fatigue. He eyed the wide expanse of bed beside Morgaine and could not bring himself to retreat to his cot. The light had faded in the room as the sun slipped behind the hills, and Alasdair let exhaustion slip through his body.

Never had he felt so alone in all his days as he did in this

moment. Perhaps cast across the centuries, definitely beyond
the reach of any he knew, and uncertain how to repair matters,
Alasdair was in dire need of the warmth of another beside
him.

And there was one in particular whom he longed to hold
close. If Morgaine was naught but a wee lass who had been
buffeted by what life had offered her, then he had naught to
fear from her.

Carefully, so as not to disturb her, Alasdair cast his kilt
aside and doffed his boots. He climbed into the bed beside
Morgaine and caught his breath when she rolled over and
bumped into his side.

But she merely curled up beside his heat with a sigh.

Alasdair eased back against the pillows and slipped his arm
beneath Morgaine's shoulder to hold her close against him.
The sweet, clean scent of her filled his nostrils and battered
down his flimsy defenses.

Though he willed himself to breathe deeply, 'twas long into
the night that Alasdair MacAulay stared at the ceiling overhead and wondered.

What if she spoke aright?

Morgan awakened with the odd sense that she had lost something, but she couldn't remember what it was. She opened her
eyes to find a suspicious warmth lingering beneath the sheets,
though Alasdair's whistle carried from the bathroom.

Morgan stretched, knowing she had slept like a rock for the
first time in a long time.

And felt very good as a result. Her sketching had gone
really well the day before, although she'd been so exhausted
she'd just fallen into bed. She looked down and realized in
horror that she had slept in her clothes.

And she was starving. Morgan couldn't exactly recall—she
acknowledged few intrusions from real life when absorbed in
her work—but she was pretty sure she had forgotten to get
any dinner.

Which was one incentive to get up. Morgan rolled across
the bed as she stretched luxuriously and thought she caught a

whisper of Alasdair's scent on the linens. Her heart skipped a beat, but another sniff was inconclusive.

Had he slept with her? If Alasdair had crawled into the bed, he certainly hadn't made a pass at her.

Which was a pretty strange change of attitude, given his sensual assault of the morning before. Morgan propped herself up on her elbows and surveyed the room, noting immediately that Alasdair's cot was rumpled.

She frowned at the wave of disappointment that coursed through her. Obviously he had gotten over his burning attraction to her.

That thought totally destroyed her good mood.

Morgan rolled out of bed with a grimace. She had a vague sense that her drawings had been examined, then returned to where she had left them, but couldn't be sure. Well aware of the merry whistling in the other room, Morgan quickly gathered up the sketches and put them away.

"Are you awake, my lady?" Morgan spun around guiltily and shoved one hand through the nest of her hair, just as Alasdair emerged from the bathroom. He nodded to her, expertly fastening the end of his kilt, then dropped into a chair to lace up his boots.

His tone was perfectly businesslike. "If you so desire, I shall seek a morsel to break our fast and discover Blake Advisor's intentions for this morning."

Alasdair was obviously in a rush to leave. Couldn't wait to get away from her. Morgan forced a smile past her disappointment. "Great. I'll be down in twenty minutes or so."

He nodded with satisfaction, then strode to the door without looking back. " 'Twill be a good thing to have an early start this day." Before Morgan could blink he was gone.

Well, not only was Alasdair not interested in her, he wanted to go home *tout de suite*. Could anyone blame him?

That's what she got for not only turning down the best offer she'd had in a long time but reminding Alasdair of the love he'd left behind.

Morgan thought about the beautiful Fenella and kicked her suitcase hard. It hurt more than she'd thought it would, and she yelped in pain. She hopped on one foot, cradling her wounded toe, then tripped over her discarded sweater and fell on her rump.

Morgan contemplated a crack in the ceiling from where she lay sprawled on the floor. Could she blame Alasdair for not being interested in her? Not really—especially when his heart was held by a dead beauty. Whether Fenella had been dead seven minutes or seven centuries was immaterial—Alasdair clearly would love her forever.

Morgan closed her eyes and wished that one day she would find a man who could do the same.

A man just like Alasdair MacAulay.

Alasdair remained distant the entire day. He sat with his arms folded across his chest as they drove, clearly focused on where he wanted to be. They all seemed to pick up on his desire to get to Lewis ASAP. It was overcast and bone-chillingly damp, but every time Blake put on the heater, the little car's windows fogged up.

So they bundled up in anoraks, shoved their hands in their pockets, and put up with it. Morgan wished they had a thermos of something warm.

There wasn't a lot of conversation in the Micra that morning. They passed Dunstaffnage Castle, where Alasdair had said the Stone of Scone had been sealed into the walls, but Blake zoomed right by. Morgan pressed her nose against the window glass and tried to catch a glimpse, but no luck.

They made Fort William by lunch and grabbed a sandwich there. Alasdair looked to the hills and the brooding skies, apparently unaware of what he ate. He stared at gas stations and traffic lights, restaurants and apartment buildings, his brow furrowed, but he never said a word.

His lips drew to a thin line as the road narrowed to two lanes once more and the hills rose high on either side. Morgan, in contrast, was awestruck by her surroundings. The scenery was spectacular in the Great Glen and would have been more so in sunlight.

Silvery water stretched beside the road on one side, and green-clad hills rose sharply on the other. Eagles circled high overhead and signs marked hiking trails. Morgan was amazed to find such an expanse of wilderness in a land that had been occupied for at least two millennia.

But Blake drove up the glen at purposeful speed.

It was teatime when they reached the coast, and Justine was trying to negotiate a stretch-and-pee break. Morgan took one look at Eilean Donan Castle and knew they had to stop. It was picture-postcard perfect, and when she chimed in, Blake reluctantly conceded.

Eilean Donan Castle occupied a small island in a narrow bay stretching eastward from the sea. The loch was as still as a dark mirror, the green-dappled highlands rose majestically around and behind the restored castle. The skies had cleared as they drove west, and now only a scattering of fat clouds drifted across the azure sky, their ends tinged with the gold of the descending sun.

The hills stretching off into the distance, one behind the other, made it look as though Scotland went on forever. The seaweed washing against the retaining walls, though, was evidence that the Atlantic Ocean was just beyond the next curve.

The tide was in when they arrived, the water high on the narrow causeway that curved out to the castle gates. The castle nearly filled the island, its high walls made of old stone. Blake parked the Micra, and the sisters practically dragged the men out to tour the castle.

Morgan was sure Alasdair would remember this place—he must have passed it centuries ago. Maybe here she could convince him of the truth.

Or at least get him to talk again.

"Do you know this place?" she asked the grim highlander. "Have you been here before?"

Alasdair shook his head.

"But we're quite close to Skye now. You must have come this way when you followed Robert the Bruce."

"We crossed to Skye and thence to the mainland near Loch Alsh," he supplied tightly.

"That *is* Loch Alsh," Morgan told him, indicating the lake to their right. Alasdair frowned and studied the hills.

He said no more, but his scowl deepened as they strode

toward the castle. Blake paid the admission, much to Alasdair's confusion.

"This is a toll?"

"No, just an admission charge."

Morgan wasn't surprised that Blake's explanation seemed to make no sense to Alasdair. She flipped through a guidebook and quickly discovered why he didn't know this place.

It hadn't been here.

"I do not understand," Alasdair muttered beside her. "What is this admission charge if not a toll?"

"Well, it's a museum, filled with things from the castle and the people who lived here, and you pay to see it."

"They show their belongings for a fee?" The highlander frowned. "Is this not a military keep? Loch Alsh is a strategic site."

"No." Morgan shook her head. "It must be a folly."

He didn't look any less confused.

"That's what they call things people built for fun," Morgan explained. "Mostly around the turn of the century. There's a house shaped like a pineapple somewhere in England and other places like that." This didn't seem to clarify anything for Alasdair, so Morgan indicated the paragraph in her book.

"See? It says here that the original keep was destroyed hundreds of years ago and no one knew what it looked like. A laird in the early twentieth century had a dream of his forebears in the castle and when he woke up, he sketched plans of the keep of his dream."

Morgan scanned ahead in the text. "Then he had it built, at considerable expense, claiming it was a perfect reproduction of what had stood here."

Alasdair snorted. "Who would know?"

"Exactly! But it says that his family actually lived here. Look." Morgan tapped the glass of a display case. "There are some of his wife's calling cards and the silver case for them."

Alasdair peered at the display, looking no less mystified. "What are these calling cards?"

"It was a Victorian thing. From the time of the reign of the English queen Victoria." Morgan glared pointedly at Alasdair, daring him to acknowledge that he had never heard of the dowager queen, but he steadfastly ignored her.

But she knew he was listening. "When you visited someone and they weren't home, you left a card with the staff so they knew who had come." Morgan saw Alasdair's doubtful expression and wondered whether he was starting to give credence to her theory.

"It went out of style in the 1920s," she added deliberately, watching his reaction carefully.

Alasdair blinked, then his gaze locked on her own. His eyes were a potent sapphire, so Morgan knew she had his attention. "1920s?"

Morgan didn't even blink. "The years between 1920 and 1930 A.D."

Alasdair inhaled sharply and straightened.

"That would be nineteen hundred and twenty years since the birth of Christ," Morgan added deliberately.

Alasdair looked about with a slight air of panic as his lips drew to a thin line. "I know naught of this 1920s, and in truth it matters little," he said, his voice tight. "I wish only to be home with all haste."

"I know," Morgan said softly. "But I don't think it's going to be that easy."

At that, the highlander spun away, his frustration more than clear.

They rounded the curve at Kyle of Lochalsh, and it became clear that the hills in the distance were actually on the Isle of Skye rising in the west. They crossed the bridge to Skye as the sun was setting in orange splendor, then passed into the shadow of the island itself as the road curved along its eastern flank. The tops of the hills glowed with the sun's last rays, while the mainland to the east was silhouetted against the first stars.

The cows were coming home, welcoming golden light spilled from kitchen windows glimpsed along the way, white sails were furled in the ships bobbing at anchor far below. Road signs were posted in both Gaelic and English, and Morgan felt the difference in atmosphere as soon as the Micra's tires touched the island.

Skye was magical, a home for fairy tales if ever there had been one. They passed mountain bikers loaded with panniers and backpackers who waved cheerfully. Bed-and-breakfast signs swung in the wind, great red hairy highland cows chewed methodically at the roadside. There were vast stretches of wild forest, and fabulously healthy roses entwined the fence posts.

The awesome power of Skye's twilight made all things possible. Morgan looked to Alasdair and found him watching her. Something had eased in his features, and she knew he felt more at home here than he had on the mainland.

And Morgan understood, because she felt the same way.

Just as she instinctively guessed that the feeling would get stronger the farther they traveled.

The next morning they caught the first ferry from Uig on the northwest tip of Skye. Alasdair's anxiety had touched them all, and they had barely taken the time to look around Skye, despite its beauty.

Alasdair was grim and silent again. Although they had shared a room once again the night before, he had not so much as spoken to Morgan. When she fell asleep, Alasdair was sitting at the window, staring at the myriad lights of the idyllic town of Portree.

In the morning he was in exactly the same position. He was obviously coming to terms with what had happened to him, and Morgan was content to leave him alone to do that.

Even if she didn't like how somber he had become.

His stoic expression didn't change as the ferry came chugging around the point of the island. Steam poured from its red stack, the blast of its horn echoed in the quiet bay. It was a car ferry, a boat of considerable size—obviously something Alasdair would never have seen before.

She noticed only the way his lips tightened.

As the ferry eased into its slip, dozens of car engines could be heard starting up. Ropes were tossed and metal ramps clanged into position. Foot passengers streamed ashore, bikers pedaled away, and a steady stream of cars drove off into the distance.

Just a few minutes after the ferry's arrival, a short man with a heavily lined face took up his position in the middle of the loading ramp. Morgan had seen him pacing the length of the queue while the ferry disgorged its incoming passengers.

He pointed to the first car in the line and beckoned.

And the loading began. Blake drove forward when the Micra was summoned, and Morgan saw that the passenger decks of the ferry wrapped around the car bay in a big U. The vehicles were nestled in the center, just below the waterline, and the little man was obviously calculating and balancing the load as he proceeded.

In fact, they had to all get out of the car so that Blake could tuck it tightly enough into the corner for the man's satisfaction.

"Heavy morning," he offered gruffly by way of explanation and then ducked off to wave a tractor trailer into position.

"They don't waste an inch," Justine added, her approval of such organization evident in her tone.

Alasdair scanned the ferry with narrowed eyes, his gaze lingering on pulleys and gears. He said nothing at all, and Morgan wished she could think of something that would reassure him.

But he was so silent that she couldn't think of a way to start a conversation.

They all went up to the deck to get out of the way and continued to watch the loading from that bird's-eye view. Morgan was astonished as three tractor trailers were parked across the width of the ferry with only inches between them. One was labeled a greengrocer's truck, one was loaded with roof trusses, and the third was a tanker of oil.

"They must have to bring everything in," Justine murmured.

"We're supposed to leave in six minutes," Blake added. Everyone looked simultaneously at the long line snaking along the dock and road. Morgan eyed the waiting vehicles and couldn't believe the man in charge would manage to get them all in, let alone on schedule.

Justine's thoughts obviously took the same direction. "There's not another ferry until this afternoon. Those people aren't going to be very happy when they don't get on."

"Good thing we made a reservation last night and came early," Blake concurred.

The loading expert indicated a car pulling a camping trailer and guided the driver to park it under the wings of the passenger deck at an angle. Another one was parked on the opposite side, two rows of individual cars were waved in rapidly to fill the space in between. Passengers scurried to get out of their cars while they could still escape.

Vans went behind the cars, a bakery truck, a good twenty bikers were dispatched to lock their mountain bikes around the perimeter. Only two Volkswagen vans remained on the dock.

"There's only room for one," Blake declared.

But the man wasn't going to give up that easily. The first van had to move back and forth seven times before he was satisfied with the angle. When he pointed to the second one, Blake shook his head.

"No way."

But the little man had obviously been doing this job for a long time. The last van ended up parked horizontally across the dock, with what appeared to be room to spare.

The loading dock rose with a creak and clanged into its locked vertical position. The loading expert nodded satisfaction and Morgan almost wanted to give him a round of applause. The ferry's engines rumbled underfoot, the ship vibrated, ropes were cast off, and they eased away from the dock.

Blake glanced at his watch and nodded his approval. "Right on time."

"Amazing." Morgan turned to Alasdair, only to find that he was gone. With the noise of the engines, she hadn't even heard him leave.

She excused herself and darted up the stairs, guessing that he wouldn't have gone into either the restaurant or the lounge. Morgan made her way to the front of the ferry, where the wind was already whipping at the few stalwart souls standing there and was rewarded by a glimpse of plaid.

She ducked around the corner and was buffeted by the wind coming off the sea. Alasdair stood with his hands braced on the rail, his feet planted firmly on the deck. His hair blew back from his face, his expression was uncompromising, and he stared into the fathomless silver blue arrayed before them.

He looked superbly alone, isolated from everything and everyone around him. The sight of him there, gold and red, every vibrant line of him such a contrast to the cold white metal of the ferry and the relentless gray of the sea, was the epitome of loneliness.

And Alasdair *was* alone, more alone than Morgan could ever imagine, a man lost from his own time, a man separated by centuries from everything he held dear.

Maybe she should paint him like this, Morgan thought before she could stop herself. The idea made a hard lump rise in her throat and she almost turned away. Morgan told herself she didn't want to intrude, but she knew that the strength of her compassion for the highlander's plight had startled her.

But Alasdair turned as though he had known all along that she stood there. The roar of the wind in her ears was so loud that Morgan knew he couldn't have heard her.

" 'Tis a powerful witchery you summon here," he finally said, though his voice was strained. Morgan heard a seed of doubt in his tone. "There was no need for such a show of wizardry."

"It's not magic, Alasdair." Morgan shook her head. "It seems like magic to me sometimes, but it's not. Just the marvels of modern engineering."

Alasdair looked to the sea again and his brows drew tightly together. "I fear, my lady"—he admitted so softly that Morgan had to strain to catch his words—"I fear that I have made a grievous error."

Morgan chewed her lip and didn't know what to do other than listen.

Alasdair took a shuddering breath. "I fear I erred in leaving my son, seven years past." He swallowed but said no more.

The confidence he had exuded since they first met had ebbed. Morgan couldn't stand to see this proud man defeated, and she quickly stepped forward, wanting only to make things right. "We'll figure it out. Things that are muddled up can always be sorted out somehow or other."

Alasdair looked dubious, but Morgan nodded with authority. "Trust me. I know."

A fleeting smile curved his lips, and the heat of his hand closed over her own. His thumb slid across Morgan's knuckles. "You do have a talent for finding a muddle and making it your own, my lady," he murmured, and Morgan's breath caught at the affectionate undercurrent in his tone.

It made her heart beat faster. "You couldn't have known, you know," she said, in a rush to reassure him. "It's not as though this kind of thing happens to people all the time. *I* wouldn't have believed it."

Alasdair flicked a fierce glance her way. "And still 'tis naught but a fear. I will know when I stand upon my own soil and see what has been wrought." His words echoed with resolve. "I will *know* the truth when I am home."

And Morgan ached at how hard the truth would be for him. Her grip tightened slightly on his arm in sympathy, but Alasdair glared down at her.

Morgan thought she saw a shimmer of tears in his eyes. "Do you consider me a feckless fool to believe only what I see with my own eyes?" he demanded defensively.

Morgan shook her head and smiled that he could even imagine such a thing. "No."

Far from it. Morgan thought Alasdair was just plain wonderful.

The simple truth flooded Morgan's heart as she held his steady gaze. Alasdair was the kind of man she'd always longed to find, the kind of man who took her weaknesses in stride and savored her strengths. There were times when he seemed to find Morgan as fascinating as she found him.

Even more important, he was the kind of man a woman could count on.

But he was a man whose heart was already claimed. Alasdair would never be happy so long as his obligations were seven centuries away.

That made Morgan suddenly want to cry, even if she didn't want to think about exactly why.

Alasdair stared into her eyes as though he couldn't look away, and Morgan wondered how much he saw. His grip tightened on her hand, as though he would reassure *her*, and her tears welled up. She stared back at him wordlessly for a long moment, then Alasdair pulled her closer, a silent plea in his eyes.

He was alone, but he didn't want to be. Morgan couldn't have denied him the comfort of a human touch. And there was nowhere else she'd rather be than here with him.

Alasdair tucked Morgan between himself and the ferry's rail, the scent of his skin rising to embrace her. Her back was against his broad chest, and Morgan trembled slightly with the power of this man's effect upon her.

"You will be cold," Alasdair murmured in her ear and wrapped his arms around her waist, folding her against his warmth. Morgan leaned back against him as they silently stared out to sea together.

And she could only hope that Alasdair was unaware of the two warm tears that meandered down her cold cheeks.

Chapter 14

LEWIS WAS STARKLY different from Skye, primal and harsh. The hills were lower, the wind was colder, the vegetation sparse. The icy bite of the north wind mingled with the tang of the sea, the colors that greeted Alasdair's eye were scrubbed to clean blues and greens.

Yet the raw, powerful curves of the land were compelling.

Alasdair felt recognition of his home stir within his very bones from first glimpse of land. He clenched the rail of the ferry as the craft slid into port and felt his anticipation rise. Perhaps the veil of Faerie was thinner here, perhaps he but drew near a critical portal.

Whatever the case, Alasdair's conviction grew with every passing moment that he was truly coming home. Not only had Blake Advisor kept his word, but Morgaine's tale of traveling through the centuries was certainly wrong.

The town Blake called Tarbert might be jostling with unfamiliar structures, but still Alasdair knew this land. The faces of the locals waiting at the landing were lined, their clothes sturdy and plain, but there was a glint of merriment in more than one fiercely blue eye. Life was challenging here, a feat for the strong alone, and those who survived oft had a powerful sense of humor.

The Micra lunged from ferry to road as though it too was

intent on seeing the highlander finally home. Alasdair leaned
forward in the seat and anxiously directed Blake across the
island. The glossy black roads followed the lines of tracks he
had walked with his sheep during days that seemed an eternity
ago.

But every curve was yet familiar.

'Twas the towns that revealed Morgaine's hand, for though
they were sited as Alasdair recalled, they bore little resemblance to the places he knew. The land, though, the land, had
escaped her magical touch and was achingly familiar on all
sides. Alasdair anticipated every mount, every valley and its
view, his excitement rising with each passing moment.

He was nearly home. His heart began to pound with anticipation. How tall was his son? What tales had his gran to tell?
How fared the cottage, the garden, the sheep? When Alasdair
glimpsed the standing stones in the distance, his heart nearly
stopped.

They alone were precisely as he recalled.

"There," he breathed to Morgaine, hating the way his finger trembled when he indicated the stones ahead. "There, my
lady, are your standing stones, as ever they have been."

Morgaine looked at the enigmatic circle, then back at Alas-
dair, a gleam of anticipation lurking in her magnificent eyes.
Her fingers closed over his and squeezed, the gesture making
Alasdair's heart leap.

Nay, 'twas only that he was nearly home. Indeed, his humble crofter's cottage lingered just over the far hill. Seven years
fell away, and Alasdair remembered pausing on this very rise
to look back one last time.

He would not consider that it might truly have been his last
time. Only now did Alasdair question the nobility of that impulse, only now did he wonder what he might have sacrificed
by following Robert the Bruce.

Had he the chance to do it all again, Alasdair vowed silently, he would not stay away those seven years. Countless
opportunities there had been to turn back and go home, but
he had pressed on, determined to see the quest fulfilled, determined to prove his honor beyond doubt.

One of those expanses of black was spread before standing

stones—as it was not in the world Alasdair knew—and half a dozen chariots parked there. Alasdair refused to accept the incongruity and directed Blake determinedly down a road just beyond.

They neared the portal between their worlds, he knew it as surely as he knew his own name. When he was safely home, Alasdair vowed silently, he would set his many wrongs to right.

The road turned to gravel within moments and narrowed with familiar ease. The surface became rougher and the Micra bounced along at much slower speed. A light drizzle of rain had begun and a mist obscured the road ahead, a road that Alasdair knew as well as the back of his own hand.

A heavy mist closed the space before them, a space where Alasdair knew the hills framed a view of the endless sea. And here, he now understood, was the place Morgaine's world touched his own.

At least, it did in this moment. Alasdair recalled well enough from his gran's tales that the portals to the world of Faerie were oft moved capriciously by immortal denizens.

But now, 'twas here.

One lone sheep glanced toward the Micra, the expression on her dark face almost knowing. Then she turned and skipped nervously along the road, ahead of the chariot. The mist swallowed her whole and she disappeared with nary a bleat.

Alasdair's mouth went dry. She was gone, home to his world.

As he soon would follow.

When they bounced out of a particularly deep rut, Blake stopped the Micra and looked over his shoulder. "Are you sure this is the right way? It doesn't look as though anyone has passed here for a while."

"Other than the sheep," Justine commented.

Alasdair would have expected naught else for a portal between the worlds. " 'Tis the right way, but I would walk this last."

As soon as the words left his lips, Alasdair knew he had made the right choice. He would return as he had left, upon his own two feet and not in some magical chariot.

He would simply walk through the mist and arrive home. Tales of those lost to Faerie returning home years after their disappearance flooded into his mind, and for the first time Alasdair feared what he would find at his own hearth.

Had a year passed for every day he had been in Morgaine's domain? Would Angus have grown to manhood? Would his gran have passed away without knowing where he had gone?

Alasdair could linger no longer without knowing the whole of the truth. Justine let him out into the rain and Alasdair suddenly wished he had his great woolen cloak. It had served him well for many a winter and he regretted casting it aside in that exploration of Edinburgh's great keep.

"I'll come with you," Morgaine declared with quiet determination.

The offer surprised Alasdair, though no less than the enchantress's resolve. "My lady, there is no need."

"Of course there is. You can't go alone."

Alasdair frowned and lowered his voice to reason with her as she came to stand beside him. "But should we pass into the land of mortals, you could well share the fate I have just survived. You could be lost from your home."

She smiled sadly and tapped a fingertip on his chest. "Surely Morgaine le Fee will only have to click the heels of her ruby slippers together to come back?"

There was a skepticism in her tone, but Alasdair refused to think again about her fantastical tale. She spoke aright about the extent of her powers, as well he knew, and truth be told, he welcomed the promise of her companionship.

For when the moment stood before him, Alasdair was not so eager to be rid of Morgaine le Fee's enchanting company. He would miss the tiny sorceress, with her intriguing blend of softness and strength, her determination and her vulnerability. Aye, he would continue in her presence for but a few moments longer before leaving her side for all time.

'Twas a weakness, no doubt of that, but one she seemed to share.

Alasdair nodded assent and folded Morgaine's hand within his own, marveling that she permitted him to touch her thus.

Morgaine nodded to Justine and Blake, and the Micra hummed once more.

"We'll find a bed-and-breadfast," Blake called cheerfully. "Meet you back here in an hour?"

An hour. Alasdair had one hour left with the enchantress before their ways parted for all time. Clearly, they believed 'twould be more than time enough for her to see him home. Alasdair's heart began to hammer in his chest.

But one hour and he would be before his very own hearth. Never would he have believed that such a fate would hold such allure. It seemed a distant dream to recall his impatience to shake the dirt of Lewis from his boots. Morgaine waved and the Micra backed down the road, spewing gravel in every direction.

Within a matter of moments, the silence Alasdair so loved pressed against his ears. The gravel faded to naught and Lewis's low grass was springy beneath his boots. He took a deep breath of the salt-laden air, caught the scent of sheep and freshly turned earth behind the swirling curtain of fog.

Home.

And Morgaine had insisted upon not only returning him but on sharing the moment with him. Alasdair was determined to show her the fullness of both his hospitality and his gratitude. Alasdair squeezed her fingers and smiled down at the uncertainty lingering in her wondrous eyes.

"Come, Morgaine," he invited with all the grace of a courtier. "Come with me and meet my son."

And with a spring in his step, Alasdair strode into the swirling mist, confident of what lay ahead.

They walked through the mist, the silence surrounding them enough to make Morgan lose what little sense of time she had. The mist was thick and white, a faint shimmer of tiny raindrops gradually gathered on her anorak. Morgan felt as though she were walking in the clouds.

An occasional sheep appeared before them, then fled in panic once it glimpsed them. Their footsteps made the only sound, until Morgan caught the steady rhythm of the sea crashing on the coast far, far ahead.

Alasdair strode with confidence, the road obviously familiar to him and the fog no obstacle to navigation at all. Morgan watched him out of the corner of her eye and caught the bright gleam of anticipation in his eyes.

If she hadn't been dreading what Alasdair would find, she might have enjoyed the walk. It felt as though they had left the world she knew and wandered in some magical realm.

Clearly Alasdair had come to the same conclusion. There was a definite spring in his step. She hoped they had a long way to go before he was disappointed, then called herself a chicken.

"I shall tell you a story, my lady," he offered, and Morgan was glad of a way to keep from thinking too much about what lay ahead.

"That would be wonderful."

"Aye, 'tis not a ditty, this one, but a fair tale nonetheless. Once upon a time, there was a smith of fair talent, who worked long and hard at his craft. He had a son, a tall young lad, who had a good interest in the smithy, and all was good within his world.

"Until one day, his son took ill. At first the smith thought little of it, for children oft catch a chill and recover with speed. But this sickness lingered on and on. The boy faded to a shadow of his former self, and the smith grew increasingly worried. He sought counsel from those in the town, without success, until the elder came and looked within his cottage with wise, wise eyes.

"The elder took the smith aside once he had had a good look at the lad and shook his head with dismay. 'I fear to tell you the truth, but 'twill out in the end. 'Tis not your son lying in his own bed, but a Faerie changeling. The fair folk have stolen your boy for their own.'

"Now, the smith was skeptical of this tale, for the lad looked exactly as his own blood, even though his flesh turned more yellow by the day. So the elder described a test to the smith that would prove the Faerie's identity. Eager to dispute this whimsy, the smith gathered the materials bidden.

"Within his cottage, the smith laid out the dozens of broken eggshells he had brought and greeted the one who appeared to be his son as though naught was amiss. Then, with great solemnity, he filled the eggshells from the water bucket, two at a time, and carried them as though they were fearsomely heavy to set before the fire. The boy watched with fascination.

"The smith continued thus, two shells by two, until the one he thought to be his son shouted with laughter. 'Never in all of my eight hundred years have I seen the like of that. Are you mad, father smith?'

"And a great fear seized the smith's heart, for now he knew the elder had spoken aright. The next morn, he raced to the elder with the news and demanded to know what he must do to rid himself of the changeling and retrieve his son.

"The elder thought long and hard, then he counseled the smith, 'Go to your home and light a large fire immediately beside the lad's bed. Make the fire burn bright and high, and when he asks you what the blaze is for, seize him and cast him into the flames. The changeling will flee screaming through the cottage roof, as surely as a wisp of smoke.'

"The smith went home and followed the elder's dictate. He lit the fire, he made it burn bright and high. The changeling asked what the blaze was for and the smith immediately seized him and cast him into the flames. And with an eerie scream, the Faerie changed to its own dark self and fled the cottage through the roof.

"Now, although this was all well and good, the smith yet wanted his own son back. He went back to the elder to ask advice, and after some thought, the elder presented him with a plan. 'On the night of the full moon,' he said solemnly, 'the Faerie folk do gather at that round green hill for their dancing. The barriers are thin between their world and ours at such times and 'tis then that you must seek your son.

" 'Take a Bible with yourself, a dirk and a crowing cock, and do exactly as I bid you, lest you never be seen on this earth again. There will be much dancing and merriment, but do not be distracted from your course. Hold the Bible high to protect yourself and go to the opening in the side of the hill from which the light will spill. Before you enter, stick your dirk into the threshold that you will not be trapped inside.'

"The old man gripped the smith's arm. 'When first you

enter, you will see your son. You will be asked why you are there and say simply that you will not leave without your son. Keep your wits about you, master smith, and you will be safely home at the dawn with your very own son.'

"Well, the smith took this counsel quite seriously and was determined not to fail. On the night of the next full moon, he gathered up his Bible, his dirk and a cock that crowed louder than most and made his way to the hill.

"True to the elder's words, there was a tremendous celebration to be heard. A golden light spilled through a doorway in the side of the hill where the smith knew there usually was none. He could hear much laughter within, as well as fey music, but he held his Bible high and approached the door. Before entering, he stuck his dirk in the threshold, then stepped over its hilt.

"He had only a glimpse of the Faeries' wild dance before he saw his own son, working at a golden forge. The smith caught his breath in the same moment that the Faerie folk spied him. The festivities halted suddenly and all manner of enchanted eyes turned upon him. 'What do you want here, master smith?' they called mockingly. 'I want my son,' the smith replied. 'And I will not go without him.'

"The Faeries laughed merrily at this bold assertion, for they knew well enough that both smith and son were on the Faeries' own soil. 'Twas they who would decide who might stay and who might leave, and none other.

"But their laughter awakened the slumbering cock, who mistook the bright Faerie lights for the sun. The cock leapt to the smith's shoulder, flapped his wings, and set to crowing. The sound was overloud beneath the hill, but naught would silence the cock. The Faeries grew agitated, but the cock crowed on and on.

"Finally, and with much gnashing of teeth, the angry Faeries cast the smith and his son and their cock out of the hill. They flung his dirk after him—the iron of the blade being as poison to them—and the doorway in the hill closed as though it had never been.

"And when father and son crossed the threshold of their

own humble cottage, the dawn was just breaking over the horizon. They lived long and happily together, the son having learned much in the Faerie smithy that he shared with his sire, and they prospered in their trade as few others do.''

The mist lifted ever so slightly once Alasdair finished his tale, and Morgan could see the silhouettes of hills on either side of them. Alasdair began to walk more quickly, his excitement obvious.

She knew it hadn't been an accident that his story had been about man and son reunited, and she ached at what she knew he would find ahead. The sound of the sea became louder as they rounded a corner, and the wind off the ocean effortlessly disposed of the fog.

A verdant valley spread before them, spilling from the hills high to the right and flowing into the sea to Morgan's left. It was touched by dew, a sparkling brook cut through the pasture on its merry dance to the sea. The fields were vivid green and spotted with hundreds of wandering sheep. It was a scene of pastoral perfection.

Much to Morgan's surprise after their walk, a glossy paved road snaked over the crest of the hills high above and wound its way to a picture-perfect gabled house. A hedge of roses grew all around the dwelling, a sign creaked in the wind before it: ADAIRA MACLEOD'S ROSE COTTAGE BED-AND-BREAKFAST.

The house had a porch all across the front and wrapped around the sides, a deep porch with plenty of room to sit even when it rained. The view of the ocean must be spectacular, Morgan guessed, even as her gaze danced over every lace-adorned window.

It was only after admiring the house that Morgan noticed the ruined walls of a single crofter's cottage beyond it to the left. She had seen these small cottages throughout Scotland, their heavy walls made of mortared stone, their thatched roofs slightly curved, with smoke coiling from the chimney. But this one had almost crumbled into the earth.

It was clearly abandoned.

Before Morgan could say anything, Alasdair was running

across the pasture. She suddenly knew exactly who had abandoned this cottage.

"Alasdair, wait!"

But he wasn't waiting for anything. To Morgan's astonishment, he continued to climb higher, ignoring the ruined cottage. He fell to his knees behind the bed-and-breakfast, where the sparkling stream burst out of the hills to meander across the valley. As Morgan watched, he pushed aside the vegetation with increasing anxiety.

He was looking for some vestige of his home. Of course, it would have eroded to nothing in seven hundred years. Yet even though Morgan had known all along that he wouldn't find his cottage, watching Alasdair claw desperately at the dirt tore her heart out.

The ruins of the other cottage were grayed and broken, all but the last foot of the outer walls gone. The remaining stones were rounded and worn by the weather, choked with moss, nearly swallowed by the long, waving grass.

A single purple foxglove bloomed in one corner, sheltered from the wind and in colorful contrast to the ruins around it. The house would have been dark inside, Morgan guessed, with few windows. But the walls would have been painted white and the peat fire would have made it cozy and warm. Now, the sunlight played on what had been the floor, and where that flower grew a stool or chest might have sat.

But it was all reverting to dust.

As Alasdair's home already had.

Morgan slowly followed the highlander, knowing that this would not be an easy truth for him to accept. As she watched, Alasdair spun wildly where he stood. He scanned the hills, the valley, the view of the sea.

The color drained from his face, and Morgan knew that this was precisely where his home had stood.

"Gone," he murmured when Morgan reached his side, as though he couldn't comprehend that fact. Then Alasdair turned tormented eyes to her, and his usual bold tone faltered.

"Morgaine, I have lost my son."

And the tears Morgan had glimpsed earlier spilled down his cheeks. He sank to the ground and stared across the valley, oblivious to his own tears, consumed by the magnitude of his loss.

Morgan didn't know what to do. Alasdair's grief was tangible, and nothing she could say would ease the sting of the truth.

She couldn't do a single thing to fix this.

Or could she?

"I left him when I should never have done so," Alasdair admitted gruffly, the words obviously not coming easily from his lips. "In my zeal to protect our honor, in my quest to set to rest the lies told of me, I failed my only son."

He looked at Morgan and her heart twisted at his despair. "I lost him as surely as if I had denied that he was blood of my own blood."

Morgan wasn't quite ready to let Alasdair be so hard on himself. It couldn't have been easy for him to see his lost love every time he looked at his child, and she couldn't really blame him for leaving. Morgan hunkered down beside Alasdair and touched his arm.

"You did what you thought was right," she said gently, but when Alasdair turned to her his eyes blazed dangerously.

"Right? To leave my son alone for seven years was *right*? To leave my gran to raise another bairn at her age was *right*? To take the dare of a wee witch was *right*?"

He shook his head savagely and bounded to his feet, gesturing wildly in the air. His voice roared through the valley at such volume that sheep skittered away.

"Nay, I acted on impulse and impulse alone, even knowing that impulse was a poor master!"

His temper spent, Alasdair hung his head and his words rumbled low. "I believed Angus in good care and thought no more upon it. Now, both he and I must pay the price of my folly."

Alasdair dropped his hands to rest on his hips, and his eyes narrowed as he eyed the valley. "Indeed, if you speak aright, Angus has already paid whatever price was due from him." His anger faded, leaving him looking more defeated than Morgan had ever seen him.

"My son," he said softly, "has long been dead. He must

have passed from this world believing that I cared naught for him. And that is the worst travesty of all.''

Alasdair's eyes clouded with tears once more, and he turned his back on Morgan. When he spoke, his words were strained. '' 'Twas some legacy I saw fit to leave him.''

And Alasdair MacAulay pressed his fingertips to his brow.

''Now, wait just a moment.'' Morgan strode to his side. Alasdair didn't move or otherwise acknowledge her presence. ''You couldn't have known that whatever you did would send you forward in time. I mean, how many people zip across seven centuries? It doesn't exactly happen every day!''

To Morgan's relief, Alasdair sent a curious glance her way before continuing his stoic scrutiny of his toes. ''I do not even know what fate befell him,'' he mumbled. ''How many years did he live? Did he wed? Did he have sons of his own?'' He swallowed. ''Did he ever forgive me for what I had done?''

Morgan touched Alasdair's arm. ''I don't think you did anything so bad as that. Maybe we could find out what happened to Angus.''

Now she had his attention. ''You can do this?''

Morgan flushed at the intensity of his gaze. ''Well, there have to be record books. It will probably take some digging to go back that far . . .''

''I cannot read,'' Alasdair reminded her in a low voice.

''I know,'' Morgan said softly. She tugged on his arm until he looked at her once more. ''But I can. We can do this together.''

Alasdair studied her for a long moment, then shook his head in disbelief. His question was gentle. ''Why do you aid me? You have brought me home and shown me with my own eyes that your tale is of the truth. Why aid me further?''

Morgan's heart stopped cold, then lunged forward at a breakneck pace. She stared back at Alasdair, then swallowed carefully. ''I guess because I can understand how you feel,'' she said finally, then turned away before Alasdair saw the truth in her eyes.

Because Morgan had just lied to him.

Maybe she *could* understand how he felt, maybe she felt

sorry for him in this predicament, but the real reason she wanted to help him was much, much simpler.

Morgan was in love with Alasdair MacAulay.

She wanted to see him happy more than anything else in the world. Unfortunately, the only way to do that was to send Alasdair back to his son, his gran, his home.

And the vivid memory of the dead woman who held his heart in thrall. It was a particularly bitter pill, but Morgan swallowed it deliberately. Then she linked her arm through Alasdair's.

"Come on," she urged gently. "We can stay at this little place. It's nice and close to your home. Let's go and meet Blake, as we planned, then come back here. Then we can start looking for those records." She squeezed Alasdair's hand. "That way you'll know what happened to Angus."

Alasdair heaved a ragged sigh. " 'Twould ease my mind to know he lived long, even in my absence."

And Morgan hoped heartily that that was the case.

Finding these records Morgaine claimed were readily available was not so easy as Alasdair had understood. 'Twas frustrating to be able to do little himself, for not only could Alasdair not read, he could not fathom the workings of the world that Morgaine occupied with such ease.

They spent the rest of the day crossing the island, fruitlessly to Alasdair's mind, rushing from here to there with naught to show for it. Blake complained heartily about people not having phones—whatever that meant—but he went as Morgaine bade him.

They returned to the inn when the sky was dark, their bellies full of sausage that Justine proclaimed too greasy but Alasdair found comforting in its familiarity. Though he was bone-tired, there was not a chance that he would sleep anytime soon.

Alasdair sat on the broad steps before the inn's door, propped his elbows on his knees, and stared at the darkening sky. The view was so familiar to him—with the road and the parked cars behind him, the valley was spread out at his toes as always it had been. Indeed, if he ignored the porch, Alasdair would never have imagined he was anywhere but home.

'Twas impossible to believe that everything he knew, everything he loved, had been swept away from him for all eternity, and that in the blink of an eye. If the evidence had not surrounded him on all sides, Alasdair knew that he would not have believed it.

But he had no choice. His home was gone as surely as if it had never been. He watched the silvery crescent of the moon launch across the sky, ached with the familiarity of the moonbeams' dancing on the sea, and wished fervently to find these records.

Alasdair wanted only to know the truth.

'Twas then that he became aware that he was not alone.

He glanced back and Morgaine smiled tentatively from the shadows by the door. She was a marvel, even more so now that he knew she was as mortal as he. The compassion that so awed Alasdair shone in her eyes, and he knew that she understood how deeply this day's events had pained him.

And she respected his disappointment enough that she did not force him to talk about it.

Morgaine sat down beside him when Alasdair moved aside in silent invitation. She mimicked his pose and heaved a sigh that doubtless was for his benefit alone.

"I can't sleep," she complained. "Could you tell me a story?"

"We should make an exchange, my lady."

Morgaine looked up with curiosity.

"I shall tell you all the tales you desire to hear, if you grant me the chance to look upon your drawings again."

She flushed in that enchanting way. "They're not done. I don't usually show them to anyone before they're finished."

"Ah, but I have had one glance and 'twas my undoing," Alasdair confided. When he looked into her eyes, he knew 'twas not the drawings that had captured his imagination.

'Twas this woman alone.

Alasdair cleared his throat and tried to tease her. "There is wizardry in your fingers. I know it to be true."

To his delight, Morgaine smiled. "I told you, I'm just an artist."

"And I tell you, I must look upon your work again to satisfy myself that no witchery conjured them before my eyes.'' She bit her lip in hesitation, and Alasdair leaned closer, his voice turning sober. ''My lady, I would have the chance to gaze upon them with leisure. If the thought offends you, then I apologize for being so bold.''

Morgaine stared at him for a long moment, then shook her head, that beguiling flush tinting her cheeks again. ''No,'' she said huskily. ''I'm flattered that you like them.'' Her glance flicked away, then back to Alasdair. She offered her small hand with a shy smile. ''A story for another look doesn't seem to be a very fair deal.''

Alasdair captured the delicacy of her fingers within his hand and smiled down at her. ''My lady, 'tis clearly to your disadvantage, but you already have accepted my terms.''

Morgaine laughed and did not pull her hand away. Alasdair looked down at their entwined fingers. Their hands were so different, yet they fit together as if halves of a single mold.

Was there more than a witch's whimsy behind Alasdair's voyage to this woman's side?

He could not think upon it, with her perfume flooding his senses and her shoulder lightly touching his arm. So, Alasdair turned to the stars, the lady's fingers secure within his grip, and began to tell her a tale.

Chapter 15

THE LOCAL POPULATION was small, so the less critical "official" capacities of local government were jobbed out to private citizens all over the island. It was much harder than Morgan had expected to find the information they sought. With every day that passed, Alasdair seemed a little less himself. He clearly believed that he had failed his son, and not knowing what had happened to Angus was eating away at him.

But Morgan had to respect him for keeping his word to her. Alasdair declined every well-intentioned offer of a drink, giving her a significant glance when he intoned that he had made a pledge. They shared a room at the bed-and-breakfast, but the situation was far from intimate. Alasdair seemed to be deep in contemplation of what he had lost, though whenever Morgan spoke to him, he roused himself to respond.

And when he looked at the drawings his stories had inspired, he smiled with a wistfulness that tore at Morgan's heart.

Seeing him so saddened by his loss redoubled Morgan's determination to see him home and happy. And so Morgan latched on to the record quest like a dog onto a bone.

It took a week to determine that the old archival records were packed into the spare bedroom of one Frances Fergusson. Frances was among those without telephone service, and the third time that they visited to find her not at home, Morgan had had enough.

"We'll just wait," she informed Blake.

He looked dubious. "You don't even know if she's around."

"Of course we do," Justine interjected crisply. "The curtains have moved since yesterday."

"And the cats are in instead of out," Morgan added. A pair of ginger cats eyed them from one window, then set to cleaning themselves, as though people waited on the porch all the time.

Alasdair sat down on the bottom step with a *thump*, the sunlight burnishing his hair like spun gold. "Aye, Morgaine speaks aright. We shall wait."

Blake hesitated. "How are you going to let us know when you want to come home? She hasn't got a phone."

Justine slid her arm through his. "We'll come back at dinnertime," she said with a smile. "Now, let's do some exploring of our own." Her glance was smoldering, and on any other day Morgan would have smiled at the way Blake jumped to head back to the car.

She slanted a longing glance at Alasdair and admitted that she had a rare talent for falling in love with Mr. Wrong.

At least Alasdair *could* have been Mr. Right—as opposed to Matt—if he hadn't been seven hundred years older than Morgan and desperately in love with a dead woman. Morgan sat down beside him dejectedly and couldn't think of a thing to say. She didn't even have the heart to ask Alasdair for a story.

Fortunately they didn't have to wait long.

A woman came sailing over the fields where peat had been cut away in squares. She carried what looked like boards under one arm and a toolbox in the other. A floral skirt swirled above her green Wellington boots, a waxed-canvas hat was jammed down on her head. She moved with surprising speed and agility, a bouquet of purple foxgloves bobbing in her grip.

Morgan noticed that the cats stood up, their gazes fixed on the woman marching closer, and twitched their tails. This must be Frances Fergusson.

When she came closer, it was clear that the boards were really canvases. Frances was a painter. When Frances smiled, waved, and tripped over the end of her driveway, Morgan felt as though she'd found a kindred spirit.

"Well, hello!" she called from the end of the path. "You must be those people looking for the records. My neighbors said you'd been here."

Morgan and Alasdair stood up simultaneously, but Frances barely seemed to notice.

"I'm sorry, but I just had to be out when the sun was exactly right. We don't get enough of it that I can afford to be picky." She laughed, dumped the canvases in Alasdair's direction—he caught them—and peeled off her hat. Her hair was the same gingery shade as the cats' but faded with age. Her smile made Morgan smile back.

Frances stuck out her hand. "I'm Frances Fergusson."

"Morgan Lafayette and Alasdair MacAulay," Morgan contributed, shaking Frances's hand while Alasdair got a better grip on the canvases.

" 'Tis indeed a pleasure to make your acquaintance," Alasdair said nobly. Morgan wasn't surprised that he had summoned his best manners.

Frances's lips quirked as she looked at the two of them. "Well, what can I do for you?"

"We're looking for records of Alasdair's family, from the early fourteenth century."

Frances whistled. "That goes a ways back." She glanced at Alasdair. "You are certain that the MacAulays were here then?"

"Aye."

"Well, then, let's have a cup of tea—I know I could use one—and we'll set to work. No doubt you know exactly what you're looking for and will know it as soon as you see it, but I can help you get your bearings in there."

And Frances bustled past them into the house. The door was unlocked, but Morgan had little chance to think about that before one ginger cat made a run for freedom.

"Stop him!" Frances cried. With his spare hand, Alasdair managed to scoop the feline up just in time.

The cat hissed at the highlander as he was dropped back inside the house. Frances closed the screen door firmly and left the animal pacing in the foyer.

She rolled her eyes. "He got out yesterday, you know, and I had to chase him all over the island once I got home."

"But he was on the porch when we came."

"Oh, yes, he only runs for my benefit." Frances dumped her paintbox on the kitchen floor. "I have no doubt at all that he sat on the porch sunning himself until he saw me coming."

The cat meowed loudly, as though he would protest this assault on his character, and Frances shot him a warning look. "Be nice to me, Balthasar. I haven't dished up dinner yet."

When she retreated to the kitchen, the cat's ears pricked up, then he ran after her like a shot. By the time Morgan entered the kitchen, he was twining himself around Frances's ankles and purring to beat the band.

Moments later, they were settled into Frances's eclectically furnished parlor. The room was a testament to a bygone age, the walls covered with a dark and busy William Morris wallpaper and hung almost solidly with framed oil paintings of everything from Lewis landscapes to still lifes and portraits.

The furniture was simple oak, Arts and Crafts style, upholstered in burgundy leather and studded with brass tacks. A vase brimming with the purple foxgloves held court on the coffee table. One ginger cat—undoubtedly Balthasar—prowled the perimeter while the other slept in the sun streaming through the window.

Morgan immediately saw that the paintings were from the same talented hand and guessed that this was Frances's work. Alasdair fumbled with his bone china teacup and lost the battle against looking painfully out of place.

"Looking for your ancestors, are you? Well, you've come to the right place, that much is for certain." Frances passed a plate of shortbread, then dropped into a morris chair, her eyes sparkling. "Although you're probably thinking how terribly difficult it has been getting ahold of me, I have to tell you that if it weren't for me, you'd not have any records to check."

She waved one hand. "These country folk, you know, their hearts are in the right place, but they just don't *understand*.

But I spent twenty years at the library of the university—
Harold was a doctor, you know—and I know how these files
have to be taken care of.'' She wagged a finger at them both.
''Things were just rotting away. I finally had to march right
into that musty old monastery and commandeer everything
before it mildewed beyond recognition.''

Frances topped off everyone's tea and pressed the plate of
shortbread on Alasdair again. He took two.

''I just knew that I had to do *something*. My Harold was
always saying how imperative it is to give something back to
the community, so I appointed myself archivist. It seemed like
a good way to get to know some people and to keep my hand
in, you know.''

Frances laughed lightly. ''But, of course, I only meet tourists, because everyone who lives here knows exactly what happened to their forebears. They've been listening to the stories
every night in front of the fire all their blessed lives!''

Suddenly she got to her feet and drained her teacup. ''But
then, you didn't come here to listen to an old woman ramble
on about nothing. Come along. I'll show you where everything
is. Hopefully, we'll be able to narrow in on the right box
quickly enough that you don't waste years in there.'' She
darted to the door, then waved at the table. ''Bring your tea
if you like.''

Morgan did.

Alasdair brought the plate of shortbread.

The women set to work with a vengeance as soon as they
entered the room piled high with cartons. Alasdair poked at
one or two, painfully aware that there was naught he could do
to aid them. He sat glumly in the corner and ate biscuits.

He fetched tea for the women, like some child bidden to
serve their wants, and waited hopefully for some news of Angus.

It took far longer than Alasdair had hoped and granted him
some heartily unwelcome time to ponder his circumstance. He
had had more than enough of that during this past week and
had come to few conclusions about anything.

'Twas apparent that he *had* traveled through time, despite

the odds, and now found himself separated from his son and gran by some seven centuries.

As though that were not trouble enough, Alasdair had left matters half done, and he had no inkling of how to go back.

But even as he itched to know his son and to repair the long years he had spent away from home, there was a part of Alasdair that did not truly want to return. He told himself that 'twas merely a case of adjusting to something he knew he could not change, but Alasdair was far from certain that that was what lay at root of the matter.

Alasdair eyed the back of Morgaine's neck as she bent over a box. She had tied her hair back in a bundle, though a few ebony tendrils had escaped to curl against her neck.

Alasdair had a sudden urge to brush them aside with his lips. What was it about Morgaine that brought out such tenderness from deep within him? What was it about her that nigh drove him to distraction, yet made him want to ensure that all came aright in her world?

What was it about her that made him want to stay and ensure that she was happy for all of her days? For truly, Alasdair was loath to leave her. If Morgaine was not a sorceress, then the allure between them could not be due to some unearthly spell.

And that had kept Alasdair thinking all the week long.

Was there a reason he had been fairly dumped into her lap? Morgaine was unlike any other woman Alasdair had encountered, with her blend of softness and strength, her passion, her laughter, her compassion and determination to do right.

'Twas true enough that Morgaine touched Alasdair as no other woman ever had. He recalled too well his gran's conviction that there was but a single true love for each man and woman on this earth, and he could not help but wonder.

Was Morgaine the woman he was destined to love? Could it be that theirs was a match fated to be, and one that not even time could stand between?

'Twas a heady thought. Alasdair caught his breath and tried to hide his response—not that either woman was paying attention—by indulging in another biscuit. He felt his ears heat and his gaze dropped to Morgaine's legs.

Was it truly so bad to be lost in this time? Angus must have grown to manhood, married, had bairns of his own. Gran must have finally passed away, after many years of health and happiness. Would it be so foul to know that they had lived the fullness of their lives, even as he had a rare opportunity to win a woman's heart?

There was naught else to draw Alasdair home, beyond concern for his loved ones and his own sense that he had erred in leaving Angus alone. Could news from these records set his mind at ease?

Could Morgaine's compassion soothe his doubts?

For Alasdair knew that if he stayed in this time, he would bend his every effort to win the heart of his Morgaine. He would make her forget this Matthew James Reilly who had treated her so poorly, he would pledge himself to her and prove himself worthy of her affections.

Alasdair would make Morgaine happy if 'twas the last thing he did.

He crunched another biscuit with resolve. Aye, Blake would not have to send his buggering advocate after him.

The light was fading when Morgaine gave a crow of delight. She emerged from the depths of a record box with an ancient bound book and a smudge of dust across the bridge of her nose. "I think this is it!"

"Oh, that's one of those books the monks did, when they transcribed all of the old records that were crumbling away," Frances said. She glanced at Alasdair. "The monks of Newcombe Abbey."

"Aye, I know them well." These were the monks who had shown Alasdair their fine books and first tempted him to learn to write.

But Frances blinked. "Know them?" She wrinkled her nose. "The abbey closed during the Reformation. It's been gone for centuries!"

"He means he knows of them," Morgaine interjected quickly. She flushed slightly at her lie, even without looking at Alasdair, and he wondered whether Frances truly believed her.

The woman could not lie to save her very soul, he thought with mingled affection and amusement.

Frances shook her head, adjusted her glasses, and leaned over Morgaine's shoulder to examine the book. ''Well, what does it say?''

Morgaine ran a finger along the text. ''It talks about Olaf the Black, King of Man and the Isles.''

''Aye. My forebear.'' Alasdair nodded approval.

''And of them coming to settle on the west of Lewis. Then there's a list of names.''

''My goodness, where to start?'' Frances murmured.

''Look for Ismay of Mull,'' Alasdair instructed. ''She wed Ranald MacAulay and bore him a son, Angus Morgan.'' Frances glanced up with surprise, but Alasdair continued undeterred. ''That man then wed Fiona Campbell, who bore him a son . . .''

''Named Alasdair.'' Morgaine's gaze sought Alasdair's and held for a long moment. He saw that she knew full well who this Alasdair was.

Finally she moistened her lips and looked back to the text. ''He married Fenella Macdonald in 1307, and she bore him a son in 1308 named Angus.''

Alasdair could not make a sound, there was such a lump in his throat.

Morgaine swallowed with an effort. ''Fenella died in 1308, Alasdair in the storming of Edinburgh castle in 1314 while he was following Robert the Bruce.''

So, they thought him dead.

''And what of that son, Angus?'' Frances demanded cheerfully, evidently unaware of the tension in the room. ''He must have had children that led to your strain of the family.''

Morgaine ran her fingertip across the page as though she would change what the script said. When she looked up at Alasdair with a glance heavy with sympathy, he had a sudden sense that he did not want to know this truth.

''He died,'' she said softly, and Alasdair prayed his son had lived long. The sorrow in Morgaine's eyes made him fear otherwise. ''In 1315.''

Alasdair blinked, but Morgaine's expression did not change.

Angus had died, at seven years of age? Impossible!

But Morgaine's eyes did not lie.

Nor did the book she held.

A hot tide rushed through Alasdair. His son had not even grown to manhood! He shoved one hand through his hair, hating that such a fate should have befallen his only child.

Aye, he had failed the boy sorely.

"Well, then, that must be the wrong family line," Frances interjected crisply, turning back to the books. "Why, you can't be descended from people who didn't have family, now, can you? Let's look a little further . . ."

Angus had died too young.

The fault for it lay squarely in Alasdair's own camp for he had abandoned the boy. Somehow, in some way, he had to make it right. He did not know where he was going or what he was going to do when he got there, but he was seized by the imperative to move.

To *do* something immediately. His gut churned with the knowing. 'Twas his responsibility to make all come right for his child, and 'twas a duty Alasdair had left undone too long.

And clearly, whatever needed doing could not be accomplished in Frances Fergusson's cluttered abode. Alasdair could not bear to remain in its cozy comfort while wrestling with the stark reality of his failure.

He had to fix the oversight *now*.

Alasdair put down the plate of biscuits with less than his usual grace. The women looked up, and he tried to excuse himself in a civilized manner. When the words would not come, he simply bolted out of Frances's home, his pulse thundering in his ears.

He barely heard Morgaine running after him.

Morgan could barely keep up with Alasdair, let alone catch him. "Alasdair!" she cried when she stumbled on Frances's gravel path, not expecting him even to acknowledge her shout.

He looked back, and Morgan's heart twisted at his anguished expression.

But he did not stop.

And Morgan would never be able to close the yawning gap

between them. She halted and watched Alasdair make quick progress across the peat, his figure rapidly growing smaller.

Alasdair must have known that Angus would be dead—it had been seven hundred years, after all!—but she couldn't blame him for being shocked that the boy had died so very young. Angus had died so soon after Alasdair leapt through time that Morgan couldn't help wondering whether there was a connection.

And she guessed that Alasdair was wondering the same thing.

Alasdair's only son, his only touchstone to remind him of his beloved Fenella, had died young, perhaps because Alasdair had been away. Alasdair probably believed he had failed the memory of his gorgeous wife.

Or maybe it just troubled him that her presence had been wiped away so quickly. Morgan wished heartily that the record had included some notation of how Angus had died.

It might have set Alasdair's mind at ease.

"Well, I must say I've never had such a strong response to finding a record," Frances commented behind Morgan.

Morgan deliberately turned away from the highlander's fleeing figure and forced a smile. "It was a bit of a surprise for him."

"Hmm." The older woman's expression was skeptical, as though she sensed that there was more to this story than she was hearing. "I suppose his family must descend from another line," she confined herself to saying, although her eyes were filled with questions. "No doubt he'll discover some other helpful details from those at home and be back."

And Morgan guessed where Alasdair might have gone. He could have gone home, where at least in his mind, he could be with Fenella and his son. It was the closest he could come to fixing what he thought he had done wrong.

But Morgan could do one better. The ideal solution for Alasdair would be for him to go back in time. Maybe then he could help his son. Maybe then he could set history to rights again.

And Morgan had the crystal that had somehow tumbled out of the Scottish regalia when Alasdair appeared. She didn't know how everything was connected, but the fact remained that Alasdair had traveled through time once. Which could only mean that he could do it again. Morgan resolved in that moment that she was going to figure out how.

The blue Micra came puttering around the corner with perfect timing, and Frances glanced at her watch. "My goodness, we were occupied for quite some time!"

"Yes, well, thanks for your help." Morgan retrieved her bag from the foyer, exchanged a few more pleasantries, then hopped into the waiting car. Blake had come alone, and Morgan barely noticed that his shirt was uncharacteristically untucked.

"Can we hurry?" she asked as she got into the car. Only then did Morgan notice that Blake didn't seem to need much encouragement to put the pedal to the floor.

Morgan waved to Frances, then stared out the passenger window as though she were fascinated by the dusk falling over Lewis. She hoped that Blake wouldn't notice she was upset.

Because Morgan knew that Alasdair would never be hers, no matter how much she loved him. Still, she had to try to make him happy, simply because she did love him.

She had to send him away.

Auntie Gillian had always said that life had no interest in playing fair, but that one had to make the best of it. Morgan bit her lip, blinked back her tears, and determined to make the best of this. She would do whatever she could to give Alasdair his one desire.

She would help him solve this, even if it meant spending the rest of her life with an aching heart.

But Alasdair wasn't at the bed-and-breakfast.

Morgan paced up and down the porch for a good two hours, purportedly watching the sun set, but he didn't show. She finally concluded that this place was too resonant of the present for Alasdair to escape to the past here.

After all, there was a tiny hotel built virtually on the site of his home.

She remembered how Alasdair had pointed to the standing

stones, the first thing he had seen that was precisely as he recalled it.

And Morgan was suddenly sure she knew exactly where to find him. He would have sought out familiarity—she knew it.

Morgan raced back into the hotel, startling Justine and Blake from the whispers they were exchanging over their after-dinner coffees.

"I need the car!" It wasn't much of a greeting, but it got their attention.

Blake frowned. "You're sure you can handle driving on the wrong side and all that?"

"No," Morgan conceded with a confidence she was far from feeling. "But it hardly matters. There's not much traffic here. It's a good place to practice."

"Uh-huh." Blake clearly didn't share her optimism.

"At night?" Justine demanded. "Where are you going?"

"To get Alasdair. I think I know where he's gone."

Blake and Justine exchanged a glance, and Blake got to his feet. "Look, I can take you there."

Morgan's tone was unexpectedly firm. "No. I need to go alone."

She knew this as surely as she knew her own name. And remarkably, Justine and Blake seemed to sense her determination because they conceded the point.

"All right. But let me show you a few things," Blake said grimly.

"And be careful!" Justine called after them.

All Morgan could think about was getting to Alasdair, but Blake seemed determined to teach her every nuance of the car's operation. She was impatient with his thorough tutorial, and of course she soon regretted it.

She particularly regretted not paying much attention to what Blake had said about using the manual choke.

Morgan did well enough on the paved road—and thankfully, divine intervention ensured that very few of the citizens of Lewis were subjected to her habitual drift to the right side of the road.

She repeatedly corrected her course in the glare of oncoming headlights.

Morgan saw the standing stones rise ahead and sighed with relief, knowing her target was close. The Micra bumbled and skipped along the gravel road littered with a jarring quantity of potholes.

Even worse, it was hard to anticipate them. Morgan was jostled and bounced in the driver's seat, she ground the gears more than once, and the little temperature gauge nudged upward as she kept her foot hard on the gas pedal.

The Micra bottomed out twice with a jolting grind, then lurched into a particularly deep hole. Morgan miscalculated whatever she should have done and stalled the car.

And couldn't get it started again. The Micra was apparently not very interested in continuing this round of torture. Morgan cranked the engine over and over, gave it a good shot of gas, and heard it choke to oblivion.

She had flooded the engine.

Morgan supposed she shouldn't have been surprised. She looked around herself, becoming aware for the first time how completely dark and silent it was here. Night had fallen with incredible speed, a night that was blacker and more complete on this island than anywhere else she had ever been.

But Alasdair was out there alone. And he needed her help. Morgan gathered up her bag and her fanny pack, then turned on the headlights to give herself at least an idea of where the road went.

A dark shape lurched across the road. Morgan's heart missed a beat and she flicked on the high beams.

Just to find a tall, golden highlander striding toward her.

Morgan collapsed against the seat in relief as Alasdair hauled open the door. He bent to duck his head inside, bracing his hands on either side of the door. Though he smiled, his gaze was somber and Morgan knew he hadn't missed her moment of fright.

"You cannot be surprised to see me, my lady," he mused, despite the opposing evidence before his own eyes. "Only this wee chariot could make such a riot of snorting and farting. They have likely heard you all the way to Edinburgh."

Morgan took a deep breath. "I came to find you."

"Aye," Alasdair said, his voice low and silky. Morgan was painfully aware of how very close he was, and her desire for his touch hummed to life.

"I came to help you go home," she said quickly, hurrying over the words before she could think about them too much. "You came forward in time, so it only makes sense that you can go back. We just have to figure out how." Morgan looked up to find Alasdair's gaze intent. "You just have to tell me exactly how you did it before."

" 'Twas the witch as done it," he acknowledged slowly. "And 'twould seem clear that you are indeed no sorceress."

There was no censure in his tone and Morgan smiled tentatively. "No. Just an illustrator."

Alasdair's smile flashed in the darkness. "There is no 'just' about it, my lady. Your talent is rare in its power."

Morgan was dismayed that she blushed so easily in his presence. "You don't have to call me 'my lady,' you know. I'm just an ordinary person, not nobility or anything."

"There is naught ordinary about you, Morgan Lafayette." Alasdair said her name deliberately, as though schooling himself to address her correctly. "And never believe anyone who tells you otherwise."

Before Morgan could absorb his words, Alasdair extended a hand to her. "Come, my lady. 'Tis time enough that you saw the standing stones that so intrigue you. The moon will rise full this night, and my gran oft said 'twas then that magic happened within the circle of stones."

Morgan looked at his proffered hand, strong and broad, and knew there was nowhere else she would rather be than with Alasdair beneath the stars.

Even if she was destined to lose him in the end.

The night sky was filled with a bewildering array of stars, and Morgan was amazed that once she stepped out of the car her eyes adjusted quickly to the darkness. There were no houses nearby and no lights other than the starlight.

Which was surprisingly bright. In fact, Morgan had never seen so many stars. Alasdair caught her elbow with a chuckle when she tripped because her gaze was so intent on the heavens above.

His touch recalled her to what she had to do. "So, what happened? What is your last memory of your own time?"

Alasdair's thumb began a slow caress of Morgan's elbow and he frowned as he walked. "Robert the Bruce had granted us the task of winning Edinburgh keep from the English. 'Twas one of two they yet held, the other being Stirling. We heard tell of a way up the outside wall and climbed beneath the cover of darkness."

"I remember the guide talking about that!" Morgan declared excitedly. "But then, once we met, no one remembered it."

Alasdair slanted a considering glance her way. "We had taken the guards by surprise and easily won the keep. We had been long at camp, and the English had ample stores of both food and whisky. We indulged ourselves, then explored the keep."

"That's why you were drunk."

"Aye. Fou as a puggie we were when we met the wee witch. She claimed we would interrupt the slumber of Morgaine le Fee, of whom we all had heard ample tales. It has long been said that her cavern lies beneath Edinburgh keep and that her pet dragon, a most ferocious beast, is doubly fearsome if awakened to defend his mistress." Alasdair grimaced. "The witch dared us to meet her mistress unflinchingly."

"And you took the dare," Morgan breathed.

"Aye. In truth, I believed it whimsy. I feared she knew another way into the keep, that she was one of the English aiming only to frighten us away."

"But she wasn't."

Alasdair shrugged wryly. " 'Twould seem not."

"What happened when you took her dare?"

"She ran. She led me to the top of a tower, then granted me the gemstone from the regalia and a tuft of white heather. She bade me turn thrice while she chanted a Gaelic ditty." He glanced to Morgan. "I believed I fell down the staircase, but I awakened at your feet."

Morgan chewed her lip. "And everything changed. The men you were with must have abandoned the keep."

"Aye. 'Twould seem so. They would be fair spooked when a man disappeared without trace."

"And that turned the tide against Robert the Bruce," Morgan mused. She tried to sound businesslike. "Well, we just have to figure out how to send you back."

"My lady, I fear 'tis impossible."

"It is not. You came forward, you can go back." Morgan's tone brooked no argument, and she heard a vestige of Auntie Gillian there. "We just have to replicate the circumstances. If it's a spell, we just need all the right ingredients to make it work again."

A twinkle lit Alasdair's eye. "For one who is not a sorceress, you sound an authority on such matters."

"I watch *Bewitched* reruns."

Alasdair frowned and his grip tightened on her elbow. "But, my lady, this is no jest . . ."

Morgan fixed him with a stern eye. "I thought you wanted to see your son again."

Alasdair shut his mouth. He was obviously still skeptical but fought valiantly against his impulse.

"Do you truly believe it can be done?" he asked finally, his tone revealing his hope.

"Yes," Morgan assured him. "And we're going to do it." She rummaged in her fanny pack and pulled out the crystal, which sparkled in the starlight. "Look, here's the stone. Which hand did you have it in?"

Alasdair hesitated, then took it in his left hand.

Morgan dug in her fanny pack and came up with a battered scrap of heather, the one that Alasdair had given her on Moot Hill. She twined it in her fingers, letting herself remember that afternoon, before she handed it to him. "And this is white heather. Or at least it was."

Alasdair's eyes lit up, and his conviction visibly grew. "And it grew near the Stone of Scone. The wee witch said as much of the piece she granted me. This might indeed be successful!"

"Well, there you go. Now, all we need is the Gaelic verse."

Alasdair's face fell. "I do not recall the verse."

"Well, then, we'll just have to do some experimenting. You must know some Gaelic verses?"

"Aye." Again that glimmer of hope lit his eyes.

Morgan's heart hurt at the evidence of how much this meant to him, and she hoped desperately that they could make it work. "Well, we'll just have to try them all. Maybe it's the Gaelic itself. Think hard—maybe you can remember at least part of the tune."

Alasdair pursed his lips. " 'Twas a merry chant. 'Twas not unlike a song my gran sang when I was a babe, though the words called to Morgaine."

"You'll just have to come as close as you can," Morgan insisted.

What other variable could they control? He could turn three times in place easily enough, although they were far from Edinburgh's towers.

The orb of the moon crested orange on the horizon and gave Morgan a sudden inspiration. "What was the phase of the moon that night? Doesn't that sort of stuff matter in these things? I mean, in the story of the smith, it was full."

"Like this night." Alasdair thought about it for only a moment. "Aye! On that eve, 'twas full and riding high."

Morgan's heart clenched because things were moving so quickly. "Okay, so if we don't try tonight, then we have to wait another month."

Their gazes clung for a long moment, and Morgan finally had to look away. She took a step back and tried to look encouraging. "Well, then, go ahead and do whatever you did then."

Alasdair's expression turned grim. " 'Tis not so simple, my lady. There was something about the tower place, she called it a portal. We need to find a portal betwixt the times."

"Like that to the domain of Morgaine le Fay."

"Aye, a place where Faeries are said to gather. I have no doubt that there was a history of odd doings in that tower."

"Like the hill in the smith's story," Morgan said.

Their eyes met in sudden understanding, and Morgan knew they were both thinking the same thing. They turned as one to eye the circle of standing stones not two hundred feet away.

"My gran oft said . . ." Alasdair began, his voice oddly strained.

"Somewhere Faeries dance," Morgan breathed.

It couldn't be a coincidence that one of the most magical places in the British Isles was right beside them. Morgan tried to swallow the lump in her throat without success. She couldn't avoid the fact that everything was falling into place with dangerous ease.

Tonight was the night that Alasdair would leave her for all time. Just the thought made Morgan feel empty inside.

"Yes," she said firmly. "That's where we have to be."

Without another word, they walked toward the standing stones of Callanish, each fighting to hide their trepidation from the other.

Chapter 16

MORGAN CLEARLY COULD not wait to be rid of him.

Alasdair fought against his instinctive dislike of that certainty. 'Twas clearly because Alasdair had never been unwelcome in a woman's company before, especially one upon whom he had lavished his rough charm.

But 'twas something more than that irking him, and in a secret corner of his mind, Alasdair acknowledged the truth.

He loved Morgan, had fallen irrevocably in love with his wee enchantress.

And he was not by any means ready to part with her company.

Not even for his son.

This might have been frightening enough—for Alasdair had never permitted anyone to have such an effect upon him—if the lady had not been so intent on sending him away from her side. What was more, the sooner that happened was clearly the better, to her way of thinking.

And that hurt Alasdair. Was it just his pride that was wounded? Or was it a sense that there was something greater betwixt them, something that twisted his innards, yet something to which she was oblivious?

For a moment he had hoped to spend an evening with Morgan, within the circle of stones, putting all the troubles aside.

He would know the woman herself, without guise of sorceress. When Morgan took his hand, Alasdair's heart had clamored with the rightness of his choice.

But it seemed the lady did not wish to put Alasdair's troubles aside. 'Twas Alasdair himself she would send away, and that with all haste.

Alasdair trudged along beside her, disgruntled and not pleased in the least that the Fates themselves seemed to be on the lady's side. 'Twas a poor time to part, in his mind, but that seemed to be of little import. Not only had she the stone and the heather he had forgotten giving to her, but the cursed moon rose full on this very night.

And the stones were far too close for chance. They were the one thing exactly the same both in Alasdair's memory and before his eyes. 'Twas not whimsy that made him conclude these stones could be the link between the centuries that he sought.

Alasdair had the sense that he was destined to leave this very night.

And he was not prepared to go.

But the delicate marvel of Morgan marched beside him, a definite briskness in her step, and Alasdair knew he had made no error. The lady could not wait to see the back of him, whatever his feelings to the contrary.

Sorceress or nay, her thorough assessment and determination had Alasdair believing she could do this thing. And 'twas true enough what she said—he had done the feat once and likely could again, were all the circumstances right.

Would Morgan forget him once he was gone? The thought was startling, but Alasdair had to consider what had happened to the tale of Robert the Bruce. Would his departure leave Morgan with the sense that he had never been?

Alasdair was more troubled by that possibility than he thought he should have been. 'Twas clear enough the lady thought she lost naught by sending him on his way—but Alasdair wished he could somehow guarantee that she would at least recall him.

He knew full well that he would never forget her.

The standing stones of Callanish etched a great circle upon

the land, and though Alasdair knew they were not the only standing stones thereabouts, this gathering was the largest. A circle of thirteen massive stones stood on end, each one of them taller than he was. In the center of the circle stood an even taller stone, its crest angled in a distinctive manner.

Lines of stones extended in the four cardinal directions from the center, the northward avenue outlined by a double line of stone sentinels. The stones themselves were weathered and gray, the rising moon burnishing the rough surfaces with deep gold.

Alasdair and Morgan entered the avenue and approached the stones. A hush seemed to fall around them as they walked, and Alasdair could near naught beyond the pounding of his heart.

It seemed they were sheltered even from the wind in this place. It had always been this way when Alasdair ventured close to the stones. The majesty of their height and the sense of ancient power contained here struck right to his very soul.

And he understood now that 'twas because his gran spoke aright. This place stood portal to domains beyond the eye. That those domains were more of this earth than Faerie was but a detail.

They halted beside the commanding center stone, and Alasdair knew he did not imagine Morgan's nervousness.

She would not look to his eyes.

"All right, you have the crystal and the heather, the moon is full and we're here." Her emerald gaze danced to him and away as she chattered. "Um, what else? You said you turned three times in place and—oh! wait! You said you were *drunk*! Maybe we should find some whisky or something." She spun away, as though anxious to find such a substance and send Alasdair away from her side.

Alasdair gritted his teeth and stood his ground. "I will drink naught this night," he said so forcefully that Morgan looked back at him in astonishment. He arched one brow and let his voice drop. "You forget, my lady, that I granted my word to you."

"But it might be part of your going home."

"I shall go with my wits about me or not at all. I have told you oft enough, a man's word must be worth something or he is as naught.''

Morgan stared at him, as though she was not certain whether to believe him. Alasdair could not tell if his assertion pleased her, and irritation surged through him.

She might want to be rid of him as quickly as possible, but Alasdair had something to say first. He stepped forward and captured her chin with one hand, stared into her eyes, and willed her to not look away.

Alasdair felt the lady swallow, but she did not flinch.

''My lady,'' he said, his voice low, yet filled with resolve. ''Before we do this thing, I would have you know that I have never met a woman the like of you. Indeed, you might as well be an immortal sorceress, for your gentle beauty entwines with your strength of will to make a beguiling combination.'' He smiled down at her. ''And your kiss is no less bewitching than the reputed power of Morgaine le Fee's embrace.''

''I'm just a . . .''

Alasdair slid his thumb across Morgan's lips to silence her protest, not the least bit interested in her modesty at this moment.

He would have his say, before he left her side forever.

''Do not dismiss my tribute, my lady. You are like the rose, which blooms in beauty all the season long, though few appreciate the challenges it overcomes to bring those blossoms to light. 'Tis a stalwart plant, a harbinger of fair weather, yet of enough strength to survive both poor soil and foul winters.''

The lady blushed. Alasdair felt his annoyance dissolve at the sight, and he could not have stopped himself from cupping her face in his hands. To his amazement, she did not pull away.

''Whereas I, my lady,'' he continued with a rueful smile, ''am but a lowly briar. Rife with doughty thorns, rough-hewn yet strong, of common persistence to the rose, but sadly without her beauty and grace. We are as unlike as two beings might be, my lady, but I would ask of you one thing ere I go.''

''What?'' Morgan's voice was soft and uncertain, her eyes were wide.

''I ask only that you remember me,'' Alasdair declared with

low urgency. "As I shall remember you for all my days and nights."

Before she could argue the matter, Alasdair bent and sealed her lips with his.

As she had before, the lady trembled within his embrace, then tentatively placed her hands on his shoulders. Alasdair's heart sang as she arched against him, and he dared to hope that he had fallen in love with a woman who held him in some esteem.

As the heat of her kiss unfurled in his loins, Alasdair faced the truth. He was smitten with a tiny woman whose life was fixed seven centuries ahead of his own. A part of him wanted to ask her to accompany him home to find his son, but a larger part of him was afraid to face her certain refusal.

After all, she had made it clear that she wanted him to go quickly. Alasdair would hold the possibility of her admiration in his heart rather than force himself to face her rejection.

'Twas not a characteristic choice, by any means, and Alasdair supposed 'twas a sign of how deeply she had affected him.

With that realization, Alasdair broke off the kiss and stepped away, refusing to acknowledge the shimmer that blurred his vision. Morgan wanted no more than to be rid of him. He had no need to hear the words.

Alasdair gripped heather and crystal, summoned the first Gaelic verse that came to mind and began to chant. He turned in place, telling himself that he closed his eyes so he might not see Morgan's relief when he left.

His heart ached with awareness of her watchful silence.

Once. Alasdair chanted with vigor and heard his voice bounce off the stones. He forced himself to think of Angus, not of Morgan, to think of his home and his gran and his debt to Robert the Bruce.

Twice. He felt the dizziness flooding through him as it had that night in Edinburgh, and he dared to hope. Alasdair took a deep breath and chanted louder, telling himself he would see his own time when his eyes opened again.

One more step. He lifted his foot, turned an increment, and made to step.

Thrice.

"No!" Morgan cried.

Alasdair's eyes flew open just as Morgan launched herself at him. He dropped the gemstone and managed to catch her, but the force of her assault sent them flying back against the great central stone.

To Alasdair's astonishment, she was crying.

"I don't want you to go!" she wailed.

But had he gone? Alasdair scanned the hills beyond the circle of stones, and his gut writhed at the gleam on the roof of the Micra parked not far away.

He was yet in Morgan's time.

Alasdair frowned down at her, slow to make sense of her dismay. "What is this? Of course, you would be rid of me! You are intent only on having me gone."

"No! I *never* wanted you gone!"

Her obvious horror that he had thought otherwise warmed Alasdair's heart. Heartfelt tears streamed down her cheeks and 'twas clear she could not stop their course. Humbled by her distress, Alasdair brushed the tears away with a gentle fingertip.

It seemed he had misjudged the lady.

"But you need to go, I understand that. Your son needs you." Morgan clutched Alasdair's shoulders as though she could not get close enough to him.

Alasdair's pulse began to thunder in his ears at this marvelous change of events, and he could not think of a word to say.

But Morgan had plenty to say. "I thought it would be easier if we got it over with," Morgan confessed unevenly, her wondrous eyes welling with fresh tears, "but, Alasdair, please don't believe that I want you to go."

And Alasdair felt the cur for ever having doubted her. He leaned back against the hard earth and gathered Morgan against his side, letting his hand slide through the ebony hair at her nape. He caressed her gently, his fingers losing themselves in the silky softness of her hair, and dared to believe what she told him.

She did not want him to go.

Morgan did not want to be rid of him.

A warmth spread through Alasdair and he felt himself begin to smile. The stars winked overhead as though they had known all along, the moon sailed high and her face turned to glowing silver. Alasdair could hear the waves of the sea crashing in the distance. He gave the woman nestled against him a minute hug and touched her chin.

"Look there," he said, pointing to the northern sky. "The Merry Dancers would have you smile again."

Morgan looked up and wiped the last of her tears, her lips rounding in amazement at the sight. "The northern lights," she whispered in awe. "I've never seen them before."

Alasdair snorted gently. "Dancers they are, as any wee lad knows, not mere *lights*."

She turned a smile on him so enchanting that it fairly melted Alasdair's bones. And he knew, as he had only guessed before, that this woman had cast a net around his heart and would hold it securely for all time.

"Alasdair," she whispered, her eyes luminous, "I love you."

Alasdair stared at her in wonder. The rose scent that she favored wafted into his lungs, the soft warmth of her pressed against his ribs, the delicacy of her hand rested on his chest. It seemed that they two stopped breathing in the same moment, and there was naught but the glow of love in the lady's eyes.

And in the wake of such a confession and all else that had happened this day, there was only one thing a red-blooded man might do. His heart swelling with his own love, Alasdair leaned closer and gently kissed his lady fair.

Morgan thought her heart would burst when Alasdair kissed her. As always, his embrace was tender, giving her the choice of how they might proceed.

And Morgan knew exactly what she wanted to do. Alasdair had taught her to trust again, taught her to let herself love, and Morgan knew that now only one celebratory act would do.

It was a perfect moonlit night, the stones surreal in their silence, the words Alasdair had uttered earlier so shamelessly romantic. The spell might not have worked this time, but Morgan knew it would eventually.

And when Alasdair left, Morgan was going to be sure that he had a compelling memory of her to take along.

So, Morgan kissed Alasdair back with a decade of denied desire, twining her hands into the wonderful thickness of his hair. Alasdair moaned when she drove her tongue between his teeth and Morgan found herself rolled to her back.

The grass was lush beneath her, like a densely knotted exotic rug, and richly green. Alasdair nuzzled her ear and ran an intoxicating line of kisses down her throat. Morgan moaned and reached for him, but the highlander evaded her embrace.

"I have waited long for this moment," he whispered with a wicked grin. Before Morgan could respond, he tucked his head beneath her sweater.

She gasped as his hands closed over her breasts, those skilled thumbs teasing her nipples to taut beads. He was so unbearably gentle that Morgan wanted more of him, everything within her melting at his sure touch. Alasdair's breath fanned Morgan's belly, he kissed her stomach and rolled his tongue in her navel.

Then, he tugged her leggings away with his teeth.

His hands followed in leisurely pursuit, sliding beneath her buttocks to lift her hips high. With his teeth, he hauled the leggings down to her ankles, teasing her with tongue and breath and fingers.

Morgan had never been so aroused in her life. She might have been shy about doing this outside, but Alasdair's confidence was more than reassuring. Alasdair was so unrestrained, so unconcerned about anything other than the magic that flared to life between them.

Morgan loved that about him, loved how he made her feel impetuous and free, loved how he was who he was, without apology or explanation. Each time they touched was explosive, yet still a bold adventure in sensation.

Morgan wanted to do this for the rest of her life.

Alasdair flashed her a mischievous glance as he cavalierly flung her tights and boots aside, his eyes darkening nearly to indigo. Then he ducked between her knees with a playful growl.

Morgan gasped as Alasdair slid his nose through her pubic hair and wanted to cry out when he pressed a slow kiss to her turgid clitoris. She trembled at the heat of his breath, then moaned as his tongue slid across the nub of her desire.

She was so wet. The strength of Alasdair's hands closed around her waist, his tongue set to work, and Morgan was left with no options but to enjoy. She closed her eyes and surrendered.

And Alasdair did not disappoint. He cajoled Morgan's response, taking her to the crest of release, then stopping to explore her navel with the tip of his nose until her need ebbed slightly. Each time, the crest was higher, each time Morgan's moans grew louder when he moved away. The heat was gathered beneath her flesh and she was twisting in desperation when the heat of his mouth closed over her once more.

And this time, Morgan knew there would be no respite. She peeled off her sweater so that she could see the moonlight play upon his hair. Alasdair glanced up, his own eyes smoldering, and Morgan rubbed herself shamelessly against him.

He caressed her expertly, laved and explored every crevice of her, tasted and tantalized. And suddenly, the quickening ripped through her and Morgan clutched at his silvered hair. Alasdair gripped her buttocks and dove deeper into her. Morgan cried out as she reached the summit and plunged trembling into the abyss beyond.

Her heart was still hammering when she opened her eyes and saw Alasdair kneeling before her. Morgan rolled over and reached beneath his kilt. The erection that she knew she would find was larger and harder than anticipated. Alasdair shuddered when Morgan's hands closed around him.

"I want all of you," she whispered and his eyes gleamed.

He was nude in a heartbeat, his skin gleaming in the moonlight, a pagan god come to life. Alasdair gathered Morgan against his chest, lifting her for a soul-shattering kiss. Morgan savored his touch, clung to the strength of his neck, then slipped her legs around his waist.

Alasdair caught his breath at her proximity.

Nose to nose, they stared into each other's eyes as Morgan slowly lowered herself onto him.

No sooner was he buried to the hilt than Morgan was again on her back, Alasdair silhouetted against the starry sky. The grass was cool and thick beneath her, Alasdair was warm and solid above.

He moved with deliberation within her, his thumb slipping between them to caress her again. Morgan writhed and twisted beneath him, she bit his shoulders, she dug her nails into his back. The heat gathered within her once again and she bucked demandingly against Alasdair, wanting every inch of him to be her own.

When she reached up and captured his face in her hands, then kissed him languorously, Morgan felt him shake with the effort of self-control. She ran her toes down his legs, rocked her hips and rubbed her breasts against him, kissing him fervently all the while.

Alasdair growled, Morgan continued her assault even as she felt her own blood heating.

When the trembling broke over Morgan again, Alasdair tipped his head back and groaned, even as he buried himself within her. The stars cavorted dizzily overhead, and Morgan gripped Alasdair's shoulders, knowing they were the only secure thing in her universe.

He fell bonelessly to the grass beside her and pulled her into his embrace. Morgan's eyes drifted closed as she felt the heat of his chest beneath her cheek, and she smiled when Alasdair pressed a kiss to her temple.

She had gone to heaven and she didn't want to come back.

Alasdair did not sleep.

He lay within the enchanted circle and held Morgan fast to his side, loving the way she slumbered against him. Aye, she was the woman he had always longed to find and more. Never had Alasdair believed that the love oft mentioned in his gran's tales was for him.

But the evidence slept within his very arms.

Some twist of fate had sent him plunging forward in time, and Alasdair was enough of his gran's grandson to know that it could be no coincidence that Morgan had been the one to find him first.

He had done the impossible, catapulted over seven hundred years, and as he lay there in the moonlight, Alasdair knew it had been so that he might find his one true love.

Morgan.

She was here and Alasdair was never going to let her go. Time would come when he recalled the right Gaelic verse, for he had a good ear and a good memory. The tune had reminded him of something, that much Alasdair recalled.

One day he would find it.

Indeed, he had little choice. Indeed, if there had been no price in coming to Morgan, Alasdair would gladly have remained here in her world with her alone.

But Alasdair was haunted by the certainty that his disappearance had changed matters for Robert the Bruce. The Scotland his son had inherited had been far from free, and the fault for that lay squarely at Alasdair's door.

Further, Alasdair knew that had he been there, Angus would not have died so young. Alasdair could not change the fact that he had left the boy so long, but he wished with all his heart and soul that he could at least have had the chance to make matters come right for his son.

Contrary to all that Alasdair had believed, it was not chanting the wrong Gaelic verse that had confounded his return home. Though it was true that the stone and the heather and the site contributed, there was one factor he had forgotten.

A heartfelt wish was the key to the witch's spell.

And in the very moment that Alasdair desired beyond all else to see his son, he was gone from Morgan's side as though he had never been.

Morgan awakened with a luxurious feeling of completion. In a hazy corner of her mind, she knew that she had found a fulfillment that she had always sought but never believed she would know.

Without opening her eyes, Morgan stretched out a hand to

Alasdair. When her fingers found only empty space, she tried on the other side.

Nothing. Her eyes flew open and she sat bolt upright.

Only to find that she was alone.

The sky was faintly tinged pink in the east, a fiery line indicating that the sun would soon drift over the horizon, but Morgan wasn't interested in that. The stones brooded on all sides, night shadows still clinging to their bases. The stars had retreated, both northern lights and moon gone as thoroughly as if they had never been.

Just like Alasdair.

Morgan tugged on her sweater and stood up to look around. In every direction the countryside was perfectly still. A patina of dew glistened on the roof of the dead blue Micra, but there was nothing else of distinctive color.

Certainly not a kilt wrapped around a golden highlander.

How could he have left her?

Morgan spun and examined the site of their tryst with mounting indignation. How could Alasdair have done this to her, after the night they had shared? After what he had said to her? Tears blurred Morgan's vision and she hated the sense that she had played the fool in love one more time.

It was only when Morgan plucked her errant leggings off a smaller stone that she realized something critical.

The crystal from the regalia was gone. Morgan searched the dirt in all directions, ran her fingers through the grass, but to no avail.

The gemstone was gone. Alasdair was gone. She looked, but already knew that the white heather was gone too.

Morgan sat down heavily as the sun peeked rosily at the world. Had Alasdair really managed to go back to the past?

There was only one way to find out for sure. He didn't have any money, so he would have had to go back to the bed-and-breakfast to eat. Morgan dressed hastily and ran back to the Micra, praying that it would start.

Evidently the car had forgiven her sins, because it did.

Justine stretched like a cat in the sun, even though it was pouring rain. She smiled to herself and stirred the sweetener into her coffee. The one thing absent from Scottish breakfast tables were those little blue envelopes that she relied upon to keep her hipline trim. At least they had been missing, until Justine sat down at the breakfast table at Adaira Macleod's Rose Cottage Bed-and-Breakfast.

And the coffee itself was divine. Justine watched Blake devour his breakfast and smiled some more as she considered how he had worked up such an appetite.

"My Mona Lisa," Blake teased. "Are you smiling about the same thing I'm smiling about?"

Justine just smiled some more. She hadn't had much sleep, but she felt very, very good this morning. She and Blake shared a hot glance of mutual adoration, then she looked reluctantly at her watch.

"I guess we should wake up Morgan," she said dreamily.

"Oh, I don't know. It's a perfect day for lounging in bed. Or drawing." Blake winked, then leaned forward and tapped his fork on the tablecloth, his eyes gleaming. "We could wander back upstairs ourselves, tell Adaira that we're packing . . ."

Adaira herself bustled into the room in a puff of frilly pink calico, clicking her tongue as she came. Justine had already noticed that their silver-haired hostess had a fondness for pink, but this apron was pinker than cotton candy at a state fair.

It was a bit of a jolt first thing in the morning.

"More coffee?" Adaira asked cheerfully, and both Macdonalds held out their cups.

"Your coffee is very good," Blake said with approval. "The best we've had in Scotland."

"Oh, Mr. Macdonald, all the handsome young men from abroad say just the same." Adaira filled Blake's cup with a flourish. "The Captain is always warning me not to go and get vain about my coffee. Adaira, he says, there's more to making a success of life than grinding your own coffee beans."

Adaira winked at Justine while filling her cup to the brim with steaming coffee. "But *I* say there's more to life than worrying about grand events that have nothing to do with our own wee lives. I would rather be having a nice cup of coffee on a rainy morning and looking upon my lovely roses than worrying myself to death about nonsense brewed up down London way.''

Justine turned and looked out at the roses in question. Adaira had a lovely hedge of pink eglantine roses hugging the perimeter of her well-manicured lawn. They were in their last flush of blooming before the winter, and Justine had admired them daily.

But today there was another bush in the middle of the lawn. Justine frowned. She knew it hadn't been there before. She'd walked around the yard one afternoon, after all.

And there was no way she could have missed this one. Blood-red blooms the size of her fist adorned the gnarled and obviously ancient bush. Around its base twined a thorny mass that had a different kind of leaves.

But before Justine could ask about it, Morgan burst into the breakfast room. She was wearing the same sweater she had worn the night before when she took the car.

''Justine! He's gone!''

Justine blinked. Hadn't Morgan come home?

And *who* was gone?

Justine had a funny sense that she had forgotten something she really should remember, but she couldn't put her finger on what it was. *He.* Hadn't there been somebody with them?

Just thinking about it made Justine's head hurt, as though she was prying at a door that didn't want to be opened. She looked at Blake, but he looked more confused than she felt.

''He?'' Justine asked carefully.

''Alasdair!'' Morgan was clearly all worked up. ''Alasdair MacAulay!''

Justine blinked, the name ringing a distant bell.

Morgan clutched Justine's hands in obvious consternation. ''Don't tell me you don't remember. You *have* to remember. The highlander, the man in the kilt, he's blond and tall and we found him at Edinburgh Castle and you thought he'd be perfect for me. Justine! That's why we came here!''

Blake cleared his throat. ''We came here because you had to see those standing stones.'' He rolled his eyes. ''Big old stones. I was thinking that we really should head back south.''

He reached down and tugged his tour book out of his jacket pocket. "I don't know how you convinced me to drive right past Bannockburn, but we have to go back."

Morgan glanced wildly at Blake. "Why do you have to go to Bannockburn?" she demanded hoarsely.

Blake impatiently tapped his pen on the table. "Morgan, do you ever listen to anything? How many times do I have to tell you that Bannockburn was the site where Robert the Bruce vanquished the English and won Scotland's freedom? It's a tremendous precedent for the referendum they just had here."

Morgan dropped into a third chair at the table, her face ashen. "Justine," she said softly. "Is that what you remember?"

Justine frowned and couldn't help looking at the red, red rose growing in the middle of the lawn. What Blake said sounded right, but she couldn't completely shake an odd sense that there had been another man traveling with them.

She remembered Blake's flatly refusing to come all the way to Callanish. Yet they were here. She knew that there had been something—or someone—that changed his mind. Justine remembered how adamant Blake was about going to Bannockburn, yet at the same time vaguely recalled his hostility about going there when they left Edinburgh.

And she had been in complete agreement with him both times.

As she was now with his insistence that they return.

How odd. It was really frustrating not to be able to remember something, especially since she usually had a mind like a steel trap. She forgot *nothing*, yet now she couldn't summon a clear picture of this highlander Morgan was talking about. She drummed her fingers on the table, ignoring Morgan's hopeful gaze, and couldn't help looking out the window once more.

Justine had an insistent feeling about that rose.

"Adaira," she called on impulse when the innkeeper bounced back into the room, "could you tell me about this red rose?"

Morgan glanced out the window and her eyes widened in surprise. "It wasn't there yesterday!"

"Of course it was!" Adaira was clearly delighted to tell the tale. "Oh, it's a lovely old story, that much is for certain, but that rose has been there for centuries. You see, there once was a man who loved a certain woman as dearly as ever a man can do. But theirs was a star-crossed match and they were doomed to part.

"When his lady love was stolen away from his side, the man pined frightfully in his loss. Finally, one day, he planted a briar and a rose together, as symbols of himself and her sweet beauty. He told all that as long as his love burned bright, the briar and the rose would twine together, each a part of the other for all time."

Adaira shrugged. "Well, the man passed away eventually, without his lady love ever being returned to him, and it is said that he was painfully lonely right to the end. Others say his eyes lit with pleasure as he passed on, and they are the ones who say he saw his lady love again in heaven's grace.

"But either way, none who has ever lived here could bear to let either plant wither away. The briar and the rose you see before you are not the original, of course, but they are the latest of countless generations of briars and roses spawned from those original plants."

She leaned closer and dropped her voice. "Truth be told, my Captain has a weak spot for the tale, though he would deny it up, down, and sideways if you asked him. Sentimental nonsense, he calls it, but he has no less than three of each plant carefully nurtured in his wee greenhouse. If one of them takes ill, the other need not endure alone."

Adaira straightened and wiped a shimmer from her cheek. "It is the least we can do to maintain a man's gesture of undying love." She hoisted the pot she held and smiled brightly. "Coffee?"

Blake accepted, then Adaira trotted away. Justine looked back to the rose with the briar tangled about it, feeling as though it was trying to tell her something. And it seemed to her that just behind the rose and briar, a little bit out of focus, she could see a tall, blond highlander with sadness in his eyes.

Blue eyes. Very blue eyes.

Everything came back in a rush, as though she had pried

open that stubborn door in her memory and forced its contents into the daylight. Justine remembered suddenly the way that very man had looked at Morgan, his insistence that he couldn't be parted from her, the way he had made Morgan laugh once again.

And then she remembered Alasdair MacAulay filling the backseat of the Micra. Justine recalled how he sang for Morgan, how protective he was of her, how dismayed he had been when she rebuffed his advances, and her heart warmed.

Justine had watched Alasdair fall in love with her sister.

She turned to Morgan, and the expression on her sister's face told Justine that the feeling was more than mutual. She covered Morgan's hand with her own and gave those chilled fingers a squeeze. "Did you tell him? Did he know how you felt?"

Tears shone in Morgan's eyes. "I couldn't . . ." she murmured and bit her lip.

Justine waited, because there had to be more.

"We made love," Morgan admitted finally with a flush, "and then—and then he was gone."

The heartfelt confession told Justine all she needed to know. Alasdair MacAulay was not the kind of man who took advantage of women or who would have used her sister for his own satisfaction. Furthermore, he wasn't the kind of rat who would run out on a woman he loved. Something had happened, something had forced him to leave, and Alasdair had had no choice but to go.

But he had wanted Morgan to know the truth, Justine was certain of it. She gave Morgan's fingers a stronger squeeze. "He planted them for you, as a sign that he loves you."

"Oh, Justine, I don't know . . ."

In that moment Justine hated Matt Reilly with every fiber of her being. He had destroyed Morgan's faith in the simple fact that she was lovable, he had stolen away a precious cornerstone of her confidence. Somehow Justine had to repair the damage.

"I know he loves you," she said firmly. "I knew he was the one for you all along."

"You remember him, then?" Morgan asked, the hope in her voice almost tangible.

"Remember *who*?" Blake demanded, but both sisters ignored him.

"Yes." Justine turned to look into her sister's eyes and used her most reassuring smile. "You have to tell me what happened so we can figure out what to do."

"Okay." Morgan exhaled unevenly and smiled a little bit. Relief surged through Justine that her baby sister wanted to share the story. "I'd like that."

"Who are we talking about?" Blake demanded in exasperation. He looked from one sister to the other and must have seen some hint of their determination because he threw up his hands in defeat. "Okay, okay. Chick stuff. I'm not listening."

Then he propped his elbows on the table. "But could we at least *think* about heading back to the mainland today or tomorrow? We're running out of vacation and there's still a ton of things to see!"

Justine leaned across the table and cupped Blake's face in her hands. "Maybe you could pack while we're talking," she suggested gently, then gave him a great big kiss.

That ought to give him enough to think about for a while. Or at least, long enough for Justine to ease the shadows from her baby sister's eyes. All she had to do was convince Morgan of the simple truth—that Alasdair MacAulay loved her to distraction and that she should take a chance on love.

Whatever that meant.

But one look at her sister's troubled expression made Justine realize that convincing Morgan of the truth wasn't going to be easy.

But that kind of challenge had never stopped Justine before.

Chapter 17

ALASDAIR FELT HIMSELF tumbling away from Morgan and the stones. He panicked as he fell but could do naught to stop himself.

Until he rolled into a tree and came to a jarring stop.

He felt the sun upon his shoulders and opened his eyes warily, for he knew 'twas still night.

Yet 'twas not night where he lay—'twas a broad, sunny morning. He must have fallen asleep in Morgan's embrace—and somehow tumbled down the grassy bank beside the standing stones. Alasdair was alone, the standing stones a goodly distance away.

He was on his feet to go awaken Morgan before he realized the Micra was gone.

Had she left him?

Alasdair spun around, seeking some sign of the blue chariot, only to realize that no black ribbon of road wound its way across the countryside. There was no pool of black beside the standing stones, no houses, no wires strung along the roadway.

And there was a crusting of frost yet lingering in the shadows. The growth was deadened, compared to where he had been, and Alasdair smelled the snap of winter in the air.

But Callanish was exactly as Alasdair knew it to be.

Even if his memory was not. Only now he became aware

of the passage of time, of the fact that he had long been without Morgan. Unfamiliar memories flooded his mind—of the barest moment lost in the keep of Edinburgh, of a string of victories beside Robert the Bruce, of an ache of loss burdening his heart. They were hollow recollections, as though they had been lived by another.

He had endured a spring and summer of knowing his lady was lost to him for all time. Alasdair's mouth went dry.

Nay! It could not be! They had just been together, Morgan had only just lain in his arms.

A primitive panic swept through him, and Alasdair's heart turned cold. A part of him knew he deceived himself, a part of him recalled the long walk home. A part of Alasdair knew that he had slept here, beneath the stars, deliberately evoking the memory of his magical night with Morgan.

But Alasdair did not want to believe it. His days with Morgan were more real than anything else he had ever known.

And he was not prepared to let her go, much less to live his life without her smile. Alasdair ran wildly toward the stones, shouting Morgan's name.

But to no avail.

He was alone, as that part of his heart had long known.

"Morgan!" Alasdair bellowed again in frustration, and a pair of young boys peeked around the stones.

"Morgan?" the fair-haired one echoed.

"He summons Morgaine le Fee!" the other one declared, his eyes round with alarm.

"I call a woman, name of Morgan," Alasdair corrected gently. The blonder boy took a step back, just as Alasdair recognized something in those young eyes.

They were of an unusual shade of dark gray, the same as Fenella's had been. A lump rose in Alasdair's throat and he recalled his last wish.

Some witchery had sent him home.

"Ha! A witchy woman indeed," the dark-haired boy taunted. "Angus knows all about Morgaine le Fee—his da was stolen away by her!" And he lunged at the fair boy in mock attack.

Alasdair liked well how quickly Angus defended himself.

"My da is a hero, no less than that," he retorted proudly. "My da helped Robert the Bruce, King of All Scots, and does not sit around with his nose in his ale all the day long."

The other boy's features contorted with rage, and the mock fight turned quickly into a real one. Alasdair waded into the midst and hauled the boys apart, gripping one in each hand by the neck of the shirt.

"I will not be watching such fighting," he declared solemnly. " 'Tis not fitting of good men to beat each other senseless over naught."

"He mocked my father!" the dark-haired boy claimed hotly.

"Not before you mocked mine!" Angus retorted. The two would have gone at it again, but Alasdair gave them a shake and held them an arm's length apart.

"And who might your father be?" he asked the dark-haired lad.

"Duncan MacIver." The boy's expression was sullen, the distinctive turn of his lips clearly the mark of his sire, now that Alasdair knew to look.

Alasdair smiled wryly. "Aye, I know Duncan well enough. A goodhearted man he is and a strong warrior, though, indeed, he has a fondness for his ale." He squeezed his son's shoulders. " 'Tis not the mark of a man to note another man's weakness instead of his strength," he said gently.

Angus hung his head. "I am sorry."

MacIver's son shook off Alasdair's grip and darted away. "But your da was still snatched by the Faerie Queen!" he cried and scrambled over the rocks. "And he is *never* coming home to you!"

Alasdair looked to his son, not surprised to find the boy dejected. This was what he had wrought by needing to see his name clear of taint.

Alasdair squatted down beside the boy and Angus flicked a glance his way. 'Twas devoid of the dark lights that had haunted his mother's gray eyes, and Alasdair ached that such a taunt should hurt his son.

"So, Robert the Bruce is a hero and King of All Scots?" he asked.

The boy looked incredulously at Alasdair. "All know it to be true," he said, without the other boy's scorn. "He defeated the British soundly at Bannockburn and my own da helped him win the day. 'Tis the only reason he went away."

Angus's defiance melted Alasdair's heart. "Aye? And who might your da be?" he asked, needing to hear the words.

"Alasdair MacAulay."

Alasdair cocked his head toward the fleeing MacIver. "Is it true what he says, then?"

"My da is a hero," Angus insisted stubbornly. "My da helped Robert the Bruce take Edinburgh keep, my gran says 'tis so." He took a deep breath. "My gran says not to listen to the tales of his being in league with Morgaine le Fee and using her dark arts to win the keep. Lies, they are, jealous lies!"

"Dark arts?" Alasdair asked mildly.

"Aye, a tale there is that my da shimmered so bright that the others could not look upon him, and that afterward he differed from afore."

Alasdair frowned, seeing the seed of truth in both the tale and his own memory.

But Angus continued heatedly. "My gran says there was never a man on this isle the like of my da and I should be proud to have him as my father." His lips tightened, and he glared at Alasdair. "And I am."

"Good for you. A man should be proud of the blood he carries in his own veins." Alasdair ruffled the boy's hair, and Angus looked up in surprise. "But 'twould be easier to be proud if the man were here, hmmm?" Alasdair murmured.

Angus looked away. "He will come home," he insisted, but there was little conviction in his words.

Alasdair frowned down at the ground. He knew full well that if he confessed his identity now, Angus would not believe him. What proof had he for the boy, after all, beyond his own word?

But there was one who knew the truth.

"I would like to meet this gran of yours," Alasdair suggested. "Do you think I might?"

Angus eyed the newcomer warily. "She talks only to

strangers who bring news from the mainland.''

"Does she now? Well, perhaps I have some news for her.''

A spark of curiosity lit Angus's eye and his excitement was
evident in his voice. "Do you know something of my da?''

"Aye,'' Alasdair admitted softly. "Aye, that I do.'' When
Angus might have asked, he shook a finger. "But 'tis for your
gran's ears.''

And to Alasdair's surprise, Angus seized his hand and ran
toward the path Alasdair knew so very well, as though he
would rush the telling that he might know sooner. The path-
way was exactly as it had been on the day he had returned
here with Morgan, and Alasdair braced himself for disappointment.

But when the pair rounded the last corner of the road, the
valley ahead contained precisely the three cottages that Alasdair recalled. A lean, silver-haired woman worked the earth
surrounding the uppermost one and now 'twas Alasdair who
urged his companion to run.

They raced up the valley as though they both were young
boys, Angus laughing at Alasdair's enthusiasm. Alasdair's
gran glanced up at the sound of their footsteps and for once,
that woman had naught to say. Her mouth fell open, the color
drained from her face, her piercing gaze faltered. Then she
flushed crimson and her eyes flashed with characteristic vigor.

"Alasdair MacAulay!'' she shouted, her voice echoing
down the valley as she braced her hands on her hips. "Where
in the devil's name have you been?''

Angus gasped, and Alasdair could not help but laugh at his
gran's response. "Aye, you have missed me, to be sure.'' His
gran snorted disdain even as he scooped her up and gave her
a fierce hug.

She clutched him tight, whispered his name as though she
could not believe he had come home, then insisted on being
put back on her feet.

Gran poked Alasdair in the shoulder, her gaze assessing.
"We heard tell you were snatched away by no less than Morgaine le Fee at Edinburgh Castle.''

Alasdair sobered. "Aye. 'Tis true enough.''

His gran's eyes narrowed, but Angus was tugging at Alasdair's hand. "You are my da?" he demanded excitedly. "Truly?"

Alasdair hunkered down beside the boy and grinned. "Aye, that I am, lad, and I have missed you sorely all these years. You've grown to be quite a man while I was gone."

Angus's eyes glowed. "And you truly were captured by Morgaine le Fee?"

"Aye, for a deadly moment."

For indeed, all those days and nights with Morgan seemed to have passed in the blink of an eye.

"Wait until Malcolm MacIver hears tell of this!" Angus was clearly as delighted with this wondrous tale as with his father's return. Alasdair silently vowed that he would change that, for truly, the boy knew naught of having a sire.

"But, da," Angus asked with no less enthusiasm. "However did you win your freedom? What price did the enchantress charge you to send you back?"

Alasdair laced his fingers together and stared at the ground, the fullness of his loss sweeping over him like a great wave. To the boy, 'twas no more than a game mortals played with the Faerie folk and one that Alasdair had won.

'Twas no more than another fanciful tale.

But Alasdair ached with the knowledge that his lady love was separated from him by a rift of centuries, a chasm far greater than any veil betwixt this world and the next.

And that he would miss her sorely for all his days.

He was home, but alone as he had never been with Morgan by his side. 'Twas a dreadful price to pay, even to see his own son again. And there would be an ache within him that Alasdair knew would never heal.

Too late he wished that he had told his Faerie Queen of his love. Now Morgan would never know the truth of it, and that wounded Alasdair as severely as the loss of her.

" 'Twas a tall price I paid," Alasdair finally managed to say hoarsely. "For the lady has kept my very heart for her own."

"Cor!" Angus's eyes went big and round. He grinned, then ran off, all legs and boundless enthusiasm, as his sire watched, no doubt to tell his friends of Alasdair's return.

But when Alasdair straightened, he met his gran's bright, steady gaze. She studied him for a long moment, then turned away with some excuse of fetching him a meal, the light in her eyes leaving Alasdair to wonder how much she had guessed of the truth.

He stood alone and surveyed the valley he had long called his home, a view so nearly the same as the one he had shared with Morgan night after night. And Alasdair wondered if he would ever look at the world without being reminded of her.

Morgan stood on the porch of the Rose Cottage bed-and-breakfast and waved at the retreating Nissan Micra. She caught a last glimpse of Justine's hand waving madly and bit her lip as the little car disappeared over the crest of the hill.

It felt as though a part of her had slipped away in the Micra. It was a much smaller part than the big chunk of her heart that had disappeared with Alasdair, but still Morgan suddenly felt very alone.

She and Justine had talked all through the night, and Justine's insistence that Alasdair loved Morgan still rang in the younger sister's ears. Trust Justine to take in stride the fact that Alasdair had traveled across seven centuries. Nothing could ruffle her sister, Morgan knew it.

Just the thought made her smile a little bit.

Justine was certain—as Justine was always certain—that Morgan should do whatever she had to do to be with Alasdair. But Morgan wasn't so sure.

What if Justine was wrong?

Because the simple fact was that although Alasdair had said a lot of wonderful things, he had never said that he loved Morgan.

And she knew he loved Fenella.

To Morgan's immense relief, even Blake had remembered Alasdair once they had checked the fate of the regalia in everyone's tour books. But it had been a fight for Justine and Blake to recall him, and Morgan ached to see Alasdair so easily forgotten.

In fact, no one else at the bed-and-breakfast had any memory at all of his presence. Robert the Bruce was a hero again,

Bannockburn had been the site of winning Scottish independence, there had been a recent referendum over establishing a
Scottish National Assembly, and Sir Walter Scott was back in
the books where he belonged. There was even a picture of the
regalia in Morgan's guidebook, complete with a quartz crystal
mounted between the gold porpoises.

It was as if Alasdair had never appeared in their time. But
Morgan's aching heart knew the truth, and she hoped that
Alasdair's return had made a similar difference in the fate of
his son.

There had to be something good about losing him.

When the car's engine faded from earshot and the silence
of the hills pressed against her ears, Morgan felt as though she
had decided much more than simply to stay on and work on
her drawings here. It seemed so final, watching the last shred
of the life she knew drive away.

But she was afraid to take a chance on the love she felt for
Alasdair. After all, experience had shown that she could make
mistakes in affairs of the heart.

Even if she could manage to follow Alasdair, what if she
was wrong?

Morgan didn't know what to do, but she did have a lot of
work in front of her. She had so many of Alasdair's stories
still to illustrate with drawings, and in one way she couldn't
wait to start. Yet in another way Morgan was afraid that once
she made all the drawings, the memory of Alasdair's resonant
tones would fade from her mind as they had from nearly
everyone else's.

Morgan wanted to cling to every vestige of his memory that
she could.

While Morgan lingered indecisively on the porch with her
jumbled emotions, Adaira came bustling through the door. As
usual, she was decked out in fuschia frills. "Miss Lafayette!
I can't begin to tell you again how delighted we are that
you've decided to stay on to work. You simply must make
yourself right at home here."

Morgan smiled. "Thank you."

Adaira fussed with the wicker chairs, moving them incre-
mentally, even though Morgan couldn't see anything wrong

with where they were. "It's a pity that your sister has taken the car, though I suppose they'll need it to get back to Edinburgh."

Adaira snapped her fingers before Morgan could say anything. "You know, the Captain is always saying that a bit of exercise does a body good, and there *is* a bicycle in the garage, whenever you want to use it. Of course, we'd be happy to drive you anywhere when we're out and about, but the Captain does tend to just pop off for a pint at the oddest moments . . ."

"Thank you," Morgan interjected, finding the idea of a bike ride enormously appealing at the moment. "The bike will be great. Maybe I'll go for a ride now."

Adaira smiled sympathetically. "A bit restless, are you? I always say as it's hard to say good-bye, though the Captain insists that partings make the gatherings all the sweeter."

Morgan couldn't think of anything to say to that. Adaira's indulgent glance revealed her thinking that Morgan was all choked up about Justine's leaving.

But it was another parting that was eating a hole in Morgan's heart. And suddenly she had to know that her pain had gained something for someone.

She had to know that Angus lived longer.

She had to know that losing Alasdair had been worth something.

Frances Fergusson was only too glad to see Morgan, although her cats were fairly indifferent to the whole affair. The two women talked about paints and composition for a few moments, then at Morgan's request, they dove back into the crowded room of records.

"Here's the box you and that Scotsman had before," Frances declared.

Morgan's jaw just about hit the floor. "You remember him?"

Frances's eyes twinkled. "Now I may be an old widow woman, my dear, but I still have eyes in my head, and he was one fine young man. A MacAulay, wasn't he?" She clicked her teeth and opened the box, popping her bifocals onto her nose. "That ledger should be right near the top. No one's been past since you were here."

Morgan sat down with a thump, and when she spoke, her voice sounded strained. "But no one remembers Alasdair except me."

Frances peered over her half-glasses. Then she smiled and gave Morgan's hand a pat. "Well, I saw the look in that man's eye, my dear, and you may be sure that he is remembering you, wherever he is." Her gaze brightened as she fingered the ledger. "In fact, I would suspect that only a very, very good reason would take him away from your side."

With that, she handed over the book and smiled. "I think I'll put on a pot of tea just now."

And Morgan was alone with the book that recounted the first of the MacAulays. Just holding it in her hands made her think of the day they had all three packed in here, how anxious Alasdair had been, the enormous quantity of shortbread he had consumed. Morgan took a deep breath, blinked away her tears, and opened the cover.

Olaf the Black.
Ismay of Mull and Ranald MacAulay.
Angus MacAulay and Fiona Campbell.

She looked at the ceiling, then moved her hand a little lower, knowing what she would see.

Alasdair MacAulay.

His name.

Morgan ran her fingertips over the spidery black writing and hid the date of his demise with her hand. She stared at the letters until her tears blurred them beyond recognition.

Alasdair MacAulay. Just the sight of his name summoned a vision of him that was almost tangible. Alasdair was in this book, as though he had been no more real than any of the others, but Morgan had held the heat of him inside her.

And now he was lost to her forever.

Did she really want to know what the book said? What if he had died young and alone? What if he hadn't really made it back to his own time? A tremor of fear claimed Morgan's heart and she almost couldn't bear to look, couldn't bear to know. She could think of a thousand possibilities, any of which would make her deeply unhappy.

Morgan called herself a chicken, took a deep breath, and moved her hand.

d. 1322—in noble defense of Scotland's borders, by the side of Robert the Bruce.

But Alasdair hadn't wanted to fight anymore! How could that be? Morgan stared at the page, and her heart stopped when she read the line immediately below.

Angus—b. 1308, d. 1315

That line hadn't changed.

A lump rose in Morgan's throat. How could Angus not have lived longer? Alasdair had gone back to help his son!

Had he gone back only to watch his son die? Morgan could just imagine how that would have eaten Alasdair up. He was so determined to make up for lost time, to compensate for the time he had spent apart from his son.

But Angus had died. Had Alasdair even managed to see the vestige of his beloved Fenella in his son one last time? What if he had gotten there too late?

Morgan looked to Alasdair's epitaph again and her heart clenched. Alasdair had gone back, but that hadn't made any difference to Angus's life. Morgan could almost feel the anguish Alasdair must have felt, to be helpless against whatever had stolen away his only son.

She scanned the listing again and saw that Ismay of Mull had died in 1320. That must have been Alasdair's gran, the one who told so many wondrous tales and who he so avidly admired.

Everyone in his life had died, and he had been left alone.

No wonder he had gone back to war. Had Alasdair ever forgiven himself for taking that witch's dare? Or had he gone to his grave believing that he had failed everyone around him?

What a horrible fate for a man who was so intent on upholding duty and honor.

At just the thought, Morgan buried her face in her hands and started to cry. Had Alasdair been the one to plant the briar and the rose? Could Justine be right? Had Alasdair pined away—loving *her*? Justine was convinced, but Morgan wasn't quite so sure.

But all the same, she hated knowing what had happened to him and halfway wished she hadn't come back here.

"Now, my dear, what can be so very wrong?" Frances came back with two steaming cups of tea, concern lining her brow. "Nothing could be so bad as that, could it? After all, everything there happened ages and ages ago! Your man and you are taking it all too personal like. Have a nice hot cup of tea, my dear, and everything will seem much better."

But Morgan just looked up at her hostess. "Why do you remember Alasdair when no one else does?"

Frances smiled sadly. "You do."

"I know, but that's different . . ."

"Because you love him?" Frances suggested softly. When Morgan nodded, the older woman sat down on the box beside her and sternly handed her that steaming cup of tea. She gave Morgan a sharp eye until Morgan obediently took a sip.

"I don't know why I remember things other people don't," Frances admitted and shrugged. "But I do. That's just how it is. And it always has been that way. For all the women in my family, actually. It goes back for ages"—she winked—"and you can be sure that there are plenty of stories of witches in my family tree. My Harold used to say . . ."

Frances's voice faded, then she waved off whatever she had been about to say. "But that doesn't matter. What does matter is that I do remember your Alasdair. And even more important, that you remember him."

Frances leaned forward and tapped Morgan's stomach as she looked into the younger woman's eyes. "Because there's someone who's going to need to know all about him one of these days."

Morgan straightened in surprise. "What?"

Frances smiled. "You've a wee bairn on the way."

Morgan sputtered in astonishment. She was pregnant? But that was impossible! It had only been two days since she and Alasdair had been together. "You can't know that!"

Frances smiled and sipped her tea. "Can't I? Well, then, I

must be mistaken. Why don't you let me know in about six weeks?''

And there was a certainty in the older woman's eyes that made Morgan wonder. Frances had said that she knew things she shouldn't.

What if Morgan *was* pregnant with Alasdair's child? A thrill raced through her at the prospect, and Morgan was filled with delight that she might have at least a vestige of him in her life.

Then her gaze fell to the book and its tragic contents. And Morgan knew with sudden certainty that the child, if there was one, wasn't for her alone.

No, she knew how much Alasdair's son meant to him, she knew how he valued the gift of fatherhood. If she and Alasdair had conceived, then Morgan owed it to Alasdair to seek him out in the past.

It would mean taking a chance on her love for him. Morgan's mouth went dry.

It would also mean losing all contact with Justine and Blake. It would mean never delivering on her book contract. It would mean stepping away from everything she knew—to find a legendary love.

If she could.

But Morgan already knew that she felt more at home on this island than she had anywhere else in the world, even Auntie Gillian's house. She liked the rhythm of the island and the way the people spoke, she loved the harsh lines of the land and the lyrical beauty of the tales they shared around the fire. It had changed so little since Alasdair's time that even he had been fooled.

And she loved Alasdair.

What if he really *did* love her? Certainly he had said some things that were at least encouraging, and he had loved her with a tender deliberation that couldn't have been accidental.

And there was the red, red rose behind Adaira's bed-and-breakfast.

What if her going back to the past could make a difference? What if she could do something to help Angus? What if she could take Alasdair another child?

What if her going back would ensure that Alasdair never

went back to war, or never died lonely and brokenhearted?

And if she *was* pregnant, didn't their child deserve to know its father? At least, if Morgan could manage to trip through time in Alasdair's wake?

But what about her book? Her sister? Her life?

Morgan was so lost in her thoughts that she jumped when Frances leaned over to give her hand a pat. "I also have a feeling you might need to know a little Gaelic," Frances confessed softly. "Come and see me, dear, if you do. You never know how an old librarian might be able to help."

And in that moment, when Morgan looked into Frances's knowing eyes, she made a decision. If she was pregnant, she would go to Alasdair.

Frances would help her.

In the time that it would take to have her pregnancy confirmed, Morgan would finish drawing Alasdair's stories.

Justine had just finished losing her lunch on a sunny November Wednesday afternoon when the phone rang. As much as she hated to answer, it might be Mrs. Fitzgerald about Lorraine's wedding invitations. They had to go out soon or not at all, but the Fitzgeralds could never decide about anything. Justine rubbed the perspiration from her brow and made her way to the phone.

But it wasn't Mrs. Fitzgerald, or even Lorraine.

"Justine?"

"Morgan! How are you?"

"Good. You?"

"Great! Well, actually I feel like hell, but that's a good thing." Justine laughed. "Morgan, you won't believe this, but I'm finally pregnant!"

Justine could feel her sister's interest sharpen. "Oh! That's terrific!"

"Isn't it? Blake's thrilled to death. You should see him, he's a classic mother hen. And I've had all the tests and everything's okay. They wanted to tell me whether it was a boy or a girl, but I want to wait. Do you think that's nuts? I mean, we could plan everything if we knew . . ."

"I think it's wonderful," Morgan said warmly. "You know, a little spontaneity never hurt anyone."

Justine grinned. "I don't know. Blake might have an allergy that we know nothing about."

"Blake?" Morgan choked back what might have been a chuckle. "What about *you*?"

Justine laughed merrily. "So, we're a little organized. The newest Macdonald will probably change all of that when he or she comes along."

"When are you due?"

"June third."

"I'll think of you." There was a somber note in Morgan's voice that caught Justine's attention.

Had Morgan decided what to do?

"Morgan, where are you?"

"Um, I'm still on Lewis."

There was a cautiousness in those words that didn't answer Justine's unspoken question. "Oh. How are your drawings coming along?"

"Good. Good. They're done."

Justine twined the phone cord around her fingers. "Oh, that's wonderful! Are you pleased?"

"Yes." Morgan hesitated, and Justine smiled affectionately. Her sister was so shy about her talents. "I think you're right that they're my best."

"I guess you were inspired."

Justine had meant the comment lightly, but when Morgan gulped, she realized she had said the wrong thing. "Oh, I didn't mean Alasdair, I meant the scenery and everything . . ."

"It's okay, Justine. I'm okay. Really."

But Morgan sounded far from okay. Justine straightened, fighting against a sense of foreboding. "Good," she said in her caterer voice. "When are you coming home?"

"Well." Justine could just see Morgan shifting her weight from foot to foot, and she didn't like the sound of uncertainty in her sister's voice. "Well, that's just it."

Silence fell over the connection, but Justine held her breath and waited.

"I'm not coming home," Morgan confessed in a very small voice.

Justine closed her eyes against a tide of mixed emotions. She had a very good idea where Morgan was going to go instead, and just the thought made her stomach feel queasy again, even though it was emptier than empty.

But the misery that had filled Morgan's voice since Alasdair disappeared tore at Justine's heart.

"I'm pregnant, Justine," Morgan confessed softly. "I have to go."

Justine gripped the phone tighter. She wouldn't think about medieval midwifery. Not for one minute. Alasdair would be the biggest and most fiercely protective guardian angel her baby sister could hope to have.

If Morgan could get to him.

"Do you think you can do it?" Justine's voice sounded too strained to be her own.

Morgan sighed and doubt filled her words. "I don't know. The stone is gone. I've learned a little Gaelic, but probably not enough." Her words faltered, and Justine ached for what her sister was enduring. "But I have to try, Justine! Tonight is the full moon and I just have to try."

Justine bit her lip. "I understand."

Morgan's voice dropped. "I just . . . I miss him." She paused, and Justine waited for the confession she knew would come. "I love him."

Justine felt the warmth of her tears tumble down her cheeks. The highlander had made a miracle happen. He had gently pried open Morgan's protective armor and fitted himself right inside her tender heart. Morgan would never be happy without him by her side—especially now that she carried his child— and Justine couldn't blame her for that.

She remembered how delighted she had been when Morgan laughed for the first time in years. There had been something between them right from the start. Something magical and powerful, something that had drawn Alasdair across seven centuries to find Morgan.

It just wasn't right that they should be apart.

Justine thought of the briar and the rose, eternally entwined as a testament of one man's love for one woman, and her tears fell in a torrent. She was so very glad that Morgan had decided to take a chance on love—even though she was going to miss her sister terribly.

"I know," Justine admitted unevenly. "Oh, Morgan, I know. And I'm sure that he's missing you just the way you're missing him."

Morgan exhaled shakily. "I hope so, Justine. I really do."

"Go," Justine urged. "Go and find out."

Morgan's next words were so low that Justine had to strain to hear them. "I love you, Justine."

"Yeah." Justine's words came unevenly. "I love you, too, Morgan. I love you so very much." Justine knew they were both very aware that they had never made such a declaration to each other before.

And she wondered why they had waited so long.

"Justine, don't forget me."

A lump rose in Justine's throat with a vengeance, and her whispered declaration was nearly inaudible. "Never."

"If you don't hear from me by . . ."

"Don't say it!" Justine took a deep breath, and the line crackled between them. "Don't even say it. I'll find out. Trust me."

Morgan then began to speak very quickly. Justine realized she was probably in the post office or some other public place and subject to a lot of interested glances. "Look, um, say good-bye to Blake for me and take of yourself, okay? Make sure you drink your milk and go to the doctor and all of that, all right?"

Justine smiled through her tears. Imagine Morgan being protective of her. "I will, don't worry. Blake has a chart on the fridge of everything I have to eat every day."

Morgan snorted. "He would."

"Oh, yeah. I'm his new project."

Morgan laughed shakily. "Well, listen to him! I'm sure he's done his research and knows more about having children than old Mother Hubbard."

"No doubt." Justine's smile broadened, and a golden moment stretched between the two sisters. "You take care of yourself, too—and tell Alasdair that Blake thinks Robert the Bruce is a hero. He's ordered some damn statue or something for his office.''

Morgan chuckled, then sniffled suspiciously. "I will.''

A silence stretched between them, and Justine knew neither of them wanted to actually say good-bye.

For the last time.

"It's okay, Morgan,'' she finally whispered. "Go and be happy.''

"I will, oh, I will,'' Morgan vowed unevenly. "And Justine? Kiss that baby for me, will you?''

Justine barely had time to nod before the line clicked.

She stared at the silent receiver for a long moment, feeling as though setting it back in the cradle would separate her from Morgan for all time.

But that had already happened. Justine's tears welled again and she sobbed inelegantly. She bit her knuckles and cried like a child, sitting with the handset still clenched in her fist. She felt torn in half, wanting nothing other than for Morgan to be happy but at the same time hurting because Morgan was gone.

Justine's stomach rolled ominously, and it occurred to her that the baby in her belly was going to give her this feeling again, and probably more than once.

Loving was about knowing when to shelter and when to set free. And Justine knew in her heart that Morgan was going to be very happy. Alasdair MacAulay would make sure of that.

She had personally picked him, hadn't she?

And Auntie Gillian would have liked him just fine.

Morgan stood in the post office, well aware that every eye was surreptitiously upon her. She sniffled, blew her nose heartily, then wiped her eyes. Even talking to Justine hadn't changed her mind. Morgan knew what she had to do.

She knew what she wanted to do.

But first things first.

She picked up the bound copy of her drawings, each one now lovingly rendered in ink and carefully colored. The bookbinder she had found in town had done a stupendous job,

turning her work into an heirloom volume that humbled her
with its beauty. The leather cover gleamed with subtle gold
embossing, the endpapers were marbled paper from Florence.

It was exactly what she had wanted. Morgan smiled as she
recalled the countless hours she had spent on this volume, her
smile broadening when she thought of what Justine's reaction
would be when it arrived.

If all went well, there would be only one copy of Morgan's
book, *Scottish Faerie Tales*. She opened the book carefully
and wrote quickly on the cover page.

> *For Justine, Blake, and (mostly!) Baby Macdonald—*
> *With all my love,*
> *For all time,*
> *Morgan*

Morgan blew on the ink until it dried, closed the book, and
took it to the postal wicket. "Do you have a padded envelope
that would fit this? It's going to the States and it has to arrive
in perfect condition."

The elderly postmaster peered through his glasses at the
book with a harumph. "A gift?"

"For a new baby. A first baby."

"Hmm." He nodded approval. "Powerful good luck that
is." Then he muttered to himself and disappeared behind the
counter as he sought the appropriate packaging. Morgan ran
her hand over the beautifully bound book and knew she was
doing the right thing.

In more ways than one.

Chapter 18

THE MOON WAS full, and a few errant clouds scurried across the indigo sky. The November winds were brisk, and Morgan's skirt swirled around her ankles. She paused when she entered the circle of stones, startled once again by the sense of warmth emanating here.

Frances nodded matter-of-factly. "It's always this way, dear. A strong force gathers here, especially on a night such as this." She handed Morgan a twig of white-blossomed heather and smiled. "I found this on my walk yesterday. It seemed a portent of good fortune."

Morgan's heart skipped a beat, and she managed a shaky smile. "I'm afraid, Frances."

The older woman sobered. "A good sensible reaction, I would think, to the prospect of traveling through time." She eyed Morgan for a long moment, then cocked her head. "Do you want to change your mind?"

"No. I have to go."

Frances nodded. "Then we have work to do." She walked around the circle of stones as she began to sing softly in Gaelic. The wind stilled, to Morgan's astonishment, although she still could see the grass beyond the circle of stones waving in the breeze.

When Frances paused before Morgan again, her eyes were

uncharacteristically bright. ''It's time,'' she whispered.

Morgan gripped the heather and closed her eyes. Was it going to work? She was stone-cold sober, she didn't have the stone from the regalia, they didn't have any idea what the Gaelic song was that Alasdair's witch had sung.

But Morgan had a funny feeling she had found a genuine witch in Frances. The woman had taken the entire story in stride and had been readily persuaded to help Morgan, who couldn't wrap her tongue around a Gaelic verse to save her life.

''Turn!'' Frances whispered and Morgan did. The older woman's voice rose in a chant that stirred Morgan's blood. In her imagination, a thousand spirits gathered around the ancient place, their ageless eyes bright with curiosity.

Once.

Morgan felt the dizziness rise within her, hardly anything new after the month of morning sickness she had had. But this was a thundering in her veins, like the pounding of the sea, that swelled up inside her and flooded her senses, making her lose track of every vestige of the world around her.

Twice.

The rhythm of the chant infected Morgan and she had a sudden soaring certainty that this could be done, that it *would* be done, that she would be with Alasdair and that he would love her for everything she was. She started the third turn with a buoyant heart and a death grip on the heather.

And just before she took the last step, cold hands framed her face. Morgan's eyes flew open and she found herself nose to nose with Frances.

It was Frances and it was not Frances. Her normally placid features were overlaid with the shadow of a woman with wild eyes and hair. Her eyes widened, she leaned closer, and she hissed, ''WISH!''

And Morgan wished with all her heart and soul to be with Alasdair MacAulay.

Three.

Morgan fell then, stumbling away from Frances, but she didn't hit the ground for a long, long time. Morgan tumbled through a black void until she thought she could fall no more, then came to a stop with a sudden thump that had her clutching at her belly.

She opened her eyes and gasped to find golden sunlight painting the standing stones of Callanish. Morgan jumped to her feet and spun around, her heart pounding erratically.

Frances was gone.

Adaira's bicycle was gone.

There wasn't a house in sight.

And on the grass, not a dozen paces away, a heart-wrenchingly familiar man with golden hair slumbered in a wrinkled kilt.

"Alasdair!"

He was having the dream again, the one that tormented him every night, the one that never let him sleep when the moon was full. Alasdair fought against it, uncertain whether he would truly rather be without these dreams of Morgan.

Because then, he feared, he might completely forget her.

But the small hands that latched on to his chemise and gave him a hearty shake were a new element of this recurring dream. Alasdair did not dare to hope as he cautiously opened one eye.

But he found his lady love crying all over him, the morning sun picking blue lights out of the joyous tangle of her hair.

Morgan!

Alasdair did not care for the details of how she had come here. He simply scooped her up, gathered her close, and kissed her with abandon. Morgan curled against him perfectly, her hands slid into his hair, she sighed beneath his embrace in a way that made Alasdair's heart race.

She was here!

Alasdair ran his hands over her curves, recalling each and every one, hating that she had lost some weight, yet loving the hint that she had missed him as much as he had missed her.

Reluctantly, he lifted his lips from Morgan's, framed her delicate face in his great hands, and smiled down at her. The lady smiled back, a shimmer of tears still gracing her cheeks. A lump rose in Alasdair's throat, and he felt a faint disbelief that the fates had been so kind as to grant his fondest desire.

Morgan was *here*.

"You came," Alasdair said simply, still marveling.

Morgan nodded shyly, those witchy green eyes luminous. "You're glad?" That she could doubt something Alasdair knew as well as his own name tore at his heart, and he could think of naught but reassuring her.

So he kissed her again.

'Twas long moments later that they parted, each breathless from their embrace. "Why are you here, at the stones?" Morgan asked.

"Each night of the full moon since my return I have kept a vigil here, in the faint hope that you might return."

"Oh!" Morgan looked across the hills again, and Alasdair had the distinct sense that there was something she wanted to ask him, something that she did not dare give voice to.

But what? He could not fathom what troubled her. They were together again!

Though 'twas clear all was not aright in the lady's heart.

Did she not mean to stay? Was it not possible for her to stay? Fear clenched Alasdair's heart and he captured her hand, almost as though his touch alone could keep her by his side.

She stared down at their interlaced fingers and swallowed awkwardly. Her words were flat. "Everything was fixed, you know. Robert the Bruce is a hero again and the crystal is back in the regalia."

"Aye." Alasdair studied Morgan, feeling as helpless as he did at his son's sickbed. What was amiss?

"What year is it?"

"'Tis March of 1315."

"Oh." Morgan looked at Alasdair, and his innards clenched with the certainty that she knew something he did not want to know. "How is your son?"

And Alasdair feared in that instant that the healer had spoken aright.

His heart sank like a stone. "He is ill and naught can aid him." Alasdair swallowed. "Do you know what fate lies before him?"

Morgan raised a hand to her lips, her tears gathering anew.

Alasdair understood that his son would die, despite his return to this time.

The book yet said the same.

Tears glazed his own vision, and now Alasdair turned away, hating that his boy would be stolen away so soon after his return home.

"What's wrong with him?" Morgan asked, the compassion that Alasdair so loved laced in her tone.

Alasdair shook his head. "He is fevered and knows not his own name. An entire day he has tossed and turned, lost in his illness. I did not intend to come last eve, but my gran fair tossed me out." Alasdair forced a smile. " 'Tis true my pacing drives her mad."

Morgan laid a hand on his arm. "Maybe I can help," she suggested softly, and Alasdair looked into her wondrous eyes.

He hated the shadows that lurked there and feared that he was responsible for them. But perhaps she could aid Angus.

And then, Alasdair would get to the root of his lady's sadness. "Come, Morgaine," he invited, in conscious echo of what he had said to her once before. "Come with me and meet my son."

The hills were achingly familiar, the sheep scurrying out of sight exactly as they had when Morgan had first accompanied Alasdair this way. Her heart was heavier, though, and she was painfully aware of the tiny burden buried deep inside of her.

And she hated not knowing Alasdair's feelings for her. He had been glad to see her, that was certain, but he had never said those three little words Morgan longed to hear.

They rounded the bend and climbed the verdant pasture. The Rose Cottage wasn't here, but there was a crofter's cottage on the site where Alasdair had searched so frantically. A wisp of smoke curled from its stone chimney, its whitewashed walls rose high and thick, its thatch was freshly repaired. Chickens pecked around the cottage, and a few early flowers bloomed.

The wind was full of tales of the sea, new grass was vividly green, the sky arched overhead like an azure bowl. It was soothing here—or could have been if all had been right between herself and Alasdair. Yet Morgan couldn't ask him how he felt, not now, not before she knew whether she could do anything for Angus.

When they drew near, an elderly woman threw open the door and stormed out to the front stoop. Her eyes snapped with vitality and her presence was commanding. She braced her hands on her hips, gave them both a stern glance, then eyed Morgan once again.

"And who might this be?" she demanded. "What is in your mind, Alasdair MacAulay, to be bringing a woman home when your own lad is lying ill on the hearth?"

"This is Morgan Lafayette," Alasdair said softly, and his gran's eyes brightened with interest. "She may well be able to aid Angus."

Gran clicked her teeth assessingly. "Morgaine le Fee herself. Well. All your blethers had a seed of truth, after all."

She didn't move out of the way when they reached the stoop, forcing Morgan and Alasdair to pause there. "Do you cook, then?" Gran demanded sharply.

There was no point in lying about it, although Morgan knew the truth wouldn't be well received. In a community like this, a woman would be expected to have traditional skills.

"No," she admitted softly.

"Ha!" Gran declared with obvious delight. She shook a warning finger, the very image of Auntie Gillian making a point. "You keep your witching from my pots, and there will be no clamjamphry mucking before the fire."

And with that, she pivoted and stalked back into the cottage.

Morgan smelled Alasdair's skin as he leaned closer, and she closed her eyes against the warm fan of his breath against her ear. "She makes a fair to do about naught at all, but you have naught to fear from my gran," he counseled quietly.

Morgan smiled. "I know. My Auntie Gillian was just like this."

Alasdair grinned. "Ah, then you have the wits to survive."

"I heard that, Alasdair MacAulay!" Gran retorted from the shadows ahead. "I am no greetin teenie, but those come to help can hardly do so without a keek at the lad."

She was right. Morgan stepped into the cottage, her eyes

adjusting quickly to the change from bright sunlight. The walls were whitewashed inside, as well, the fire casting a warm glow over the cozy contents.

But Morgan's glance flew to the pale boy sleeping before the fire. She touched his brow, under Gran's sternly protective eye, and didn't like the feverish feel of his skin.

"The healer says he is to die," the older woman said flatly and Morgan saw her fierce love burning in her gaze. She loved this child beyond all else, probably loved Alasdair the same way.

Just as Auntie Gillian had loved Morgan and Justine.

Morgan rummaged in her fanny pack, hoping she had the tiny box of aspirin that she forgot all too often.

She did.

"This might help break his fever."

Gran's eyes flashed and she took a step back. "Witchery!"

Alasdair plucked the box from Morgan's hand and glared at his gran. "Medicine, from farther afield than our healer has been."

Gran's suspicion cleared instantly and was replaced with curiosity. "Aye?"

"Aye." Alasdair's tone brooked no argument. He slanted a glance at Morgan. "Tell us how it should be granted."

"We'll give him two for now, maybe a couple more later." Morgan hoped she was right. "With soup. Chicken soup, if you have any."

"We will soon enough," Gran declared and lifted a hatchet from its hook on the wall.

Morgan didn't watch.

She had, after all, agreed to stay out of the kitchen.

The shadows had drawn long and Alasdair had nearly paced a trough in the floor. The heat in Angus's cheeks had gone, and it seemed that he slept easier than he had when Morgan arrived. Gran sat close to him, her knitting needles clicking in the silence, her eagle gaze bright on her ward.

When Angus finally opened his eyes, Morgan nearly fainted in relief. His vision was clear, his eyes a distinctive shade of dark gray, completely unlike Alasdair's vivid blue.

Morgan's mouth went dry at the sight. Fenella might as well have drawn up her own chair at the hearth.

But Angus, unaware of her doubts, widened those eyes when he saw Morgan sitting beside his bed. His gaze danced wonderingly over her hair, her eyes, her clothing, then he looked to his gran in confusion. Morgan was dimly aware that Alasdair's pacing had fallen silent.

" 'Tis Morgaine le Fee herself, come to aid you," Gran declared matter-of-factly, her brisk tone giving no hint of the concern that had creased her features just moments past. "You had best give your thanks to such a fine lady."

"Morgaine le Fee!" Angus breathed wonderment, his gaze clinging to Morgan once again. " 'Tis true, then! You do know my da!"

In both the biblical and the casual sense, but Morgan didn't think this was a good time to make that clear. "Yes," she admitted simply.

"Cor!" The boy's eyes were nearly round. "Have you come to bring back his heart, then?"

His heart?

A lump rose in Morgan's throat and she glanced at Alasdair. He lingered a few steps away, with uncharacteristic uncertainty, his features hidden in the shadows. He was stunningly, eerily silent, his manner far from reassuring.

What had he told his son about her?

"I think your mother holds that honor," Morgan said softly.

Gran's snort reverberated through the cottage, but Angus settled back against his pillow and his eyes drifted closed. "I think you should keep it," he murmured so quietly that Morgan had to lean close to catch the words. "As long as you give him yours in exchange."

Morgan kept her gaze fixed on the dozing boy and felt her cheeks heat. "He has it already," she confessed.

And Angus smiled like an angel before his breathing deepened.

Morgan smiled herself, knowing the sound of a healthy sleep when she heard it. She touched Angus's brow and found that all the alien heat had left his skin.

When she looked up, she inadvertently met Gran's flaming gaze.

"His dame?" the older woman snapped. "That woman has no right to my Alasdair's own heart, there is the truth of it!"

"You will not say anything against the dead in my home," Alasdair retorted.

"I shall say what needs saying, especially as you are not inclined to tell the truth yourself!" Gran bounded to her feet and cast her knitting aside. She jabbed a finger through the air at Alasdair, her voice low and angry. "That Fenella was a peck of trouble and a greetin teenie, if ever there was! There was naught she liked better than to set all tapsal-teerie for no more than her own enjoyment!"

Alasdair straightened and his words were wooden. "She gave to me a son, against her own will, and paid dearly for the doing." Morgan ached to hear how Alasdair still blamed himself for this.

Gran spat on the floor. "She gave you naught but grief!"

Alasdair inhaled sharply and strode across the room. "My son is not grief!" he declared, his voice low and hot.

Gran pointed to the sleeping boy and her voice dropped lower. "Make no mistake, Alasdair, this boy is not your son!"

The color left Alasdair's face in a rush, and Morgan caught her own breath at this unexpected blow, but Gran continued in a fury. "Aye, 'twas against her will to be round with a babe, that much is for certain, since the lads have no affection for a ripe woman and she was vainer than vain, that Fenella."

Gran glared at Morgan. "Trouble she was, trouble from the first we saw her, and he knew it as well as I. Hers was a beauty not even skin-deep, for her heart was black as coal." Anger and pride combined in the older woman's tone as she flicked her head toward Alasdair. "But duty-thirled is my Alasdair and naught would come in the way of any word he had granted."

"When did you know?" Alasdair asked stiffly.

"I suspected from the first, but was not certain until you were gone away with the Bruce. And now," she smiled down at the sleeping boy, "he is as our own and there is little point in the telling."

"But tell you did," Alasdair observed.

Gran shrugged and her gaze sharpened. "Are you expecting me to stand by and watch you err again?" She sniffed and stared at her grandson, who still stood stiffly to one side. "Any man with his wits about him could see that this one is as different from Fenella as sea from shore. You said yourself that Morgaine le Fee held your own heart fast," she said softly. "Do you not imagine the woman deserves to hear the truth fall from your own lips?"

And with that, Gran scooped up her knitting with a vengeance and sat down heavily before the hearth. The sound of Angus's even breathing was nearly driven out by the pounding of Morgan's heart. She stared at Alasdair, hoping that his gran knew the truth.

Alasdair offered Morgan his hand. "Come, my lady," he murmured, his low voice making her heart skip in anticipation. "Come. There is something I would show you."

Morgan looked into the fathomless blue of his eyes and put her hand in the warmth of his.

The first stars were out, the view to the sea still streaked with orange and pink. Alasdair led Morgan behind the cottage with a surety of purpose. She caught her breath when she spied two freshly planted vines, one rife with thorns, the glossy green leaves of the other very familiar.

Alasdair *had* planted the briar and the rose.

But for whom?

Morgan glanced up to find Alasdair's blue, blue gaze steady upon her, and her heart gave an unruly thump.

But he didn't say anything, just guided her closer to the plants. He paused beside them, bending to tuck the dirt carefully around their roots, her fingers still firmly captured within his hand.

"These I planted but yesterday," he confessed hoarsely. "And though there were those who doubtless thought it foolish, it suited me well to mark the loss of a love, a love that still burned bright within my heart."

Morgan didn't even dare to breathe.

Was he talking about Fenella?

Alasdair's thumb slid across the back of her hand, then set to tracing little circles around her knuckles.

"My lady, I am not a man who surrenders any matter readily, but I must confess that this was to be my last night at the circle of stones. This was to be my final tribute to the ache in my heart before I left this place for all time."

He was going to leave here?

" 'Twas when the healer came and gave her ill portent for Angus's health that I knew I could remain here no longer and dream of what might have been." Alasdair impaled Morgan with a look. "She said he would die and I vowed then that if he did, I would return to battle with the Bruce."

"But you'll die!" Morgan burst out. She clutched at his hand. "You can't go! I read it in the bo—"

Alasdair placed a resolute thumb over Morgan's lips to silence her and his lips quirked. "My lady, I have no intent to go," he assured her softly, his eyes glowing. "All has changed this day." He raised one hand and stroked her cheek, his smile broadening. "You have saved my son, and for this, you have my eternal gratitude."

Gratitude was a far cry from what Morgan actually wanted. "But he's not your son," she felt obligated to point out.

Alasdair shrugged. "It matters little. The boy rests as securely in my heart as though he were my own blood, and in my mind he is. My gran's tales can change none of that. Angus is my son."

Because Angus was Fenella's son, at least, and Alasdair was still in love with Fenella, regardless of her faithlessness.

Disappointment flooded through Morgan. She had been a dope to come back here, an idiot to imagine that her pregnancy or even she herself made any difference to this strong and gentle man.

They were of different times, and Morgan knew now that she should have stayed in her own. She turned away, not even caring where she went. Maybe somehow she could find her way back to Justine, but Morgan wasn't sure.

One thing was for certain—she had bet the farm and lost.

"My lady! What is this you do?"

Morgan looked back at Alasdair and tried to smile. "I'm leaving. Of course."

"Of course?" Alasdair frowned as though he could make no sense of this. "But you have only just arrived!" He gestured to the entangled plants behind him in frustration. "Does this mean naught to you?"

Morgan shook her head sadly. "I'm sure Fenella is delighted, wherever she is." And she turned once more to leave. "I'm sure she's thrilled that you'll love her forever."

"Fenella?" Alasdair's voice sounded strained, but Morgan didn't stop. "This has naught to do with Fenella!" he declared hotly.

No, Morgan admitted, it probably has more to do with Angus. Alasdair's son. She thought about the tiny baby in her own belly and her tears rose. She forced herself to just keep walking.

Until the cry of a mad boar made her jump in fright. She pivoted to find Alasdair closing in on her.

Fast.

"My lady Morgaine, if you imagine for one clarty moment that I will stand by while you walk away, then you know naught of the measure of man I am!" he bellowed.

Morgan froze. Alasdair's eyes flashed, and he flung his hands skyward as he stormed toward her. "Does it mean naught to you that I love you beyond all else? Does it matter naught to you that I have no reason to wake each day without you by my side? Did your pledge of love to me mean naught in the end?"

Morgan went all cold, then felt a flush rise over her cheeks. She gaped at the furious highlander as he came to a stop before her, his eyes blazing sapphire.

"You love me?" she asked incredulously.

"Aye, that I do!" Alasdair roared. "Have you listened to naught I have told you this night?"

"But you love Fenella."

"Fenella?" Alasdair looked horrified by the concept. "Never did I give a care for that flighty besom! A sound whack on the bahookie was what she deserved, but so long left undone, 'twas not easy to fix.'' His expression turned wry. ''My gran speaks aright in this, at least.''

''But you married her.''

Alasdair arched a fair brow and folded his arms across his chest as he regarded Morgan. '' 'Twas my duty,'' he said quietly. ''I have told you this afore.'' He stepped closer while Morgan absorbed this and took her chin in his hand, his voice turning gentle. ''And did I not tell you when last we were together that you were as fine as a red, red rose, while I was no better than a doughty thorn?''

Morgan nodded.

Alasdair smiled. ''Then how can you doubt the meaning of the rose and briar, my lady? My heart is as securely in your keeping as ever a man's could be.'' He leaned down and brushed his nose across hers, his voice husky. ''I love only you, Morgan. Do not leave me.''

The truth shone in his blue, blue eyes, as always it did.

''Oh, Alasdair! I don't want to leave.'' No sooner had Morgan made that confession than Alasdair scooped her up in his arms and kissed her thoroughly. She reveled in his touch, secure in the knowledge that she had made the right choice.

And then she began to cry that she had ever doubted him.

''Tears, my lady,'' he whispered, wiping them away with an indulgent thumb. ''Is it so dire as that to pledge to me for all eternity?''

''We didn't make a pledge.''

Alasdair snorted. ''An omission to be righted, to be sure.''

Morgan smiled through her tears. ''I suppose that would be the right thing to do,'' she mused. ''Since I'm pregnant.''

''Pregnant?'' Alasdair's eyes widened in joy, and then alarm. ''And what foolery is it that has you out in such chill air? And nary a morsel for your supper to warm the babe's belly?'' He growled as he carried her directly back to the cottage. ''My lady, did I not know better, I should think you had need of a keeper . . .''

Morgan kicked her feet playfully. ''Good idea. Know anyone who might be interested?''

Alasdair looked at her intently, and his grip tightened possessively. "There will be none taking that task. 'Tis mine and mine alone, and well do I intend to fulfill it."

"Are you giving me your word?" Morgan teased.

Alasdair's eyes gleamed as he stared down at her. Morgan felt as though the world stopped when he paused on the threshold of his cottage to gather her closer.

"Aye, my lady," he murmured with a smile. "Aye, that I am."

And he bent to kiss her with a thoroughness that made Morgan's heart sing. She twined her arms around his neck, thinking of the rose and the briar tangling each about the other, the vines becoming as one.

Inseparable for all time.

And Morgan liked the sound of that just fine.

Epilogue

JUSTINE'S FINGERS TIGHTENED on the envelope when she saw the postmark, and she tore it open without another thought. She dropped onto the stool beside the phone in her sunny white kitchen and read hungrily.

May 23, 1999

Dear Mrs. Macdonald,

Thank you so very much for your lovely letter. The Captain and I were delighted to hear that you are expecting a child. Know that all of our warmest congratulations are with you.

Per your request, I did trot over to Frances Fergusson's and have a look for the record of your forebears. You will be pleased no doubt that Frances does have a thorough record in her files and you may wish to see it yourself whenever you are back this way.

It seems your ancestor Alasdair MacAulay did indeed marry twice, as you had suspected. His first wife was a Fenella Macdonald, who gave to him a son, name of Angus. By the dates, Frances guesses Fenella died either in childbirth or shortly thereafter.

How blessed we are that such matters are less risky

*in our times! I trust that all will go well on your day
and that you will be feeling quite yourself again shortly
thereafter.*

*But to return to the tale, this Alasdair did wed again
and remarkably, Frances knows quite a bit of his second
wife. Her name was Morgaine, though there is no clan
listed for her, so we cannot tell from whence she came.
Named for the great sorceress herself, if you can imagine the cheek of that! But all the same, she seems to
have been uncommon lucky—the pair of them had four
bairns, two boys and two girls, not two years between
any of them. The man must have been smitten with her
charms indeed!*

*Then it is that Alasdair had five children: first Angus
in 1307 by that first wife, then a boy, Caillen, in 1316,
then you'll no doubt be surprised to learn that the first
girl has your own name, though it was uncommon
enough in those times. Justine was born in 1318, followed by what appear to be twins, Niall and Isobel, in
1320. All the children lived to a doughty age, as did
their parents, living as they did until . . .*

Justine firmly put her thumb over the dates. She didn't want
to think about Morgan being dead for several hundred years.
She pulled out a calendar and tried to figure out the dates of
the babies' births instead.

Well, Morgan had been pregnant when they last talked and
that baby had presumably been Caillen, born in 1316. So, for
Morgan, right now, it was sometime in 1316.

Justine patted her ripe belly and smiled. Morgan was probably just as pregnant as she was right now. Justine could just
imagine how Alasdair would fuss around her.

He'd probably be even worse than Blake had been.

She bit her lip, told herself not to cry, then read on.

*But what is truly remarkable is that there are several
letters preserved at the monastery between Morgaine
and the abbot there. It seems that she had a gift for
painting miniatures. The abbot's letter makes it clear*

that although this is most unusual, a lack of talent within the monastery had him hiring Morgaine's abilities to illuminate the Bibles and Gospels that they copied there. Several sentences lead Frances to believe that Morgaine was not allowed within the perimeter of the monastery because of her gender, but that she had a rare and mutually profitable relationship with the monks of the abbey.

Isn't that remarkable? I must confess that curiosity sent me myself down to the town library, where the last of the monks' illuminated books are preserved, and the librarian let me have a wee look. Mrs. Macdonald, if ever you can come back this way, I would strongly suggest you treat yourself to a look at these marvelous books. She may only have been named for a great enchantress, but it is more than clear that your forebear could put magic on the page. Not surprisingly, her spouse, Alasdair, had somewhat of a reputation as a man of letters—some of those between himself and the abbot are also preserved.

As for your question about the briar and the rose behind the hotel, well, frankly I cannot imagine why you need to hear that tale again. Goodness, Mrs. Macdonald, how often did I tell it to you?! But here it is again, as you requested.

There was once a man living in this very valley who loved his wife with all his heart and soul. One day, she bore him a son and it seemed to him that nothing could be more right in his world. To commemorate his lady's struggle to bring the babe to light—for in those days, it was no easy task—he planted a rose and a briar behind their home. The plants twined together and grew ever stronger and taller, as the man proclaimed did his love for his lady fair.

They lived long and well together, happy all their days, and when they passed, that very son tended the briar and the rose, so that the legacy of his parents' love might continue on in the garden as it did within his own heart. And so, through the years, each master of

*this house has tended the plants, ensuring that always
there is a briar and a blood-red rose growing together
on the selfsame spot that the man chose to salute his
beloved wife.*

*I hope this has answered your questions. Again, all
the best from the Captain and me. We look forward to
seeing you again whenever you are back this way.*

> *Sincerely,*
> *Adaira Macleod*

Justine read the letter again and folded it carefully. Adaira
was right—Morgan did have a rare gift. And the body of her
strongest work was bound and waiting in a cheerful yellow
nursery upstairs. One day Justine's child would learn to read
magical tales of Scotland, tales illustrated with the fairies that
had tumbled out of Morgan's pen.

A key turned in the lock and Justine started at the sound.
"Anybody home?" Blake called from the foyer.

Justine glanced to the clock in surprise. "It's only four!
What are you doing here?"

Blake grinned and dropped his briefcase in the hall. He
scooped up Justine and gave her a thorough kiss. "Had to
come home and see the most beautiful woman in the world,"
he declared.

Justine poked a finger in his chest, trying to hide how
pleased she was by both his appearance and his compliment.
One week past her due date had left her feeling as attractive
as a hippo in a tutu. "What about work?"

"Screw work," Blake said with a cavalier wink. "I've got
a family that needs my time."

A year ago, Justine would have been scandalized by this
attitude, but pregnancy had changed the rhythm of the Macdonald home. It was amazing how much time Blake now took
just to be with her. Justine once had been convinced he would
burn water while trying to boil it, but he learned a few tricks
while she had had that morning sickness and couldn't even
look at food.

Justine got no further in her thinking than that before the

first contraction took her to her knees. Her water broke, the sight of it spreading across her sparkling floor nearly giving her a heart attack.

But it was Blake who remembered everything from the pre-natal class. "Okay," he said with easy assurance. He grasped her chin and winked at her again, his manner easing Justine's panic. "Don't freak out on me. Remember, this is what we've got to do next."

And Justine was very, very glad she had married a practical man.

Too many hours later, Justine lay in the maternity ward of the hospital cuddling her very red, very new son. She still couldn't get over how absolutely perfect he was, the tininess of his fingers and toes, his eyelashes and fingernails.

"Hi. Ready for company?"

Justine smiled to find Blake loitering in the doorway. He'd been great, right beside her the whole way. "You don't fool me," she teased. "You came to see your son."

"Well . . ."

The baby squirmed and cried, and they exchanged a glance. "He knows you're here," Justine accused.

Blake grinned unrepentantly. "It's a guy thing."

He came closer and eyed the baby, Justine's wonder echoed in his expression. "It's really amazing, isn't it?" he whispered with awe as the baby settled against Justine again.

"Yeah, it is." Their gazes met and held over the child's bald little head, and Justine felt her tears well.

They had a child, and it was because Morgan had made it possible. Morgan had given them an important lesson on mak-ing time for each other, a lesson that Justine was never going to forget.

She wished they had learned to appreciate the magic of what was between them a little sooner. Silently, she thanked her sister for giving them this gift before it was too late.

Blake's next words made it clear that his thoughts must have turned in a similar direction. "Hey, I had this idea." Something in his tone warned Justine that this was important.

"About what?"

"Naming the baby." Blake's gaze locked with Justine's. He shoved his hands in his trouser pockets, and his expression was somber. "Let's call him Morgan."

Justine's tears rose unexpectedly, she was so surprised by the suggestion. Yet, at the same time, it was so apt that she couldn't believe she hadn't thought of it before.

"Oh, Blake, that's a great idea!" She reached up and gave her husband a sound kiss. "You're a wonderful man, you know that?"

"So I've heard," he said and tweaked her nose. "And that's a good thing, too, or I'd never be able to hold on to a wonderful woman like you."

They smiled into each other's eyes for a long, warm moment, then Morgan let out another cry of protest.

Blake winked. "See? Competition at every turn. I'm not the only one who wants you."

Justine rocked the baby and cooed to him, feeling like she was less than instinctive mother material. Blake, though, seemed impressed. Morgan's eyes opened blearily, and they already seemed to be a little less blue than they had been just a few hours ago.

His eyes would be green, Justine knew with sudden certainty.

Morgan.

"Hello, Morgan," she murmured and tickled his chin. He gurgled and nuzzled against her breast, his mouth working hungrily. "One day, I'm going to tell you all about the auntie you've been named for," she whispered.

And in that moment, Justine suddenly remembered her last promise to Morgan. She bent and gently kissed her son's temple, wondering if Morgan was simultaneously pressing a similar kiss to Caillen's brow, somewhere across the eons.

That was how she would think of it, she decided. She and Morgan were living their lives in parallel, day for day. Justine would mark Morgan's babies' birth years on the calendar—she could figure it out—and celebrate each one's arrival as though it had just occurred.

And when her Morgan passed each threshold in his life—lost a tooth, took his first step, smiled his first smile—Justine would know that Morgan and Alasdair were watching Caillen do exactly the same.

Justine smiled and cuddled her baby close under Blake's indulgent eye, knowing she had more than one precious treasure to hold within her heart.

And so, she knew, did Morgan.

Auntie Gillian would be proud.

Author's Note

EDINBURGH CASTLE WAS retrieved for Robert the Bruce in March 1314, but the assault was led by Bruce's nephew, Thomas Randolph, not the fictional Alasdair MacAulay. Interestingly, the daring route was suggested by one William Francis, who had used it while stationed in the keep to make discreet jaunts into town for his romantic liaisons.

Robert the Bruce died—after uniting Scotland beneath his hand—in 1329 in Cardross above the Clyde at fifty-five years of age. Ironically, he died before word of a papal bull pronouncing the legitimacy of his kingship could reach him. That kingship, so arduously won, would not continue smoothly in his absence, and ultimately Scotland would surrender to England's rule once more.

There are many wonderful stories surrounding Robert the Bruce—including that of the spider—though it is uncertain how many of them are true. One of my favorites is Robert the Bruce's reputed final request, which was for his heart to be taken to Jerusalem and buried near the Holy Sepulchre.

Sir James Douglas took the heart as pledged, but got no further than Granada (in modern Spain), where he was killed in battle with the Moors. Bruce's heart was purportedly returned to Scotland by another knight, still in its lead casket, and buried beneath Melrose Abbey. Recently, a lead casket matching the description has been discovered in the abbey, and early tests indicate that it likely contains an embalmed heart.

All of Alasdair's stories are truly Scottish folktales or ballads. Many of these were collected by Francis James Child in his nineteenth-century volume *The English and Scottish Popular Ballads*.

The story of Thomas Rhymer is included here with some anglicization of its Scots dialect. The actual Thomas of Erceldoune (also known as True Thomas, or Thomas Learmont— c. 1220–97) was a poet who claimed to have been captured by the fairy queen and released with the gift of prophecy.

Erceldoune is now called Earlston and is in the Eildon Hills southeast of Edinburgh, coincidentally quite close to Melrose Abbey. The Eildon Hills are also considered by many to be where King Arthur and his knights lie in an enchanted slumber, waiting to be awakened by the summons from a magical horn.

The Stone of Scone remained in Westminster Abbey from the time of Edward Plantagenet's seizure in 1296, with the exception of a brief interval in the 1960s when the stone was captured by Scottish nationalists. In 1996 it was returned to Scotland by the British government. Interestingly enough, although the stone is reputed to have been brought from Tara in Ireland by the Picts, some seven centuries before Edward's plunder, geologists maintain that the stone is red sandstone, and quarried near Scone.

The Scottish regalia have a long and colorful history—including being "found" by Sir Walter Scott in the nineteenth century—but are much as is described here. They are on permanent display in Edinburgh Castle—and the scepter still does have a crystal mounted in it!

Finally, the quest for Scottish independence was sought long before and continued long after Robert the Bruce. As I finished this book—in September 1997—the Scottish people had just voted strongly in favor of establishing a Scottish National Legislature once more. It appears that Robert the Bruce's dream of independence—and that of countless other Scots—will come to fruition before the turn of the millennium.

Perhaps this time his legacy will endure.